Joseph E. A. Smith

Taghconic

The romance and beauty of the hills

Joseph E. A. Smith

Taghconic
The romance and beauty of the hills

ISBN/EAN: 9783337344658

Printed in Europe, USA, Canada, Australia, Japan

Cover: Foto ©Andreas Hilbeck / pixelio.de

More available books at **www.hansebooks.com**

THE ROMANCE AND BEAUTY

OF THE HILLS.

BY GODFREY GREYLOCK.

"Thou shalt look
Upon the green and rolling forest tops,
And down into the secrets of the glens
And streams, that with their bordering thickets strive
To hide their windings.   Thou shalt gaze at once
Here on white villages and tilth and herds,
And swarming roads, and there on solitudes
That only hear the torrent and the wind,
And Eagle's shriek."

BRYANT.

BOSTON :
LEE AND SHEPARD, PUBLISHERS.

NEW YORK :
CHARLES T. DILLINGHAM.

PITTSFIELD:
S. E. NICHOLS

1879.

EPISTLE DEDICATORY.

FRIENDS : —

From Vermont upon the north to Connecticut upon the south, for fifty miles along the eastern border of New York, extends Berkshire, the most western county of Massachusetts. It is a region of hill and valley, of lake and stream, of woodland, farm and field. Its beauty is world renowned; for the pens of Cullen Bryant and Catherine Sedgwick early made it their favorite themes, and in later years Holmes and Longfellow, Hawthorne, Melville and Thoreau have invested it with the halo of their genius. Within its limits lie Monument Mountain, Icy Glen, the Stockbridge Bowl, Green River, October Mountain and a thousand other scenes of storied or of unsung loveliness.

Bounding the valley on the north, from innumerable points of view, the double peaks of Greylock rise majestically three thousand five hundred feet into the air, the mountain summit of the Commonwealth. Along its western borders, in curves of marvelous grace, lie the dome-like hills of the Taghconic range. Less graceful in outline, but even more romantic with broken and precipitous ascents, wild glens and tumbling brooks, the Hoosacs shut out the world upon the east. Within this mountain-walled amphitheatre lies cradled the upland valley of the Housatonic, with all its fertile farms, its mansion homes, and frequent villages. Somebody has called it the Piedmont of America. I do not know how just the appellation may be, but I do know that if Piedmont can rightly be called the Berkshire of Europe, it must be a very delightful region.

What we most admire in Berkshire scenery is its freshness, boldness, and variety. Our hills boast no astounding grandeur; there is nothing about them of an Alpine character; they possess few scenes which can properly rank with the sublime. The highest mountain tops, the most precipitous cliffs — sufficient to claim our admiration, wild enough to be the marvel of tourists from the tame coast country — cannot, for a moment, compare with similar scenes among the White Mountains, or the Alleghanies — not to mention more unapproachable wonders of Nature. Our deepest ravines, often penetrated by smooth, flower-bordered roads, are very different things indeed, from the earthquake-rifted chasms of other lands.

If the traveller seek some object for a day's or a week's wonder, some tremendous cataract or " Heaven piercing Cordillera," he must seek it elsewhere. But if he asks for a retreat among wild and picturesque scenery, adorned by much that is pleasant and refined in his city life, but far removed from its heat and turmoil; where he can draw closer the silken cord of social intercourse, and yet throw loose some of its galling chains; where nature ennobles by her greatness but never chills with a frown, he may find it all amid the varied beauty of the Berkshire Hills.

The inexhaustible variety of our vistas is wonderful. It is marvellous in what an endless series of combinations, mountain, valley, lake, stream, rock, field and wood, present themselves. Wherever you go, you meet a constant succession of changes which at once charm the eye and delight the heart. At every turn

> "You stand suddenly astonished,
> You are gladdened unaware."

Through the long summer months you may daily seek, and not in vain, some new object of beauty or of romantic interest. But it may chance that you will not. It often happens that a few spots become so dear that one revisits them again and again, leaving others of equal or surpassing charms for those to whom *they* have become like a familiar friend.

So profusely indeed has nature scattered her wealth of beauty in this fair county that, to many, it seems a useless labor to search out her more choice and hidden gems; and they remain concealed from those who pass their lives within a rifle-shot of them.

The traditions, too, which used to attach to most of these scenes are rapidly fading with the fading years of grey-haired men. "Yes, there was a story"

I have been often told, " Old Deacon Whitehead or old Captain Grey used to tell it; but they are dead and my memory of it is dim." * * * * * * *

And now to you, whom I have presumed to call my friends, and for whom these brief pages were more particularly designed, I commend for your kindness what is done. Every word was written in sympathy with your admiration of these glorious hills; a sympathy which seemed to ripen into personal friendship with yourselves. If I shall point any of you to scenes of Nature's gladness, to which you would otherwise have been strangers; if I shall contribute one moment of happiness to your summer hours; if I shall hereafter recall more vividly to your mind these rural scenes, when they shall be a little faded, I shall be amply repaid; how much more, if I shall add one pleasant thought to mingle with your own, as you gaze upon the grand, the noble, or the beautiful, in our dear mountain valley.

OLD FRIENDS : —

Many years ago, in words like the above I addressed to you a little volume, which, somewhat changed in form, but not one whit in sentiment, I now offer to you again. If the words I then wrote were warm with the glow of first love, they seem tame to express the affection which, in the intercourse of years, has been inspired by each fair scene, each now familiar mountain peak: so many of them now inseparably associated with pleasant or tender memories.

Do you remember — it was but yesterday — standing on the beetling cliffs of Monument Mountain; clambering through the rock-cumbered recesses of the Icy Glen; lingering in pleasant Mahaiwe, blest of nature and of art; watching the moon and the sunrise on the shaggy shoulders of Greylock; wading and stumbling through the rushing brook up the marble ravine that leads to the Natural Bridge; dazed by the superb over-view from Perry's Peak; climbing the cliffwood recesses of South Mountain; letting the long summer days melt deliciously away, with discourse of books and nature, on the leafy summits of Osceola and Yocun's Seat; in storm on Otancaque, in sunshine on Constitution Hill; floating half sadly on Lake Onota or the Stockbridge Bowl; in merry masquerade on Pontoosuc or the Lily Bowl; listening to the lonely dash of Wahconah's Falls, or the mirth-mingled murmurs of Lulu Cascade; watching the summer-flash of life and fashion into the romantic solitude of Lebanon; puzzling over the potent charms of Lenox, loved of the literati; rapt in the noble memories of old Stockbridge on the Plain, and the no less noble memories of Poontoosuc, home of patriots; lingering in many a nameless nook or shaded woodroad, to be, perhaps, thenceforward dearer than all? You cannot have forgotten all this, for you know it was but a little, a very little while ago when it all happened.

And of tale and tradition; how have they on every hand answered to our seeking, and clothed every scene anew, with old life. To be sure, I have not deemed it necessary to severely criticise every tradition that has been preserved. Enough that it accorded with the spirit and the customs of the day of which it was related, and did not knock its brains out against some hard and ugly fact. Nay, I will even make a more startling confession. When in some dry old documentary history, or original document yellowed by age, I have found a glimpse of real life and real story, I have not been ashamed to call in the spirit of any old fellow, whom I supposed cognizant of the facts, to help me fill out the chronicle. Living for years half buried in accounts of these departed heroes and among the papers which they wrote — all the while striving with all my might to do justice to their memories — I should have thought it hard indeed if they could not now and then tell me a little story at midnight, when other spirits bestow their time so freely upon those who have no claim at all upon them. My old heroes were not so ungrateful. It does not seem best, however, to quote these spiritual authorities in foot notes, as e. **g.**

[1] Interview with Capt. Konkapot and Wampenum.

[2] Spirits of Captains Aupaumut and Solomon.

[3] Thus Coochecomeek, but Mahtookamin seems to think otherwise ; however, M. did not seem perfectly *en rapport*.

I am afraid this sort of thing would not do at all for the Methuselah Society for the Perversion of History. Nevertheless the testimony **of eye‑wit‑** nesses of, or actors in, scenes which took place, over two hundred years ago, is very satisfactory to right-minded people; and if they are willing to leave their happy hunting grounds or other places of comfortable spiritual abode and pleasure, to tell old tales of their old home, I for one am grateful. If you think otherwise, we will not quarrel about it: you shall have the stories all the same, just as the dusky shades of the heroes already quoted, and also Unka-met, Honasada, Wanaubaugus and the gentle Wah-conah, told them to me.

But, from whatever sources I may draw the incidents and legends associated with the scenery of Berkshire, I shall endeavor that none are inconsistent with the most accurate history; that nothing shall be told, but which at least "might have been." And I trust that none of my readers will be so dull as not 'to be able to detect what is literally true and what partakes of the infirmities of tradition. In the description of scenery my aim will be in all cases, without affecting any Pre-Raphaelite precision, to paint a faithful likeness. If I err it will not be in the intention.

I said that I address these little sketches to those to whom they were first dedicated; but, with the words, comes the thought that, of those favoring eyes to which I should have looked for the kindliest judgment, many have closed forever on the scenes of earth; that there are some spots, once the most joyous, which if we visit them for the purposes of mirth, seem strangely changed:

> " Happy places have grown holy ;
> If we went where once we went,
> Only tears would fall down slowly,
> As at solemn sacrament."

And yet we know that those whom we miss would have grieved sorely had they believed that their departure would leave a shadow, their memory could not brighten, upon the scenes that we enjoyed together. For us who remain, it would have been their wish that that memory should shed upon each spot with which it is associated, a purer and holier, but not less gladsome, light. To the living who have lingered with me in loving admiration among the hills of our dear old Berkshire, and to the memories of our dead, I then dedicate these pages.

We are most of us, still far from having lived out the life which it is appointed for man to live; still farther perhaps from having thoroughly earned the grave which we would not willingly owe to the charity of a soil to which we have given less than we have received from it. And upon him whose duty it is to live and strive, rests equally the obligation to enjoy; for he who works sadly, works at ill advantage; nor without enjoyment can there be any genuine and heartfelt gratitude for the gifts of the Creator — of which none speak more directly of Him than these grand mountains, these noble hills, these fair and fruitful valleys; among which let us hope that our rambles are not yet ended.

Godfrey Greylock.

Pittsfield, *June 1st*, 1879.

TAGHCONIC.

I.

OUR TOWN.

To be sure, the first claim which our town has to notice is that it *is* ours. The *propriâ* affords a paramount and never-to-be-disputed title to our affections. *That*, all clear-sighted persons admit. The very idea of property is genial to our hearts, even if it be only in the travelled streets of a town, with so much of Heaven's universal gifts as one can there possess, use and enjoy, in common with some thousands of copartners. Says Thoreau, with philosophic acumen — and Southey has the same idea, somewhat enlarged, in " The Doctor " — " I think nothing is to be hoped from you, if this bit of mold under your feet is not sweeter for you to eat than any other in this world — or any other world." " Mine " and more intensely " mine own," are terms of superlative endearment in the *patois* of the novel writers.

So inherent indeed in the human heart, is this correspondence between ownership and affection, that no sooner do we conceive a liking for our neighbor's house, horse, or, anything that is his, than an uneasy, feverish desire to transfer the possession betrays that our hearts are out of unison with the harmony of nature.

Nowhere is this natural law of relationship more religiously honored than in the love which the good people of Pittsfield bear to their beautiful town. But, waiving this claim, which is in its terms not binding upon a stranger, our town has a title to affectionate admiration, which not the most crabbed traveller ever yet desired to impeach.

It is indeed a fair town; and, standing in the center of that magnificent panorama of hills which encompasses the county of Berkshire, it is embosomed in beauty — in beauty, whose excess and overwhelming profusion, in some of its broader and more comprehensive presentations, often raise it to the level of the sublime. Branching from its central elm-shaded green, delightful avenues invite into the most picturesque regions. Through long vistas of elms, lindens and maples, you look longingly away to tree-flecked and grove-checkered hillsides, dappled also, it may be, with passing cloud-shadows; to wooded mountain tops, the nearer brightly green, the more distant sometimes dimly, sometimes darkly, blue, as the fickle powers of the air may ordain. Over valleys lying in goldenest sunshine, you look away to glens deepening into mysterious gloom, and — yet beyond — to pastures, stretched at intervals along the topmost heights, upon whose bright verdure the sunlight lingers longest. Enchanted land, you will think those Hoosac pastures, when, after a summer shower, the rays of the setting sun suddenly burst upon them, while they are overhung by such a rainbow as is possible only among the mountains; its glorious arch, gemlike in the living depths of its color, resting upon pillars of shadowy splendor which find their bases among the foundations of the everlasting hills.

Regions these, one would say, in which much of man's and much of nature's story must lie hid. Very enticing regions they are in truth; the whole broad landscape one grand volume of song and legend, bound in the most gorgeous green and gold. But, before we permit it to lure us away, I have a story or two to tell, which must be told right here, under this little cluster of elms; and nowhere else.

II.

STORIES OF A TREE, AND OF ITS PRE-SERVERS.

" Wise with the lore of centuries,
What tales, if there were tongues in trees,
That giant Elm could tell!"

You must have heard of the old Elm of Pitts-field Park. It has its place of fame among The Trees of America; and has had this many a year. It is not long since it rose here, among the young green growth, the scarred and seared veteran of centuries. Straight into the air it sprang, one hundred and twenty-six feet; a tall grey pillar, bearing for sole capital a few green branches, and a few withered, shattered and bare limbs. From Greylock to Monument Mountain there was no inanimate thing so revered and venerable. Nor had it grown thus without a story, and one with which the stories of other, and human, lives were closely entwined.

When it stood, a graceful sapling, in the forest, wherein as yet no white man had his habitation, the spot which is now our peaceful green, with a little neighboring territory, was an upland wood surrounded, except for a narrow space upon the north, by impenetrable swamps: a most defensible camping ground; such as the red engineers knew well how to select.

And here the St. Francois war parties, returning from their merciless raids into the valley of the Connecticut, were wont to bivouac, binding their way-worn and woe-worn captives to the lithe but firm-set young trees. Many a sorrowful sight must have been witnessed by that lone oasis among the hemlock thickets, but one tradition only speaks of individual suffering and adventure.

Peril the First.

Once — as this half forgotten old story goes — there came, among a group of captives, the daughter of one of those God-fearing pastors who, rather than bow the knee to Baal and Archbishop Laud, forsook their quiet and comfortable livings in Old England to become the living springs of the New England churches. Fair with the light of "Sunny Devon by the sea," and graced by culture imbreathed with the odor of honeysuckles and roses in the old moss-covered rectory, Isabel Walton carried sunshine, melody and joy into the bare log cabin prepared by the puritanic settlers for her widowed father, in their narrow forest clearing.

But, one murderous night, torn from the dead body of that father, and spared by the caprice or avarice of the savages, she was brought thus far on her way to Canada. Here, broken with grief and fatigue, she was doomed to death, as an encumbrance to their march, and to death by fire. She was already bound to the sapling Elm, and the faggots piled about her feet, when, happily, the party was joined by a small detachment of French soldiers under the command of a young lieutenant. Touched by the maidenly modesty, as well as by the brave and almost saintly bearing, of the victim, this officer interposed so vehemently that, partly by threats and partly by pledges of ransom, she was rescued; and with her the young Elm escaped its first peril at the hand of man. Supported with tender care and reverent regard by her manly preserver, Isabel reached Montreal in safety. And the garrulous old tradition, after the absurd manner of such ancient chronicles, thinks it necessary to add that weak, captive, and bereaved, as she was, she did not find the long march altogether without its consolations, or indeed at all tedious. I preserve this addendum solely for the benefit of elderly philosophers in search of psychological data. I am quite sure, at least, it will not be needed by any of my fair readers who ever passed an October day in Berkshire woods, rustling through the crisp carpet of many colored leaves, tumbling over criss-crossed and tangled roots, lunching sociably in sunny glades, climbing paths so arduous that the liberal support of strong arms was not to be dispensed with; and withal performing feats which would have made their teacher of calisthenics open her pretty eyes very wide.

And now I must tell you of one thing which I fear some of you will not so well like. But, ah me !

in any veracious narrative unpleasant facts will out.
Naturally there came a time in their wooing when
Pierre and Isabel spoke together of their difference
in religious faith. This was certainly after their
betrothal, but I think, the weight of evidence indicates that it was before their marriage; which the
records of the cathedral church fix with great precision at just one year after their arrival at Montreal.
The anniversary is a holiday with their descendants
even yet. But, whatever may have been the precise time when the lovers ventured upon this delicate topic, it was not until Isabel had become so
accustomed to yield to the persuasive tones of her
preserver and guardian, that the protestant pastor's
daughter forsook the faith for which her father
suffered — for which she, as well, was ready to
suffer — and adopted that in whose communion she
could walk with her husband. Mightier than Laud's
power of prelacy, or fiercest Torquemada persecu-
tions, are the soft persuasions of love. I beseech
you not to think too unforgivingly of the young bride
for this love-led back-sliding of hers. Rather than so,
I could wish you to disbelieve the story outright;
although that, besides being painful to my own feelings, would be deemed impolite by the whole long
descended Lanaudiniere family of Montreal, who
would consider it little that their great-great-great
grandfather — be the degree of his grandfathership
more or less — had rescued their grandmother in
like degree, from the flames of savage torture, had
he not also saved her from more enduring torments,

Should you visit them — these ancient Lanaudinieres — in their ancient Montreal home, they will
show you, in a richly gilt frame, still more richly
adorned with the precious tarnish of two hundred
honorable years, the portrait of a young woman with
very blue eyes very widely expanded; with very
yellow hair, and plump cheeks, in which very red
roses meet the very white, but very, very decidedly
refuse to mingle. A silver crucifix, or it may be of
ivory — envious time has here blurred the coloring a
little — rests upon a very full and a very fully displayed bosom; while the faint suspicion of a halo,
half retiring into the obscure back-ground, as if
doubtful of its right to be there, hovers above the
yellow hair.

You will guess this remarkable picture to be
enlarged from a saintly feminine figure in the old
family missal; the "specimen piece" perhaps, of
some accomplished Lanaudiniere damsel of an elder
generation; or possibly, a study by some artistic cadet
of the house, turned monk. Lacking the corrective
contemplation of living models, the imagination of
the cloistered artists, in their lonely cells, was wont
to play strange freaks with saintly personages of the
gentler sex; not excepting her lovely majesty, the
Queen of Heaven, herself.

But your guesses will be all wrong; as my friends,
the Lanaudinieres, will tell you, as politely as the circumstances will admit. And they will add, with
half offended pride, that this is the portrait of grandmother Isabel; a gift to grandfather Pierre from a

renowned Jesuit missionary, who painted it with his own pious hand, that the world might not lose the memory of the miracle of a New England Puritan converted to the old faith. Many a year of patient and fruitless labor among hundreds of that stiff necked race, " captivated " and brought to Canada, had taught the good father what a miracle that was. He believed that it was, and would be, unique. But you must remember that he was a celibate.

This preposterous painting is prized beyond measure by the present generation of Lanaudinieres, although, in their hearts, they know as well as I do, that it is not in the least like gentle grandma Isabel; save perhaps in the modest halo, which may indeed have glimmered above her golden hair, if saintly heads are ever crowned with such manifestations of Divine favor.

The neighbors of the owners of this portrait — the Protestant neighbors I mean — maliciously aver that the last genuine likeness of their ancestress departed from the Dominion of Canada, when, after a ceremony that was not performed cathedral-wise, another Isabel Lanaudinere sailed away, the bride of a young lieutenant-commander in Her Britannic Majesty's Sloop of War, The Whirligig — The Whirligig of Time, the Protestant wits of Montreal called it. It will be considerate in you when visiting these really excellent, but rather over-sensitive, people, to avoid all allusion to Her Majesty's naval service. I trust to your discretion, also not to repeat, what I mention in the strictest confidence, that their much prized Jesuitical portrait is but a sad caricature of features even too delicate for perfect beauty; of eyes as guiltless of a stare as the violet's; of cheeks which, never round or rosy, paled more and more to her young dying day.

Alas, not all the endearments of husband and children, not the fond affection of new friends, nor the charms of a new home, could altogether banish the memory of what had been in Old, and New, England.

Meanwhile, troubled by no memories, the young Elm grew and flourished. Memory never troubles things of growth and living verdure. If it should seem to you that any of the woodland scenes to which I am leading you back, are " sicklied o'er" by any " melancholy cast" of that kind, be assured it is but a sickly fancy of your own. Take boldly with you those to whom you have loved to forecast their charms. They shall tell you, the hills of Taghconic are as green, the sheen of their lakes as sunny, the echoes of their valleys as joyous, as even you can have portrayed them. The woods remember little of last year's wild flowers — nothing at all of those which perished long ago. It is the stern old rock, wrinkled by the convulsions, hardened by the fires, and furrowed by the storms of infinite cycles, which forgets not the most gossamer-like veining of the slender fern which, in his far off youth, lay upon his bosom and faded there.

But, unmindful even of the buried leaves which nourished its young life, the Elm, quivering with new joy in the new verdure of each new year, grew in beauty and in stature.

"How straight it grows!" said the Mohegan maiden.

"Straight as an arrow!" echoed the young warrior, himself almost as arrow-like.

Peril the Second.

But not the young Elm only, grew and exulted in the strength of its youth. The young commonwealth — the Province of Massachusetts Bay — also grew apace. And, by and by, some century and a quarter ago, the white man got himself sufficiently established in the Indian's Poontoosuck, to think of clearing the highways, which, many tumultuous years before, had been laid out 'very broad and straight; as the Great and General Court at Boston prescribed.

Here was indeed danger for our Elm. On this much tyrannized globe, there is not another despot so obdurate to every appeal for justice or mercy, as that enemy of the vested rights of nature in her own loveliness — the old-fashioned New England highway surveyor: of whom too many yet remain, to cumber the earth, and scrunch out her delicate graces with their hobnailed heels. Witness a thousand turf-robbed, shade-bereft waysides, whose dust this torrid summer shall rise up in judgment against these ruthless ravagers of their comeliness — these soulless deformers of the lawn-like knolls, which nature, with all her marvelous forces, had toiled for a myriad years to round into perfect grace.

Remorseless rascals, they were, for the most part,

those old tyrants whose resistless scepter was that hideous relic of barbarism, the ox-goad: and to their most legitimate rule, our dear young Elm was as clearly subject as ever hapless ward to heartless Suzerain. Something savoring of the miraculous was needed to save it alive; and something very like a miracle happened.

He to whom that cruel, proding scepter was first confided in the young plantation of Poontoosuc — so they called then, what is Pittsfield now — was a stout farmer from Wethersfield in Connecticut, who had become lord of some thousands of acres scattered here and there among the green hills. Tradition has preserved a world of racy and romantic stories about him, which we must not now stay for. In the Indian wars then just ended, he had been a stout soldier; and, afterwards, when the time for that came, he was as stout a patriot; bold alike to resist the encroachments of kingly power and the crude license of a newly enfranchised people. Honor, always, to his memory for these things; but, here and now, chiefly that, one summer day — doubtless one of those perfect June days, which still come in Berkshire, bringing all that is best in a man to the surface — with that sweet summer day softening the harshness of his rude work, he saw reverently, what in those forest-hating years, it required a rare eye to see, even with the aid of the most heavenly light, that God had made this tree passing fair; a thing to be loved and honored of many generations, and not to be rooted up like a pestilent weed.

Shall we praise such a man as this under a pseu-
donym? Leave him a mere backwoods *nominis
umbra* — an unsubstantial ghost of a name; to
wander, as dimly remembered, in the dim shades of
forgotten forests? I trow, not we! Honor then to
the name of Captain Charles Goodrich!

As was fitting, he *had* honor; had it for many a
year after that genial June day when he saved the
Elm alive; until, well nigh a century old, he died,
and was borne under its shadow to his neighboring
grave. But long before that, the tree had met its

PERIL THE THIRD.

From which, to use the pious phraseology of that
day, Providence again raised up for it a worthy preserver.

In that grand year, 1775, the most soul-stirring in
all Massachusetts story, a gallant and spirited youth
was enrolled, among the students of Harvard college,
as John Chandler Williams; a name indicating his
kinship with two families of considerable standing
in the scale of the Provincial gentry. Any quiet
study was at that time sadly unattainable in the
classic shades on the banks of the Charles; but the
young gentlemen were not, on that account, necessarily idle. In fact, several of them were notably
busy, one well remembered April day; having found
occupation with some, thenceforward world-renowned, farmers.

Young Williams was among them; and must in
some way have distinguished himself; for, not many

days after, he was summoned to the Provincial
Congress, then in session at Cambridge; by whom
he was as speedily dispatched, with a single companion, upon a secret and delicate mission; every
friend of the liberties of the Province being officially
enjoined to help him on. This mission was no less
than to secure the correspondence of Governor
Hutchinson with the enemies of those liberties on
both sides the Atlantic.

These important documents, having been left with
singular carelessness in Hutchinson's country-house at
Milton Hill, it required only a rapid and secret
movement to secure them; and they revealed all His
Excellency's secrets, about which the congressmen
had so lively a curiosity.

The congressmen were delighted; thanked their
messenger warmly; voted him the liberal and precise
sum of £4. 4s. 6d.; and then probably thought no
more of him. But he, poor fellow, had brought to
light other, and more, revelations than he looked for ;
as you shall see.

Student-wise, John Chandler loved his cousin; a
fair and stately cousin, who was daughter to a
grand and stately old father. Now this father —
Colonel Israel Williams of Hatfield, once a famous
commander of the Indian-fighting militia on the
Western Border, and afterwards Chief Justice of the
Common Pleas for the old county of Hampshire —
had, before the open rupture with the King's Governor, and indeed afterwards, been one of the few
friends of Parliament in the General Court. None

of the acts of government which had surrounded him with a population of enraged and rebellious Whigs, had served to shake his own loyalty to the British crown; so that, in the year previous to his kinsman's exploit at Milton Hill, Governor Gage appointed him one of his thirty-six councillors. *Mandamus* councillors, they were called, being created by the Royal writ, and not elected by the Representatives of the people, as was the old charter privilege. Thus, nothing was more hateful to the patriots than a *Mandamus* councillor. Resolved that their venerable judge should not become this odious thing, they — as a mild form of persuasion — shut him up in a small school house, closed the windows, built a huge pitch-pine fire in the ample fire-place, and then blocked the chimney-top. The judge, although a brave, and withal an obstinate man, succumbed — as who would not ? — and signed a renunciation of his office, with whatever other pledges his tormentors saw fit to dictate.

There were a good many hesitating persons made excellent Whigs by processes like this. But Judge Williams was not a hesitating person; and, having settled it in his judicial mind that pledges made under duress were not binding, he, like a prudent judge, reserved his decision, and went on his way, but covertly, the same old servant of King George. Trumbull has commemorated his pertinacity in his queer old Hudibrastic, "McFingal," where he makes that hero taunt his persecutors with the futility of their methods:

> " Have you made Murray look less big,
> Or smoked old Williams to a Whig?
> Did our mobb'd Oliver quit his station,
> Or heed his vows of resignation ?"

Hutchinson's unfortunate letter-book rendered Judge Williams's prudence of no avail, and made it apparent that he had furnished the royal governor with the most dangerous information, and, still worse, had urged the severest measures against the unruly provincials.

The Whigs can hardly be blamed that, upon this discovery, they threw him — even him, one of the " River gods" of the Connecticut — into Northampton jail. It is what follows, that shows us how even zealous patriots, and possibly, although that is not fully established, gallant soldiers, may come short of being in the least chivalric gentlemen, or even passable Christians. The jails of a century ago were miserable places at the best: not at all like the comfortable structures in which modern criminals recruit their exhausted energies, and take lessons of infinite value in their after-rascal-life. The most favored prisoner could not congratulate himself on a prolonged residence in the Northampton jail of 1775 ; and Judge Williams was not a favored prisoner.

We might forgive that, too, remembering the fate which he had contemplated as fitting for his jailors. In our distant, latter-day view, it would no doubt have been well had his venerable years and many services to his people softened resentment a little; nay, even turned aside a little the severity which the safety of the country seemed to require against those whose loyalty was not towards her. But we will not complain that the rigors which he would have visited upon others, recoiled upon his own head. The something which will not be forgiven while the story lives, lies beyond that also.

His fair and stately daughter, for all her beauty and all her stateliness, was as loyal to her father as he to his king. Proud, brilliant, and with a wit which could be grandly used in wrath when the occasion demanded wrath, towards him she was gently and devotedly affectionate as only a strong warmhearted woman can be. With her Roman name —. have I said that she was called, Lucretia ?— she had some noble qualities of the Roman dames.

Daily, after the incarceration of her father, this noble and beautiful girl visited him in prison and ministered to his wants. And daily, as she passed to and from his place of confinement, she was subjected to taunts, and insulting threats against him she loved so well, from the baser fellows who, either in official positions or as loiterers, hung about the jail. The favorite councillor of the renegade Governor Hutchinson, and the chief Tory of Western Massachusetts, could not have looked for extraordinary leniency from the exasperated partizans who held him in their power; but Northampton was the home of Hawley and other of the more high-bred and courtly leaders of the people, who could hardly have known and sanctioned the unmanly treatment to which those who had such claims upon their courtesy as the Tory chief and his daughter, were subjected. I believe that, after awhile, they did interfere. The judge was liberated; and, under the surveillance of some local Revolutionary committee, was permitted to live, with such comfort as in that way he could, until the close of the war; and afterwards, for some years, in peace and freedom.

In the western counties it was too much the custom to leave the "handling of the Tories,"—as proceedings against the loyalists were quaintly called, to violent partisans, who, well knowing that the powers above would never finally consent to extreme punishments, were accustomed to provide for their prisoners a little purgatory, by placing them in the custody of coarse and vindictive jailers, who were glad to undertake the ungracious task in order to gratify some ancient pique — as often of a private as of a public origin. It was not alone in Revolutionary France that, under the cloak of patriotic zeal, vulgar envy sought, in its coarse way, to humiliate those who had been its social superiors, and low crime to avenge itself of its high-born judges.

What was the exact nature of the insults heaped upon the proud Judge Williams and his prouder daughter in Northampton jail, we can only conjecture. Whatever was their character, the latter curbed her resentment for the time, for her father's safety, but it never ceased to rankle in her heart. To her the name of Whig was always hateful: the glorious Revolution was always the "Rebellion," and the theme of her bitterest wit; and, to her life's end, she proclaimed herself the loyal subject of whatever "Sacred Majesty" filled the throne of Great Britain.

How, in this temper, she arranged matters with the lover kinsman who had so large a share in bringing about her family misfortunes, the parties interested discreetly kept to themselves: as I had occasion to remark, a few pages back, love has his own way out of all perplexities. But we hear of no more patriotic exploits recklessly performed by the young John Chandler, who went sedately back to college; graduated with high honors in 1778; studied law with the Honorable, and very conservative — John Worthington at Springfield; and, in due time — himself became a conservative counsellor, and Federal politician at Pittsfield.— And yet the spirit which led him to Lexington and Milton Hill was not quenched; years afterwards, among his fellows of the bar, he was still "Mad Chandler, the Wild."

The offended, but tender-hearted, Lucretia, of all the world, understood perfectly the nature of the change which had come over the young man; and she must have considered it as meeting her at least half way. At any rate, they commenced married life, about the year 1783, in the fine old gambrel roofed mansion — then fresh from the hands of the carpenters — which you still see among the Elms, across the park; still in all its pristine dignity. And there they lived, happy and prosperous; there died honored and lamented by all around them, notwithstanding the lady's political idiosyncrasy.

If you ask, "what has all this to do with the perils of The Old Elm?" I answer, "Much every way."

You will infer with me that such a woman as Lucretia Williams would love bravely where she loved warmly, even though the object of her affections were but a rock or a tree. She was indeed a true lover of the beautiful in nature; and its undaunted defender, as well, against all the evil fashions of her day. To her we owe yonder cathedral-like colonnade of elms, with whose long succession of gothic arches she surrounded her home; first resolutely levelling the poplar grenadiers, whose stiff plumes, being of the latest importation, were *a-la-mode* for all courtly court-yards. Perhaps they reminded her unpleasantly of militia sentinels pacing around Northampton jail.

For seven long years, however, she consoled herself, for looking through these objectionable bundles of lank twigs, by the luxuriant foliage and graceful form of the fair elm on the green beyond. She had learned to love it well; and the better after Captain Goodrich — a frequent and congenial visitor at the conservative Williams fireside — had told her something of its story. Then, in the seventh year — or, to be precise, *Anno Domini*, 1790 — came the Elm's Third Peril.

The town had hitherto worshiped in a little brown meeting house, rich in grand memories, but poor as it well could be in every other respect. Now they resolved to build anew, in splendor commensurate with their increased wealth and larger figure in the world's eye. A famous Boston architect — one Colonel Bulfinch — furnished a most ornate design evidently suggested by Faneuil Hall, but intended to eclipse that renowned edifice: and, after the manner of his craft, sent a superbly colored representation of it, with a profusion of scrolls, brackets, pillars, arches and what not, which at the suggestion of Dame Prudence were largely omitted in the completed structure.

When this astonishing "design" was handed around among the congregation at the next Sabbath nooning, the admiration was so intense that there was danger lest, as in some modern instances, the new building would become a House of Worship in an equivocal sense. But the immediate, the "imminent deadly," peril was to the Elm. There was then around it neither park nor public square — nothing but a little grass plot, kept from the public travel in the broad street by immemorial custom. On the outer edge of this green, and well into the legal highway, by the grace of God inspiring Captain Goodrich, the Elm still kept its place, with the little old meeting-house almost, or quite, under the shade of its spreading branches. It was intended to place the new building upon the site of the old; but, with the excitement created by its architectural promise, came a desire for a more conspicuous location.

A large share of the more resplendent glories of the proposed edifice were concentrated in the tower and belfry; and these, it was discovered, would delight a majority of the citizens when on their way to church or market, if only they were thrust a few feet into the highway. True, this would mar the fair proportions prescribed for the street by the esthetic old legislators at Boston, and, what at this distance seems quite as bad, would involve the destruction of the Elm. But, then, incontestibly, the street would still be wide enough for all the purposes of travel; and were there not innumerable elms in the near forest? We have lately cut off the superb vista of the same street by an ugly brick railway station house; and it will hardly do to call that vandalism in the fathers which must be taste and culture in the sons. At any rate, whatever we may call it, the people, in town meeting assembled, determined to make the sacrifice; although not without stout opposition from Captain Goodrich, "Squire" Williams, and others who held God's beautiful creations to be esteemed beyond man's fairest handiwork. If the Elm's indwelling dryad had not before been exorcised by the prayers or frightened away by what passed for music in the old church, she must have shuddered in the deepest recesses of its trunk, at the horrid speeches and resolutions of that town meeting.

In the Williams mansion there was grief, consternation, lamentation, indignation; and then a determined purpose to resist the barbarous edict, so far at least as it concerned the Elm. Madam Williams did not melodiously request the woodmen to spare her favorite tree; partly, perhaps, because there was no ballad to that effect in her *repertoire;* but chiefly, no doubt, that such was not the lady's manner of aiding her friends in their extreme distress. It is of tradition that once in her girlhood she threw herself, with triumphant daring, between her father and a raging mob of exasperated Whigs. The story is not verified beyond historical doubt, but it is likely enough to be true. By a resort to similar feminine tactics, she certainly saved the Elm; placing herself resolutely before it when the ax men came to perform their fell task.

Here was a curiously sad dilemma for the puzzled executors of the town's wicked will. Had almost any other woman thus stood in the path of municipal wrong-doing, she would have been thrust aside with small ceremony; if not with a sharp threat of some of those ingenious and highly civilized punishments contrived by the keen-witted New England fathers, lest the impulsive sex should rush madly from their sphere.

But with a lawyer's spouse it was quite another matter; that is, if man and wife were in perfect accord, as the Williamses were to a proverb. In those superstitious days, a gentleman of the green bag was held a most uncanny person to deal with at odds. It was grewsome to think what dread processes he might evoke from the mystic depths of that weird receptacle of the law's imperious *dicta* and *scripta ;* or from the still more occult and awful recesses, where he sat, among massive and inscrutable tomes, well known by their potent words to have charmed many a man out of a fair estate, and into a foul jail. Not that Squire Williams was known ever to have wrongfully used his abstruse learning. On the con

trary he was counted a rather benevolent sort of
dealer in the law's black art; given to the defense of
the poor, the protection of the widow and the father-
less, and to bringing the counsel of the wicked to
naught: still there was no telling what latent fiend-
ishness might be developed even in so benevolent a
wizard; for was he not an attorney after all?

There were therefore none to lay violent hands
upon Madam Williams, even with the town's most
puissant warrant.   Nay, even the Selectmen felt that
a dreadful weight was lifted from their mighty
breasts, when they found that the Squire would take
only a generous advantage of their ludicrous predicament.

As I have said, there was, around the Elm, no
green or public square, such as adorned a few of the
more aspiring villages of the Commonwealth; but a
vision of such a glory had danced before the eyes
of some of the more ambitious citizens; and especially
dazzled the not inconsiderable number who held com-
missions in the militia, and already in imagination
saw themselves resplendent upon a parade ground
worthy of their most gorgeous array.   The un-
sophisticated chieftains would have stared at the
suggestion of coping and curbing it into an out-of-
door parlor.

Mr. Williams shrewdly seized the opportunity to
offer for a village green, so much of his land south
of the Elm, as the town would devote to the same
purpose from their domain on the north, used for a
meeting-house site and burial ground.   Under these

conditions, it would be hard to guess how far the new church would have receded, had not a great part of the burial-ground been already well filled with graves. The old puritanic folk held it idle, or worse, to consecrate their cemeteries; nor did they cover them with conservatories, or convert them into driving parks. I fancy they would have eschewed the word, cemetery, as savoring of paganism. But they held sacred so much at least of the dust in their plain grave-yards as had once been animated by living spirits; and they shrunk from making money, or saving it, by secularizing the soil with which the ashes of their dead were inseparably mingled. So they were fain to content themselves, in this instance, with a village-green of moderate dimensions.

It chiefly concerns us, however, that, by the bravery of Madam Williams and the timely generosity of her husband, the Elm was again saved.

And now the love of the people began to go out more and more towards it. Fond associations clustered faster and faster around it; growing more tender, and gaining a richer flavor with age — as may always be expected of such luxuries, as well as of others of a less sentimental caste. Children pursued their noisy sports under the tree's expanding shade, pausing often to form fabulous estimates of its size and centuries; which, for the most part, their later years never found time to revise. In the near academy, the village boys and girls played their pretty prelude to life's drama. Here were the athletic games whose best remembered feat — entitling the youth who performed it to a place in the town's little Valhalla — was to hurl a ball over the Elm's loftiest branch. Here lovers lingered a precious moment in their moonlight walks. Here were the Fourth of July celebrations, the cattle shows, and all the country gala-days which bring boyhood back to the most prosaic citizen who has a heart in him; even if it glow only at these long intervals — as some fanciful people aver that comets periodically revisit the sun to replenish their stock of "caloric," wasted by measureless wanderings in coldest space. And, while the noble tree was thus sending its roots deep down into the hearts of the town's-people, it was also growing up to fame; for travelers celebrated it in their books, and poets in their verse.

And thus it came about that when any "to the manor born" went out into the great world beyond the mountains, the Old Elm was the center around which clustered all their memories of home; and when any stranger visited the village, it was the first object of his search — unless, as was most likely, it had been the first to greet his approach.

Doom.

But, escaping all peril, to trees as to men, comes at last that which is not danger, but doom. And, as with man, so with the tree to whose mortality the sacred writers so often liken our own, the life which aspires the most loftily best chances to meet a noble death. It so happened with our Elm. A thunderbolt fell crashingly upon it, and darting straight down its tall trunk, ploughed a wound of ghastly whiteness from stricken bough to seared root. The fiery fluid dried up the juices in its old veins, and the whole tree, although cared for with almost filial tenderness, began slowly to perish. But, even in its death it was fortunate. The long white streak pencilled by the scathing lightning in its smooth bark, caught the eye of Herman Melville, who, in his wonderful story of "The White Whale," thus interwove it in his strong-lined portrait of Captain Ahab:

"Threading its way out from among his grey hairs, and continuing straight down one side his tawney scorched face and neck until it disappeared in his clothing, you saw a slender, rod-like mark, lividly whitish. It resembled that perpendicular seam sometimes made in the straight, lofty trunk of a great tree, when the upper lightning tearingly darts down it, and without wrenching a single twig, peals and grooves out the bark, from top to bottom, ere, running off into the soil, leaving the tree still greenly alive, but branded."

There you have a graphic picture of the old Elm in its decay. And thus in its death-stroke, it found a new life: as the ancients fabled that they who were slain by Jove's thunderbolts thereby became immortal.

The brave old tree had clearly received his death wound, and remained "greenly alive" but for a space, and only as to a few scanty boughs. Still, grandly wearing this meager coronal, and erect as when the Indian maiden likened it to her warrior lover, it looked as if proudly conscious of the veneration which it inspired; as I have seen some white-haired citizen walking beneath it, in a vigorous old age, full of the memories of a gracious youth and a beneficent manhood. And, each spring when the young grove about it began to put forth its buds, the question, "Will the old Elm survive this year also?" was anxiously asked by a whole people whose love for it in its grand decrepitude and decay, exceeded even that of Lucretia Williams for its leafy prime.

Twice again it " midway met the lightnings," and then, one summer morning, the whisper passed along the street that the Elm was bending to its fall.

The axe — in kindness now — gently aided its slow descent, until in the afternoon it lay prostrate: while men whom the world does not accuse of immoderate sentimentality, stood aloof, literally weeping; and the more mercurial crowd rushed eagerly to secure a chip, a leaf, a twig, a branch — any relic of their old friend. Soon wherever they who had held it in reverence were scattered abroad, bits of its wood set in gold, appeared among their richest jewels; or, in less costly guise, were treasured in the most sacred reliquaries of their thousand homes.

And, lo, when the tree's inmost heart was laid open, there preserved, were found the tokens of its earliest perils and, pervading its whole tissue, the unbroken memories of all its summers, and all that they had done for it. Said I that the woods remember nothing?

THE GREY OLD ELM OF PITTSFIELD PARK.

Tell us a tale, thou grey old tree,
  A tale of thy leafy prime;
For thine was a home in the forest, free,
  Ere our bold forefathers' time.
Thou sawest the wild-wood all alight
  With the bale-fire's direful glare,
Where now the murkiest gloom of night,
  Our household fires make fair.

    Then tell us a tale, thou grey old tree,
      A tale of thy leafy prime,
    Of the wild-eyed red man roaming free,
      Or our fathers' deeds sublime!

Say, when the gorgeous laurel flowers
  And sweet-briar's bloom were gay
If here, in the forest's fragrant hours,
  Some dusky loves would stray!
Sadly, we know, the captive's sigh
  With thy murmuring sound was blent :
Oh tell of the love and the courage high
  That the captive's bondage rent.

    Ay, tell us a tale, thou grey old tree,
      A tale of thy leafy prime,
    Of the wild-eyed red man roaming free,
      Or our fathers' deeds sublime!

Tell us the tale how the forest fell
  And the graceful spire arose;
And, charmed by the holy pealing bell,
  How the valley found repose.
Our heritage here, with the blow and prayer,
  Was won by the good and brave,
While over their toils, like a banner in air,
  They saw thy branches wave.

4

Then tell us a tale, thou grey old tree,
   A tale of thy leafy prime,
Of the wild-eyed red man roaming free,
   Or our fathers' deeds sublime !

Ah, dearly we love thy wasting form,
   Thou pride of our stern old sires,
Though torn by the rage of the darting storm,
   And the lightning's scathing fires ;
And dearly the sons of the mountain vale
   Wherever their exile be,
Will thrill as they list to the song or tale
   If it speak of their home or thee !

      Then tell us a tale, thou grey old tree,
         A tale of thy leafy prime,
      Of the wild-eyed red man roaming free,
         Or our fathers' deeds sublime !

III.

ANOTHER STORY.

What came of, and to, Chandler Williams's Village Green.

"For the soldier's trade, verily and essentially, is not slaying, but being slain. This, without well knowing its own meaning, the world honors it for. A bravo's trade is slaying; but the world has never respected bravos more than merchants; the reason it honors the soldier is because he holds his life at the service of the state. Reckless he may be — fond of pleasure or adventure. All kinds of bye-motives and mean motives may have determined his choice of a profession, and may affect (to all appearance exclusively) his conduct in it; but our estimate of him is based on this ultimate fact — of which we are well assured — that, put him in a fortress breach, with all the pleasures of the world behind him, and only death and his duty before him, he will keep his face to the front; and he knows that this choice may be put to him at any moment, and has before hand taken his part — virtually takes such part continually; does in reality die daily."— *Ruskin*.

And, of the spot whereon the Old Elm once stood, what? Other stories, and grander than the simple tales, I have ventured to tell, early ennobled it; but must nevertheless have the briefest narration here.

Near yonder very prosaic brick corner, bounding

one of the most park-like, and least prosaic of streets,
stood, a hundred years ago, the quaint old gambrel-
roofed tavern of Colonel James Easton; the commander of the Berkshire Militia, and Ethan Allen's
lieutenant in the capture of Ticonderoga. And, to
its hospitable door, late on the dark and rainy evening
of May-day, 1775, came Captain Edward Mott and
his little band of sixteen Connecticut men, stoutly
resolved, by the Grace of God, and with the help
assured them among the Green Mountains, to wrest
"the Key of North America" from the grasp of
Great Britain. At midnight in the most secret
chamber of the old inn, although the bar-room had
long been emptied of its tonguey revellers — while
the great raindrops dashed and spattered against the
pigmy window-panes, and a generous tankard of
aromatic punch steamed before each wet and wearied
guest — the Connecticut leaders held council with
five or six bold and true men of the vicinage; among
them their host, and his neighbor, Ensign — afterwards Colonel — John Brown; a member of the Provincial Congress, who, being specially charged by
that body with efforts for the acquisition of Canada,
was the projector of this present expedition, as well
as of many another daring adventure afterward.

Before dawn, not to endanger the secresy of their
plans by adding to their company here, Easton and
Mott crossed the Taghconic ridge, and passing up
the secluded and romantic valley of Hancock (it
will well repay you to do the same, even with a much
less stirring errand) they were joined by twenty-

four stalwart minutemen, with Capt. Asa Douglas —
a "Douglas, trusty and true" — at their head. In
the meanwhile, Ensign Brown and the remainder of
the party, starting also under cover of the darkness,
drove up the Berkshire-valley to Williamstown,
where they were joined by fifteen other bold and
trusty yeomen. Then all began their march to join
Ethan Allen and the Green Mountain Boys. All the
world knows how that march ended. The spot where
the men of Massachusetts and Connecticut first met
in council concerning it, in the home of one of the
earliest, the bravest, and the truest of Revolutionary
patriots, should be held as sacredly memorable as
those resting places in old, renowned pilgrimages
which royal piety marked with monumental crosses.

And, on yonder other corner, where, among ancestral trees, a massive mansion marks the site, stood the
modest dwelling in which lived and died the Parson
of Bennington Field. In the little brown meeting-
house under the branches of the Elm, year in and
year out, he preached that the Gospel of Liberty
was part of the Gospel of Christ; and much fruit
came of it: sweet and bitter, but for the most part
wholesome. Potent to-day beyond much which
struggles visibly — and all too audibly — for power,
his spirit still lives and walks abroad among these
hills: and not here only, but far away in ever-ex-
tending paths.

A hundred years ago the pulpit of the little meeting house was indeed the seat of power; so that
when the patriot soldiers gathered on the narrow

green before its door, it seemed as if their hearts had been verily touched with a live coal from its altar. And, from this holy rallying place, inspired anew by solemn prayer and fervent exhortation, they marched away to Canada, Bennington, Saratoga, Stone-Arabia, or wherever else Berkshire blood flowed for freedom.

Where they thus assembled, the national independence which they helped to achieve had been commemorated, with rural, but not unmeaning, pomp, for well nigh a hundred years, when treason assailed the nation's life. Then, on the same spot where the fathers met to consecrate their lives to the service of their country, the sons assembled for the same holy purpose. Even while the tall Elm still waved its branches — a tattered banner — above them, the minute-men of 1861 responded to the first note of alarm as eagerly and promptly as the minute-men of 1775 sprang to arms when the reveille, beaten by drums as far away as Lexington Common, announced the dawning of the Revolution.

The old tree fell: but, year after year, often and often, the peal of other than church-going bells, and other music than that of the organ and the choir, deepened the solemnity of the Sabbath, and summoned the people to high conference in the young grove which succeeded to its honors. How vivid is the memory; yet how distant seem those strangely awful Sabbaths, and those anxious nights when the lurid glare of torches fitfully lit up the over-hanging foliage and the endangered flag, while eloquent voices from some rude rostrum, told the danger of the hour to those whose souls were already heavy with the consciousness of it.

At hours like these, or when, at busy noon, the clangor of bells and trumpets hushed the more sordid sounds of trade and traffic, what new and conflicting emotions struggled in every breast, as those most full of life and life's longings were adjured to risk all in the defence of that which was dearer than all. Duty, religion, a pure patriotism, a noble ambition ; how fervently each was urged in its turn. What promises of life-long honor, and tender regard, to be shared by none — what prophecies of enduring fame, glowed upon the lips of the orators ! And, ever and anon, as the young and faithful-hearted — glorifying the plain tables at which they sat into sacredest altars — enrolled themselves in the Grand Army of the Nation's Defenders, how the ringing plaudits, bursting from the full hearts of the people, seemed borne by the rolling echoes of drums far into the promised future.

What other memories, in the lives of any of us who did not share in the actual conflict of arms, can compare in grandeur, with the recollection of those sublime moments; and of others, intermingled with them, when regiment after regiment with sad, but proudly unregretful, farewells — and not without solemn prayer and fervent exhortation, as of old, from reverend lips — marched hence to do or to suffer that for which they had set themselves apart?

Then, whatever gloom might overhang the hour, we knew that the old heroic spirit, which, in the foolishness of our hearts, we had thought passed away forever, had come again in all its fullness; and that the old triumph was assured.

Here and there a taint of mean ambition, or meaner avarice, you may have detected in those who received these plaudits, although I hope that you were better minded than to be seeking for it. An army of purely unselfish men, marching in any array, were conceivable only in an age which shall be free of all armies; in that, namely, when nations "shall beat their swords into plough shares, and their spears into pruning hooks."

For this present, be content that, as to all who enrolled themselves, and — with whatever ulterior reward in view — did become actual soldiers, we come, at least, if to nothing better, to Mr. Ruskin's "ultimate fact" of the soldier's soldierly fidelity to the state under whose flag he has enlisted.

But, on the other hand, in how many did you discover a purity of purpose and of soul, a stern subjection of self to duty, an unboastful heroism so unlooked for, an intellectual strength in quarters so unsuspected, that they seemed like a new and sudden inspiration from Heaven. So illy do we read that which lies behind the eyes into which we daily look. Nay, the revelation vouchsafed to our great need, seems in these less exalted days so incomprehensible that we are fast losing it in clouds and doubt.

Yet surely such men were — and are — and they

did in verity shed a luster upon our arms beyond that of conquest. They did exist; enough of them in almost every New England village, to ennoble its name — if their story could but be worthily told.

Their ideal, but deeply truthful, type, wrought in enduring bronze, surmounts yonder monument, the memorial of those who marched hence, to sacrifice their young lives in the defence of their country. I pray you mark that statue well: it is no common work; but the tribute of genius, to heroism, patriotic devotion, and much else. It represents simply a color-sergeant of the Union army, standing in line-of-battle, and looking eagerly and thoughtfully into the distance. The figure is erect, but slightly supported by the staff of the colors, which it grasps with both hands — the right also gathering the flag into graceful folds. The work is correct in detail as well as truthful in its grand effect; but these are its minor and prosaic merits; there is more in it than these. Both face and figure are of a peculiar military type — as unique and readily recognized as that of the French Zouave or the Cossack trooper — which the war for the Union developed from material which it found rough-moulded in every Northern village. You will see, as you study his work, that the sculptor's ideal was a bold, frank, generous man; resolute rather than defiant, of valor without ferocity, of gentle heart, without weakness; self-reliant, but modest; capable of either commanding or obeying; looking into the future as well as the distance; a man with such stuff in him as poets and orators and statesmen, as well as conquering soldiers, are made of.

They dedicated this memorial one genial September day, with much memorable eloquence, and much military and other pomp, of which I will only here recall, that, among those who had large part in it by word or work, was he

> "As Galahad pure, as Merlin sage;
>   What worthier knight was found
> To grace in Arthur's golden age
>   The fabled Table, round?
>
> A voice, the battle's trumpet note,
>   To welcome and restore;
> A hand that all unwilling smote,
>   To heal and build once more.
>
> A soul of fire, a tender heart
>   Too warm for hate, he knew
> The generous victor's graceful part,
>   To sheath the sword, he drew.
>
> The more than Sidney of our day,
>   Above the sin and wrong
> Of civil strife, he heard alway
>   The angel's advent song."

Him, I may single out, not invidiously, from those who on that September day joined in consecrating this monument to its hallowed purposes; for, even while mingling his monitions to his surviving comrades, with laudations for the dead, his enfeebled frame prophecied but too truly that his life, too, would soon be added to the great price of the nation's unity.

But you are restless, that I detain you so long upon this contracted spot; and we will leave it; taking with us, however, as I hope, this lesson; that he who, like Captain Goodrich and Chandler Williams, graciously preserves a thing of mere grace and beauty, may well expect that, in due time, much of the grandly and nobly useful — nay, much of sublime human action — may cluster around it, and mingle their memories with his own.

IV.

REMINISCENT.

The memory of great men is the noblest inheritance of their country.— *Blackwood's Mag.*

You have been very patient with me — have you not? — in my long-time weakness of lingering by this old park; and perhaps I ought to reward you with an excursion to the lake-side or mountain-top. But I pray you to be patient yet a little while, as we take a walk among the pretty village houses, with their luxuriant gardens, and court yards green with shrubbery — a delightful summer promenade. To the towns-people the older of these dwellings are all pregnant with associations of the past; each has its story. They tell you — these good citizens — as you pass along, now pleasant, gossiping histories; now low-hissed scandals, mouldy and soured, which ought long ago to have been in their graves; and occasionally you hear a tale of open or proved guilt such as you would rather not believe could have its dwelling in such innocent-looking homes.

You hear them speak names which call up no image in your mind, and which have long since ceased to receive an answer in these streets. They call places by appellations unfamiliar to your ears. The iron horse has brought new wealth, prosperity and hope to the thriving town. There are groceries where there used to be gardens; mansions where there used to be meadows. The town is richer and handsomer than it was; but in many hearts, for whom the old quiet used to be full of joy and peace, the new wealth and crowd and noisy prosperity cannot but sometimes awaken painful longings. In the stillness of the evening — when the shrill cry of the steam-whistle pierces the ear and goes echoing into the breathless distance, like the shout of a drunken man on the solemn midnight — you listen to their touching reminiscences of the past, and are moved by laments for which the eager, throbbing heart of common life has no chord in unison.

But, for the present, we will pass scandal and retrospect, except so far as the latter recalls the memory of two men whose wide-spread fame has become identified with that of their homes, and whom I have not mentioned with others who have brought honor to it — George Nixon Briggs and the Rev. Dr. John Todd. Whether there is romance in the lives of either of them or not, there is certainly beauty in their memory, among the hills; and beauty that is seen afar off. I need not speak in detail of either. Their memoirs, written with rare ability, have been long published to the world; and I only desire here, by a few reminiscences of their lives, to give a pleasant tinting to our scenery.

And, first, of the much-loved Governor Briggs,

whose beautiful tomb in our beautiful cemetery is the spot there most sought by the visitor. You will observe that, conspicuous upon it, is a large white marble cross. He loved well that simple symbol of the Christian faith, so long proscribed in New England; and it was his influence which placed it on the spire of the village Baptist church in which he worshipped. But I shall only have room to give you a few reminiscences, illustrating one of the qualities which won for the good governor so universal popularity, and which were remarkable as mostly referring to incidents which occurred within the compass of a few days.

In the spring of 1851, I chanced to occupy, one day, a seat with Governor Briggs in the cars of the Boston and Albany Railroad. The train was excessively crowded, many being compelled to stand; and when we reached Westfield there entered our car, at the door most distant from us, two women evidently much wearied; one of whom carried a child. None of the gentlemen in their vicinity seemed to notice their condition; but Governor Briggs went forward, invited them to our seat, and aided the one with a child to reach it. Instantly many seats which had not been vacated for the weak and tired women were placed at the service of the Governor of Massachusetts; but he remained standing, talking kindly to the women and at times soothing the child which had been made restless by its unaccustomed position. There was nothing in this, you may say, more than any true-hearted gentleman ought to have done.

True; but, out of a whole car-full, Governor Briggs was the only one to think of doing it.

We passed on, and as we approached the Brookline Bridge, near Boston, found that a collision had taken place upon, it, blocking the passage with the wreck of two trains, which hung by a fearfully precarious hold over the water. It was necessary for the passengers to clamber over and through the wreck, to reach the relief train, while their baggage was sent to the city by the highway. But, among them, was an old Irish woman, one of those wrongheaded, as well as ignorant, people who can never be made to see the necessity of anything out of the ordinary course. She would not and could not be separated from her trunk — a rude, hair-covered chest. Most men would have been merely amused by, at least indifferent to, her troubles; but ludicrous as was her grief, it was piteous and real, and such, however uncouth and groundless, never failed to touch the heart of the governor. So when, having passed from one to another, imploring aid, she came to him, perceiving at once the uselessness of attempting to reason with her, he quietly took hold of one end of her trunk, and helped her carry it over the tottering wreck. The profuse and quaintly expressed thanks of the woman, and her still more profuse and quaint apologies — when, with all her old-world awe of dignitaries, she found whom it was she had made play the porter for her — were extremely amusing. But there were few who witnessed the scene who did not envy Governor Briggs

his satisfaction in relieving the distress of even so
rude and uncouth a creature, by so simple a piece of
thoughtful kindness.

Leaving the governor at Boston, I pursued my trip
to Martha's Vineyard, where I employed a man to
carry me from point to point in search of certain
varieties of clay — a plain, but intelligent and quick-
witted person, of much shrewdness and criticism,
which he applied freely to public men, as we rode
along. But, happening to learn incidentally that I was
from Pittsfield, he checked his horses suddenly, and
exclaimed. "Pittsfield; why Governor Briggs lives
there !" Somewhat surprised at his apparent emotion, I assented; and he continued: "I love that man;
I always shall. You know I am a Democrat; but I
always put in my vote for George N. Briggs. He's
got a heart — he has !" I asked him how he found
that out; and he replied, that once, when the governor was reviewing the militia at New Bedford,
he was standing directly behind him, with his little
daughter in his arms. The child begged hard to
see the governor and the troops, while the crowd
and his position made it difficult to show her either
to her satisfaction; but the governor, happening to
hear her entreaties, turned around, took her in his
arms, and placing her before him on his horse, showed
her the soldiers, and then, with a kiss, returned her
to her father — a pleased child and a grateful father,
you may well believe. "I have loved him for that,"
he said, "ever since;" and I always shall."

At a later time, arriving at Pittsfield with a

travelling acquaintance from the west, he asked me, while the train was accidentally delayed for a few moments, to show him the residence of Governor Briggs, who had then been some months dead; and I took him to a point where he obtained a view of the trees which conceal it. As he seemed deeply interested in the view, I remarked carelessly, " So you are a hero-worshipper." " No," he replied with evident emotion, " I loved the man — I had good reason to ! " I had no time to learn the cause of this feeling — whether it arose from some of those minor acts of kindness, such as I have related, and such as the governor was constantly performing — or from some grander benefits, for which occasion more rarely presents itself: but the tone and manner of the speaker were more earnest than would probably have been caused by any trivial beneficence.

How many friends would be made by a public man whose life was filled with acts of kindness like those I have mentioned, and governed always by the spirit manifested in them, I leave you to judge.

You will pass the Governor Briggs homestead on your way to Lebanon or Lake Onota, a little way beyond the Railroad Station in Pittsfield ; a handsome mansion with fine grounds, and rich in portraits, busts and relics of its former owner.

The parsonage, once the home of Dr. Todd, is not very far from the Park ; but it is so changed from what it was that it hardly suggests a memory of him. When I first came to Pittsfield, the first thing I looked for was the author of " The Student's

Manual ; " and I had no difficulty in singling him out from a number of *distingué* figures in the village streets. He was the homeliest good-looking man, I ever laid eyes on ; and, withal was unmistakably marked with the impress of thought and feeling. Mindful of certain ridiculously ineffectual attempts to mould myself upon the systematic model prescribed by his famous book, I held him in almost grewsome awe ; and it was a great consolation to find afterwards that he was not nearly so formal a man as I dreaded, but one who did an immense amount of work, simply by attacking it lovingly, and with a loving purpose. You may recollect that he became an author, so that he might add to his means of supporting an aged and infirm mother.

He was the most contented man I ever knew. Living comfortably and handsomely, if not luxuriously ; loving and loved, not only by his own people, but by the whole community ; glorying in and enjoying the natural beauties and the pleasant fortunes of his home ; surrounded by a social circle perfectly adapted to his tastes ; honored at home, and famous abroad ; with admirers to welcome him, wherever he went ; with the means and the taste to fill up his vacations with healthful woodland sports : Thus favored of fortune, there was no good reason for discontent, and Dr. Todd was not the man to seek evil ones. Of sorrow and pain, he, like other men, had more than enough; but they were the incidents of his manhood, not of his position in life. They might be sources of grief and bodily agony ; but not rightly of discontent.

Seeing the man thus living and, as it seemed to me, living beneficently, and in the tenderest love for all the world, I came — although I had little sympathy for what I supposed to be his abstract theological opinions — to share in the kindly feeling which he inspired in all about me. In this comfortably Christian mood, I was shocked to find the truculent Theodore Tilton, who had been taken somewhat sharply to task by the good doctor, going about insisting that the following lines, by Longfellow, were intended as his portrait :

> " The parson, too, appeared, a man austere,
>   The instinct of whose nature was to kill ;
>   The wrath of God he preached from year to year,
>   And read, with fervor, " Edwards on the Will ;"
>   His favorite pastime was to slay the deer
>   In summer on some Adirondac hill.
>   E'en now, while walking down the rural lane,
>   He lopped the wayside lilies with his cane."

" Good lack ! " I thought, "can this be the man who, to our uninspired eyes, seemed the very soul of gentleness ? who seemed to have a child-like love for the meanest flower that blooms? who sorrowed for a loved tree, as for a friend ? Where had that austerity been hid for so many years; that it never scared the village children who hung upon his smile just as though it was benignant. Had all of us really been, for near forty years, ascribing the kindest of humane souls to one whose instinct was to kill, and who did not even spare the lilies in the Berkshire lanes — if any grow there; which I very much doubt, unless somebody, like Dr. Todd, has planted them for the wicked pleasure of cutting them down. There really seemed to be a sad misconception on somebody's part — Mr. Tilton's, as I hoped, since it could not much harm him.

But let us see, item by item, wherein the likeness of the picture to the Pittsfield pastor consists. Item first: The scene of the poem is laid in the village of Killingworth; and Dr. Todd was born in the village of Killingworth in Connecticut, but was never pastor there. Item second : The Killingworth parson was a "man austere ;" there the likeness fails altogether — Dr. Todd was anything but that. Item third : This austere parson "preached the wrath of God from year to year ;" and I suppose that, like thousands of other ministers of religion, the world over, Dr. Todd preached upon that theme as often as he thought it to be his duty ; which was certainly not "year in and year out "— for he delighted much more in preaching the Creator's tender mercies, that are over all his works.   He rested firmly upon the orthodox Congregational creed — the faith of his fathers — and died steadfast in it ; but he loved best to repose upon its sunny side ; and, ever, as his religion ripened with his mellowing years, his charity grew broader, and his appreciation of God's loving kindness keener and deeper.   Item fourth : The poet's objectionable preacher read with fervor " Edwards on the Will: " Dr. Todd was at one time pastor of a church in Northampton which was an off-shoot of that which in 1750, by a majority of one hundred and eighty, refused utterly to have the stern Calvinistic moralist any longer to be their servant—or, as he would have had it, their master — in the Lord.   However, the children had long ago repented of the sin of their fathers — the offending minister having risen to a great height in the esteem of his co-religionists. And so, when they sent out a colony to found a new church, they called it "The Edwards;" and Dr. Todd, who became its first minister, gave the same name to his first-born son.   Doubtless he held his celebrated predecessor in reverence; but I had it from his own lips that he deemed, not only the much objurgated and much-admired Treatise on the Freedom of the Will, but all metaphysical theology whatever, unprofitable reading, while we have the Bible, and the great book of Man and Nature is spread wide-open at its less abstruse pages.   I do not believe that he read a page of "Edwards on the Will," with fervor or otherwise, after he left the Theological Seminary. Item fifth : The favorite pastime of the Killing-worth Cruelty was to slay the deer in summer, out in the Adirondack country.   And so did Dr. Todd love to hunt the deer there, and elsewhere ; as hundreds of very worthy people still do.   The pleasures of the chase would bring little but pain to myself ; and the cold-blooded ruthlessness with which Kingsley in his "Idylls" gloats over the skillful "killing" of trout ruins half my pleasure in that otherwise charming book.   But that, I take to be a constitutional peculiarity ; and it would be absurd in the extreme for me, on the strength of it, to assume a virtue above that of Canon Kingsley, Isaack Walton, Shakespeare, Adirondack Murray, and a host of other renowned trout-killers and deer-slayers, lay and clerical.

But, to be fair, I suppose that the gist of Mr. Long-fellow's accusation, if it be an accusation, lies in the innuendo — "in summer" — intending thereby that the reverend defendant slew the deer, out of season, wantonly, and contrary to the recognized although unwritten laws of venery. And Dr. Todd did pursue the chase on the Adirondack hills in summer. He could not well have done so at any other season ; but he obeyed the law in its spirit, if he broke it to the letter : for he scrupulously refrained, however much in need of venison, from firing upon a fawn or a nurs-ing doe, and never at any season killed for the pleasure of killing, but rather with pity for the pain inflicted.

There seem to be some wide divergences between Mr. Longfellow's portrait, and its assumed original ; but there is sufficient vraisemblance to justify the as-sertion that Dr. Todd was the clergyman whom the poet had in his mind, when he wrote "The Birds of Killingworth ;" and it seems equally certain that he was misled by the reports of certain jealous and rascally Adirondack guides — as is very well shown by Dr. Todd's biographer. And it is to be mourned that the most amiable and gentle of our great poets — one to whom the love of all English-speaking people gives such power of reproof and condemnation — should have allowed himself to be led into injustice by such base and vulgar slanderers. I will not believe that he was the more readily induced to give them credence by the memory of Dr. Todd's old polemical pastorate — a half a century ago — in Groton. The *odium theologicum* could hardly rankle so long as that in the celestial mind of the author of so much noble and manly verse. But well says old Selden, speaking of judges who hold the power of life and death : "Let him who hath a dead hand take heed how he strikes."

Here have I been spending this time which we might have given to pleasant reminiscences of Pittsfield's great pastor in a probably needless defence of him against a random and unworthy charge : but perhaps I have been able in this way, as well as another, to show how he appeared to one out of his own theological pale. How he looked to one of his own household, both in the faith and according to the flesh, is graphically painted in the full and frank biography published by his son.

V.

PONTOOSUC LAKE.

The memory of one particular hour
Doth here rise up against me.— *Wordsworth.*

Oh, thou most rare day in June, whose rain of golden moments fell so preciously by the green borders of Pontoosuc; there shall be few like thee in the gladdest summer month !

With L. and two other friends from the dear tri-mountain city, and with one laughing daughter of the Berkshire soil, I went that faultless morning, to pass the " lee long summer day " by the clear waters of our favorite lake : the popular favorite, although, fair as it is, I confess that it has a rival in my own esteem. But this is lovely enough to satisfy any reasonable craving. And so is the approach which brings us to it. Passing the neat and tasteful factory village, whose busy wheels have been turned by the waters of the lake for more than half a century, you enter a piece of winding, willow-shaded road, on the left of which the ground descends abruptly to the rocky bed of the Housatonic river, which issues from the lake a few rods above. Just below, it falls in a cataract, whose worst fault is that it is artificial,

Alas, on this whole romantic stream, from the mountains of New Ashford to The Sound, there is not one waterfall which has not been disturbed by art. But water, and especially dashing, sparkling, foaming water, is always beautiful, and this broad, smooth sheet of crystal, rolling over its table of massive marble, to be broken into infinite sparkling drops thirty feet below, is worth at least a passing glance. If you so honor it, you will observe that the smooth water, at frequent intervals in its fall is bent, across its whole width, into rippling curves parallel to its upper surface. The cause is simple enough, but it took us, bright ones, a long while to hit upon it that June morning. No, I shall not tell it here; for it is the prescriptive privilege of the Berkshire friend who first drives you that way, to propound the problem for your bewilderment.

Before you have solved it, a slight rise in the road will bring in view the blue surface of the lake, in glassy stillness or sparkling in broken light, dotted only with two emerald islets. Mere dots, now : in that elder day, before the dam-builders — observe that, as I spell it, dam is a noun substantive — before the dam-builders had raised the surface of the lake and spoiled some of its prettiest outlines, these islets were quite conspicuous islands; the commodious resort of frequent jolly chowder-parties. At a still earlier day, as you will see by and by, they had a story.

You catch your first glimpse of the water between gentle declivities covered by a fine growth of pine, with, here and there in the intermediate opening, an elm, a hemlock or a beech. As you pass through these woody portals — or better, if you stand in the grove on the southern bank — the view expands. The farther shores rise gradually to hills; to mountains. Not far off, in the west, they terminate in the ever-graceful Taghconic domes; every summit of which, in a calm clear day, is mirrored by the unruffled lake. You should see them on such a day in their brave June verdure, or in their October splendors, every height, every hue, glowing double, hill and shadow, as perfectly as ever Wordsworth's swan.

On the north, the long valley, a little broken by the bold, fair hills of Lanesboro', stretches away until it finds its barrier in that superb culmination of so many Berkshire landscapes, grand and graceful Greylock.

You would pause, as we did, to admire the almost artistic arrangement of the stately grove of pines, the single elms, and beeches, and the twin hemlocks scattered along the lawn-like slope between the road and the lakeside ; but I know not how much of all these the encroaching waters will leave for the delectation of future visitors. There was a very joyous and soothing beauty in the scene as, driving slowly along, with the gently rippling waters upon our left and the cool evergreen grove on our right, we stopped here and there; now to gather splendid bouquets of the rich red columbine, which then grew here in profusion, and now to try, for the most part in vain. to catch a glimpse of the birds, who from their hiding places, joined with most melodious energy in the carolings of M. and F.

Dismissing our carriage at the northern end of the lake, we sauntered back, lingering by the pebbly shore, where the dashing of the wavelets reminded us all of the great billows that beat upon the Atlantic beach one other summer day. It was strange this mimicry of the great sea by the little mountain loch. F. said she had once been startled in the same way by recognizing the tones of a great orator in the lispings of his infant grand-child. Such are the trifles of which talk is made on summer excursions.

Then we sat awhile under the great pines, and let that mischief of a Grace — she of the Berkshire Hills — inveigle every one of us into a promise to read there, on our return, verses in their honor, composed during the day. I confess that I was, for a reason which will appear by and by, the first to assent to this nonsense. But, having assented to it, our wisdom recovered itself, and espying across the lake, an inviting grove familiar to all our lovers of picnic, we determined to make it our camping ground for the day. I have since seen a fanciful array of gaily bannered barges moving thither in long procession bearing the semblance, at least, of kings and queens, cavaliers and court ladies, priests and bandits, harlequins and columbines, monks and outlaws, clowns, savages, fairies and all the masquerading fraternity, while pealing music echoed among the astonished hills, and the dwellers on the farther shore wondered what on earth was coming now.

In our time the lake fleet was somewhat more scanty ; but, by the courtesy of the gentlemen of the neighboring factory, we were enabled to reach the haven where we would be in a luxurious boat, once the property of Audubon who had used it in his studies of the rich ornithology of the Berkshire-lakes. We were soon quite at home in a nice nook of the grove, where, by the aid of L's flute, F's guitar, the fun of the madcap Grace, a book or two of poetry, and a plentiful supply of cold chicken and other " creature comforts," we passed hours which are not lightly to be forgotten in lives which have few such.

Then, too, there were rough rambles, to the grievous detriment of Grace's flimsy drapery ; although, on my soul, I believe the gypsy tore that gown with malice prepense, for the sole purpose of bringing an unhappy victim within range of her wit. At any rate he came, an l, as she was repairing damages with an infinitude of pains and pins, impertinently asked what she was about ? " Collecting my rents, stupid ! " And as Grace was the owner of houses and lands in quantities, we all laughed. It is so easy to be witty at picnics.

" And to laugh at the wit of an heiress any where," do I hear you add ? Well, perhaps, Monsieur Le Sauer; but that has nothing to do with our lake-side merriment. You haven't an idea what a balm there is in woodland odors. I half believe a day or two in these Berkshire woods would take some of the grimness out of even your visage. The experiment is worth trying, for the curiosity of the thing, if for nothing more. I wonder how you would look with a gleam of real genuine happiness in your eye. So come right along, old fellow, and we'll take you all about : make a new man of you as like as not.

There are fanciful legends about this Pontoosuc lake; among them an old tale that a shadowy bark with a shadowy boatman is often seen to flit over its midnight waters, as if in quest of that which it is doomed never to find. What it is this restless phantom seeks, whether lost love or hidden foe, I do not know that legends tell. I have often passed that way at the accredited witch-ing hour : sometimes when the pale moon shed a very ghostly light upon the waters, while the shrieks, screams and howlings that hurtled discordant upon the air, defied all my 'ologies to assign them to any known beast, bird or reptile ; sometimes when only the lurid lightnings fitfully lit up the night, and shim-mered a thin and sulphurous blue from shore to shore; sometimes when fisher's skiffs, a red torch glowing at every prow, looked sufficiently infernal ; but neither in ghostly moonlight, by lurid flash, or by glare of torch, can I rightly say that I ever caught sight of his flitting ghostship.

"You never did ! well that shows how much of a seer *you* are. Now, that ghost's as real as — as real as anything. Why there are two of them."

It was that saucy Grace who said this, when she read my humiliating confession. The simple fact is that Grace belongs to one of the old story-telling Berkshire families. One of her ancestors was prime chum to Hendrick Aupaumut, tradition-keeper-in-chief to the Mohegan nation, almost two hundred

years ago; and that veracious chronicler indoctrinated
him in all the legendary lore of which he was master.
Of course his pretty descendant has a tale to fit
every romantic scene among her well-loved hills. I
do not know that any of her story-telling ancestry
were ever guilty of fathering the wild children of
their imagination upon old Aupaumut. If they did,
nobody suspected them of it: for they were all
"honorable men." or at least were always so desig-
nated in the political columns of the county newspapers. I have, however. sometimes suspected that
their quick-witted daughter. rather than let any
favorite spot go unstoried. would on the instant in-
vent a tale to meet its exigences: and if a ghost were
needed would e'en haunt it herself. I have gleaned
from her a good deal of the material for the Indian
legends of this volume: but in order to secure the
accurate truthfulness. which. as you perceive. charac-
terizes them. I have been obliged to correct her
vivacious narration by the aid of graver authorities;
frequently summoning Hendrick Aupaumut from
the Happy Hunting Grounds for that purpose. and
sometimes consulting the historical collections of
Dry-as-Dust LL.D.

In most cases I have thus scrutinized her stories
so closely as to leave little doubt of their perfect
truth: but in this Pontoosuc affair. I shall devolve
that task upon the reader. and tell the tale just as it
was told to me.

SHOON-KEEK-MOON-KEEK.

"She loved her cousin ; such a love was deemed
  By the morality of these stern tribes
Incestuous."— *Bryant.*

In the first place you must know that Pontoosuo
was not the aboriginal name of the lake now so
called. That is a corruption of the Mohegan word
Poontoosuck — "a field for the winter deer," by
which the tribe called all the Pittsfield valley, indicating that it was their abundant hunting ground.
When the factory of which I have spoken was built,
it received the name, simplified for the sake of
convenience, and it was gradually extended to the
lake itself.

The Mohegans, who loved the lake well, called it
Shoon-keek-Moon-keek. Why they did so, you will
find out if you listen with a little better attention
than you gave those phantom voices across the water:
loons, herons, owls and foxes, I haven't a doubt.

Although at certain well-defined seasons of the
year, this valley, in the old Mohegan times, used to
be all alive with hunters and trappers, its permanent
population was exceeding scant. The Indians did
not greatly affect solitary wigwams, but the little
clusters which passed with them for villages were
small indeed; and it was one of the smallest which
stood in the sunny recess among the hills, seventy
or eighty rods below the lake and on the west side
of the outlet. You can hardly mistake the spot.
They found some ghastly relics of the aboriginal

owners not far from the site of their village, not many years ago.

The great men of this little community were two brothers, probably not very conspicuous in Mohegan annals, for their very names are forgotten now; and all else concerning them except this faint legend. It happened one bright day in June, three hundred years ago, that to one of these brothers was born a son, and to the other a daughter; the prettiest little papooses that ever came to light in all that region. Their names, Shoon-keek for the boy, Moon-keek for the girl, seem to have signified their parent's appreciation of that pleasant fact, although I cannot give you a literal translation of the words.

One shudders to think of the barbarous physical and moral training those young things underwent. No boarding school miss ever had her back straightened by such heroic processes as gave uprightness to the children of the woods, and I dare say the mental and moral processes were equally rude and effective. The motto was "kill or cure;" the weaklings always gave in, before they made much trouble in the world. As the cousins did not die, the presumption is that they graduated, perfect specimens of the Indian youth and maiden: indeed the tradition hints as much.

The other result might have been better for them; but no such gloomy premonition overshadowed their joyous childhood.

> "The morning of our days
> Is like the lark that soars to heaven, all happiness and praise;
> The earth is full of beauty, rose .bloom is on the sky,
> And hope can never fail us, and love can never die."

And so Shoon-keek and Moon-keek revelled together in all the joys of childhood; gathered for each other the arbutus in spring, the laurel in summer, and all pretty wild flowers in all flowery months ; together filled their birchen baskets with the luscious berries of the woods, together chased birds or butterflies; and as they grew older fished on the lake in the same birch canoe.

It was very pleasant for the fathers to see the children thus absorbed in each other — just brother and sister, as it were : which, considering the stern moral law, I have quoted above from Bryant's famous poem, seems to me much like playing with edge tools ; cousins are so liable to discover that they are only cousins. Not that any consciousness of wrong disturbed the pure happiness of Shoon-keek and Moon-keek: even when they were both thrown into consternation by the matrimonial advances made by divers young men of the tribe to the maiden, they did not suspect the nature of their common grief. Little the simple ones deemed that the affection which, in those pleasant places, had grown up as sweetly and naturally as the may-flower and the violet mingle their perfumes, was unholy.

So natural and so innocent was their intercourse that, not until the keen eye of jealousy discovered and its subtle tongue pointed it out, did the fathers of these poor children suspect the love, which they called guilty; nay, not till the voice of parental authority had forbidden their precious meetings did the lovers learn the nature and ardor of their own passion.

Parental authority had some rather effective means of asserting itself among our predecessors in this valley. But not for that did the cousins consent to forego each other. The means of evading parental oversight were also abundant in those thick-wooded days. There were hidden recesses in the islands of the lake, in its sedgy shores, in its inlets and outlets, all very tempting to opposed lovers who could both speed the light canoe. Then, as now, at night as well as by day, the surface of the lake was constantly dotted by the little skiffs of the fishermen — and fisherwomen. And then as now, the busy plyers of the hook and line little noted at night if one or another skiff, dipping its torch quietly in the wave, suddenly darted into some narrow hiding place. But then it unfortunately happens that all who go down upon the lake in little boats are not busy plyers of the hook and line, but sometimes, rather, busy-bodies in other men's matters: a sort of people, who, though specifically classed by Holy Writ among the wicked, persist in existing in all ages. And they always make mischief wherever you find them. Nockawando was the mischief-maker on Pontoosuc Lake three hundred years ago; and as he was, not only a prying busybody, but also a jealous lover of the pretty Moon-keek, you may be sure he was not long in making known to her father the secret of her clandestine nocturnal meetings with her forbidden cousin: and a pretty lecture the old fellow read her ; with a promise of such further measures as on examination he might find the case to demand.

My dear young lady reader: that threat suggested something much more serious than being locked up in your own room, even on a meagre diet of bread and water. But, if love laughs at locksmiths, what could be expected of a flimsy wigwam, without so much as a latch to rattle or a hinge to creak, in the way of restraining a brave girl's wayward fancies? The lovers had planned a meeting that very night upon the island in the lake; and they had it. They had before determined to fly from Mohegan-land and ask adoption into some eastern tribe whose marriage code was less absurd than their own; precisely as an Englishman, resolved to marry his deceased wife's sister anyhow, just takes her across the Atlantic. The idea was a capital one; and, under the pressure of Nockawando's terrible. discovery, they determined to carry it out the very next night. They should have started right off on the instant. I wish they had, even if the lake had waited to this day for a story and a name. But, even with the primitive wardrobe and diet which prevailed three centuries ago in Mohegan-land, some little preparation seems to have been needful. And, then, Moon-keek's stern parent had intimated that he would wait the return of his brother from Esquatuck, before proceeding to extreme measures.

But delays are dangerous, as even our sanguine lovers seem to have been aware; for they made sad provision for the possibility of failure. They had

not faith enough in the moral code of their nation,
to make themselves mangled martyrs to it, like
Bryant's monumental maiden, by jumping down a
five hundred feet precipice into a hugh pile of
jagged and splintered flint rocks. They declined
martyrdom singly, even in the milder form suggested
by the deep waters of the lake. But, however rebellious against the more austere deities of their
nation, they were sworn subjects of whatever imp
in their mythology played the role of Cupid.

Before leaving the island, they, therefore, solemnly
pledged themselves, that, if any fate should interpose
to prevent their flight, and threaten to separate
them forever, they would meet beneath the cool
waters, and part no more. It was a fearful vow;
and yet lovers, educated in a more enlightened faith,
have been known to make, and faithfully perform,
essentially the same. There was nothing in it, save
the cousinly relation of the parties, that was re-
pugnant to the superstitions of the forest. Yet hear
what befell those who preferred the worship of the
little god, Cupid, whatever may have been his Mohegan name, to the behest of the Great Manitou.

You will have anticipated that fatal disaster befell
the cousins in their proposed flight: fatal indeed
it was, and fearful; but it may be briefly told.
Shoon-keek, gliding stealthily across the waters to
his island rendezvous, died by a treacherous arrow
from the bow of Nockawando; and his body, pitching
from the canoe, sank with strange swiftness. No
breath of life, no spark of soul, lingered to buoy it

for an instant; but the shadowy semblance of him who had sat there, kept his seat, and the skiff sped on, faster than when driven by mortal arms — towards the island, past the island, into the dim night.

The expectant maiden discerned it as it passed, and the piteous tone in which she shrieked the name of her lover pierced the heart even of Nockawando who was approaching the point upon which she stood. The response came back as piteously, from afar, " Moon-keek ! " The lover — now a phantom, could then hear and answer the loved voice; but, though his arm seemed to drive on the skiff, another power inexorably guided its course.

It needed but this, and the sight of the murderer, to tell the frantic girl all that had happened. Nothing remained but to fulfil her vow. Springing into her canoe, she darted it madly from the shore, singing a wild and plaintive death-song. Nockawando hastened to pursue ; but, as he drew near, the song ceased and such a supernatural silence prevailed that, in the terror of a guilty soul, he would have fled; but flight was no longer possible. He came nearer still: the maiden, like her lover, was a shade. What more he saw or heard, was never known, except that, as he looked, the canoe of Moon-keek, without apparent motion, was afar off. He returned to the village, a gibbering idiot. Neither hunting-ground or war-path ever knew him more. The dusky maidens gazed upon him, shuddering — but pitiful ; and he fled from them as from some remembered horror. The tribes-men dealt charitably with him as with one stricken of heaven; but he went ever feebly moaning strange syllables: the wise men said, they were the parting words of the phantom maiden.

Death at last came to his relief. But not so ended the punishment of those who loved not wisely ; that is, not according to the traditions of their people. If legends do not lie, it was decreed of Manitou, that so long as the lake shall dash its waves, so long shall their restless shades flit over them with responsive but bewildering and illusive call and response, while, led by the hope that maketh the heart sick, they nightly seek that meeting, no more to part, to which they impiously pledged themselves in the madness of unlawful love.

With rightly attuned ears, you may, on almost any night when the lake is not frozen, hear those piteously plaintive voices, calling to each other from ever-changing points, and if you are a right ghost-seer — a sort of gifted folk much more rare than they used to be — you may sometimes faintly discern a shadowy canoe flitting, spectre-like, over the waters; vanishing here, appearing there, in an altogether supernatural way: like an aboriginal Flying Dutch-man in miniature. Such are the phantoms of the Mohegan's Shoon-keek-Moon-keek, and our Pon-toosuc.

"If I were rich enough, I would have that cruel lake drained," cried F., her blue eyes filled with tears.

"Don't," said the laughing story-teller, "It would ruin some of the finest water-power in the county."

And yet one could see with half an eye, that she was proud to have had one sympathetic auditor.

"And now," she continued, "now for the pine grove and our improvisings!"

Oddly enough no one owned to giving a thought to that rash promise of the morning, except Grace and my unhappy self — why unhappy, you shall see by and by.

The pine is rather a rare tree in this region; but there are a few fine groves; this by the lake-side being the finest, although but a relic of that which the records proudly boasted, a hundred and fifty years ago. It looked very grandly as we paused on our way home, to pay it our tribute of verse.

Grace, as the proposer, was first called upon for her offering; and gracefully accepting the situation, read:

Pinos loquentes semper habemus.

"Lowland trees may lean to this side or to that, though it is but a meadow breeze that bends them, or a bank of cowslips from which their trunks lean aslope. But, let storm or avalanche do their worst; and let the pine find only a ledge of vertical precipice to cling to, it will nevertheless grow straight. Thrust a rod from its last shoot down the stem; it shall point to the center of the earth, as long as the tree stands." * * * * Other trees tufting crag and hill yield to the form and sway of the ground; clothing it with soft compliance, are partly its subjects, partly its flatterers, partly its comforters. But the pine rises in serene resistance, self contained.— *Ruskin.*

All hail to the pine, to the evergreen pine,
   The pride of our forest, the boast of our story:
   A health to his tassels; still green let them shine,

To remind the new times of the old fields of glory !
'Twas he to our fathers, on Plymouth's bleak shore,
  The first shelter gave and the first welcome bore :
Then a health to thy tassels our own native pine ;
  A halo of glory, above us they shine.

All hail to the pine, o'er our heroes that waved,
  Ere plumed was our Eagle or starry flags floated !
On field and on fortress where tyrants were braved,
  The pine on our banner the victor denoted.
It marched in the van where our minute-men met,
  Its folds with the blood of our Warren were wet ;
Proud voices of story are evermore thine,
And we thrill to thy murmur, O, eloquent pine.

All hail to our-pine, fadeless type of the true !
  The changeless in beauty, unbending, undaunted ;
The banner of green, to the May breeze he threw,
  In the gales of December as bravely are flaunted.
He meeteth the blast when the tempest is high,
  Nor faints in the heat of the scorched summer sky.
Grand poet, pure teacher, high priest of truth's shrine,
  Thou art evermore with us thrice eloquent pine !

When Grace rolled out that Latin quotation-title in her fullest and richest tones I opened my eyes wide and stared at her in a half dazed way — glared at her, as she tells it; and got a provokingly saucy smile for my pains. But, as she read on with melodious calmness, my blood fairly tingled; partly with amazement, partly with vexation and perplexity.

"There was nothing in the verses so startling as that comes to," you remark.

No indeed ! but the fact is, I had spent some weary hours, the day before, preparing to extemporize those very lines, which the minx was coolly reciting as dashed off by herself in our pic-nic hubbub. But scolding would have been absurd, especially as, to tell the truth, she read my poor purloined verses, so charmingly that they sounded almost like real poetry. To make a formal claim to the authorship was at least dangerous, in view of the probability that this was the very ambuscade into which my fair foe was trying to lead me, and once there I should be at the mercy of her merciless wit.

There was only one road out of the scrape; and luckily I took it — I overwhelmed her with the most outrageous praises of *her* poem, and wondered that it could have been written in the brief and broken intervals of such a day. I had never suspected her of such genius. Then I tore my own manuscript to shreds, declaring that it should never be brought into comparison with such a transcendent work.

The rest of the party, astounded at my extravagance, fancied that I was crazed by love, or something else equally far from my heart; and even the marvellous equipoise of Grace was a little disturbed. But she quickly regained her composure, and we both kept our counsel for that day.

Of course the truth came out in the end, and I received the credit which that eloquent reading gained for my verse. Now I am rash enough to throw it away by printing the thing. I wont spoil a story for relation's sake, even though the relationship be so close as mine to myself. And, from the first, I determined to describe this particular pic-nic with reasonable fulness, just to show the uninitiated what a Berkshire pic-nic really is. I shall not need to depict another so minutely, unless it be of a different class.

But this is not yet ended. Some sunny hours of the June day yet remained, and, as our party was to be broken on the morrow, we were tempted to crowd as much as possible of pleasant adventure into the present excursion. We therefore resolved to extend our ride to a wonderful rock of which we had heard much, and which could be reached by an additional drive of perhaps two miles, around the north end of the lake. There is a nearer road to it from Pittsfield village; but this, by and around Pontoosuc, is far the most picturesque.

The Balanced Rock.
Dropped in nature's careless haste.— *Burns.*

Passing again the lakeside, we turned, by a cross-road towards the west, and rolled through a quiet rural country, whose inhabitants, whose fields and cattle, even; nay, whose very houses and barns; seemed as much in exuberant enjoyment of the day as ourselves.

> " Every clod feels a stir of might —
>   An instinct within it that reaches and towers,
> And, grasping blindly above it for light,
>   Climbs to a soul in grass and flowers;
> The flash of life may well be seen
>   Thrilling back, over hills and valleys;
> The cowslip startles in meadows green;
>   The buttercup catches the sun in its chalice,
> And there's never a leaf or a bud too mean
>   To be some happy creature's palace."— *Lowell*

A hill on this road affords fine prospects in various directions; especially looking backwards upon the lake, which has a wilder picturesqueness than when viewed from any other point. The Taghconics, too, loom up grandly in front.

When the sun wanted an hour of his setting, we passed a few scattered chestnut trees in a field, and entered the grove which concealed our sphynx.

The Balanced Rock is a huge mass of white marble — grey upon its weather-stained surface — weighing many tons; rudely triangular, or still more rudely oval, in its shape; and so nicely balanced on a pivot of a few inches, that, although, by the aid of a lever, it may be made to slightly oscillate, no force yet applied — and it has been tried with more than reasonable effort — has been able to overturn it.. Of course it is not impossible to accomplish this vandalism; but fortunately the means are not within easy reach of ordinary wantonness. The great danger is from greed; if this curious work of nature should come into the possession of men of different character from those who have hitherto owned its site. It should be public property; and one of its recent owners offered to make it so, with sufficient surrounding land, on condition that the public would take measures for its preservation.

The belief used to be that the mass was immovable, which was an excellent reason for calling it the Rolling Rock, by which name it was first introduced to me. But I can bear witness that, on the occasion of a certain notable visit to the spot by the combined

scientific associations of Troy, Albany and Pittsfield,
certain venerable savans, by the aid of a friendly
fence-rail, did obtain distinct vibrations.

The same learned gentlemen determined, rather
more doubtfully, that the great rock was not perched
up there — where it looks like the roc described by
Sinbad the sailor — as certain other huge boulders
were strewn about the county, by being thrown over-
board from ice-bergs or ice-floes, several million ages
ago. It seemed to them, on the contrary, that the
Balanced Rock grew where it stands, and that the
mass which originally enclosed it had been worn away
by innumerable floods. On the other hand, a more
recent geologist, after a more complete survey than
the pleasure excursions of science can afford, discards
all theories of floating ice, and holds that all these
boulders, the Balanced Rock included, were deposited by fields of ice, several thousand feet thick,
slowly grinding over the ancient surface of the
valley.

They appear to have done some thorough work —
those old ice giants — crushing, as in an emery mill·
quartz, slate, mica, corundum, jasper, marble, horn-
blende, green-stone, iron, and every rock that could
be gathered from the neighboring mountains, into all
required sizes from that of the Balanced Rock and the
Alderman, to the dust that grits in your teeth and
sends a cold shudder through you when the ther-
mometer is raging among the nineties. You may see
fine specimens of ice-age-work carefully assorted in
the curious strata of any of our Berkshire gravel-

beds; and it will be well worth your while to make a study of them.

But, as these explanations of the phenomenon of the Balanced Rock refer to obscure dates far back in the infinite eons; and the record, whatever the geologists aver, may not seem to you indisputable, perhaps you may prefer something within the range of authentic history, as related, for instance, by those grave chroniclers, Hendrick Aupaumut and Grace Scheherazade. And it is but reasonable that you should have it.

I assume that you know something of the Atotarhos of the Iroquois, or Six Nations; a line of kings or emperors, of whom each, when he succeeded to the office, took also the name of the founder of the dynasty, just as the Roman emperors were all Cæsars. Individuals of the line were gifted with diverse divine, or at least supernatural, attributes and powers; all being esteemed demi-gods of one estate or an other. The first, a truculent old fellow, had a complete table service made of the bones of his enemies; and he had an imposing way of receiving even friendly deputations, clad in an entire panoply of living and venomous serpents. I have seen a portrait of his majesty in that royal costume. Most of his descendants, although invariably wise in counsel and mighty in war, were of a more gentle kind. The particular Atotarho, with whom we have here to do, was ordinarily of even feminine beauty and delicacy; and devoted himself to the cultivation of the milder virtues among his people. A white

poet has even ventured to fable that this gentle ruler
was the daughter of Count Frontenac, stolen in her
infancy, and palmed off on the confiding tribes by a
childless predecessor. But the Iroquois were not
the sort of people to see any divinity in a woman,
and they aver that, if occasion required, he could
assume gigantic proportions and unlimited strength.
And this assertion is fully borne out by the story of
the Balanced Rock.

I need not tell you that the Indian youth were
severely trained to athletic sports,— quoits, clubs and
the like,— and you may or may not, have heard
that a favorite game, was one which, under the name
of " duff," was a favorite also among my own school-
fellows, who played it with paving stones. It consists in placing one stone upon another, and then
attempting to dislodge it, by pitching a third from
such distance as the player can; a feat which requires
more strength and nearly as much skill as the kindred game of quoits.

It was a long, long while ago that a party of
Mohegan youth were excited over this sport in the
neighborhood of the Balanced Rock. Words ran
high and indeed blows seemed exceedingly imminent
when their attention was diverted to a slender
youth who stood leaning against a neighboring tree
in admiration of a sport in which he seemed ill
adapted to take part. Had the elders of the tribe
been present, doubtless the courtesy to a stranger
required by Indian etiquette would have mitigated
the rudeness of the youngsters' wit; but, left to them-

selves, and taught to despise effeminacy, the strange youth appeared to them a fair mark for their raillery, and they did not spare him, notwithstanding his modest and manly responses.

But the loudest laugh was when, as if provoked beyond endurance, he accepted a taunting challenge to a trial of strength and skill. The laugh was brief, and changed to cries of terror, when they saw the slender but lithe figure grow to giant size. Then they knew the Atotarho of their masters, the Iroquois; and when he hurled the huge rocks about, as you still see them, they would have fled had not his glance held them fast. At last, seizing the largest boulder to be found, as one would a pebble, he fixed it where you now marvel, and the geologists blunder, over it — the Balanced Rock.

Then, resuming the slender figure, to which the frightened youth were now quite reconciled, he gave them a lesson in manners and morals, which was handed down through all after-generations of the Mohegans, whose tradition-keeper-in-chief yearly repeated it from the top of THE ATOTARHO'S DUFF.

Now, does not that sound a vast deal more sensible and truthful than all that stuff about icebergs floating round Perry's Peak, or glaciers five thousand feet thick in the Housatonic valley? Methinks I hear you say; "*Now, actilly, don't it?*"

Well, one thing is certain; whether this old rock got its marvellous poise at the hand of enchantment or by the still more wondrous workings of nature, we came to visit it, that June afternoon, with min-

eet merriment and astonishment. M. rushed to it with a ringing laugh, declaring she would push the monster from the seat; he had kept longer than was right. Her gay, fairy-like figure present against the rude, grey mass with such minute weight, reminded me of a task assigned, in some elfin tale, to a rebellious hand-maiden of Queen Mab.

We had a little intellectual amusement in discovering the names of innumerable Julias and Carolines, Rosalinds, Janes and "Rarmy Augustus," inscribed by affectionate jack-knives upon the bark of the surrounding trees. Some classic gentleman, doubtfully desirous of a day, had carved among them the words "Mamson," and "Perceval." I have since heard the story of the merry boat when "Memnon" was inscribed by a hand which has written many a witty and clever volume. Indeed, indeed there must have been a deal of witchery in the amusing priestess who made that scene did not breathe such mysterious and enchanting music.

> "Can any mortal creature of earth's mould
> Breathe such divine enchanting ravishment?"

I should think not. Was it a wood-nymph then with her music box! Was there ever anything in that broken champagne bottle at the foot of the statue! And do wood-nymphs drink champagne! This grove is very questionable and full of marvels.

When we had clambered with a world of pains on to the top of the rock, we too had music — merry and sad — "music at the twilight hour." Then, as the evening shades deepened in the wood, came too-spoken words of memory and of longing for those far away. Alas! if all whom we invoked had come, the grave and the sea must have given up their dead.

With voices softened and mellowed by deeper feeling, my companions sang an "Ave Maria," and we bade farewell, not gaily, to a scene mysteriously consecrated by memories not its own. So, often, in scenes and hours when we invoke the ministers of joy, other spirits arise in their places, and we do not bid them down.

8

VI.

LEBANON SPRINGS — A DASH AT LIFE THERE.

So when, on Lebanon's sequestered hight,
The fair Adonis left the realms of light,
Bowed his bright locks, and fated from his birth
To change eternal.—*Darwin's Botanic Garden.*

Down in the hilly valley, beyond the Taghconics, is Lebanon — New Lebanon: the capital of the Shaker world, the seat of the mineral springs, the most delightful of watering places, the birth-place of Samuel J. Tilden, and our Gretna Green. All the world knows Lebanon, but much of it about as accurately as the knowledge-seeking traveller who, on the morning after his arrival, desired to be shown the cedars for which he was told the place was famous. Lest any of you should waste your time in antiquarian research for the point where "the fair Adonis left the realms of light," I may as well tell you at once that it was the door which opens from the gay parlors of Columbia Hall out upon the long balconies on a moonless night. Lebanon Adonises "bow their bright locks" to the brighter eyes of the belle of the season; and, as there is likely to be a new one every two or three months, they are fated to eternal change. That explains the fable.

The Springs are a very Mecca for summer pilgrims.
The first June heats bring the habitués with their
quiet quite-at-home air. A little later, others, catching a feverish impulse from the city miasma, rush
away like mad to flirt awhile with Nature and Hy-
geia among the mountains. Still others take a season
here after their Saratoga; like hock and soda-water
after champagne. At all seasons — midwinter
even — the people of all the region-round-about love
their little trips to The Pool.

"The Pool:" that was the neighborhood name in
the simple days of old. Catharine Sedgwick, who
then, and always, well loved this resort, delighted to
speak of it as The Pool, and that is what Miss Warner
also calls it in her charming novel, Queechy. Queechy
Lake, by the way, is one of the prettiest features in
Lebanon scenery, and the ride to it is a favorite drive.

This valley was the Wyomanock of the Mohegans,
and the name still clings to the stream which flows
through it. Very lovely are both vale and stream.
If natural beauty were the sole test of excellence few
watering places would rival Lebanon Springs. But
they have other merit than this. It is claimed that
they are the oldest watering place in America; and
village tradition will tell you that, a hundred and
seventy years ago, or about the close of the last French
and Indian war, a certain Captain Hitchcock, then
stationed at Hartford, finding himself afflicted with
a grievous malady, was induced to try these waters.
"He came," says an interesting local writer, "with
one servant and a company of Indian guides, and

was carried from Stockbridge to the Springs on a
litter, and by an Indian trail, there being no roads.
He found a large basin filled with water, and, from
appearances around it, judged it to be a bathing place
for the natives." Captain Hitchcock camped for
several days near the springs, and received great
benefit from their use. After the peace he returned
to New Lebanon as a permanent resident, and his descendants still live there.

Before the Revolutionary war, the Springs had
become noted. In the early part of the present
century they continued to grow in repute, and
towards its middle, society there was subjected to
the praises of Nat. Willis, the sarcasms of Mrs.
Trollope and the judicious criticism of Miss Sedgwick.
But why bother with the old life at the Pool while
the living world of the Springs so provokingly
challenges us to read it — if we can. It were an
infinitely curious study to enquire what brings each
individual into the respectably-motley throng; but,
unfortunately for psychological science, the so-
journers at fashionable hotels are the most incommu-
nicative of beings; reticence being the primal law
of society — technically so called. Lamentable as
that fact is, we need not, however, despair; having
a ready resource in that supreme faculty of guessing,
which makes us, Yankees, from Emerson to Andrew
Jackson Davis, the incomparable philosophers, we all
are.

It is a pleasant and profitable recreation to exercise this precious and peculiar faculty, of a lazy

summer afternoon, on the long verandahs of Columbia Hall. Laziness is the mother of at least one school of philosophy, and guessing at the foibles of one's friends is always delightful: their virtues, I take it, guessing philosophy generally leaves to be proved.

There are some hundreds of human beings about the huge hotel, most of whom may be supposed to have some motive, not of a purely sanitary character, in coming here; and to have also some notion, more or less definite, of the nature of the place and the part they are to play in it. In the old times of the Pool, we might have gone straight to the point, and asked people what they thought of things in general, and themselves in particular; but, since Mrs. Trollope, Capt. Hall and the Dickens have snubbed inquisitiveness out of American manners, that won't do at all. It might reap the reward of impertinence. No matter; a tolerably shrewd guess may do as well. Let us guess then.

It would not require a Connecticut Solomon to discover that the student-looking young man, with an orange-colored face and sea-green spectacles, thinks himself in an enormous hospital, or perhaps only a mammoth apothecary's shop. I dare say he spends his most contented hours in the famous medicine factory of the Tildens, two miles down the street. He deems those gorgeous, flaunting dames, of whose bright presence he is rather vaguely conscious, of no more real value — since they will not nurse his invalidship — than the colored waters in the apothecary's window opposite.

Those gay ladies themselves, of course, view the matter in a very reverse light. Take one of them, for example — that flirting, chatting, jewelled thing, Madame, the wife of the Wall Street millionaire. With both those clear-orbed eyes wide open, she can see little in this magnificent panorama of hill and valley, and this, its life-throbbing heart, more than a splendid ball room or gorgeous saloon; as indeed, for that matter, she would like the wide, wide world to be — and is vastly annoyed that misery, with her discordant shrieks and disgusting deformities, should presume to spoil the music and mar the decorations.

That blinking exquisite in those outrageously stunning habiliments — him with the eye-glass painfully squinnied in between bloated cheek and villanously low forehead; him with his nose turned up, as if in scorn of the poor moustache struggling for life in the exhausted soil below it : he has graduated from Paris; and the dazzling, dancing dames hold him a prodigy of intellect. But you note that he has all the external symptoms of being a thoroughbred donkey; and I think a practiced guesser would have little difficulty in making him out a weak cadet of one of those families to whom the Jenkinses of the New York press have given brevet rank as "aristocrats."

Look again. You would call yonder a frank, freehearted, undesigning girl. Hear with what joyous, summerly forgetfulness she throws off those snatches of unstudied song; and see how ingenuously the blush rises in her cheek, now she remembers that she is not alone. You would not dream now — would you? — that she looks upon this fair spot only as a mart in which she is to dispose of that dear little commodity — herself — to the best possible advantage? Yet I'll wager you a small farm I have in the clouds, that every note of that outgushing melody was aimed, point blank, at the handsome gentleman who has been conversing, these two hours past, with the pale girl in black. I only hope the minstrel will not be malicious enough to say, the pale girl is "setting her cap" for the handsome gentleman.

Why don't she turn her thought to drive away the cloud which has settled in the eye of the gloomy-browed man who is pacing the verandah so heavily? Bless us! the summer sunshine glances off from him, and leaves not a trace of light; he has never sold *his* shadow to Satan. Yet I misdoubt; and so we go on, doubting and misdoubting, guessing and mis-guessing: sure enough — if we would consider it — of two things; that we shall always hit wide enough of the mark, and never too near the charitable side of it. "Wise judges are we, of each other's actions!"

This Lebanon is not without its vein of romance. How could it be, when youth and age, folly and wis-dom, joy and sorrow, love and hatred, life and death, make it their yearly rendezvous? How strange a rendezvous, oft-times! Of those who seek here new thought, new hope, new feelings, how many find only what they bring — a jaded mind and a palsied heart? Mind cramped to the puny pursuit of puny

things will not always, upon the mountains, expand
and glow with the widening horizon and the purer
sunlight. Passion, born luxuriously in the crowded
city, grows and strengthens, and will not die, in the
bracing upland air. Yet is there forgetfulness of
lighter woes and less corroding cares, in the gay
saloons and woodland drives, as well as marvellous
virtue for the diseased body in the bubbling waters
and fresh breezes. Care-worn men and women
worn with ennui, do get new elasticity of thought
and frame; but in what do they seek a balm for
the wounded spirit, who bring hither the broken
hearted also — like thee, fair and gentle L. — or was
it that thy pure spirit might wing its way to Heaven
through purer skies than overhang thy native city?

I said Lebanon had its vein of romance. A
bachelor friend of mine, who has been a lounger at
Columbia Hall every summer these ten years past,
has a rich fund of stories — humorous, melo-drama-
tic, and tragical — about those who have fluttered,
flattered, flirted, and flitted here in that time. With
him, half the demoiselles who have "made their
market" under his eye, are heroines of a quality
which would surprise themselves not a little to know,
and their husbands a good deal more. It is often a
matter of discussion with us, whether, among other
connubial revelations, the arts and devices whereby
he was entrapped are usually disclosed to the husband.
In the absence of data from which to conclude, we
always end in the same mists in which we set out.
One of my bachelor friend's stories I will venture to

repeat, although I perceive it loses half its flavor, for lack of the gusto with which he would dwell upon it.

She Would be a Gentleman's Wife.

"More beauty than ever at Lebanon this year," I remarked to my friend, as we sat together one evening, about a year since; it was a common observation, and I thought myself particularly safe in repeating it.

"Hey! what's that you say?" he ejaculated, after a pause, in which it seemed my words had been following him far down into the depths of reverie. "More beauty than ever! Let me tell you, my dear fellow, that you know nothing at all of the matter. It's one of the stupid common-places of stupid common people."

I bowed to the compliment, and the bachelor went on with a half sigh, "Ah! you should have known us in the reign of the bitter and beautiful Lizzie B., or in that of the wonder-working Mrs. M."

Here the bachelor again relapsed into reverie, and I had time to remark to myself that this hankering after faded flowers, when the world was full of fresh, was an ugly symptom that my friend's own hey-day of beaudom must be on the wane. When people begin to complain that they can find no beauty, now-a-days, like that which they used to meet, look if they don't wear wigs, and other falsities of decoration.

"But the most charming season," resumed the

bachelor, emerging again into the present, " was that
of 185-, when Kate L. was in the ascendant. She
was far enough from beautiful, was Mrs. L., but such
a winsome way she had with her that we all, to a
man, acknowledged her sceptre — and the most
dazzling belle in her realm was ready to die with
envy: envy, by the bye, was a vice Mrs. L. was especially free from. Never was woman more ready
to recognize and exhibit the charms of her rivals.
She surrounded her throne with a constellation of
lovely women from far and near, and would let none
be eclipsed. A kind-hearted creature was she, and a
sensible to boot; a tithe part the jealousy we en-
dured from the splendid Lizzie B. would have made
Kate look as ugly as a Bornese ape.

" But it was of her throne-maidens that I was going
to boast. I wish you could have looked in upon one
of our gala nights; we have none such now — (that,
entre nous, was a fib of the bachelor's). There was
a floral ball we had one night in July — I have some
reason to remember it, but no matter. Mrs. L. had
made more than usual exertions in getting up this
festival, which was the opening one of the season.
The arrangements were perfect; — the floral decorations unique and profuse; the music superb; and the
supper just what it should be. But our Lady
Patroness was too true a genius to give to these concomitants the monopoly of her attention. With a
magic little crow-quill by way of wand, she summoned from all manner of retreats, the most brilliant
assemblage of fair women and distinguished men

that I have ever beheld among these hills; and when Mrs. L. summoned youth and beauty, you might be sure there was something to be done. I am going to leave them to do it, while I tell you of my cousin Ellen, the fairest of them all.

"You remember Nell—my uncle Fred's Nell—the merriest girl that ever hid deep design under careless laugh. Uncle Fred., you must know, left her an orphan at twenty — with exquisite accomplishments, unrivalled tact, and four thousand dollars, with which to make her way in the world, as she best might. Her guardian—a staid, business-like old gentleman, guardian to half the heiresses in the county, as well—when her year of mourning was over, advised her to buy a share in a boarding-school, and earn her living by teaching. 'With your accomplishments and talents, my dear,'— the good, fatherly old man was going on, when he was astonished to find his pretty ward cutting short his speech with —

"'With my accomplishments and talents, my dear guardian, I don't intend to squeeze my brain like a lemon, to give flavor to some insipid school-girl, while I might as well be rivalling her mamma. No! I'll invest in — a husband!'— and here her little foot came down with a will.

"The guardian stared; but he was too sensible a man to oppose a woman whose will was up; and so, under the nominal chaperonship of his wife, Ellen opened her first campaign at Lebanon.

"That night of the floral fête, she stood, the centre of an admiring group — a slight, aerial figure, but full of elastic life and vigor; her face transparent with changing light, and her eye overflowing with a flood of love and laughter. She was dressed with wonderful artistic skill; for the life of me I could not imagine how she contrived to arrange her mist-like drapery so that she seemed always on the point of rising into air. I have since heard that it is no mystery among mantua-makers. Among the crowd of women, laden and over-laden with all kinds of flowers, native and exotic, Nell had only twisted in her hair a few snowy, star-shaped blossoms — the spoil of a mountain excursion. Not a fold of her robes, not a tress on her head, but seemed too spiritual for mortal touch. I have since learned that the artistes call this style of dress, *la Gabrielle.* It is a triumph of genius; but I would not advise any lady weighing over two hundred to attempt it.

"Frank Leigh was conversing with my etherial cousin in a composed tone, and with a gaze of mere earthly admiration which I could not then have assumed for the world, although Nell and I had been playmates from infancy. I almost shuddered — so strangely had the fancy possessed me — when Frank took her hand, to lead her to the piano, lest she should indeed prove a spirit, and dissolve into thin air.

"'Ellen should be a gentleman's wife,' said a pretty and brilliant widow by my side.

"Wife! so she was human. 'A gentleman's wife,' I repeated aloud, 'and pray what is a gentleman? — and why should Ellen, more than another, be a gentleman's wife?'

"'Why,' replied the widow laughing, 'a gentleman, in Ellen's vocabulary, is a man of elegant manners, with at least one hundred thousand dollars, and a disposition to spend his income in graceful and fashionable follies. Ellen's expensive tastes demand such a husband — and I hope she may get him.'

"'Oh, now I am enlightened,' I said.

"'I am glad to hear it,' rejoined the widow, merrily. 'But come with me out into the balcony, and I'll let you into a secret or two.'

"Of course, such an offer was not to be resisted; and before we returned, I was put in possession of much recherché gossip, known only to the initiated.

"There had come that year to the Springs, a fine looking young man — generous, spirited, of captivating address, and great reputed wealth — Frank Leigh by name; the same who was in attendance upon my cousin Ellen at the floral fête. Of course such a god-send was not to be neglected by anxious mothers, and daughters no less anxious. Mrs. L., finding him clever, fond of sport, and prompt to forward all her gay schemes, had taken him up at once, and installed him her prime minister. Ellen, I need not say, was quite as ready to acknowledge his merits.

"Frank was universally declared to be a 'sweet man,' in the ball-room and drawing-room; but he was not a bit of a dandy; there was nothing of the exclusively ladies' man about him, nothing effeminate in his habits. On the contrary, his tastes were eminently manly. He had yachted on the Atlantic coast, hunted moose in a Maine Winter, and even

9

taken a run after buffaloes into the Sioux country. Here, among the quiet hills, his exuberant spirits found vent in a passion for wild horsemanship. Jehu was a child to him, with the whip; he was sure always to choose some unmanageable foal of gunpowder, that nobody else would come within a rod of; men, even of strong nerves, were of opinion that safer pleasures existed than a seat beside Frank Leigh, on one of his break-neck drives; and as for the women, not a soul of the dear creatures, who would have given their eyes to secure him for a partner at the last night's ball, could be persuaded to trust their ivory necks with him and his 'Lightning' next morning.

"To all this was one most remarkable exception — my brave cousin Nell, who had come out all at once a perfect Di. Vernon. Ah! but it was an inspiriting sight, to see her mounted on her brown steed, leading her panting admirers an aimless race over fields, brakes, briers, and fences, till half the chase foreswore all pursuit of her thereafter.

"But Nelly's favorite seat was in Frank's light buggy, of which she enjoyed undisputed possession — her rivals thinking it a particularly 'bad eminence.' Of course she was the constant companion of our Jehu, and a fit one, as it looked. Travellers marvelled enviously, as Frank's chariot dashed by them, to hear Nelly's clear, ringing laugh, or rattling song; or even at times to see her slight figure braced back, her loose curls flying, and her little hands holding

fast the 'lines,' while she urged the foaming horses
to yet more impossible speed; —

> ' Like a dream doth it seem,
>   When I think of the past ;
>   Up the road gallantly dashing along,
>   Driving two noble steeds, square built and strong ;
>   Firmly her little hands grasping the reins,
>   Held them as firmly as lovers in chains.'

"I think the echoes of her merry voice must linger
yet among the old woods which skirt the Hancock
road. Sure I am that the dwellers in the road-side
farm-houses yet remember Frank Leigh's dashing
equipage, and the gay couple with whom it used to
fly by their doors, at such flashing speed.

"Beside his equestrian fancies, Frank was exceedingly prone to romantic excursions, and by the aid of
the good-natured Mrs. L., who was nothing loath, led
us upon a hundred wild adventures among the hills,
to the great detriment of patent leather and super-
fine broadcloth. Here, too, Nell was the co-leader
with the rattle-brain heir ; never a ramble ended
until she had joined him in one mad-cap feat or
another.

"All this you may be sure gave ample room and
verge enough for bitter tongues; but the sage conclusion of one shrewd lady, that 'some folks could
do what other folks couldn't,' soon came to be in substance the universal sentiment. Indeed, with all
Nelly's faults and follies, it was impossible, when you
knew her, to think her capable of anything very
wrong.

"One opinion, at least, every body held, and that was, that she was just the girl to charm Frank Leigh—and that she had charmed him to some purpose. Every body but my friend the widow, who, while she admitted the boldness and vigor of Ellen's attack, had a doubt or two as to its success. 'Ellen,' said the widow, 'has a splendid genius for business, but very little experience. Do you not notice that Frank of late has another companion sometimes on his rides?'

"'What! the timid and femininely delicate Miss P.?'

"'The same—and with what tender care he curbs his speed when she is his companion?'

"'It is very kind and considerate of him; the jolts and racing in which Ellen delights, would be the death of Miss P. I am sure it is good in him.'

"'Oh, very! And yet is it not possible that she who tames the steed may tame the master?'

"I admitted the noteworthiness of the fact, but trusted to the genius and address of my fair kinswoman for a successful issue of her summer campaign. Indeed, as the season waned, her star seemed to rise yet higher into the ascendant, while she relaxed no whit of her zeal, but cut madder freaks, rode more daringly, was more than ever the constant companion of Frank, who, although he daily took a quiet drive with Miss P., seemed more than ever devoted to her dashing rival.' Everybody said Frank had proposed, was about to propose, or at least was in honor bound to propose, to my cousin. He was set down as certain of the fair hands which so gracefully reined in his fiery coursers. Only the widow shook her curls and Miss P. said nothing.

"One bright morning in September, just before the close of the season, Ellen was sitting in the drawing room, surrounded as usual by a group of loungers — among whom were Mr. Vinton, a gentleman of singularly reserved and quiet manners, and said to be very timid — and a Miss Phœbe N., a young lady who, in spite of nose and eyes equally awry with her temper, was supposed to be about to seize the quiet gentleman, *vi et armis.*

"'So Frank Leigh has taken us all by surprise, and married,' said some one, joining the group.

"'Married !' 'No ?' 'You don't mean it. 'How !' 'When ?' 'To whom ?' exclaimed a dozen voices at once — the speakers, of course, fixing their eyes considerately upon Nell: except Miss N., who was enabled to turn only one of hers that way, but answered:

"'Oh, to that stupid Miss P. I saw them depart this morning.'

"'I am sure you would not so speak, if you knew her,' said Ellen, indignantly. 'On the contrary, she is a sweet, sensible, and witty girl.'

"'Rather too quiet for me,' mildly remarked the very quiet Mr. Vinton.

"'I don't see why you should defend her,' snarled the amiable Phœbe to Ellen. 'She has carried off the prize we all assigned to you.'

"'To me !' exclaimed Ellen with real laughter

and well affected surprise; 'I am sure I am much
obliged to you all. Frank is a noble fellow; but do
you know, I should have an unconquerable aversion
to being rivalled by dogs and horses ? — and of
course ' Lightning' and ' Ney ' will hold equal place
in Frank's heart with his wife.'

"'But we,' began Miss N., with a malicious look —

"'But me no buts !' exclaimed Ellen, interrupt-
ing her; 'I would sooner marry a cobbler than a
horse-jockey, be he never so rich !'

"Mr. Vinton looked radiantly happy; Miss Phœbe
darkeningly the reverse, for it was her 'one woe of
of life' that her father had begun his ascent to wealth
in the respectable calling of a cobbler. Ellen saw
where her shot hit, and then cast a penetrating
glance at Vinton, in whose face she read more than
she had suspected."

Here the bachelor paused for breath. "And so,"
said I, " Miss Ellen lost her summer's work."

"Not at all," he replied resuming; "you shall
hear. Frank Leigh did not choose to fall in love
with a woman who rivalled him in the accomplishments of which he was most proud. Even so sensible a fellow as he had a spice of human vanity —
quite enough to cause him to prefer Miss P.. who
admired his daring feats. to Nelly. who demanded
that he should admire hers. and showed. moreover,
to all the world that they were not beyond the attainment of a very slight-framed woman. Besides. he
could too readily understand all that Nell felt. said,
and did: it is not the near view which charms.

"Poor Vinton, however, looking on from a distance, became every day more enamored;—the qualities which Ellen displayed proved so much the more fascinating from their very strangeness to his own nature. But it is in vain to philosophize about these matters; Vinton, like many a sensible fellow before and since, contrived to get hopelessly into the meshes before he thought of asking how; and the moment he saw the field clear, resolved to occupy the vacant lovership.

Our light-hearted Ariadne I suspect was secretly piqued at her desertion; at all events, she gave the new lover a world of encouragement. Indeed, so rapidly did affairs advance, that the same afternoon Mr. Vinton, in a tremor of fear, made a formal proposal—and was at once accepted. Still more to his joy, Ellen consented—if Miss Phœbe is to be believed, proposed, that the union should take place that same evening. So soon after the demolition of her hopes, Ellen reached their consummation, and was a 'gentleman's wife.'"

"A queer wooing," I said, when the bachelor had concluded. "Was the result happy?"

"Why, the chances were rather against it," he replied; "but fate often treats us better than we deserve. The result, I believe, was happy for both."

"And how about the widow and yourself?"

"Is not that the moon rising yonder?" said the bachelor.

VII.

ON PERRY'S PEAK.

Profit and pleasure, then, to mix with art,
T'inform the judgment, nor offend the heart,
Shall gain all votes.— *Anatomie of Melancholy.*

Of all pic-nics in which many people join, commend me to a scientific field-meeting. I do not compare that, or anything else, with hours like those we passed by the lakeside. The things are too diverse for comparison. Nor do I mean to say that, for once in a while, a merry masquerade in the glamour of the woods, or among the weird rocks of Icy Glen, has not unique charms. But a little science gives a zest always fresh, and a flavor always piquant, never cloying, to the enjoyment of large bodies of fairly well-educated excursionists.

To go out with a multitude in the vague expectation of a day's pleasure, even in the most romantic regions, often results in pure weariness of spirit. We are all true heirs of the old hunter races. Our joy is in pursuit; and the more definite the object of the chase, the keener the pleasure. That is what makes him who has an aim in life the happy man. That is what inspires alike the gold-hunter in the sands of California and the planet-seeker among the stars of heaven. It is the old instinct inherited from Nimrod and his fellow huntsmen. Or shall we trace it, far back of these, to progenitors in the Darwinian eons? Surely my highly civilized cat shows indications of sharing it, when she leaves the rodent trophies of her chase untasted, to partake of my own meal. Clearly her enjoyment is more purely in the pursuit, than is his who kills the deer, and eats the venison.

But the point from which I have wandered, is this; an excursion-pic-nic should, if we would gain the most and the highest enjoyment from it, have a more distinct purpose than the mere passing of a few hours among pleasant or romantic scenery.

I have already attempted to paint the delights of the genial, unrestrained social intercourse of a few friends in the freedom of the woods; but in a multitudinous picnic there is no place for that — every hindrance to it. The snobs who affect it are mere kill-joys and mar-plots. The pic-nic excursion should have an aim common to all its members; and all should join in it. I will take it for granted that you would not desire that aim to be attendance upon a cock-fight, a pugilistic mill, a horse-race, or a Fourth of July celebration. A camp-meeting might do; but even if one were at hand, the spirit is not always willing, however it may be with the flesh: just reversing the scriptural dilemma. The field-meeting, as conducted by the scientific associations of several New York and New England towns and cities, seems

to meet the want precisely, furnishing interesting
objects of pursuit to all intelligent persons, and, for
the most part, eliminating all others from the pic-nic.

This is a peculiarly American device, essentially
differing from the lawn-meeting of an English village
institute, as described by Tennyson in his introduction to The Princess: And the difference well illustrates that in the genius of the two nations. The
associations under whose auspices our field-meetings
are held do not seek a patron in any neighboring
great or rich man; nor are their pic-nics designed to
teach the rudiments, or exhibit the common wonders,
of science to rustic villagers. The leaders are often
leaders, as well, of scientific opinion, investigation
and progress, while their associates are generally
qualified to aid intelligently in their labors.

These field-meetings — designed partly as a relaxa-
tion in the intervals of more severe study, and partly
to keep alive a popular interest in science — are held
in neighborhoods where there is a chance that new
facts may be elicited, or which present features, intimate acquaintance with which is in itself culture:
which contain spots either picturesque, possessed of
interesting historical associations, or inviting as a
field for scientific research. Generally they combine
all these attractions.

The addresses which close and crown the day, are
no dry rehearsals of book-lore, but vivacious description and discussion of what the day has brought to
light. There is of course no time for minute investigation or profound study, but clews are struck, to

be followed up afterwards, valuable collections are made; and, above all, "thought is quickened and awakes."

Doubtless there is also a great deal of fun and flirtation not strictly scientific; nor yet, perhaps, wholly otherwise: ending sometimes, I am sure, in the illustration of an entirely natural science, to which so renowned a philosopher as Plato long ago gave his best thought, and a name which is too often taken in vain. But when were hundreds of people, mostly young men and women, ever thrown together in pic-nic, even of the Sunday-school variety, without something of that kind happening? It was said of old:

> "Who marks in church time others symmetry,
> Makes all their beauty, his deformity."

And yet I have heard of rash young men, even in New England, "making eyes" across the most Puritanic of meeting-houses at blushing girls who, blushing, made eyes back again: both utterly reckless of any resultant ugliness.

But, so far from there being any precept against love-making at a scientific pic-nic, there is absolutely a formula provided, suited to the occasion:

> " I love thee, Mary, and thou lovest me,
>   Our mutual love is like the affinity
>   That doth exist between two simple bodies:
>   I am potassium to thy oxygen. —
>   'Tis little that the holy marriage vow
>   Shall shortly make us one. That unite
>   Is, after all, but metaphysical.
>   Oh, would that I, my Mary, were an acid,

A living acid; thou an alkali.
Endowed with human sense, that brought together
We might coalesce into one salt,
One homogeneous crescile.* * * * *
And thus, our several natures sweetly blent
We'd live and love together until death
Should decompose this fleshly tertium quid,
Leaving our souls to all eternity
Amalgamated.   Sweet, thy name is Brown,
And mine is Johnson, wherefore should not we
Agree to form a Johnsonate of Brown ?"

The scientific field-meeting being a pot-pourri of solid meats, rich juices and spicy relishes, you will readily believe is among the choicest of our Berkshire pleasures; especially when it is enjoyed in such good fellowship as the famous Essex and Albany Institute and the Troy Scientific Association can furnish. The meeting to which I am going to invite you, however, shall consist of only our own home association, with a few pleasant friends from Stockbridge, Lenox, and Richmond: a sort of family dinner as it were.

Perry's Peak is the highest summit of one of the largest mountain masses in the Taconic range, which, like many of the others, has several minor prominences. It rises one thousand and thirty feet from its base, which itself has an altitude of one thousand and fifty feet above the sea level. A large part of the upper surface of the mountain, including the peak, is bare of trees, and often of soil also; and as the neighboring hills do not press very close upon it, it affords some of the broadest, grandest, and most picturesque views to be witnessed from any point in Berkshire, extending to Greylock on the north, Mt. Washington on the south, the Catskills on the west and the Hoosacks on the east.

In the south the Taghconics proudly raise their noble dome against the sky, while nearer, for an interval, they present the appearance of pyramidal summits, the conventional form in which the abstract mountain range is represented, but which this rarely assumes to the eye, and never in reality. The far-off Catskills can sometimes hardly be told from the massive clouds which overhang and mingle with them. You will be told that, from the Peak, steamers can be seen passing on the Hudson: but, for that purpose, you may as well be provided with a good field-glass; and, unless the day be very favorable, with the eye of faith also. No doubt it is well to keep the latter aid to vision in constant practice: you will find it as needful at a field, as at a camp, meeting. But I see little good in straining the natural eye in an attempt to discern, doubtfully at best, objects of merely curious interest, when such a grand and beautiful world lies within its easy range.

For example, here at the western foot of the mountain gleams Whiting's Pond, better known to "the wide-wide world" as Queechy Lake, one of the prettiest lakelets among the hills. Upon the other side we look down upon Richmond Lake, another pretty sheet of water, and moreover a favorite of sportsmen. Eight miles away we see the spires of Pittsfield. Scattered all about are points of individual interest; but it is the grand *coup d' œil*, which it affords in several directions, that gives Perry's Peak its celebrity.

Until recently one could easily and safely drive to the very topmost summit; but a few years ago a summer tempest sent raging torrents down the mountain-side,cutting huge ravines out of the road, and burying acres of meadow under barren gravel-heaps: an interesting study for one inquisitive as to the Berkshire drift system, but distressful to the industrious farmer and the lazy excursionist. There is still, however, a tolerable road for the greater part of the height, and you may accomplish the rest without much trouble by driving " across lots." For equestrians, there is no difficulty. As I once approached the top of the Peak it was crowned by a well mounted group whose graceful figures " darkly painted on the clear blue sky " made a striking picture which I should be sorry to think it impossible to repeat.

Thus easy of ascent, and temptingly accessible from Lenox, Lebanon Springs and Pittsfield, it is no wonder that the Peak has long been a favorite mountain resort, although it has no such romantic interest as that with which Bryant has invested Monument Mountain, nor such poetic fame as Dr. Holmes, Mrs. Kemble and Thoreau, have conferred upon Greylock. It remains unsung, although a poet of no mean powers and with hereditary obligation to do it honor, was born almost at its foot. The reason possibly is that its charms are in the views from, not of, it. Its individuality, although decided, is not of the character which at once strike either the eye or the imagination.

The celebrity of the Peak is in the world of science, and there it has hardly a rival among the hills of New England; its fame however, to confess the truth, being less due to any startling wonders of its own than to the puzzling geological phenomena of the region of which it is the conspicuous head and centre. It was these, together with its superb overviews, which led our Scientific Association to select Perry's Peak as the theater for their celebration of the one hundredth anniversary of the birth of Alexander Von Humboldt. Think of a celebration which extended from the crowded capitals of Europe to the lonely mountain tops of New England. When did kingly conqueror have glory like that?

The most uniformly delicious week in the Berkshire year is the second in September. "Then, if ever, come perfect days." And the day of our anniversary — the fourteenth of the month, was absolutely perfect. The universal voice proclaimed it entitled to the biggest boulder of the purest quartz on Crystal Hill, if ever day deserved to be "marked with a white stone."

By the courtesy of the occasion, the party which ascended the mountain, that bright September day, was presumed to be an intellectual one, but it required no presumption to pronounce it a glad company, and the merriment was no worse for the attempt to give it a learned flavor. The result, whether a failure or a success as to the original intention, was always .

funny enough to provoke a laugh that was genuine, if the wit was not.

Reaching the summit we assembled on a spot marked by the coast survey, as 2089 feet above the sea level. All around us the bare ledges were scored with parallel groovings on broadly polished surfaces, and bore other distinct marks of glacial action. Within a few rods were strewn those wonderful boulders whose story has puzzled so many learned heads. And there, with the tumbled ridges of four grand mountain-chains in view, and the purest of sapphire skies over-hanging all, we found as fitting a spot as could be desired to commemorate the centennial birthday of the great naturalist.

The formal exercises of the celebration, if they could be called formal, were brief and simple. Professor William C. Richards — poet, orator and naturalist — displayed a superb photograph of Humboldt — taken at Berlin and approved by its subject — and, with a brief introduction, read an appropriate ode full of poetic thought and feeling.

Then, after an inspection of the evidences of glacial action on the Peak, we betook ourselves to a cool and pleasant grove, in which lay one of the largest of the famous Richmond boulders: and there, with appetites of mountainous proportions, discussed our pic-nic dinner.

While thus agreeably engaged, we learned that the Peak took its name from the Rev. David Perry, who owned lands here and elsewhere in the town of Richmond, in which he was the second minister of the gospel. Mr. Perry was rather a liberal as liberality went with the New England clergy of his day: that is, although a Federalist, as it was natural for a Massachusetts Congregational minister to be, he kept on good terms with his clerical brother of the next town, who was a flaming Democrat; I have no doubt that he could, and did often, dine with the only Episcopalian rector in the county, without any conviction of a neglect of duty in failing to smother him in his own popish surplice. Nevertheless, I fancy it would have given the good old gentleman a strange sensation could he have dreamed that profane philosophers would come from the ends of the earth to find, in his own personal and ecclesiastical domain, evidence that the world was no more made in six days than Rome was built in one; and I do not know what would have happened to him had he foreseen that one of his own descendants, in no very distant generation, would give himself to conducting a newspaper so devoted to the fleeting pleasures of this life as the New York Home Journal. It is fortunate, after all, that even ministers are but short-sighted mortals. I dare say that, if the sainted pastor is now able to look down and see all that has come about so strangely, he regards it with the same equanimity which his successors in office manifest.

The dinner over, we devoted ourselves to the more strictly scientific work of the day, first listening to the story of the boulders from the lips of their venerable discoverer. But, as I purpose to go into that story somewhat at large, I will make it the subject of another section.

VIII.

THE RICHMOND BOULDER TRAINS.

"One must go back to an age before all history; an age which cannot be measured by years or centuries; an age shrouded in mysteries and to be spoken of only in guesses. To assert anything positively concerning that age, or ages, would be to show the rashness of ignorance. ' I think that I believe,' ' I have good reason to suspect,' ' I seem to see,' are the strongest forms of speech which ought to be used, over a matter so vast and as yet so little elaborated." — *Kingsley's Idylls.*

TEN MILLION YEARS AGO.

It may have been only one million years ago that the events I am to speak of occurred; but I put it at ten to cover accidents. It may have been less, or perhaps more; the record is not so precise as could be wished if title to real estate depended upon it. But for our present purpose the vague measurement of the unnumbered eons of geology gives a more adequate conception of their immensity than could be obtained from the most definite statement in numbers, even if we knew it to be exact: the mind is so apt to fancy it has a full appreciation of such a statement whereas it really has not the slightest.

Let me give you a general outline of the physical

geography of our hills as described by Dr. Palfrey in his History of New England, on the authority of Professor Guyot.

"Only moderate elevations present themselves along the greater part of the New England coast. Inland the great topographical feature is a double belt of highlands, separated almost to their bases by the deep and broad valley of the Connecticut River, and running parallel to each other, from the south-south-west to the north-north-east,till, around the sources of that river, they unite 'in a wide space of table land, from which streams descend in different directions."

"To regard these highlands, which form so important a feature in New England geography, as simply two ranges of hills, would not be to conceive of them aright. They are vast swells of land, of an average elevation of a thousand feet above the level of the sea, each with a width of forty or fifty miles, from which asfrom a base, mountains rise in chains or isolated groups to an altitude of several thousand feet more."

"In structure the two belts are unlike. The western system, which bears the general name of the Green Mountains, is composed of two principal chains [the Taghconics, or Taconics, on the east. the Hoosacs on the west], more or less continuous, covered, like several shorter ones which run along them, with the forests and herbage to which they owe their name. Between these, a longitudinal valley can be traced, though with some interruptions, from Connecticut to Northern Vermont. In Massachusetts and Connecticut, it is marked by the Housatonic [and the Hoosack]; in Vermont by the rich basins which hold the villages of Bennington, Manchester and Rutland, and farther on by valleys of less note. * * *

"The mountains have a regular increase from south to north. From a height of less than a thousand feet in Connecticut, they rise to an average of twenty-five hundred feet in Massachusetts, where the majestic Greylock, isolated between the two chains, lifts its head to the stature of thirty-five hundred feet. In Vermont, Equinox and Stratton Mountains

near Manchester are thirty-seven hundred feet ; Killington
Peak, near Rutland, rises forty-two hundred feet ; Mansfield
Mountain, at the northern extremity, overtops the rest of the
Green-Mountain range with an altitude of forty-four hundred
feet.

"The rise of the valley is less regular. In Connecticut its
bottom is from five hundred to seven hundred feet above the
level of the sea. In Southern Berkshire it is eight hundred
feet ; it rises thence two hundred feet to.Pittsfield, and one
hundred more to the foot of Greylock ; whence it declines to
the bed of the Housatonic in one direction and to an average
height of little more than five hundred feet in Vermont on the
other. Thus it is in Berkshire county that the western swell
presents, if not the most elevated peaks, yet the most compact
and elevated structure."

Besides the shorter ranges, mentioned by Dr.
Palfrey as lying along the Taconics and Hoosacs, the
Berkshire valley is everywhere broken by spurs from
the main chains and by hills, often of magnitude.
The mass of up-tumblings and down-pullings which
meets the eye that looks down upon it from some
elevated point, is a marvel and a joy to the geologist.
We have locally been accustomed to regard the underlying rocks — chiefly mica schists of different
grades, crystaline limestones, quartzite and green-
stone — as belonging to the very earliest formations.
Thirty or forty years ago, Professor Emmons
maintained a hard fight against cruel odds, to establish that theory, and we fancied his victory complete. But now comes a newer, and very high, authority, Professor Dana, and relying upon the evidence
of certain Vermont fossils, denies to our rocks any

antiquity greater than the earliest period of the older
Silurian epoch; not much, if at all, more than a hundred million years: and that likely to be fearfully
cut down if certain still later theorists upon the ages
prevail.

I suppose I shall be told that we must submit to
be thus deposed from our high estate and ranked
among comparative parvenues; mere rocks of the
second order. But

"On what compulsion must we? Tell me that."

The newest geologist is only infallible, while he *is*
the newest; an arrant brevity. Never, within all the
borders of Berkshire, in schist or quartz, in marble or
greenstone, in dyke or bed-rock, ice-ground gravel or
unburied boulder, was there ever found the slightest
trace of organic forms, animal or vegetable: and
shall our pure azoic rocks be robbed of their virgin
fame because the Rev. Augustus Wing has detected
the slip of a frail distant relative up in Vermont, a
hundred million years ago? Worse accidents than
that happen in the most primitive families.

To be sure, our rocks have been greatly meta
morphosed, and there is indisputable evidence of
violent heat in their impressible youth; but does that
prove that their metamorphoses were like Ovid's?
My Berkshire blood is up, and, if I were younger, I
would myself ride a geological tilt in their defense
as it is, I summon some youthful champion to put on
his armor of proof, and try a joust with this renowned
knight of the hammer. Let him show that our old
mountain ridges are the very "bones of time;" not

fossil bones by any means, but the veritable rock-ribs of mother earth. But, until such champion shall appear, we will, for the sake of peace, and in submission to the geologic ruler of the hour, admit that we are only Silurians. It might have been worse; for, after all, the Welsh is a good old stock.

At any rate, the rocks are there in very palpable mountains, Azoic or Silurian as you please; and they are covered far up their sides, if not to their very summits, by immense deposits of drift, composed of rounded and rolled fragments of all sizes from the huge boulder to the finest sand. The same drift covers the valley ; stones of all sizes and of every variety which could be torn from the neighboring hills, being jumbled together in utter confusion as to size, the largest often being at the top; as you may see finely exemplified on Jubilee Hill in Pitts-field and elsewhere. But, with regard to the prevailing rocks which compose it, the position in which they lie, and in other particulars, you will find the drift of different localities marked by distinct individual characteristics. Even in regard to size, confusion is not absolutely universal: you will find many gravel beds beautifully stratified in this respect: but, as compared with the great mass of drift, these are exceptional. These queerly tumbled beds and piles of drift afford an altogether curious study; and one in which there are few adepts. I commend it to you as a summer recreation on the whole preferable to trouting; although, if you persist in gratifying your murderous propensities, you may pleasantly combine the two.

Scattered all over this loose, stony formation, which clothes the rocks of hill and valley as muscles clothe bones, is still another deposit of boulders, generally of considerable size and often very large. They are easily distinguished from the underlying drift; not being, like it, either buried, smoothed or rounded, but exposed, rough and angular, except when sometimes, their upper surface is worn to a rude dome shape. Neither the boulders or the drift are at all peculiar to Berkshire. Similar formations cover a large portion of the Northern hemisphere. The phenomenon which has drawn hither so many eminent geologists is the occasional arrangement of the exposed boulders in well-defined trains; which is exceptional, if not unique, so far as observations have been made and published.

These remarkable trains were discovered, about the year 1840, by Dr. Stephen Reed, who, as President of our Scientific Association, led our field-meeting on Perry's Peak. When the feast was over, that day, and we had fraternized with our genial and hospitable Richmond hosts, we listened to local story, told by venerable speakers from Lenox and Stockbridge, concerning Parson Perry, the second minister, and his parishioner, Col. Rossiter, who, as second in command of the Berkshire militia at the Battle of Bennington, did good service; recalling his men from plundering to fighting, and thereby saving the day which was well nigh lost after it had been once won.

When we had thus done due honor to some of the old-time local worthies, our venerable president — who might well have served the most fastidious painter as a model for "an old geologist" — told the story of his discovery, illustrating his method very simply. "If," said he "you should see a cart loaded with apples of a peculiar variety, which, dropping from a leaky tail-board, were strewn all the way back to a certain orchard which alone bore that kind of fruit, you would have no difficulty in determining where that apple train came from."

By a similar process it is easy to trace the principal, and most perfect, of the Richmond Boulder Trains to its source; since it is an exceedingly well defined and nearly continuous succession of large angular masses of a peculiar chloritic schist, wholly unlike the general bed-rocks of the vicinity, and also differing totally from most of the neighboring boulders.

Following up this train, Dr. Reed found it terminate, three miles north-west of the Richmond meeting-house, on the summit of Fry's Hill, the highest, and almost the central point of the Canaan Mountains in Columbia county, N. Y.; one of the short ranges which run along the Taconics. The top of this hill is composed of a chloritic schist, precisely like that of the boulders, and unlike any other bed-rock in all that region. Of course no doubt remained of the source of that train, and its discoverer, retracing his steps, continued his investigations until he had followed it in the opposite direction across the towns of Richmond, Lenox and Lee, some ten or twelve miles in all. He believed that it reached still further, and perhaps even to Connecticut. I think he afterwards obtained some evidence that this supposition was correct, but of how conclusive a nature I cannot say. Subsequently he found another train of the chloritic schist, originating, like the first, on the Canaan Mountains, and five of limestone derived from the Taconic range; but none so complete as the first.

In 1842, Dr. Reed published an account of his discovery in the "Lenox Farmer," predicting for the boulders a host of distinguished visitors and a wide fame; a prophecy which has been amply verified; for during his life he piloted among them, Dr. Birney of Boston, Professors Chester Dewey, Hitchcock, Hosford, Hall and the Brothers Rogers, Sir Charles Lyell, Count Pourtales, and Professor De Saurre.

Dr. Reed, in his first paper at least, contented himself with simply describing the boulder train. The apple-cart by which it was strewn had long disappeared, and he did not attempt to restore it from his imaginings, doubtless knowing full well that, if he did, the next geologist who came along would make it his first business to upset it.

Some of his visitors, however, were not so discreet, and the result has been a dozen or more learned essays, of which the most interesting are those of Sir Charles Lyell and Rev. John B. Perry.

Lyell in his "Antiquity of Man," gives a spirited account of his visit and a graphic description of the rocks, making some very fascinating reading. His theory, to use the condensation of another, is that "at the time of the drift period, the highest points of the Canaan, Richmond and Lenox ranges formed chains of islands in an ocean; and that the gaps in the Richmond and Lenox ranges were straits through which floated ice-bergs bearing the chloritic blocks from the exposed parts of the Canaan range, and dropping them in their present positions." So strongly did this notion impress itself upon Sir Charles, that he illustrated his work with a view of the islands, and the rock-laden ice-floes — not ice-bergs — floating between them. He has also given views of some of the larger boulders, and a diagram of the seven trains.

Mr. Perry "divides the boulders which rest upon the surface of the drift into two classes, according as they are rounded or angular: those which make up the trains being rounded, while the angular are distributed without definite arrangement. He considers that the trains owe their formation to the movement of the general ice-mass which rested upon the region during the glacial period; the boulders, which are found in trains: and which he believes to be rounded [dome-topped?] having been torn from prominent peaks, and forced along under the ice-sheet, while the scattered ones were transported to their present position much later, when the ice-mass had become so much reduced in thickness that the peaks in question projected above the surface, so that masses of rock could be lodged upon the ice as well as dragged along under it.

Since Dr. Reed's death, which occurred in 1876, Mr. E. R. Benton, of Boston has made an exhaustive survey of the locality of the boulders and a thorough study of their phenomena, and has published the result in a pamphlet of forty-two pages, forming Number Three of the Fifth Volume of the Bulletin of the Harvard College Museum of Comparative zoölogy. Odd, is it not, that of the three best treatises upon these rocks — which, however we may class them, show not the slightest vestige of animal or vegetable life — one should be found in a work upon the antiquity of man, and another in a bulletin of zoölogy? Is then the absence of life the complement of its presence, as well before as after its existence upon this earth?

But, wherever we may find Mr. Benton's paper, let us be thankful for it: for it is the most complete, satisfactory and philosophical essay upon its subject, which we have, or are likely to have, unless he himself pursues it further.

Having given a concise resumé of the statements and opinions of his predecessors, Mr. Benton proceeds to a geological and topographical description of the Boulder Region, which is illustrated by maps showing the contours of the hills, their bed rocks and

the course of the trains. I condense his description
of the principal and best defined train.

The crest of Fry's Hill in the town of Canaan, has
an elevation of six hundred and twenty feet above the
track of the Boston and Albany railroad in Richmond, which is one thousand and fifty feet above the
level of the sea. This crest, extending one hundred
and fifty feet down from its summit, is composed of
a fine-grained foliaceous mica chloritic schist, very
tough and of a green color. It is identical with the
boulders of the main train, is of narrow extent here,
and has been found, in place, in only one other locality
on the range. To its limited extent Mr. Benton attributes the distinctness of the train, whose width varies
from two hundred and fifty to five hundred feet; the
difference being caused apparently by the varying
contours of the hills in its path.

From the summit of Fry's Hill the train descends
in a south 54° east direction; then bends gradually
to the southward till, at the base of the range, it
has a south 27° east direction. Thence it extends
just south of the North Family of the Shakers, and
up the face and along the crest of a westerly spur
of the Richmond range, called Merriman's Mount,
to the crest of the western branch of the range.
In so doing it gradually changes its direction, to
south 68° east; and so crosses the Haskell valley and
begins the descent of the Richmond range. In
making this descent, it bends considerably to the
south, crossing the main road in Richmond two
miles north of the railroad station, till it attains a

south 25° east direction, where it crosses the railroad. From the railroad the train continues on across the Richmond valley, but curves to the eastward as it mounts the western slope of the Lenox range crosses its two parallel ridges and descends into the Lenox and Stockbridge valley, where its direction is south 50° east. A half a mile south-east of Mr. Luther Butler's house, near the Lenox and Stockbridge line, the train seems to lose its continuous character; the chloritic schist boulders in the same line, to the south-east, being few, small, and widely separated.

Far the largest boulders of the train, averaging fifteen feet in length — are found on the eastern slope of the Canaan range; two of them measuring ninety and one hundred and twenty-five feet in circumference respectively, and being about thirty feet in hight. On the western slope of this range there are no chloritic schist boulders. Near the Lebanon Shakers they average twelve feet in length; one having a circumference of seventy-five feet. Lyell mentions two with circumferences of seventy and one hundred and twenty feet respectively, and a hight of twenty feet above the soil, lying two miles north of Richmond station. Thence there is a constant diminution in size until, in the Lenox and Stockbridge valley, the average length does not exceed two feet.

By the Richmond range, Mr. Benton means that portion of the Taconic Mountains which lies in Richmond and the adjoining town of Canaan on the west; and is separated by a narrow valley from the Canaan or Columbia range. Fry's Hill is two and half miles south of Douglas Knob, the picturesque elevation which almost overhangs Columbia Hall, and forms the northern terminus of the range.

The Lenox range is a spur thrown off by the Taconics at Egremont, which, broken by the Williams River at West Stockbridge, extends north-eastward to Pittsfield, where it terminates in South Mountain and Melville Hill. Its domes and peaks form some of the most striking and beautiful features in the views, looking north from the Lenox, and south from the Pittsfield valley; while its southern extension, reaching to Stockbridge, is filled with the most delicious scenery.

But to return to the Boulder trains; Mr. Benton examined three others, all less continuous and composed of smaller blocks than the first; but he failed to find the chloritic schists, in place, upon the points in the Canaan range to which they led, and this, as well as the imperfection in the trains, he attributed to the early exhaustion of the knobs of this rock which formerly crested this ridge at intervals, but were of inferior thickness to that on the summit of Fry's Hill.

He speaks generally of certain other curious but promiscuously scattered boulders, and of limestone trains; but appears to have been discouraged as to the latter by the inaccuracies of previous writers. All the three ranges mentioned exhibit marks of glacial action wherever their beds are exposed; but none of them send out trains of boulders except the Canaan, as few others anywhere do. The explanation is found in the sharpness and narrow limits of Fry's Hill, and of the other, now obliterated, knobs of chloritic schist, in which the trains, undoubtedly had their origin.

In accounting for the transportation of the boulders to the positions in which they are now found, Mr. Benton discards Lyell's theory of floating ice, since it implies that, during the period in which they were deposited, the level of the ocean stood above the crest of the Canaan range, or sixteen hundred and fifty feet higher than it now does. Other writers have shown that the same line of reasoning which leads to Lyell's conclusions would require a depression of parts of the glaciated region to a depth of five thousand feet below their present level: a depression which all the evidence indicates did not exist.

Mr. Benton's own solution of the problem is based upon the fact, now generally admitted by geologists, that in the Post-Pliocene age, this region, in common with a large part of the northern hemisphere, was covered with an ice-sheet several thousand feet thick, which had a slow motion in this district from the north-west to the south-east. But he shows that the boulders could not have rested, and been borne along, upon the upper surface of this ice-sheet; since that pre-supposes cliffs upon the Canaan range which towered above that surface, whereas an ice-sheet which could move

across valleys six hundred feet deep, without being
materially deflected from its course, must have
covered the highest land to the depth of many hundred feet. Nor could the boulders have been dragged
along under the ice-mass, without leaving marks of
abrasion of which none are to be seen.

It is probable, he thinks, that the boulders were
torn from their original bed by the ice sheet, and
became imbedded in its mass instead of being dragged
along under it. The sharpness of the knob called
Fry's Hill favors this supposition, since boulders torn
from its upper part would be at least one hundred
feet above the lower surface of the ice along the
neighboring parts of the crest; and the mass, closing
again as soon as it had passed the sharp knob, would
hold many of them firmly in its grasp, without al-
lowing them to reach the rocks below, until the ice-
sheet had ceased its grinding march and was in
process of dissolution. Nevertheless, under the in-
cessant influence of gravity, the imbedded fragments
would be constantly working their way downward,
and many of them, finally reaching the under surface,
would be ground up by the crunching, superincum-
bent, moving mass; and the farther from the source,
the greater would be the amount of material lost to
the trains, and added to the underlying gravel beds.

In condensing a portion of Mr. Benton's essay, I
have occasionally departed from the order of arrangement pursued by him, and have interpolated, now
and then, matter of my own, but I believe that I have
given correctly the facts and theories presented by

him, so far as I have attempted to give them at all;
often using his own language. But he enters much
more into detail than it would be possible or proper
for me to do here, and touches upon some allied topics
to which I have not even alluded. His pamphlet
should be in the hands of every student of the boulder
phenomena, or of the superficial geology of this
locality.

The boulder and drift deposits in the valley at the
base of the Taconics, north of Richmond, offer a
fresh and interesting field of investigation. At
some points there are indications of arrangement in
trains; but, whether or not if followed up those indications should lead to discoveries of that character,
they could not fail of valuable and curious results.
Some of the local deposits of boulders are strikingly
suggestive. I have already spoken of the Balanced
Rock group. In the romantic town of New Marlboro',
next east of Great Barrington, is another rocking
stone, quite as firmly based, and with a more pronounced and easy oscillation. Between Onota street
and Lake Onota, in Pittsfield, some most singular
boulders are strewn. One variety is composed of
what appears upon the surface to be a net work, but
in reality is a honey comb, of quartz cells filled
with a hard schist. Sometimes cells, which were
probably filled with a softer rock, are empty, leaving
a skeleton of quartz walls. Another variety of soft
rock encloses rounded pebbles sometimes six or
eight inches long. I think some summer or autumn
days could be pleasantly passed in tracing these

queer erratics to their source, and trying to imagine
how they were made; and when; and why.

I fear I may have wearied some of you by dwelling so long upon a theme in which you perhaps take
small interest. But, when you think of it, is it not
after all a wondrous thing? As strange as any marvel
of the genii and, at the same time, if we can rightly
read it, telling a tale as true as Holy Writ. If Sir
Thomas Browne could properly call the moor-logs
and fir trees found under ground in many parts of
England, "the undated ruins of winds, floods and
earthquakes," of what are these Berkshire boulders
the ruins; and where is their date recorded?

And now, one word more; that I may have the
credit of, for once, closing a story with a sound moral
lesson. The study of these rocks will aid you in the
clear and conscious recognition of a truth, which I
dare say you know already, but perhaps only in a
dreamy, unthinking way. It is this, that in those
immeasurable ages, matter was composed of the same
elements and obeyed implicitly the same laws, which
at this moment compose and govern it, both on this
little spot of earth and in the illimitable heavens.
Whether there were intelligent eyes to watch them
or not, rising and setting suns measured the days;
and, if not here, by reason of cold, yet at our antipodes, the procession of the Seasons marked the
coming and the going of the year. For as yet we
have only begun to approach that epoch, when science
and revelation alike require us to believe that the
earth was without form and void, and darkness was
upon the face of the deep.

IX.

THE WIZARD'S GLEN.

Right well I wote, most mighty soveraine,
That all this famous antique historie
Of some the abundance of an ydle braine
Will judged be, and painted forgerie,
Rather than matter of just memorie. *Fairie Queene.*

A four miles' drive from our village brings the excursionist to a deep gorge, now called the "Gulf," but known in the earlier and less sceptical days of the settlement as the "Wizard's Glen." It is the wildest scene in our immediate neighborhood. A narrow valley is enclosed by steep hills, covered far up their sides with the huge rectangular flint rocks which mark this whole mountain range. You see them scattered everywhere, from Greylock to Taghconic; but nowhere else — unless, perhaps, at Icy Glen or Monument Mountain.— piled up in such magnificent and chaotic profusion. It is as though an angry Jove had here thrown down some impious wall of the Heaven-defying Titans. Block lies heaped upon block, squared and bevelled, as if by more than mortal art; for of such adamantine hardness are they that never hand nor implement of man could carve them into symmetry.

In their desolation they seemed charmed to everlasting changelessness; storm and sunshine leave few
traces upon them; the trickling stream wears no
channel in their obdurate surface; only a falling
thunderbolt sometimes splinters an uplifted crag, and
marks its course by a scar of more livid whiteness.
No flower springs from, no creeping plant clings to,
them for support, save when the rare Herb Robert
would fain cheer them with his tiny blossom; or
some starveling lichen strives to shroud the livid
ghastliness of their hues.

It is a stern-featured place; and yet of a warm
summer afternoon, one — no, not one, it is too intensely sombre for that — but a party can pass a
merry hour there, in the cool depths of the ravine.
There are some books too, written in a spirit akin to
the fantastic and demoniac grandeur of the place,
which can be read there with a double zest. Perched
in the angle of a cleft boulder, I once keenly enjoyed some scenes in "Faust." "Manfred" would
not be out of place there, nor would some parts of
"Festus."

But the best is, to mark how the most humanly
merry laughter and the gentlest of gentle voices
catch a fiendish echo from the rocky hollows. There is
diablerie in the very air; the fairest form I ever knew,
as it rose from behind one of those enchanted rocks,
looked weird as Lilith, the first wife of Adam. He-
cate herself could not have emerged from Hades
with half the infernal grace and beauty; I am sure
the place is bewitched.

Tradition indeed says that, before the decay of
the native tribes — of whom a scanty remnant were
found by the white man in the valley of the Housatonic — this used to be a favorite haunt of the
Indian priests, or wizards. Here, it was said, they
wrought their hellish incantations, and with horrible
rites offered up human sacrifices to Ho-bo-mo-ko,
the Spirit of Evil. One broad, square rock, which
chanced to stand alone in the midst of a conveniently
clear space, had the credit of being the Devil's altar-
stone. Some crimson stains marked its upper surface,
upon which the earlier settlers could not look without a shudder. They were believed to come from
the blood of frequent victims — although, now-a-
days, a sceptic with no analysis at all would find
little difficulty in resolving them into " traces of
iron ore." For my part, until the analysis is made,
I hold fast to the older and better opinion of those
who believed that around this ensanguined shrine a
spectral crew of savage wizards nightly reënacted
the revolting orgies of the past.

I met, not long since, an old man of ninety
winters — perhaps the last believer in their superstitions. He had heard the story of the shadowy
sacrifices from an eye-witness, and related it with a
credulous simplicity very difficult to gainsay.

Not far from the year 1770 (as he said), one John
Chamberlain, a brave man and a mighty hunter, of
Ashuelot (now Dalton), at the close of a hard day's
chase, overtook and slew a deer, somewhere within

the Wizard's Glen. While he was dressing his quarry, a terrific storm of thunder, lightning, and hail arose — as Chamberlain averred, with supernatural celerity, as such often seem to do among the mountains. A thunder-storm, even in the ordinary course of nature, is not just the thing to be coveted in this place, by the hardiest deer-slayer; but come what will deer-slayers must make the best of it. Seeking out, therefore, a spot where the rocks were piled one upon another, with cavernous recesses that formed a sort of natural caravansary beneath, he drew his deer under one boulder and ensconced himself snugly under the shelter of another.

Thus protected, he betook himself to such slumbers as he might get, which turned out to be not the most peaceful. The thunder crashed, the lightning glared and the wind howled in a manner which seemed to our poor John altogether demoniacal. Sleep, in such a hurly-burly of the elements, was out of the question; so, raising himself up, he looked out among the rocks, as he could very well do by the aid of the scarcely intermittent lightning.

You may be sure that, with all his courage, our hunter was not quite pleased to find himself in full view of the Devil's altar-stone. It was an ugly predicament, to say the least of it; but there was no help in the case, and he had only to make the best he could of this also: which turned out to be bad enough again. His eyes once fixed upon it, the haunted spot kept them riveted by a terrible fascination, while Chamberlain reflected upon his position in a state of mind which was doubtless far enough from that of philosophic calmness.

Very soon, however, his reflections were interrupted by a wilder rush of the storm, and a yet broader and more vivid flash of lightning, which illumined the whole valley and revealed the horned Devil himself, seated upon a broken crag and clothed in all the recognized paraphernalia of his royalty. Chamberlain thought him a very Indiany-looking devil indeed, which rather pleased him afterwards to tell, for he was no lover of the Indian race.

This was apparently a gala night with Satan, although none of the guests were yet arrived. He was not now going to battle or to work, but rather to hold a royal drawing-room, by way of enjoying himself and receiving homage. His sable majesty has been too long intimate with earthly majesties and their courts, not to recognize the value of a becoming stateliness on the part of those who rule states, whether their capitals be here or below: their subjects civilized or savage. He sat, therefore, on this occasion enthroned with a very commanding and royal grace, while the arrowy lightnings shot in circles around his head — very much, I judge, as you may have seen the swallows dart and soar of a summer evening, around an old church steeple.

His Majesty had not long to wait for his loving lieges, for suddenly from the darkness a huge, gaunt-framed wizard leaped out and mounted the altar-stone. If Chamberlain has not painted him blacker than he deserves, this high priest of Satan was a most villainous-looking rascal. His raw-boned and ghastly visage was painted in most blood-thirsty ugliness; scalps, dripping with fresh blood, hung around his body in festoons; on his own scull, by way of scalp lock, burned a lambent blue flame; his distended veins shone through the bright copper-colored skin as if they were filled with molten fire for blood — and, as for his eyes, they glowed with a fiercer light than those of the arch-fiend himself; whence Chamberlain maintained that an Indian priest was at least one degree more devilish than the Devil himself.

The present was evidently a very potent magi-cian, for at his call a throng of ghastly and horrible phantoms came pouring in from every nook and cranny of the valley — each with a shadowy toma-hawk and a torch, which did not burn with the honest and ruddy glare of pitch-pine, but with a blue color and sulphurous odor, that revealed un-mistakably at what fire they had been lighted.

Every ghost, as he came, made a profound obeis-ance to the rock-throned Satan, and then took his place in the circle around the altar-stone. By and bye, the chief priest set up a wild, howling chant, and away went the whole rabble rout, yelling and rushing round the altar in a mad, galloping sort of dance, in which they lifted their feet all the while, as if treading upon burning coals or red-hot iron — a step which is only learned in the dancing-schools down below. Many more such diabolical antics they cut, which, as they would neither be profitable by way of example or warning, it does not matter to tell.

At last they paused, and Chamberlain thought it about time for them to take themselves off. But they were far enough from that: on the contrary, two barbarous looking phantoms — who might in life have been familiars to a savage inquisition — presented themselves, leading between them a beautiful Indian maiden, robed only in her own long black hair. At another moment the beholder might have admired her graceful proportions and regular features — as he did when he afterwards remembered them — but now his senses were too much absorbed by horror. Not a word the poor girl spoke, but, stupified and silent, looked around from one unrelenting face to another, as if at a loss to comprehend what it all meant. Alas! she soon knew; for one of the familiars, seizing her rudely around the waist, placed her upon the altar-stone before the priest. Then she shrieked — so wildly that the hunter declared the echo never ceased ringing in his ears to his dying day;— what part she had to perform there was no longer doubtful. But she shrieked not again nor spoke — only looked up into the fiery eyes of the priest so piteously that it seemed his heart should have melted, had it been formed even of flint like the stone on which he stood; but it had been hardened in more infernal fires.

So he took up his demoniac howl again, and went capering madly around the maiden. Then, suddenly pausing before her, he raised his hatchet and the whole phantom circle gathered closer around him, as if to gloat more nearly over their victim's pangs. It seemed the sacrifice was about to be consummated; but as the weapon was raised, the maiden's eyes (averted from it) met those of Chamberlain. The kind-hearted hunter, in whom compassion had overcome fear, could no longer restrain himself; so, taking out his Bible, he pronounced the great Name — and with a terrific crash of the elements the whole scene vanished, leaving him in impenetrable darkness — for although the lightnings ceased, as if they had accompanied their master in his flight, yet the rain fell faster than ever.

When the morning came, Chamberlain would have taken it all for a dream, for, exhausted with fatigue and excitement, he had fallen into a deep sleep; but he found that the wizards, unable to harm him, while protected by the holy volume, had revenged themselves by stealing his deer, and perhaps giving it to their familiars, the bears — for there were bears in those days — so that there can be no manner of doubt as to the truth and accuracy of Chamberlain's story.

There is many another legend of this haunted dell; as for this, I hope you place the same implicit confidence in it which my old informant did.

Passing through the gorge very late, one piercing cold winter night, the place looked very weird to me. The frozen air was still as death; the white moonlight was reflected from the snow, as I fancied with more of pallor than of brightness, and I heard a shriek which I tried to believe came from the maiden victim. But it may have been the scream of some far-off locomotive. Confound those "resonant steam eagles!"—there's never a shriek, from Cape Cod to the Taghconics—though with the ghostliest ring to it—but they get the credit.

X.

UNDINE'S GLEN.

Page—Apelles, you must come away **quickly, with the** picture. The king thinketh, now you have painted it **you** play with it.

Apelles.—If I would play with pictures I have enough **at** home.

Page.—None perhaps you love so well.

Apelles.—It may be I have painted none so well. [**Exit** page.]

* * * O Campasne, I have painted thee in my heart; painted! nay, contrary to my art, imprinted, and that in such deep characters that nothing can rase it out, unless it rub my heart out.—*Alexander and Campasne.*

It had been a week of rare sultriness with us—the fierce dying flicker of summer's life-flame. The maple leaves had lost the last remnant of their glossy freshness; the cattle stood cooling themselves under the willow trees in the still pools of the river; long ago the birds had ceased their songs and fled into the deeper recesses of the woods; we, human idlers, lay listlessly under the shade of the nearer groves in dreamy reveries, or feeble speculations upon the destiny of some little cloud which might chance to speck the horizon—the forlorn-hope of a thunder-shower. At evening we broached the mildest possible topics of conversation. The nearest approach we made to vigorous effort was when a necessity arose for throwing cold water upon any chance theme or project which might heat the blood.

On the most fiery day of that fiery seven, came a friend who, then of all times, must climb to Washington Mountain. No flaming sword of the elements could fright him from his purpose, and all the chivalry of friendship forbade me to leave him to the chances of being roasted, alive and alone, on some sun-burnt exposure of quartzite: a very possible fate for him who in his scientific ardor lingers too long on those natural gridirons. My friend had passed the livelong summer in New York, and minded our mountain heats no more than Monsieur Chaubert did a furnace only heated three times, instead of seven.

Washington Mountain is the higher portion of that part of the Hoosac range which lies in the town of Washington, and is to be carefully distinguished from Mount Washington, the grand mass of Taconic hills in the south-western corner of the county. The point which we were to visit, was the shore of a pretty and lonely mountain lake, which lies seven miles east of Pittsfield and seven hundred feet above it, or seventeen hundred above the sea-level. The bed-rock here is pure quartz, which is a good thing for the Pittsfield people, who get their luxurious abundance of pure water from the lake, and from mountain streams which flow over the same insoluble formation. It takes here the form of granular quartz — which mineralogists, absurdly to my thinking, nickname

quartzite. When distintegrated, naturally or artificially, it becomes the silicious sand of the glass
manufacture. A very valuable bed of this sand lies
on the eastern shore of the lake: of which, more by
and bye. I mention it now, merely to confess that
it was some speculative interest in the money-value
of its contents, and not any fanatical devotion to
mountain scenery which led us to undertake that
pilgrimage which threatened to be so like that from
Morocco to Mecca: what ever of a romantic character
finally attached itself to the excursion, was purely
subsidiary. But in Berkshire, if there is any sus-
ceptibility to the romantic in you, you can hardly go
to market for a pig without its betraying itself.

' Thinking to escape the more violent heat, we set
out at a very early hour, but the air was already intensely sultry, and, still worse, was filled with a fine
white dust, that completely penetrated eyes, nose,
and mouth. We could neither see, breathe, nor
speak, with comfort; and the gritty particles between
our teeth sent a nervous shudder through the whole
frame. As we ascended the mountain we came upon
a fine breeze which never fails there, and which at
the same time aggravated the plague of the dust,
and inspired us with vigor to devise and execute a
remedy.

Ever and anon, by the road-side, appeared glimpses
of a deep, rocky gorge. Up this, L. proposed to
ascend the mountain by a path familiar to him, and,
accordingly, sending our horse forward by a willing
youth — who, I rather doubtfully hope, did not seize

this rare opportunity to violate the precepts of the society for the prevention of cruelty to animals — we plunged down a steep descent, thick beset with brambles. At the bottom, a little brook came tumbling and purling down the hill, and, yielding to its suggestions, we indulged in a series of luscious ablutions. None but those who have experienced the like, can know the thrilling vigor and elasticity which penetrated us with the cool mountain air when the burning and inflammatory dust was once removed from the pores.

Filled with new life, we pushed eagerly up the brook, now clambering over huge angular blocks of flint rock, now sauntering along smooth patches of green sward, and anon pushing our way through a thorny hedge of blackberry bushes, hanging full of the ripest fruit. Still L. led on, till we came to a little level spot of green sward, around which the brook swept in a graceful curve, while a thick leaved maple overhung it. We were here shut out from all sight of human habitation. The only traces of man's ravages were the weather-beaten stumps, which stood, ghastly memorials of his parricidal war with nature, like the bleached sculls which the ploughman turns up on an ancient battle-field. The precipitous hills, on either side, were yet shaggy, although not as of old, with the maple, the beech, the fir, and the hemlock. Just up the gorge, the streamlet leaped down a black ledge in a silver white column; while, beyond, the glen was dark with narrowing cliffs and over-hanging trees. Bravely, but in vain, the gorgeous sunshine darted its arrowy rays into that Thermopylæ of gloom.

L. flung himself at full length beneath the maple, and I was glad to follow his example. "Do you know," he said, "this is Undine's Glen? Shall I tell you the story of how it got its foreign name?"

One day in June, some ten years ago, there came to the village hotel in Pittsfield two ladies; the one, Miss Helen V., an heiress, and what was more, a spirited, brilliant, and natural girl. The other was her maiden aunt, Miss M., neither young nor pretty, yet a little romantic and not a little stiff in her manners. Miss M. held moreover the responsible office of guardian to her niece, which that young lady took the best care should be anything but a sinecure.

Riding, walking, and reading, the lone dames whiled away a week or two; when, provokingly enough, just as the last page of their last light reading was cut, there came a rainy, dreary day, as such days will come, even in June. At such desperate junctures, solid literature and re-readings, are not to be thought of; so recourse was had to the land-lord. That functionary was anxious to serve his fair guests, but unfortunately his shelves were but meagerly filled. Suddenly his face brightened with a new idea. Among his boarders was one Dr. M., who, to enliven his hours in the country, had brought with him from New York a curious library. This gentleman was summoned, and made his appear-ance — a very personable young gentleman, and a clever. The wants of the ladies were made known to him, and he invited them to examine his library for themselves, and some pictures which he prized, as well.

Helen was delighted, although she did not exactly say so then; Miss M. hesitated, with some secret misgivings, but finally, overcome by the fiend ennui, and the frank bearing of M., she, courteously enough, accepted the. invitation. Evening was upon them before they had completed the survey; for, besides his paintings by other artists, M. modestly displayed his own portfolio, filled with sketches of foreign as well as neighboring scenery. Helen eagerly turned them over, and M. had an enthusiastic word for many a remembered scene. After Miss M. had several times reminded her of her prolonged stay, Helen selected De La Motte Fouqué's delightful romance of "Undine" from the library, and that evening M. read it aloud to them in their parlor. Before they parted, the ladies had consented to accompany him on the morrow to this spot, of which he was going to complete a sketch. So does friendship ripen when the right sun-light falls upon it.

They came hither; the artist fixed his easel and wrought upon his sketch. Helen, seated at the foot of this maple, read "Undine" to her aunt. But both found an interval to wander up the glen; so with reading, sketching, romancing,— and most likely eating — the day wore away and the night came,— a moonlight night and a moonlight ride home.

Some days passed, in which M. gained hugely in

the good opinion of his fair friends, who continually teased him for a sight of his sketch — which he declared should not be seen until it was completed.

Thus, something of an air of mystery had woven itself around the picture when at last he brought it out, altogether with the air of a man who knows he has done a nice thing, and is rather proud to have the world see it.

Never was pride more completely dashed, or lover more completely puzzled. Helen blushed and smiled, but looked strangely and heartily vexed. The guardian aunt frowned unequivocally — not to say scowled. Poor M. turned from one to the other in most innocent and ludicrous bewilderment; but finally settled down into a fixed consideration of the cloud which had so suddenly gathered on the old lady's brow — as a summer storm sometimes will over the placid surface of Lake Ashley. The summer storm is transient, but Miss M. seemed to have an inexhaustible magazine of wrath behind her wrinkled forehead. So, taking a hint from Helen's eye, at the first growl of the thunder, M. fled.

The tempest was brewed in this wise. The good old lady, with all her romance and stateliness, had a spice of puritanism about her, and the special phase in which it showed itself was a prudish modesty in the matter of pictures. Why it took this form, more than any other, might be discovered, perhaps, if we could pry into the crooks and crannies of her early history. At present it only concerns us to know that it was there, and that in consequence of it she issued a husky edict for M. to "take his vile picture hence."

Now this vile painting was neither more nor less than a simple and spirited sketch of this scene, into which the artist had interwoven a portrait of Helen in the character of Undine. All very well — only the painter, with the modest assurance of his art, had changed the maiden's chaste garb for a bit of flimsy drapery, which displayed the ivory neck and swelling bosom, the taper leg and rosy foot, as circumstantially as though he had had the original all the while before him for a model. O fair and false imagination, to steal away so fair and true a reality !

Miss M. would have thought her ward's character irreparably compromised by interchanging a word more with the immoral young man M. had proved himself, in her estimation. Helen thought quite otherwise. Fortunately for M. there was another difference in their notions. The aunt loved her morning pillow — the niece her morning walk — and this taste of the damsel's now acquired a new strength that would have charmed Dr. Alcott. In another point of view these sunrise excursions to South Mountain and Mellville's Lake might have been thought alarmingly frequent. The young lady could not have been expected or desired to make her walks solitary, but one who saw how demurely they met at the breakfast table would not have surmised that the painter had been her companion an hour before.

But the end was not yet; walking, it seems would not content them — they must ride as well. So one balmy morning in the gray twilight, a pair of spirited greys were reined up at the south door of the Berkshire House, while our young friends took their places behind them; and then, heigho for Lebanon! "They'll have fleet steeds that follow, quoth young Lochinvar." Gallant champions of Love, those same fiery greys! Before then, and since, they have borne beating hearts up the hills and down the valleys of that seven miles of Hymen's highway which lie between the jurisdiction of the puritan publishment laws and the marriage-encouraging state of New York. I wonder if any where in this western world more visions of happiness have been dreamed, more passionate pulsations throbbed, than between the tall Elm of Pittsfield and the all-curing Springs of Lebanon. The very murmurs of the groves have caught the soft tones of lover's vows; the sparkling streams reflect the ardent gleam of expectant bridegroom's eyes.

Over this hymenial highway, that balmy morning, our happy couple were rapidly whirled, and before the sun was up, the words were said which bound them in that union which no words can unloose. I doubt if their steeds were urged as impatiently on their return, but they reached their hotel again while the careless guardian, fatigued with the last night's novel, yet slept. How they ever reconciled matters with her I never heard; but it was done, for last week she sat quietly by, while M., in a little recessed back parlor in Brooklyn, told me the story of his wooing. On the wall, too, he pointed out to me the identical "vile painting;" and by her mother's side a little Undine of eight summers shook her sunny curls and laughed. I don't think the painter ever regretted his day's sketching in the wild glen he christened "Undine's Gorge."

"Can you believe the doctor was ever guilty of such nonsense as that?" said Mrs. M., laughing and blushing, as she handed me a delicately tinted and perfumed paper. It was one of her husband's effusions in the days of their courtship, and I noticed that his nonsense had been carefully copied in her own neat penmanship. "And will you believe that those silly lines once had the power to make me tell my poor aunt a little fib, and then walk half a mile to meet the saucy fellow, by Elsie's Haunted Pool? What weak things girls are!"

Of course I could but beg a copy of the verses; and here they are:

GREEN HILLS OF TAGHCONIC.

All sounds are hushed to silence,
   Save the insect's lulling drone
And the murmur of the brooklet
   O'er its bed of pebbled stone.
Far off, the green hills of Taghconic
   In the glow of the sunset lie,
Entwined with a chaplet of roses
   And clasped in the arms of the sky;
For, round as the bosom of beauty,
   They swell from the vale in the west,
And, catching the rose hue of twilight,
   Seem blushing to be caressed.

One wreath of a silvery vapor
   That awhile on the hill-top hung,
Like a gossamer scarf by a maiden
   O'er her ivory shoulders flung,
Is gone ; for the sky — a right lover —
   The beautiful wearer kissed,
And drew to himself for a token
   The scarflet of silvery mist.
But lo, for the token he taketh
   A token more fair he bestows,
For, see, on the brow of the mountain
   A starry diamond glows.

To-night by earth and heaven
   Alike is love-lore taught,
And the air with the sweetest wisdom
   Of happiness is fraught.
Then come to our tryst in the gloaming,
   Our tryst by the whispering beech,
And we'll con the lessons duly
   That the sages of nature teach ;
While near us the clear Housatonic
   Meandering flows to the sea,
And sounds, with the silence harmonic,
   Are blended in melody.

The story told, and a bumper drained to the health of the heroine — again up, still up, the cool gorge, till it diverged to the north, while our path lay southward.

XI.

WASHINGTON MOUNTAIN AND LAKE ASHLEY.

"A lonely mountain tarn."

Emerging from Undine's Glen, and reclaiming our carriage, we soon reached the shore of Lake Ashley, a pretty sheet of water, but more remarkable for its elevation, its loneliness and its unrivalled purity, than for any beauty of contour. The cold, pure serenity of its dark waves, as we looked upon them that day, was indeed exquisite. Lined on all sides but one by unbroken woods, fed only by fountains which gush from below, with neither speck nor boat on all its tranquil surface, it seemed, as we rode along its eastern border, the very waters of solitude. It should be so, for since the Indian's graceful bark is gone forever, there remains none which would not disturb the calm beauty of the scene.

In long delicious draughts of the cool, sweet wave, we drank deep to the mountain maids, and certain maids of the valley: to the spirits of earth, air and water — to all kindly spirits whatever; not forgetting those who were then planning the grand project, since grandly perfected, of teaching these solitary and secluded waters to thread their way through the homes, and sparkle in the fountains of thirsty Pittsfield. They are as refreshing there as a lively, bright-eyed country girl in a Fifth Avenue parlor. Bless them both, girl and mountain stream !

And then we got down — or, rather, up — to the solid business of the day. Washington Mountain, as I have said, is composed largely of quartzite. On the western slope it lies in laminated strata, of which some, from three to six inches thick, are quarried for flagstones and like purposes.

In the earlier days of the settlement they were occasionally used for grave-stones, although of such adamantine hardness as almost to defy the sculptor's most irresistible chisel. You may see, in the "Pilgrim's Rest" of the Pittsfield cemetery, some curious specimens, a hundred years old, on which the inscriptions, whose depth is almost imperceptible to the eye, yet look as fresh as if cut yesterday; so little has a century done to smooth the thin, white roughening, the painstaking old sculptor was able to effect.

From these rude quarries, the people of old time called this "Rock Mountain;" a name quite as distinctive and appropriate, to say the least, as that which it now bears. In other parts of the mountain the quartz is of finer grain, and not stratified. Still, like the quartzite boulders you find all the way from the Canaan range to the Hoosac, it appears compact; but, crush it under a hammer or in an iron mortar — or throw a heated fragment into water — and you shall see it fly into a sand identical with that used by the glass-makers.

In Cheshire, Lanesboro', and other localities along the Hoosac range, this quartzite is found naturally disintegrated, in immense and valuable beds, from which large quantities of silicious sand are annually taken for the local glass-works and for exportation; for it is very widely used. It is altogether probable that the light by which you read these words comes to you through material which once lay in our Berkshire sand-beds, now transformed to window glass and lamp chimneys. I had learned that one of these precious deposits lay under a little well-wooded noppit which rose not far from the eastern shore of Lake Ashley. It supplied silicious material for glass-works during the war of 1812, but afterwards fell out of use, and almost out of mind. There was now a new demand for it; and hence our haste in seeking it that torrid summer day. A small recess in the side of the noppit was the only trace which remained of the labors of the old miners; but there were sufficient indications of a rich deposit. I shall have more to say hereafter of the beautiful and curious quartz formations of Berkshire; but for the present it is enough to add, concerning this peculiar bed, that the indications of its wealth were not deceptive. It proved among the best in the country, both as to extent and quality; and has long been the source of supply for the famous glass-works at Lenox Furnace.

Such investigations as we had the means for mak-

ing were soon finished, and we had still time to seek
for an extended mountain view. Knowing nothing
of the region, we found this a task of no small difficulty; but there was a great reward. By mere ac-
cident we came upon an outlook open on every side
to the surrounding mountains, but cutting off every
glimpse of valley.

     " Nunc coelum undique et undique" montes!

Although there are many similar views among our
Green Mountains, there are few in which the seclusion of sky and mountain-tops is so complete as in
this. To the north-east a wild billowy sea of mountains stretched far away — a taller peak sometimes
dashing its splintered crest into the sky, and a white
village spire, or a red farm house, appearing here and
there, a floating waif upon the waste. Upon a
lofty point, miles away, the pretty village of Mid-
dlefield glittered in the light of the setting sun.
On the north and on the south as far as the eye
could reach, extended the long, rolling, billowy swells
of the Hoosacs. On the west, the ever beautiful
Taconics; and, looming far beyond them, the shadowy
Catskills, looking like huge ghosts of perished mountains — long ago murdered by crashing earthquakes
or smothering ice-sheets.

The fastnesses of Washington Mountain were
among the last strong-holds in Massachusetts where
the defeated, but not yet wholly desperate, insurgents of the Shay's Rebellion took refuge; and met
with new disaster. The sad case of men " who
have been in arms against the government," and by

failure are placed at the mercy of insulted and vindictive law, has long been one of the most touching themes of historical romance. In this instance,
to be sure, the triumphant government, doubtless
conscious that it was itself not without sin in giving
cause for the revolt, was more merciful to the treason than it had been to the poverty which provoked
it; but at the time of the rally on the heights of
the Hoosacs, this clemency was by no means well
assured, and I doubt not that there was enough
of dread and suffering and sorrow there, to touch
our deepest sympathies could we but recall their
story.

An excellent road — the old Boston and Albany
highway, leads to "Washington Center," and thence
another runs southward along the crest of the mountain, through a level pastoral country, affording a
charming, invigorating drive with frequent bold and
striking prospects. If your imagination is potent to
bring back a ragged squad or two of those forlorn
old rebels, to enliven the foreground, it will improve the picture. In default of that, a trim school
mistress in a jaunty hat, a bronzed and bright-eyed
ploughman, and perhaps a grim and grizzled wood-
chopper, must serve.

XII.
MARVELS OF THE TUNNEL CITY.

Make straight in the desert a highway for our God:
Every valley shall be exalted, and every mountain shall **be**
    made low ;
And the crooked shall be made straight, and the rough places
    plain,
And the glory of the Lord shall be revealed.—*Isaiah.*

The chariot shall be with flaming torches, in the day of his
    preparation ;
And the fir trees shall be terribly shaken ;
The chariots shall rage in the streets ;
They shall jostle, one against another, in the broad ways ;
They shall seem like torches ; they shall run like lightnings.

Nahum.

Whither shall we go this fine morning ? For one I am inclined to extend our rambles a little: and an hour or so on the rail will enable us to spend a long day in any of those delightful localities, brimful of interesting objects and associations, which cluster thickly around Williamstown and North Adams on the north, Sheffield, Great Barrington and Stockbridge on the south, and in the rich mineral fields of the Corundum hills on the border of Hampshire county. Or we may take the wings of " the resonant steam eagles," and fly away to towering, sparkling, splashing, darkling, Bash-Bish. But I think bright, busy, bustling dashing North Adams, with its lively streets and peculiar surroundings, will show off well in this cool, clear atmosphere: hot and hazy, or **wet** and misty, days do not favor them much.

To my mind, the most notable thing in this fine old town, or its bright new village, is the people: not to disparage some very noble scenery, or perhaps the most remarkable natural curiosity in the commonwealth; and, least of all, to speak lightly of the grand Tunnel. But North Adams is, I verily believe, the smartest village in "the smartest nation of all creation:" the concentrated essential oil of Yankeedom. As you pass through its streets, you see the evidence of this great truth everywhere; in the shops, in the manufactories, in the hotels: and, if these do not convince you, there will be no room for doubt when you come to the Hoosac Tunnel, which is almost as much a North Adams product, as the shoes made by the aid of Chinese cheap labor, or the textile fabrics woven by more costly imported help.

We look with admiring awe upon the engineering skill and persistence which penetrated from side to centre of that enormous mountain-mass, in exact conformity with their intention; but not less skillful and persistent was the engineering which carried the Tunnel measures through that solid, but ever-fluctuating body, the Great and General Court; which, like the demoralized rock of the Hoosac Mountain, was all the more difficult to manage for the instability of its constituent material. You think that.

14

the waters of the Deerfield river generated the power which bored the Tunnel. Doubtless, in a secondary way, it did; but not until a rill from the state treasury had become a helpful tributary of the Deerfield. The primary motive force was furnished by that bold engineering which dammed the treasury, and turned a golden stream Tunnelward; and North Adams furnished the engineers.

Do not misconceive me. I do not use that word, engineering, in an offensive sense, although I admit it to be, in some sort, slang. Slang is often, as in this instance, only metaphor vulgarized by the newspapers. Every public movement must be engineered; not one, that I know, was ever so non-antagonistic to private interests, or so self-evidently for the common good, that it would engineer itself — move off spontaneously; and, by virtue of its own native goodness, finish its course triumphantly. Even a revival of religion is not achieved that way; and I seem to have read somewhere that our American Revolution was adroitly "worked up." As for those who, by engineering or otherwise, helped on the boring of the Hoosac Tunnel, I fully believe that they deserve, and will in due time receive, the gratitude of every unselfish well-wisher of the commonwealth.

Having read in the old records that, after the Boston and Albany Railroad was opened, its managers were in great doubt whether freight enough would ever be offered, to require the use of the two locomotives which they had placed between Springfield and Pittsfield, I have the courage to find, in the great traffic which already seeks an avenue through the Tunnel, the promise of an adequate direct return for the State's vast expenditure there. But, even if that promise fail, I have the faith in reserve that the deficiency will be more than made good, indirectly, by increased wealth and population.

But what have we to do with profit and loss, in our search for romance and beauty? Of romance, we shall surely find enough in the undertaking and accomplishment of that stupendous Tunnel enterprise; and, if there be any lack of beauty — of which I am not sure — it will find abundant compensation in the grandeur of the work; a much more rare attribute of Berkshire marvels.

The Tunnel, however, as well as the glories of the scenery around North Adams, has been celebrated by a pen so much more competent than mine, that it would be presumption for me to attempt more than the briefest glimpses at them; a barley-corn of quit-rent, as it were, in acknowledgment of homage due.

The Hoosac Tunnel project is of no recent birth. It is more than sixty-five years since the Massachusetts people, provoked to good works by the success of the Erie canal, conceived the idea of making the Hudson River climb over the Berkshire Hills and run down to Boston; or if, under the protection of certain laws not subject to repeal by the General Court, or to be evaded by its engineers, the waters of the great river obstinately refused to run up hill, then to take from them the ever-increasing burden of western commerce, which they perversely carried to New York, and turn it eastward by means of a little Yankee Hudson — to wit, a canal — to be manufactured, until it crossed the Hoosacs, out of the lakes and streams of Berkshire.

One proposition for carrying out this scheme, was to follow nearly what is now the route of the Boston and Albany railroad; but there was some doubt whether Pittsfield and the neighboring heights could furnish an adequate supply of water; and, besides, as one can readily believe, the "rocky nature of the ground between Pittsfield and Blandford was discouraging."

On the route now followed by the Troy and Boston railroad, the engineer found no very troublesome obstacles, except that, immediately east of North Adams, the Hoosac Mountain reared a barrier fifteen hundred feet high, and, at his very moderate computation, four miles thick.

Here was something that, even with our advanced scientific and material engineering facilities, would give the boldest projector pause; but if it intimidated those old enthusiasts at all, it must have been only for a brief space. Late in the winter of 1825, Governor Eustis appointed Nathan Willis of Pittsfield, Elihu Hoyt of Deerfield and H. A. S. Dearborn of Boston, commissioners, and Colonel Laomi C. Baldwin, engineer, to consider the possibility of the scheme for a canal from the Hudson to Boston; and in January, 1826, they reported it to be perfectly practicable, by means of a tunnel through the Hoosac Mountain, nearly at the point occupied by the present tunnel. The proposed dimensions were four miles in length, twenty feet in width and thirteen and a half in height; requiring a total excavation of two hundred and eleven thousand cubic yards. The elevation of the mountain ranges which still remained was to be overcome by a series of locks, whose total rise and fall were to be three thousand two hundred and eighty-one feet. The commissioners estimated the cost of the canal, one hundred and seventy-eight miles long, at about six million dollars, including that of the tunnel which they put at less than one million.

Colonel Baldwin was probably the daring spirit who first conceived the idea of this gigantic undertaking — far more gigantic than he, in his professional philosophy, dreamed. But, whoever was father to the thought, the people of the Tunnel Region eagerly adopted it; and, though for a time it seemed to others to die, they knew that it only slept; and never lost sight of it until a locomotive, instead of a canal boat, emerging from the bowels of the mountain, rejoiced their waiting eyes.

In 1826, a Boston newspaper-writer demonstrated, to his own satisfaction at least, that, on the commissioner's own showing, it would require fifty-two years to complete the proposed excavation. Nevertheless, had it not been for the timely introduction, at that very moment, of steam as a motive power on railroads, there is much reason to believe that the state would have undertaken the tunnel. It is certain, at least, that there would have been a strong party in favor of its so doing.

And now, if you will consider what chemical and mechanical appliances were at the command of the engineer in 1825; what was the cost of labor, and what the pecuniary resources of the state, I think you will concede some grandeur to the courage that did not flinch from a work which has since, under far different conditions, almost frightened some very solid economists from their propriety.

The successful use of steam on railroads effectually cured the canal fever, which was raging with symptoms very threatening to the public purse; and attention was diverted from the Hoosac Mountain — the highest mass of the Hoosac Range — to the more moderate grades of the same chain in Central and Southern Berkshire; which, at no ruinous cost, could be made available even with such locomotive power as the skill of that day was able to provide.

The tunnel project, thus put to rest, slept an unquiet slumber, until it was re-awakened in 1848, by the charter of the Troy and Greenfield railroad with a capital of three million five hundred thousand dollars. A proposed capital only; for the arbiters of finance did not look kindly upon the scheme, and it languished — in a morning nap perhaps — until its friends, in 1854, secured a loan of two million dollars from the commonwealth.

The tunnel work was begun with energy in 1856. But I am not going to attempt the story of its troubles and its triumphs. What with demoralized rock and demoralized legislators; with the rudest inexperience to be transformed to accurate practical knowledge; with useless, followed by the most efficient, machinery; with inadequate, and then with almost too violent, rending power; with sad waste of treasure; with still sadder sacrifice of life — there was enough, both of obstacle and the overcoming of it. But the final victory came at last; and, as I think, that first locomotive which, on the first of March, 1875, thundered through the vanquished mountain, was the proudest triumphal car that had ever celebrated conquest.

If you think my estimate exaggerated, what will you say of Rev. Dr. Todd, Pittsfield's quaintly eloquent, but thoroughly orthodox, divine, who found in our railroad era the fulfilment of the sublime prophecies which I have placed at the head of this article? This was in that glow of feeling excited in the warm-hearted pastor by his official participation in the golden welding of those iron bands by which the Pacific railroad binds together the east and the west; and I am not sure whether he counted his words well grounded doctrine, or merely the play of his bold poetic fancy. But you and I have heard many a less plausible interpretation of prophecy gravely propounded by reverend lips.

Well, there the Hoosac Tunnel is — not at all the visionary thing it seemed to many eyes, even a quarter of a century ago; but a very palpable fact; so palpable indeed that you can feel the darkness within it. You may visit it; but, before you do so, consider well the strength of the old Titanic mountain wall, which, so far as it was a barrier to commerce, it has thrown down; consider the wealth of treasure and of intellect, of human labor and human life, which have gone to its construction; get some conception, if you can, of the mighty flood of travel and traffic which rolls through it in ever-swelling volume. Thus prepared, you may feel the grandeur of the Tunnel; otherwise you may almost as well spend eleven minutes in your coal-cellar. Unless, indeed, you chance upon an hour when the cavernous walls are, for some special purpose illuminated; then, I dare say, you will experience some curious sensations; it may be of an exalted nature.

And now let us return to the Tunnel City: where, however, I shall not attempt to paint for you Mount Hawkes, Williams, Adams or any of the grand hills which look down upon it. They have already been gladdened by a more golden light than I could throw upon them. But I cannot resist the temptation to repeat a visit which I made many years ago to The Natural Bridge: a piece of carving by the Water Nymphs, which I do not find surpassed by any thing which Dame Nature's eccentric work-people have effected anywhere in New England.

Some years ago I took a walk, with a noted traveller, along the bending valley of the Hoosac, to North Adams and Williamstown; thence to the summit of Greylock, down its most precipitous side into one of its wildest recesses; and down the valley of the Housatonic to Pittsfield. You will wander long before you meet another route so rich in admirable landscape or in objects of marked individual interest; but none of them were impressed on my memory so vividly and pleasantly as this bridge, and the ravine by which it is best approached.

Reaching the vicinity by a winding road which afforded superb views towards the south and east, we entered the ravine at its lower terminus. We made no measurements, but the following description, furnished by Rev. John W. Yeomans for the "History of Berkshire" published in 1829, perfectly accords with my impressions.

" About a mile north east of North Adams village, Hudson's brook has worn a channel thirty rods long, and in some places sixty feet deep, through a quarry of white marble. The ledge terminates at the south in a steep precipice, down which it seems the water once fell ; but, finding in some places natural fissures, and in others wearing away the rock, it has formed a passage from thirty to sixty feet below its former bed, and with a mean breadth of fifteen feet. Across this chasm, two masses of rock — one ten or twelve feet above the other — lie like bridges. The upper is now much broken : under the lower, which is beautifully arched, the stream has sunk its bed nearly fifty feet."

The walls of the ravine are perpendicular cliffs of pure white marble, highly crystaline in coarse granulation — a dolomite, if I recollect rightly, susceptible of a fine edge under the chisel. They are mottled all over, from top to bottom with indentations of various shapes and sizes: but oftenest circular and concave, like a saucer, with an average diameter, at a rough guess, of eight or ten inches: making a very pretty Arabesque fret work. But,

small or large, the indentations were evidently made
by rolling pebbles kept in motion by the waters of
the sinking stream.   Frequently one of the niche-like
recesses has almost its exact counterpart precisely on
the opposite side of the chasm; as though a marble
mass — in which was a hollow space, like an inverted
cauldron or old-fashioned dinner-pot — had been
sharply rent in twain, and the sides withdrawn fifteen
feet apart: an explanation which has sometimes been
rashly made.   The phenomenon seems rather to indicate where a ledge of fixed rock extended nearly
across the bottom of the brook, forcing the grinding
pebbles against the wall on each side.

Ask the sculptor who makes gravestones of that
marble, how long he thinks it took the water nymphs
to carve out that ravine and fret its walls so curiously.

Entering the lower opening of the ravine, we waded
squarely into the brook, which we found easily
fordable; and as it was a warm summer day, we went
merrily splashing our way almost to the bridge;
whereby we got the best possible appreciation of
the whole thing.   And a high appreciation it was,
as my companion expressed it in an animated
speech when we had ensconced ourselves in opposite
niches in the marble walls.

XIII.

LANESBOROUGH SUNLIGHT AND SHADOW.

Man has two minutes and a half to live — one to smile, one to sigh, and a half to love: for in the midst of this we die. But the grave is not deep; it is the shining footprint of the angel who seeks us; and when the unknown hand throws the fatal dart, man boweth his head, and the shaft only lifts the crown of thorns from his wounds.— *Jean Paul Richter*.

Nestled closest in the bosom of our hills lies the little village of Lanesboro' — the very fondling of Nature. Thither turns never the good mother her wrinkled front; near pressing as the mountains clasp the narrow valley, you must not look among them for frowning precipices, or earthquake-rifted chasms. High into the air their summits press, but not in jagged peaks — only with the full, round swelling of loving breasts, upon which you may repose, if you will, in the gentlest of summer reveries.

There is one eminence — in patriotic gratitude they call it Constitution Hill — with such a winsome, neighborly look to it, that in our streets, miles away, it seems near as your own garden. If you have in you any yearnings at all after beauty, I am sure you cannot look upon, and not be irresistibly drawn to it, to be lifted up gently and humanly, above the baser things of earth. Lying under its druidical oaks, or seated, farther up, upon a pearl-white quartz rock, in the shade of a whispering birch, you will see below you, groves and farms, and broad, fresh meadows, with laughing lake and winding rivulets — like silver embroidery on the green banner of Erin.

Many fair villages, as well, will dot the scene, whose names — if you do not know — I hope you will never ask, but be content to remember, that under each roof of them all, human lives are wearing themselves out. Then let your own heart interpret for you what the overlooking woods whisper. If you know well the story of one hearth-stone, think what a thrilling tale it is; and if, in your reveries upon the hill-tops, you multiply that marvellous but common story into the thousand dwellings of the valley, the resultant mass shall be mightier than the mountains which encompass it.

I could point you to an antique mansion — a grey spot it appears in the far distance, with no overhanging cloud to distinguish it — at whose story I am deeply moved, as often as I look upon it. The splendors and the shadows, which have by turns darkened and illumined its chambers, pass and repass in spectral reiteration, over my spirit. Whether I will or not, come the ghosts of fleeting joys, irradicable sorrows; the loftiness of human pride and the lowliness of pride's abasement, which have passed and left no record there; and yet that grey old homestead is no accursed roof, devoted to misery

from its foundation, but one even such as its fellows
are. Ah ! if we could look within the seemly exterior of any home — if we could penetrate the heart's
chambers of any man, what might not meet us there ?
Those glowing windows which gleam so cheerily on
our evening path, by what funereal torches may
they not be lighted ? Those radiant faces which
meet us smilingly in our noonday walk, by what infernal passions may they not be driven on ? So,
under the green and smiling earth, lie pent the hidden
fires, and help the genial sun to quicken the blossom
and ripen the fruit.

This Constitution Hill must be a great promoter
of reverie. I have a friend — a bachelor friend —
who, no sooner is he seated upon it, than off he goes
dreaming over the whole valley, in a very marvelous
way. I do not believe there is a dwelling in sight,
from Greylock to Yocun's Seat, that he has not, at
some time, made himself *pater familias* in it. Bring
him up hither, and his respect for the Tenth Com-
mandment vanishes like the mist of the valley.
Another friend of mine — an artist — never looks
down from this hill, but — presto ! change ! — the
hard work of a century is all gone, and the red
Indian comes back again, with wild-wood and wigwam, council fire and hunting ground. So you, if you
come within the charmed circle of our hill's shaven
crown, may, perchance, work some wonderful phan-
tasmagoric changes.

I do not know how it all comes about. Perhaps
some good genius has cast a spell upon the spot — a
15

mode of solving such difficulties to which I confess myself prone, being naturally of a superstitious as well as lymphatic turn of mind.

It may be only another fancy of mine, but the leaves here seem to have a perfection of beauty not attained elsewhere. Nature's work is finished with more care; the curves are cut with a more accurate grace, and the green more faithfully laid on. In the Fall, too, the rich enamellings are done with greater depth of coloring, and without shrivelling up the work in the process, as the careless elves are very apt to do in other groves. The specimens of their workmanship which I have seen here were perfect gems in their way. You shall not desire to see a more gorgeous sight than Constitution Hill in October.

Just on the western declivity is a good sized cavern, which, a witty lady thinks, may be the home of these elfin workmen; but in spite of the high authority, I must doubt; such underground tenements are more fit dwelling places for bears, wolves, and such like ugly gnomes, than for any gentle spirits whatever. **No,** ours are

> "Some gay creatures of the elements,
> Who in the colors of the rainbow live
> And play 'i the plighted clouds."

Descending from the hill, you may wander up the stream which flows at its base. If a follower of the "gentle craft of angling," you will not neglect to lie awhile where some thick-leaved maple overshadows a deep pool, where you may drop your line with the reasonable hope of bringing to shore a dozen fine fish — perhaps even the " Hermit Trout " himself who is believed to haunt these pools, and only dimple the shallows in the pale moonlight;—a wary old fellow he,

> " Too shrewd
> To be by a wading boy pulled out!"

But I trust you are no patron of this treacherous sport. You were better to sit on some warm bank of green-sward, or dangling your feet over some rustic bridge, to watch the smoothly gliding current, and

> " The shadows of sun-gilt ripples
> On the pebbly bed of a brook."

There is no wine, or oil of gladness, which has such a balm for the wounded spirit as the soft murmurs of a rural brooklet.

Wandering on, you may, if you are fortunate as I have been, sometimes catch a glimpse into dreamland — like a vignette to an old romance, of a youth seated under a spreading elm, with a guitar in his hand and a maiden by his side; or even catch Titania shooting grasshoppers with elfin arrows among the ox-eyed daisies and buttercups. When I was a citizen I used to think such things confined to poetry and Spain; but here, in the quiet days of summer, things often occur which convince one of the truth of Hood's remark, that " it is dangerous to swear to the truth or falsehood of a romance, even of one's own making."

On a gentle hillock, by whose side the stream flows
in deep willow shade, is the village grave-yard. Do
not fail to enter it. Among its thick-clustering
monuments you can linger with best profit, undisturbed by quaintly ludicrous epitaphs, or monstrous
heraldries of death. The touching inscriptions on
the simple marbles bespeak alike the chastened spirit
and the cultivated mind. What wild woe — paternal,
filial, fraternal, and conjugal — this narrow spot has
witnessed, I shrink from recalling. The marble bears
record only of the subdued grief and the Christian
hope; the story of the early woe, when the one joy
of life perished — when "the young green bole was
marked for fellage," is not told to the stranger's eye,
and is sacred from the stranger's pen. Yet, for that
stranger is the place deeply consecrated; how holy,
then, to those whose best of earth is mingled with its
dust. I am here often reminded of a beautiful
thought of Richter: "The ancients had it, that not
even the ashes of the dead should be embarked with
the living, for fear of the storm which would be sure
to follow. We have learned better, and know that
to be accompanied on the voyage of life by the
memory of the dead brings calm and not storm; he
who always feels one loss, will be less accessible to
new sorrow."

The Old Worshipper.

In this grave-yard I once witnessed a scene, so
touching and solemn, and yet so far removed from
any agony of woe, that to speak of it can open anew

no half healed wound. It was one of those occasions when the sorrows of earth are so gloriously transmuted into the joys of Heaven, that we, who remain "of the earth, earthy," look upon the transfiguration in far-off wonder; while philosophy strives in vain to characterize emotions, in which the consoler, Christ, enables the mourner to mingle — as in His own mysterious nature — so much of human sorrow with so much of Divine confidence.

Not far from the village grave-yard, is the church— a modest gothic structure, built of the grey stone of the country. This was once, for many months, my own place of worship; and still, on a pleasant Sabbath morning, I love to stroll to it. The bracing walk of some half dozen miles, through a delightful region, is no unworthy preparation for the devotions of the sanctuary; and, through the day, the voices of woods and waters seem to mingle with the deep responses of the congregation. Nature, with her thousand voices, joins in the jubilant chorus, and in subdued tones echoes the supplications of the solemn litany.

The first morning upon which I entered this church I was struck with the venerable figure of an old man, who sat in front of me, completely absorbed in worship. Never had my ideal of Christian devotion been so completely filled; no painter could have desired a finer model. His whole soul seemed informed and penetrated with the spirit of the liturgy, in whose eloquent words he poured forth his soul to God.

His veteran form was tall and martial in its bearing; in the deep lines of his countenance you could
not mistake the characters of strong intellect, self
respect, and unbending firmness of purpose. You
would say he was one not likely to yield much ob-
sequious homage to his fellow man; but here, in the
presence of Jehovah, his whole bearing was con-
formed to the most lowly, yet manly, humility.
Nothing could be more impressive than the earnest
tones with which he joined in the services of the
church.

Sabbath after Sabbath, my eye sought and found
him — the most noticeable figure in the room —
until one summer's day, when I entered, the people
were waiting, in that hush of expectation which in
a country congregation tells one that a funeral is
about to take place. On my way to the church I
had lingered a few moments, as was my wont, in
the grave-yard — and had found an open grave in
the lot of the venerable worshipper. I now looked
to his pew; it was vacant; and I at once guessed
that it was he who was about to enter the sacred
portals for the last time. But it was not so: a
whisper from a neighbor informed me that it was the
wife of the old man who was no more — the wife of
his youth.

Presently, as the procession entered, I saw the
widowed husband following close behind the coffin,
his head a little bent, as if to approach nearer the
form of the sleeper, and his voice a little more tremu-

lous than usual, as he joined in the Scripture appointed to be then read.

The coffin was laid before the altar, and the old man took his seat, with that forced calmness where the quivering lip shows the struggle hardly yet over, and the victory only half won.

As the sublime promises of future reunion were read; as the sympathizing tones of consolation fell from the lips of the preacher, I thought the few remaining clouds vanished from the aged face, and a perfect serenity overspread it. When the sermon was ended, with an aspect almost cheerful, he rose up, to follow to her burial-place all that remained on earth of her, with whom, for more than fifty years, he had walked, in sunshine and in storm. What emotions were at work within, none could read — the fixed eye, the firm-set lip, revealed nothing — the prying eye of curiosity, the anxious gaze of friendship, returned alike baffled. And yet, with what overwhelming power must the busy memory of that lonely old man have brought back the thick-crowding events of half a century, from the first thrilling meeting to this last brief parting! It is such moments which must disclose most viv'dly to the mind of Eld what this life is, which passeth like a dream. Such might have been the retrospect of the mourner of three score years and ten, as he took his few brief steps from the temple to the tomb — or, perchance, his better spirit reached forward to a glorious meeting in that home to which sorrow and parting can never come.

The coffin was lowered to its place; the people
gathered around. The pastor began that beautiful
service, in which the church commits earth to its
kindred earth, and proclaims the spirit returned to
the God who gave it. There, at the clergyman's
side, stood the tall and veteran form of the mourner,
his thin grey hairs streaming in the mountain wind,
as he repeated, firmly, the proper responses. For a
while he looked steadfastly down into the grave —
but as the pastor read: " And the corruptible bodies
of those who sleep in Him shall be changed and
made like unto His own glorious body," the de-
pressed eyes were raised to Heaven with an expression of most triumphant and joyous hope. The
struggle was over. The grave had lost its sting;
"Death was swallowed up in victory." It was a
spectacle most touching and sublime.

Yet a few moments, and the grave was closed;
the people separated to their homes — and the
mourner, likewise, departed to his — but for not long.
He was soon missed from his accustomed seat in the
sanctuary. With the fall of the leaf, he went down
into the grave — and the grass which in the spring
grew upon his wife's mound, waved over two.

There is another and older graveyard in the town,
white with its multitude of marble testimonials.
Here there used to be a tomb, carved with masonic
symbols, and having a heavy iron knocker on its
door. Here, often at midnight — whether the still
moon shed her pale light on the ghastly tombstones,
or the dark and howling tempest was on — a crazed

woman used to enter the grave-encumbered ground, and strike such a peal on the ringing iron that the sleepers in the near dwellings started trembling from their slumbers. There is something terribly significant to me in that gloomy visitation of the tomb. What earnestness of agonized longing for their repose, may have impelled that wild nocturnal summons to the dead. "Wake! wake! ye peaceful dwellers in the tomb," perhaps that weary, brainsick woman said: "Open your dark portals and give me rest beside ye. Wake!—the living turn from me, and do you also spurn me?—me, who shudder not at any loathsomeness of yours?"

But cheerier thoughts for the cheerful light of summer—and, passing the mildewed realms of death, do you hie away to some beautiful hill—Pratt's, Prospect, St. Luke's, or "The Noppit;" or to some fair valley—whither I may not stay to accompany you.

Lanesboro was the birth place of that queerest and wisest of humorists, the Yankee Solomon, Josh Billings: *neé* Henry Savage Shaw. The people of the village used to affect a certain rural English style, and the older inhabitants still love to speak of it as "The Borough." Hon. Henry Shaw, the father of our humorist, and one of the ablest statesmen who have represented Berkshire in congress, was the Lord of the Manor, and quite held his own in most of the traits which are conventionally ascribed to that class of gentry in England. But there was one notable variation; he was no Episcopalian, but always occupied with his family, the square and spacious pew of state in the Congregational meeting-house.

The rector of St. Luke's, although bearing the same name as the squire, was proud of his descent from the old Brentons, and clung fondly to. the customs of his ancestral church, as well as to its doctrines. Overflowing with genial wit, charitable, given to hospitality, and devoted especially to the kindlier duties of his priestly office, he might have furnished Goldsmith or Praed, a model for their delightful pictures of the English country clergyman. A man greatly to be loved.

In matters of religious dogma and form, there was not that happy accord between the squire and the rector, which usually prevails between similar classes in England; but, although both seemed to belong to another state of society than that which prevailed outside of the Borough, each seemed exactly fitted for the niche in the great temple — the world — in which it had pleased his Maker to place him. That is, so far as his home in the Borough was concerned — outside of that the squire, at least, who took a large part in public affairs, fared like others who mix in the mad whirl of politics and finance, and get more or less of their deserts, as it may chance. But in their retired niches at home, each would gladly have preserved every dear antique ornament, however grotesque, of the life which surrounded him. But the well-born and polished clergyman and the stately, courtly squire were not the only original characters in the Borough: it was full of them, from these conspicuous specimens down to the sardonic dealer in oysters and poultry — nay, to the very blackest picker of black-berries in " The Gulf."

Such was the early home in which Josh Billings meditated fun and — I have not a particle of doubt — mischief. Here he made curious observation of the odd people about the village, and perhaps treasured up the wise and piquant sayings for which the squire and the parson were renowned, the county over. I will cite one of the squire's, which he ejaculated with some emphasis, although he had the smallest possible personal experience of its truth: " Confound "— that is not exactly the word, but I translate —" Confound poverty: it never did any body any good ! " What do you think of that for truthfulness, compared with the old sentimental philosophy on the same point ?

XV

LAKE ONOTA AND ITS WHITE DEER.

Can I forget? no, never, such a scene;
So full of witchery —*Rogers' Italy.*

I said, the other day, that Pontoosuc is not quite
my favorite among our mountain lakes.   Onota is.
Of all the hundred lakelets of Berkshire — exquisitely
lovely as many of them are — I think there is not
one which equals this in grace of outline, or in its
rich back-ground of wood, field and hill.   It lies in
an elevated valley only two miles west of our main
street ; and, if you will come with me to the commanding elevation upon its south-west shore, and
look across its broad and tranquil surface, towards
Constitution Hill and Greylock, you will confess that
I have not too highly extolled its charms.   I am
sure, at least, that I never heard such an admiring
shout over any other piece of landscape as went up
from scores of Stockbridge and Albany field-meeting
visitors when this view was suddenly revealed to
them, one glorious summer day.   I should have bid
you, as you approached the lake, take note of the
twin elms which crown the hill upon its eastern
side and form a perfect arch — St. Mary's Arch, they

call it. But you may observe it from many points in the village.

When I first wrote of this lake, I said with truth "Of all our enticing groves, none are more perfect than the woods upon the eastern shore of Onota. Few have so hermit-like a solitude, yet none are so far removed from a desolate loneliness. These shades are sometimes very solemn, but one need not be very sad in them. A merry company might be very gay." As to a large extent of wood, this description still holds generally true, although costly mansions have arisen by the lake-side, and streets are creeping towards it. We must still ramble through woods, and for a little space scramble through brambles, to reach its northern shore.

But it is worth the trouble; for the view southward is wild and picturesque. I have heard artists commend it as the best to be had of the lake. I cannot so think; but its peculiar formation is certainly here displayed to the best possible advantage, and is very curious. At about one-quarter of its length from its northern end, it is divided by a narrow isthmus; the northern portion being the work of those industrious and skillful engineers, the beavers — who formed it by building a dam across a small stream which still runs through it, overflowing their embankment in sufficient quantities to turn the wheels of large factories at some distance below. The main or southern lake is fed by springs and Taconic mountain-brooks.

The fringed gentian, the cardinal and other gor-
16

gcous wild flowers, grow in profusion at the north of the lake. The more pleasant resort, however, is upon the south, where, of a dreamy summer after-noon, one can recline in luxurious reveries, as he watches the image of the mountains, sharply re-flected in the clear waters; sometimes in the green leafiness of June, sometimes in the melancholy gor-geousness of autumn, or better still, when the haze of the Indian summer invests them with hues of pearly delicacy and richness.

Perhaps, while you look, a broad-winged eagle will appear above you, soaring and sweeping in the silent sky, till it vanishes into the heavens; or a blue king-fisher will perch awhile upon yonder blasted bough, and then suddenly darting into the water bear away its writhing prey to some hidden haunt. Other gentler birds will sit a-tilt on the lithe green branches — and, if it be in early summer, serenade your slumberous car.

Near by, the cattle will stand in groups on a pleasant point of land which runs out into the lake, and which they seem to love better than other spots.

Around these shores were some of the earliest settlements; and, before the intrusion of the white man, they were the favorite haunt of the Indian. A gentleman digging into a bed of peat and marl, upon his farm on the east of the lake, found, at great depth, stakes pointed artificially — evidently the remains of wigwams built ages ago, when, perhaps, the marl bed was a lakelet as crystal clear as Onota. Remains of the rude arts of the later Indians used to be found in the neighboring fields; but now they are rarely, if ever, turned up by the plough.

Upon the eminence to which I first took you, a fort of some pretense was built, during the second French and Indian war, for the protection of the settlements at the south and east; and relics are still occasionally found of the regiments which rested here on their way to the campaigns which ended in the conquest of Canada. There were four of these forts in Pittsfield, garrisoned partly by soldiers sent by helpful Connecticut; and partly by the settlers, who, compelled to abandon their log cabins, took their families with them to these places of refuge. And a jolly time they seem to have had of it, shut up there cozily together — a perpetual tea-party.

The commissariat accounts are, some of them, still preserved, and afford us a peep at the housekeeping on Fort Hill a century and a quarter ago. They tell us that the larder of the garrison was plentifully supplied with venison at five pence a pound; wild turkey at a shilling, and beef at twelve pence. Trout were to be had by the hundred for the catching, and partridges for the killing. But the old accounts are chiefly occupied with charges for spirituous liquors in drams of rum, bowls of punch and mugs of flip. Persons of the lower rank took their drams; their superiors revelled in punch; while the more temperate, and the ladies, were generally content with the mild beverage, flip. On some days merriment grew merrier, as on a certain second of November — perhaps thanksgiving day — when the gallant

Captain Hinman, of the Connecticut troops, is charged with several punches for himself, and "a mug of flip for Mrs. Piercy." And, just below, we are startled by this entry: "The wife of Deacon Crofoot, for a mug of flip — a kiss." A merry party of fair women and brave men, there must have been that chill November evening in the old fort; maugre the possibility that a legion of Onuhgungo fiends would be howling for their scalps before morning. But antiquarian research dissipates any visions of the "rosy juncture of four melting lips" as a result of that charge against the Deacon's wife, by showing that the good dame was then sixty-six years old. Which doubtless is the reason that the account is not recorded to have been ever liquidated.

There are a couple of legends about this Onota, perhaps worth the telling. The first is well authenticated, and the other not improbable, as legends go.

THE LEGEND OF THE WHITE DEER.

There is hardly a country where a deer ever trod in which there does not linger some legend of one or more of these graceful animals, either wholly or in part of a supernatural whiteness. It is a fancy which seems to spring spontaneously in the rich soil of a woodman's imagination. The "White Doe of Rylston," and Bryant's "White-footed Deer, will occur to every one, as instances of the use to which these forest tales have been put in poetry. Traditions of a similar character are said to exist in many tribes

of American Indians, and among others, those of the
Housatonic valley.

A gentleman tells me that in the old witch times —
long after the Salem delusion ended — there were no
firmer believers in that sort of supernaturalism than
the people who lived about Lake Onota; one of
whom was his own grand-father, of whom he relates
the following anecdote:

Coming in one day from an unsuccessful day's
hunting, he was surprised to see a white deer stoop-
ing down to drink at Point Onota — the little cape
which extends into the lake at its south end. Instantly his rifle was at his shoulder; but before he
could pull the trigger, his dog howled, and the
startled deer fled into the wood. The marvellous
story of the white deer of the Mohegans at once
occurred to him, and it entered into his head that
his dog was bewitched; or rather that an old hag
who lived in "The North Woods"—a section on
the north-western side of the lake — had assumed
his form; which, among other freakish powers, she
had the perilous reputation of being able to do. With
never a doubt, therefore, that he was all the while
belaboring the witch, our disappointed hunter waled
his poor hound till the woods howled again with his
piteous cries.

This done, he posted away in hot haste to the
cabin of the old crone, and demanded that she should
show him her back — never doubting that he would
find upon it the marks of the stripes he had inflicted
upon his miserable beast. Of course the old woman

was in a tempest of wrath when she learned the errand of her visitor; and it is believed that he made a retreat more discreet and rapid than valiant, under a sudden shower of blows from that notorious article of house-hold furniture which was supposed to serve its mistress the double purpose of a broom by day and an aerial steed by night, and which now answered another very excellent turn.

Another gentleman, to whom I mentioned this anecdote, tells me an aboriginal legend of this same White Deer.

"Long before the Englishman set foot in the Housatonic valley," he said, "the Indians used to notice a deer, of complete and spotless white, which came often, in the summer and autumn months, to drink at Onota. Against this gentle creature, no red man's arrow was ever pointed; for, in their simple faith, they believed that with her light and airy step she brought good fortune to the dwellers in the valley. 'So long,' the prophecy ran, 'So long as the snow-white doe comes to drink at Onota, so long famine shall not blight the Indian's harvest, nor pestilence come nigh his lodge, nor foeman lay waste his country.' In the graceful animal, the tribe recognized and loved their good genius. He among them who dared to harm her would have met swift punishment as a sacrilegious wretch and traitor."

Thus protected by the love of her simple friends, year after year, soon as the white blossoms clothed the cherry, the sacred deer came to drink at her chosen fountain; bringing good omens to all, and especially to the maiden who first espied her, glittering brightly among the foliage. Finally she brought with her a fawn, if possible, of more faultless purity and grace than herself; and that year more than the usual plenty and happiness reigned around the lake. Not long after this, the first French and Indian war broke out, and a young French officer — Montalbert by name — was sent to incite the Housatonic Indians to join in the league against the English colonies.

In his sacred character as an ambassador, he was welcomed to their lodges, had a seat at their council fire, and listened eagerly to their wild and marvellous tales. Among others, he heard the story of the White Deer; and, however incredulous of her sanctity, sufficiently admired the description of her beauty. Among those reckless and ambitious adventurers who set up the standard of France in Canada, it was a passion to carry away some wonderful trophy of the forest domain, to lay at the feet of their sovereign. Even the persons of the savages had thus been presented at the Court of Versailles, and royal favor had not been niggard in rewarding the donors of the more unique and costly trophies of barbaric splendor.

It was for such reasons that an uncontrollable desire to possess the skin of the White Deer took possession of Montalbert. He already enjoyed, in imagination, the reward which could not fail him who brought so rare and beautiful a peltry to the splendid Louis.

Not fully aware of the veneration which the Deer received from the natives, he first offered liberal rewards to the hunter who should bring him the coveted spoil. For half the proffered price, the chiefs would, perhaps, have alienated their fairest hunting-grounds; but the proposition to destroy their sacred Deer was received with utter horror and indignation. It was gently hinted to Montalbert that a repetition of the offer might ensure him the fate he designed for the Deer.

But the Frenchman was not of a nature to be so baffled. He had noticed that one of the native warriors — Wondo, by name — was already debased by the use of the white man's fire-water, of which Montalbert possessed a large supply. Concealing his purposes for a time, the adventurer sought out this Wondo, and shortly contrived to foment the poor fellow's appetite to such a degree that he became the absolute slave of whoever had it in his power to minister to his desires.

When the hunter was thought to be sufficiently besotted, Montalbert ventured to propose to him a plan to secure the skin of the White Deer. Depraved as he had become, Wondo at first recoiled from the thought, but appetite at length prevailed and he yielded to the tempter.

Years of unmolested security had rendered the Deer so confident in the friendship of man that, when at last treachery came, she proved an easy victim. Before conscience could awaken in the sacrilegious hunter, the gentle animal was taken and slain, and the ill-gotten fur was in the possession of the white man.

No sooner had Montalbert secured his prize than, concealing it in his baggage, he set out for Montreal; but the legend hints that he never reached the French border, and the beautiful skin of the Indians' sacred deer never added to the splendors of French royalty.

Among the natives, the impious slaughter was not suspected until the fire-water of the slayer was expended, and a returning consciousness compelled him to confess his deed of horror, and to meet the speedy vengeance which atoned for it.

Long and earnest were the supplications which the frightened natives sent up to the Great Spirit, that He would avert from the tribe the punishment due to such a crime; but its prosperity never again was what it had been, and its numbers slowly wasted away.

XVI.

ROARING BROOK AND TORY'S GLEN.

Fear God, honor the King.— *St. Peter.*

The powers that be are ordained of God.   Whosoever therefore resisteth the power, resisteth the ordinance of God; and they that resist shall receive to themselves damnation.— *St. Paul.*

And what saith the Koran ?   "**Speak** truth to thy Prince."— *Blue Beard.*

"Every state and almost every county of New England has its Roaring Brook — a mountain streamlet, overhung by woods, impeded by a mill, encumbered by fallen trees, but ever rushing, racing, roaring down through gurgling gullies, and filling the forest with its delicious sound and freshness; the drinking places of home returning herds; the mysterious haunts of squirrels and blue jays; the sylvan retreat of school-boys, who frequent it in the summer holidays, and mingle their restless thoughts with its restless, exuberant, and rejoicing stream."

Thus speaks Professor Longfellow of one of the most charming features of our hillsides.   Our Roaring Brook, I think must be familiar to the poet. Indeed, it is shrewdly suspected that it is the original of that where Churchill and Kavanagh passed so delightful a day with Cecilia, Alice, and the schoolmaster's wife. If not, it might well have been, for the description is perfect; and there is every reason to believe that the author was familiar with the original. There is a shorter road to it now; but that over which the author of Kavanagh must have driven, is both so pleasant and so rich in memories that I prefer it still; and so will you. We will not hurry over it.

Passing down the broad elm-shaded, old-fashioned, courtly street which leads east from the Pittsfield Park, we come, at the distance of a few rods to a bold and picturesque knoll, upon which stands one of those square old dwellings, such as it was the fashion of the New England gentry to build seventy-five or a hundred years ago: and which still delight their descendants, although, like antiques in other branches of art, they seem to defy modern imitation. This was long the country seat of Hon. Nathan Appleton of Boston, whose wife was a daughter of the builder of the mansion, and whose daughter became the wife of the poet Longfellow. On the landing of the broad stairs at the end of its long entrance hall, stood the old clock so touchingly commemorated by him:

> " Somewhat back from the village street ·
> Stands the old fashioned country seat ;
> Across its antique portico,
> Tall poplar trees their shadows throw,—
> And from its station in the hall
> An ancient time piece says to all —
> > Forever, never,
> > Never, forever."

The mansion, now the residence of Mrs. Thomas F. Plunkett, has been to some extent remodelled externally, but it preserves all the features noted in Mr. Longfellow's poem.

A couple of miles further south, on what is known as the old road to Lenox, is the villa built by Oliver Wendell Holmes, in which he resided for several years. Dr. Holmes had an hereditary interest in Pittsfield; his great-grand father Col. Jacob Wendell of Boston, with his kinsman, Philip Livingston of Albany, and Col. John Stoddard of Northampton— "the great New-Englander" — having been equal owners of the township, six miles square, before its division by sale among the first settlers. These great proprietors — or at least Stoddard and Wendell —reserved some of the best lands for themselves; and Col. Wendell making choice of the farm on which Dr. Holmes afterwards built, either he or his son, Judge Oliver Wendell of Revolutionary fame, erected a mansion upon it for a country seat. In the fierce political feuds, before and during the war of 1812, Judge Wendell was a great stay and consolation to the Pittsfield Federalists to whom he gave much support, moral and pecuniary. The First Church still cherishes among its precious relics, a baptismal basin of solid silver, which he presented to the Federal section when it was divided on political issues. I will continue the story in the words of Dr. Holmes's speech at the Berkshire Jubilee in 1844:

" One of my earliest recollections is of an annual pilgrimage made by my parents to the west. The young horse was brought up, fatted by a week's rest and high feeding, prancing and caracoling, to the door. It came to the corner and was soon over the western hills. He was gone a fortnight; and one afternoon — it always seemed to me a sunny afternoon — we saw the equipage crawling from the west towards the old homestead; the young horse, who set out so fat and prancing, worn thin and reduced by the long journey — the chaise covered with dust; and all speaking of a terrible crusade, a formidable pilgrimage. Winter-evening stories told me where — to Berkshire, to the borders of New York — to the old domain ; owned so long that there seemed to be a sort of hereditary love for it.

"Many years passed, and I travelled down the beautiful Rhine. I wished to see the equally beautiful Hudson. I found myself at Albany ; and a few hours brought me to Pittsfield. I went to the little spot — the scene of the pilgrimage — a mansion — and found it surrounded by a beautiful meadow, through which the winding river made its way in a thousand graceful curves. The mountains reared their heads around it. The blue air, which makes our city pale cheeks again to deepen with the hue of health, coursing about it pure and free. I recognized the scene of the annual pilgrimage and since that I have made an annual visit to it."

Three or four years after the Jubilee, Dr. Holmes built, upon a round knoll or hill, near the old mansion, a neat plain villa, commanding a fine view of the whole circle of Berkshire Mountains and of the Housatonic winding its serpentine way through the Canoe Meadows; so-called because the Mohegan Indians used to leave there their frail barks, perhaps to visit one of their burial grounds in the vicinity, or perhaps considering this the head of canoe navigation. The knoll was barren enough when the poet-professor

built upon it, but his liberal planting has covered it
with rich turf and an abundance of trees and shrubbery. The place is however chiefly notable as having
once been the home of Oliver Wendell Holmes, and
the spot where he performed work, the fame of
whose results is now sure to be as lasting as it is
universal.

Some of these results are closely associated with
the name of Berkshire. Among those locally most
highly prized is Dr. Holmes's poem at the dedication
of the Pittsfield Cemetery: equally charming in its
way is "The New Eden," which was read before
the Berkshire Horticultural Society at Stockbridge,
in the September following the excessively **dry**
summer of 1854, when

> " We saw the August sun descend
>   Day after day with blood-red stain,
>   And the blue mountains dimly blend
>   With smoke-wreaths on the burning plain.
>
> " Beneath the hot Sirocco's wings
>   We sat and told the withering hours,
>   Till Heaven unsealed its azure springs,
>   And bade them leap in flashing showers."

In a still finer vein is "The Plough-boy," which
was written for the anniversary of the Berkshire
Agricultural Society in October, 1849. Dr. Holmes
was chairman of the committee upon the ploughing
match; the large old church was, as usual on such
occasions, crowded almost to suffocation, and when
his turn came, he mounted half-way up the pulpit-
stairs and read a report of which I quote a part:

"Time and experience have sanctioned the custom of putting

only plain, practical men upon this committee.   Were it not so, the most awkward blunders would be constantly occurring. The inhabitants of our cities, who visit the country during the fine season, would find themselves quite at a loss if an overstrained politeness should place them in this position. Imagine a trader, or a professional man, from the capital of the state, unexpectedly called upon to act in rural matters. Plough-shares are to him shares that pay no dividends.   A coulter, he supposes, has something to do with a horse.   His notions of stock were obtained in Faneuil Hall market, where the cattle looked funnily enough, to be sure, compared with the living originals.   He knows, it is true, that there is a difference in cattle, and would tell you that he prefers the sirloin breed.   His children are equally unenlightened ; they know no more of the poultry-yard than what they have learned by having the chicken-pox, and playing on a Turkey carpet. Their small knowledge of wool-growing is lam(b)entable.

The history of one of these summer-visitors shows how im-perfect is his rural education.   He no sooner establishes him-self in the country than he begins a series of experiments. He tries to drain a marsh, but only succeeds in draining his own pockets.   He offers to pay for carting off a compost heap ; but is informed that it consists of corn and potatoes in an un-finished state.   He sows abundantly, but reaps little or nothing, except with the implement which he uses in shaving, a pro-cess which is frequently performed for him by other people, though he pays no barber's bill.   He builds a wire-fence and paints it green, so that nobody can see it.   But he forgets to order a pair of spectacles apiece for his cows, who, taking offense at something else, take his fence in addition, and make an invisible one of it, sure enough.   And, finally, having bought a machine to chop fodder, which chops off a good slice of his dividends, and two or three children's fingers, he con-cludes that, instead of cutting feed, he will cut farming ; and so sells out to one of those plain, practical farmers, such as you have honored by placing them on your committee, whose pockets are not so full when he starts, but have fewer holes and not so many fingers in them.

It must have been one of these practical men whose love of his pursuits led him to send in to the committee the following lines, which it is hoped will be accepted as a grateful tribute to the noble art whose successful champions are now to be named and rewarded."

Dr. Holmes then read the poem now known to fame as the " The Plough-man," which, in his reading, all must have recognized as grand poetry. But I suspect that not one of the applauding audience — and probably not even the author himself — realized that they were listening to what would afterwards be recognized by the world's great critics as the finest georgic in any living language, or perhaps in any language whatever. I have my doubts if many understood to the full even the exquisite fun of the " report."

Yielding to his own good nature and the soft persuasions of a committee of ladies, Dr. Holmes once contributed a couple of poems to a fancy fair in Pittsfield. The writer does not gather them into the fold of his published collection, and I do not know that it is quite fair to print them here; but, of course, they got into the newspapers of the day, and I cannot deprive you of the pleasure of reading at least one of them, even if the poet does consider it a trifle, too light for preservation.

Each of the poems was enclosed in an envelope bearing a motto; and the right to a first and second choice, guided by these, was disposed of in a raffle, to the no small emolument of the object of the fair.

I think that the two pieces are now represented by
at least a square yard of the quaint ecclesiastical
heraldry which illuminates the gorgeous **chancel**
window of St. Stephen's Church.

The motto of the first envelope ran thus:

> " Faith is the conquering angel's crown;
>   Who hopes ror grace must ask it;
> Look shrewdly ere you lay me down;
>   I'm Portia's leaden casket."

The following verses were found within.

> " Fair lady, whosoe'er thou art,
>   Turn this poor leaf with tenderest **care,**
> And — hush, O hush thy beating heart;
>   The One thou lovest will be there."
>
> " Alas! not loved by thee alone,
>   Thine idol ever prone to range:
> To-day all thine, to-morrow flown,
>   Frail thing that every hour may **change.**
>
> " Yet when that truant course is done,
>   If thy lost wanderer reappear,
> Press to thy heart the only One
>   That nought can make more truly dear!"

Within this paper was a smaller envelope, con-
taining a dollar bill, and this explanation of the
poet's riddle.

> " Fair lady, lift thine eyes and tell
>   If this is not a truthful letter;
> This is the one (1) thou lovest well,
>   And nought (0) can make thee love it better (10).
>
> Though fickle, do not think it strange
>   That such a friend is worth possessing:
> For one that gold can never change
>   Is Heaven's own dearest earthly blessing.

You see now, in part, why our people claim a sort of joint ownership with Cambridge and Boston in Dr. Holmes and his fame. They have moreover a real affection for him, which leads them even to condone his irreverent sneer at Pittsfield's Old Elm, as "sadly in want of a new wig of green leaves :" and the charity which covers a multitude of sins could stretch its skirts no further than that. He has so much human nature in him that, in spite of some social and educational impediments, he, every little while, gets right down to the heart of things. That is the Berkshire version of the "one touch of nature that makes the whole world kin." And that is what makes Dr. Holmes the most popular of scholarly writers. Do you suppose the world would tolerate so much learning in any body else ?

A very few rods beyond the Wendell Farms, we come to Arrow-head, the fine estate formerly owned by Herman Melville. Mr. Melville is a grandson of that Major Thomas Melville, who, a few generations ago, was known to all Bostonians as the last genuine specimen of the gentleman of the old school left in the city, the last wearer of the costume of the Revolution, and the last survivor of the Harbor tea party. His son, of the same name and rank, was commandant of the military post at Pittsfield during the war of 1812, and, after the war, president of the Agricultural Society, and otherwise a leader of men in Berkshire, besides being a man of rare culture. With him, his nephew, Herman, was domiciliated for a time, while in his youth, he, played school-master in a wild district — under the shadow of Rock Mountain, I think.

It was probably the memory of this early experience which led Mr. Melville in 1850, in the first flush of his literary success, to retire to Pittsfield, and soon purchase a fine estate with a spacious old house; adjoining, in the rear, the farm of his early residence with his uncle. This quaint old mansion, he made the home of the most free-hearted hospitality; and also a house of many stories — writing in it Moby Dick and many other romances of the sea, and also "The Piazza Tales," which took their name from a piazza built by their author upon the north end of the house, and commanding a bold and striking view of Greylock and the intervening valley. "My chimney and I," a humorous and spicy essay, of which the cumbersome old chimney — overbearing tyrant of the home — is the hero, was also written here. And so, of course, was "October Mountain," a sketch of mingled philosophy and word-painting, which found its inspiration in the massy and brillian tints presented by a prominent and thickly-wooded projection of Washington Mountain, as seen from the south-eastern windows at Arrow-Head, on a fine day after the early frosts. Mr. Melville was almost a zealot in his love of Berkshire scenery, and there was no more ardent and indefatigable excursionist among its hills and valleys.

And now, let us drive on to the Roaring Brook, which — as you may possibly recollect — we set out to visit. Our way lies through pleasant rustic scenes and the pretty agricultural hamlet of New Lenox.

Passing this, and guided by the sound of the brook, we come to the mouth of the Tory's Glen, through which its waters leap, tumbling down.

From the broad summit of Washington Mountain, the brook comes dashing down the deep ravine, smiling in the rare sunshine, glooming in the frequent shade, brawling with the impeding boulders, toying in amber pools with the mossy banks; but for the most part rushing impatiently from fall to fall, for five restless miles, until, just without the glen, it loses itself in the indolent curves of the Housatonic, which here puts on its gentlest mood.

It must be a sweet relief to the water — vexed and wearied by its rough passage among the sharp-angled flint rocks, and by its arduous labors in turning mill wheels — thus to repose at length in the flower-bordered bed of the river, and wander about the meadows, in what leisurely and graceful curves it will.

Just below the entrance to the Tory's Glen, at a point in the road where it winds around the base of Melville's grand October Mountain, the curves display themselves in a breadth of beauty which they rarely exhibit north of Stockbridge, and help make up a much admired view. It is the beginning of that system of beauty which distinguishes the Stockbridge valley, and affords a kindly relief to the eye, if it wearies of mountains, lakes and waterfalls.

One warm October day, many years ago, a three miles walk in pleasant company, brought me to the smiling and fertile valley, just without the glen, and following directions given with kindly zeal, we soon entered it mentally contrasting the courtesies of rustic life in New Lenox, with the urbanities of Broadway, not to any flattering extent in the interest of the city.

You can see the black opening in the mountain side which indicates the location of the glen from many points in the village of Pittsfield, and if you ask the people what it is they will perhaps tell you, if they are of the fanciful sort: "Oh, that is the Jaws of Darkness;" and you will reply, "Oh yes, I · see it is!" And, although you would not be quite correct, the contrast between the cheerful light of the hamlet and the wild, sombre solitude of the mountain gorge is strikingly impressive. From the shadeless field, you enter upon overarched paths — among mossy trees, along precipitous rocks, under the shadow of overhanging mountains. The heart feels the change instantly, and conforms itself instinctively to it.

Here we find again those adamantine blocks of flint-rock which characterize and rudely adorn this whole mountain range. Sometimes they lie confusedly upon the mountain's steep slope; then, again, they impede the rushing course of the brook. In the bed of the stream, the ever-rolling current, in the course of ages, has polished the surface and rounded the edges of even these obdurate masses. It is startling to think by how many years of constant attrition the soft flowing wave accomplished its purpose. How many centuries ago did the savage stoop to

drink at this mountain stream, and think of nothing
but the cooling draught — least of all that the
smooth, gliding fluid was bearing away a portion of
the solid rock whereon he stood, to form a soil for
a conquering race !

These rocks form the bed of the brooks; and are
piled up along its banks in mad confusion, with
crevices and dens between and beneath them, which
in former days sheltered a tenement-house population of wild beasts. In one cave which lies under
the road, Revolutionary tradition affirms that an
outlawed Tory, one Gideon Smith of Stockbridge,
once found refuge for weeks. It is a dreary habitation — not in the ornamented style of grotto at all —
a couple of small rude chambers built of huge over-
lapping flint-rocks, without a pendent stalactite or
sparkling encrustation, nor even a grotesquely
shapen fracture, to relieve their barren walls. Not
a desirable residence, in any respect; and, since the
war has been ended for a hundred years, and it can do
the country no harm — and, especially, as he is dead
and it can do him no good — I sincerely pity that
hunted Tory, driven out to make his home among wild
beasts. Although, I dare say, he came out, as often
as he dared, to sun himself, as the badgers do, in the
openings of the wood, if he could find any in that
shady retreat.

I do not know what offense had made him especially obnoxious to the committees of vigilance, to
which the safety of the young republic was en-
trusted; but there is a touching anecdote of him,

which, if it was known, ought to have softened even the asperities of war times. It is to the effect that, when concealed in some hiding-place at home, he made his wife cause all his children to pass daily before the crevice which supplied him with light and air; so that he might see their innocent faces and be comforted with the knowledge of their health and safety. Not a bad man at heart, that!

Smith seems to have been often a "hunted" man. In May, 1776, he harbored a certain Captain McKay, a British prisoner of war, who had escaped from Hartford, by the aid of John Graves, a Pittsfield Tory. Smith's treasonable hospitality becoming known to the committees, the hue and cry was raised against him; and a party, of which Linus Parker, a famous Pittsfield sharp-shooter, was one, repaired to his house. His family reported him not at home, but the seekers, confident that he was in the barn, summoned him to surrender. He appeared at the half-open door, peered curiously around, and, after some parley, gave himself up. Smith and Parker were nevertheless personally upon friendly terms; and after the war, the former being, with his wife, on a visit to Parker's house, Smith reverted to the incident described, and said that when he opened the barn-door, being an extraordinary runner, he felt certain of making good his escape; but, seeing Parker with his famous rifle in hand, he was afraid to make the attempt.

"And now, Parker," he added, "I want to know if you really would have shot me?"

"As quick as I ever shot a deer!" was the reply.

"Then it would have been all over with me," exclaimed his friend, feeling that he spoke in truthful
earnest, and trembling at the memory of the danger
which he had escaped.

Such are the amenities of civil war. There were a
good many Tories in Berkshire county, as in every
other; made so doubtless, as in all civil conflicts men
range themselves, both on the better and the worse
side, some from base and selfish, some from pure and
noble, but most from mixed, motives. The Tories
of Berkshire — it might be courteous to call them
"loyalists," but it would hardly be distinctive, since
loyalty to the crown meant treason to the people —
the Tories of Berkshire were mostly of the wealthier,
the magisterial, and the more refined, classes; and of
those in other grades of society who were bound to
them by one tie or another. Not that all, or even a
majority, of these classes failed under the test which
tried men's souls: but, as ever, wealth and official
position proved powerful persuaders against revolution: and, early in the war at least, the leading Tories
evidently believed in the prophecies which they uttered so unctuously that, to Whig ears, they sounded
unpleasantly like threats: to wit, that the king's
generals would come down upon the rebellious colony
from Canada, with his resistless army and his savage
allies; and that Berkshire would be the first county
to feel his vengeance, as it had been the first to provoke it by suppressing his courts. It was a prudent
error which made most of the Tories; they knew not
what this means: "he that seeketh his life, shall lose

it "—lacked the virtue which risks all in conflict for the right; and had neither the daring wisdom nor the wise courage which plucks the flower, safety, from the thistle, danger. Before the war was over, most of them were — often by rather heroic remedies — cured of their perversity — at least as to its external manifestation. I fear the cure was not always radical; but it sometimes was, as in one instance which I am going to cite for you.

No doubt, however, many were religiously sincere in their loyalty: and all were able to make a very plausible, even if hollow, defence from Holy Writ.

When a man has made up his mind to do a mean, vicious or cruel thing in his own interest, a text of scripture, which seems to commend or justify it, is very soothing. I think some of us can recollect when the garbled text "servants obey your masters," and St. Paul's injunction to a fugitive slave — Onesimus by name — salved the conscience of almost an entire nation, sorely lacerated by all the rest of the New Testament, to say nothing of the Decalogue, the Declaration of Independence and the great book of nature. The Tories could make out a much better case than that; as you see by glancing at the head of this article. Those of them who were, or had been, magistrates or officers in the militia had moreover taken the most iron-clad of oaths, not only to bear faith and true allegiance to King George, but to the best of their power, to defend him against all traitorous conspiracies, and to make all such known to him. "All these things," said the

subscribers to this oath, "I do plainly and sincerely
acknowledge and swear according to the express
words by me spoken, and according to the plain
common-sense and understanding of the same words,
without any equivocation or mental reservation
whatever: " and, however the majority of good men
might find that in the conduct of " the man George,"
which released them from the obligations of that
oath, and discharged them from all allegiance to
him, I hope that you will not bestow unmitigated
reprobation upon those whose tender conscience, and
the loyalty to "His Sacred Majesty," sedulously in-
stilled by education into their heart of hearts, refused to be so relieved.

I am speaking of moral condemnation only: however tenderly we may appreciate the sentiment of
natural, but mistaken, loyalty which governed the
conscientious adherent to the royal cause, the committees of safety and vigilance could take little account of it. Stern necessity, and duty to a holier
cause, imperatively demanded that it should be repressed with a strong hand. And it was done;
harshly perhaps and unwisely at times; but effectually, and not with half the vindictiveness and cruelty
which would surely have been visited upon the
committee-men had the Revolution failed.

Pardon me for this prolixity; but I am heart-sick
of the overstrained magnanimity, falsely so called,
which concentrates all its charities and praises for
the defeated champions of the wrong, and reserves
all its censures and denunciations for the triumph-

ant defenders of the right. If I recall some of the traits which relieve somewhat the odium justly due to even conscientious support of tyranny and antagonism to freedom, or something of the imperfections which marred the record of the patriots, let me not be construed as denying that, to the memory of the rudest sincere Whig, honor and glory are due which that of the most refined and conscientious Tory must never share.

And now let me to my stories, the first of which I heard from that best, and most abundantly supplied, of all Berkshire story tellers, Governor George N. Briggs; who, by the by, I am sure would have sanctioned the sentiments I have just expressed.

In the early part of the Revolution there lived in Lenox a staunch old Tory, who openly professed his allegiance to King George, and his hostility to the rebel cause; but, as he confined his opposition to words, and was greatly respected and beloved by his fellow citizens, for his many excellent qualities as a friend and neighbor, he was allowed for a long while to enjoy his opinions unmolested. But the contest between England and the colonies waxed every day more bitter, and the Committee of Safety began to be troubled with doubts if it were consistent with their duty to permit one who so loudly vaunted his toryism to live among them, and encourage others to commit outrages of which he would not be personally guilty.

The matter was often a subject of deliberation, but the committee were reluctant to act. At length,

however, in some dark and trying hour — perhaps
in the bitterness of defeat, perhaps after hearing of
the horrors of Wyoming — they resolved to move.
Or, perhaps, as happened in some emergencies, their
zeal was quickened by orders from head-quarters.
At any rate, paying a visit to the Tory, they informed him, they had come to the conclusion that
his example was too pernicious to the cause of
liberty to be any longer permitted. They regretted
the circumstance, but their duty was imperative; in
short, he must take the oath of allegiance to the
colonies — or swing.

The oath was peremptorily and unhesitatingly refused; and the next step was an extemporaneous
gallows, erected in the public street, beneath which
the recusant was placed, and the rope tightened
around his throat, but immediately loosened and the
oath again proffered, and again declined. .

All arguments and threats proving abortive, the
contemptuous loyalist was again drawn up, and
left to hang until he became purple in the face —
care being taken to lower him and apply restoratives,
before life was extinct. Consciousness being once
more restored, the oath was again tendered, and he
was entreated to yield to the necessity of the case:
but his stubborn spirit was not yet broken; he refused to renounce his allegiance to the Crown.

Things had now come to an awkward pass; and
the committee, who possibly were by this time sorry
they had taken the matter in hand, retired to the
tavern for consultation. The New-England com

mittee-man could no more deliberate without his mug of flip than the New Amsterdam burgher without his pipe of tobacco. But whatever counsels of mercy there may have been under that genial influence (of which the prisoner was not denied his consoling cup) it was finally resolved that, having put their hands to the plough, it would never do to turn back. Regard for dignity and the authority of the committee forbade it. In short the good of the cause required that the prisoner should take the oath, or suffer death for his contumacy.

The loyalist received their decision with unflinching determination not to yield a hair's breadth in what he believed to be the right. The committee were equally resolved, and he was again drawn up — perhaps with some angry violence. And at once it seemed that the work of death had been too effectually done.

It may be that the committee had not designed to carry their measures to so extreme a length. Possibly they doubted if the authority given them to "handle the Tories" was sufficient to warrant them in it, for, although the people of Berkshire, from 1774 to 1781, would admit no courts of law among them — submitting only to their own committees — there was a tacit exception of capital cases, which were tried before the Supreme Court at Springfield. But, whatever may have been the feeling or intention of the committee in their anger, the sight they now witnessed might well bring back their old affection for a tried friend and kind neighbor. They hastened to cut down the body, and use every effort to undo their fatal work.

There seemed at first little hope of reanimating the senseless clay; but at length the limbs slightly relaxed their rigidity, the eyes moved, and the livid hue began to disappear from the cheek. Consciousness slowly and painfully returned; the victim sat upright — and the question was again asked: " Will you swear ? " " Yes," faintly responded the half-dead convert to patriotism.

A few moments afterwards, as he was sitting before the tavern fire and a glass of steaming punch — furnished by the order, if not at the expense, of the committee — warming himself after his dangerous exposure to the chills of the shadow of death, he was heard to mutter thoughtfully to himself — " Well ! this is a hard way to make Whigs — but *it'll do it !* "

And, accordingly, from that day to the close of the war, he was one of the most zealous and unwavering of the patriots.

Another story illustrates still more remarkably the same trait of unflinching integrity. It was told to me by the late Hon. Henry Hubbard, who was well versed in Berkshire traditions; but I remember to have read it in my childhood, and, although I cannot recall the name of the book in which I found it, it is likely that I have used some of the phraseology which was impressed upon my youthful memory.

It seems that, at some time during the Revolution, one Nathan Jackson of Tyringham — a romantic and beautiful farming town of Southern Berkshire — was accused of the crime of high treason against the United Colonies, or States. The trial was to be at Springfield, but the court did not sit for some weeks— during which interval Jackson was confined in the Berkshire county gaol, at Great Barrington, which was in so dilapidated a condition that he might easily have escaped at any time, had he not scorned an act which might indicate cowardice, or reluctance to suffer for his principles. Unwilling, however, to waste his time in idleness, he applied to the sheriff for permission to go out daily to work, promising to return faithfully to the prison every night. So well was his character for integrity established, that, although he was committed on a capital charge, and did not deny the facts alleged against him, the sheriff did not hesitate to comply with his request. And so well was that confidence deserved, that the prisoner never failed to return to his quarters punctually every night to be locked up.

What follows is a still stronger proof of the reliance placed upon his word. The court was to be held at Springfield, and the journey to it was then a weary one, over rough forest-roads. Jackson was the only prisoner to be carried on, and the sheriff complained bitterly of the trouble to which he was subjected, particularly at this busy season of the year. The Tory told him that it was quite unnecessary for him to go — he could go just as well by himself; and again he was trusted, and set out alone and on foot, to go fifty miles through the woods to surrender himself to be tried for his life, upon a charge where he could not hope for an acquittal, and by a tribunal whose right to judge him he could conscientiously deny. Surely, if ever a man had an excuse to palliate a violation of confidence, it was he; the idea, however, seems never to have occurred to him.

Luckily for him, on his way he was overtaken by the Hon. Mr. Edwards, then a member of the Executive Council, to attend a session of which body he was then on his way to Boston. This gentleman entered into conversation with Jackson, and, without disclosing his own name or official position, learned the nature of his companion's journey, and something of his history. Pondering upon what he had heard, Mr. Edwards pursued his way to Boston; and Jackson, trudging on, soon reached Springfield, and surrendered himself, was tried; did not deny the facts alleged against him, and, as a matter of course, was found guilty and condemned to death.

In due course the petitions for pardon of persons under sentence of death, were considered by the Honorable Council which then exercised the supreme executive authority in Massachusetts. After all had been read Mr. Edwards asked if none had been received in favor of Nathan Jackson of Tyringham. The reply was that there was none; and a member of the council, who had been present at the trial, remarked that the case was one of such undoubted and aggravated guilt, and the attachment of the condemned man to the King's cause was so inveterate, that there could be no reason for granting a pardon in this case, unless it was extended in every other.

Mr. Edwards, in reply, related his adventure with Jackson on the road, and also his story, which he had taken pains to have substantiated by the sheriff of Berkshire. A murmur of admiration went round the council board; it was unanimously agreed that such a man ought not to die upon the gallows, and, after some brief discussion, an unconditional pardon was made out and dispatched to Springfield.

The stories suggested by the Tory's Glen have led us far away from it; and we will return only for the purpose of passing again through the pleasant village of New Lenox and its sunny valley; and to answer a question asked me by a companion with whom I once rode through it: "Has so pretty a place no story?"

To be sure it has; but of that kind which is best told in verse.

SUNNYVALE.

One sunny summer afternoon,
The gladdest in all joyous June,
Happiest man beneath heaven's dome,
A farmer brought his young wife home;
And, as they reached the mountain's brow,
And saw his cottage smile below,
He bade his bonnie bride mark well
How gaily there the sunshine fell.

June came again — a babe was born.
It came once more — the child was gone:
Yet, though the farmer's face grew sad,

A smile of new-found peace, it had,
He strove the mother's grief to calm,
And said the June days brought a balm;
For something more than sunshine fell
From where their child had gone to dwell.

June came again — the farmer's wife
Was passing from our mortal life;
They laid her in our sunniest glade
Before its frailest flowers could fade.
That year the farmer did not mark
If earth or sky were bright or dark,
Yet still the careless sunshine fell
Gaily, as if all things were well,

June cometh now.   From scenes the dead
Had left too lone, the farmer fled;
And strangers, from his lonely hearth,
Dispel the gloom with household mirth,
While not a tone in any voice
Says some have wept, where they rejoice;
And still the blithesome sunlight falls
As gaily round those cottage walls.

XVII.

BASH-BISH AND THE DOME.

Doubtless the wildest and most awe-inspiring gorge among the Berkshire Hills is the deep and shaggy recess in the western side of Mount Washington, into which the famous cascade, Bash-Bish Falls, comes dashing in a striking series of bold leaps and plunges. Speaking of the passage downward, along the side of the little cataract, a writer familiar with the Alps, but a little inclined to startling statements, says ; " the descent over the rocks, along the awful rent made in the mountain, was wild as an Alpine gorge, and even more perilous."

Mount Washington is the huge mountain pile — a portion of the Taconic Range, which fills the south-western corner of Berkshire. In grandeur it is rivalled by Greylock alone among our hills; the inhabited portion having an elevation of from fifteen hundred to two thousand feet above the level of the surrounding valleys, while the summit rises to an altitude five or six hundred feet greater. Its grandeur, however, comes from other peculiarities as well as from its height. It has also long been famed for scenes of picturesque beauty; and has of late gained new renown and interest as the locality of Sky Farm; thé romantic home of the charming child-poets, Elaine and Dora Goodale.

If you chance to be in the vicinity of Great Barington, or if you desire, and have leisure for, a prolonged drive, your better way to Bash-Bish is through that town and Egremont, past Bryant's Green River and over Mount Washington. That is certainly the old fashioned poetic route; but I am going to tell you how the falls looked, one day, to a field-meeting of certain scientific associations of Troy, Albany and Pittsfield.

Bash-Bish lies at an equal distance from Albany and Pittsfield, and an hour's ride on the Boston and Albany railroad brought the excursionists to Chatham, midway between the two — while another hour on the Harlem road carried the united party to the pleasant village of Copake, renowned chiefly for its iron works.

The location of the village is unique: with an outlook over the smiling fields of New York, on the west, while the frowning mountains of Massachusetts almost over-hang it on the east.

The falls are about a mile and a half from the village, and not many rods east of the state boundary line. The road to them is delightful. Indeed the first glimpses of it were so enticing that a majority of our party preferred to walk over it, although our hosts — the Troy and Albany Associations — had provided liberally for riding, and the kindly people who welcomed us, gave warning that the ladies, at least, should reserve all their strength for the falls.

After lingering awhile in the village, we moved on, to the great stone stack of the iron blast-furnace: the most picturesque of manufacturies, and the only one which adds to, rather than mars, the attractiveness of a region like this.

A little further, and we came to the handsome and finely located Swiss cottage of Mr. Alfred Douglas, of New York, the proprietor of Bash-Bish and its romantic surroundings; where, by his hospitable invitation, we wandered at will through the spacious grounds and deliciously-filled conservatories. Even after leaving this charming resting place, most of us did not heed the hurrying summons we began to hear in the impatient roar of the cascade; but dallied listlessly in the park-like groves, by the shady wayside, or on the banks of the stream whose dashing, flashing, gleaming rocks and amber pools reminded us of our own Roaring Brook.

Still the day was not very far advanced when we came where the gorge, widening a little, throws up its barriers into bare cliffs and shaggy, precipitous, or pillar-like, eminences. Through the top of the central cliff, the stream has worn down its way, leaving its walls on either side like huge horns. Between these in no very great volume — but snowy, silvery, summer coud, foam-like — its waters come

down in a succession of bold leaps, divided midway
by a rocky shelf into "The Twin Falls." A column
worthy, almost, of the Alps or the Yosemite. One
peculiarity of the basin at the foot of the falls, is the
great variety of views which it affords of the cascade
and the rocks which mingle grandly or grotesquely
with it. And, wandering from point to point in
search of these — now standing on the rudest of
rustic bridges, and now on slippery rocks; here on
bare and gravelly beaches, and there under green
branches — scores of laughing groups helped to fill
up and enliven the landscape for each other. This
for half an hour, or more; then ambition seized them.
"By that sin fell the angels "— Shakespeare's angels;
and the danger seemed imminent that it would have
a similar result for ours. But the first effect was
quite the reverse: it carried them right up — almost
straight up — the steepest of all possible log-and-
rock-encumbered paths, to the Eagle's Nest, Prospect
Rock, and all manner of preposterous places. And
grosser mortals, whether laden with scientific lore or
otherwise, went along per-force.

It was impossible in the brief time of our visit to
make a thorough survey of the falls, and I therefore condense the detailed account of President
Hitchcock, who devoted three visits to it:

From a spot upon Mount Washington whose beauty the
President glowingly eulogizes, one descends, two thousand
feet, to find himself by a noisy stream, about a rod wide,
which for a short distance, tumbles rapidly down between
perpendicular cliffs of talcose slate, a hundred feet high.
Soon, striking a huge barrier of this rock, the brook turns, at

right angles, to the left, and for fifty or sixty rods, rushes down a declivity of eighty degrees. Here the water has performed its greatest wonders. Sinking its bed for unknown ages, and at the same time beating with its waters on the edges of the slate, it has worn a dome-shaped cavity to the depth of one hundred and ninety-four feet. At the bottom of this cavity, one is at the foot of a vast wall of rock [the base of "The Eagle's nest,"] which encloses him on the east, south and west; and as it rises, curves outward. So that, looking upward, he sees it, at the height of nearly two hundred feet, projecting full twenty-five feet from its base. From the uppermost fall, the stream leaps in several smaller cascades perhaps sixty feet in the aggregate, half hidden by huge boulders and over-hanging trees. At length we arrive at the principal fall. The water divided in twain by a huge boulder poised upon its brink, falls over a nearly straight and perpendicular precipice, about sixty feet, into a deep basin. Any single view, as this detailed description shows, can take in but a small portion of the scenery of Bash-Bish Gorge. President Hitchcock estimates the perpendicular height from the top of the highest precipice to the bottom of the lowest fall at three hundred and twenty feet.

Among the striking prospects offered by these stupendous heights, there was a very clear one that some unfortunates would glance off the paths, slippery with the needles of evergreen foliage, and, going sheer down that fearful distance, get undistinguishably mashed upon the bare rock beneath: which, for the moment, would have been disagreeable, however much of pleasing interest it might have added to the scene for future visitors. But the day passed with no more thrilling incident than a sudden plunge from an insecure plank into the cold stream. Never was so adventurous climbing with so little of startling adventure.

As the afternoon wore to a close, we gathered for the favorite landscape of the gorge: that from Sunset Cliff, which rises a few rods below the fall. Here the view is down the gorge, westward. For a mile, there is a wooded glen with the stream threading its silver way through it, while at its termination two abrupt hills — Cedar and Elk Mountains — rise on either side, like Herculean pillars, to the height of more than a thousand feet. Near the end of the glen we see the fitly placed cottage of Mr. Douglas, with the American flag floating in grace and beauty by its side. But this bold and pleasing picture is only the foreground to the grand view of the Catskills, which are seen to loom up in the distance lofty, majestic, dim and cloud-like. In perfectly clear days their outlines are sharply cut on the blue sky or sunset clouds. One may doubt which of the two aspects is the most to be enjoyed. We were enraptured with that which was vouchsafed us.

The explorations of the day over, carriages were more in request than they had been in the morning, although an enthusiastic minority preferred to stroll back as they came. Then we dined luxuriously in the rude but comfortable freight depot: the Albany and Troy Associations still being our hosts; and Mr. H. S. Goodale, of Sky Farm, adding to the fare two fat turkeys, one of them including in its dressing a witty poem of welcome, and the other a mineralogical tribute in the shape of a superb specimen of kyanite.

Finally we gathered in the tasteful little church, to ascertain what anybody had done for science during the day. I had not observed that any soul had cared for anything except, with might and main, to enjoy the scenery, the scrambles, the rambles, the climbing and all the rest of the woodland jollity. Somebody has said that notes to a fine poem are like an anatomical lecture upon a savory joint; and I greatly feared that some such comparison would fit a scientific report upon Bash-Bish. But those field-meeting savans, with their eyes trained to special observation, are at home everywhere with their minute philosophy ; and everywhere find sources of rare enjoyment which, however they may have before been " caviare to the multitude," they contrive to make the multitude enjoy with them.

In some departments, Bash-Bish had proved a rich field. Professor Peck, the State Botanist of New York, and a specialist in fungi, had detected in the gorge five species which were new to him, as well as some rare and beautiful varieties of the fringed gentian. Mr. Homes, the State Librarian, had made a study of the peculiar and valuable hematite ores. Others contributed their share of scientific discussion: so that the day was found to have been not altogether squandered in pleasure.

The notes to the poetry of the occasion were furnished, in anything but an anatomical style, by.

learned and quaint Professor Tatlock of Pittsfield.
"They might be epitomized, said a writer in an
Albany newspaper, by the line of Horace:

Nullus argento color abdito in terris :

or, in other words, what is all the beauty of
nature that we have been admiring, without men
and women — and especially the Albany Institute
and their friends — to admire it ? "

There seemed nobody to say anything for the
really very interesting local history of Mount Washington and its vicinity. I might indeed, myself,
have told the little story which I am now going to
tell you; but there were reasons why I should avoid
doing so.

THE SWISS LOVERS.

You may have read — or, at any rate, whether you
have read it or not, it is true — that, at a very early
date, there was a Swiss colony of iron-makers upon
Mount Washington. Miss Sedgwick asserts that
they gave the name of Bash-Bish to the cascade —
that being the patois of their canton for a small water-
fall. But I have my doubts as to that: first, because
two or three Swiss gentlemen of whom I made inquiry
were not aware of anything of the kind; and,
secondly, because Dr. O'Callaghan, the New York
historian, once pointed me to an old vocabulary of
the language of some western Indian tribes — in
Illinois, I think — in which Bash-a-Bish is given as
signifying a water-fall. Still Miss Sedgwick may
be correct, as she had visited in Switzerland, and was

the intimate friend of the historian, Sismondi, and his family. A resident of one canton in Switzerland is not necessarily familiar with the patois of another, and makers of Indian vocabularies are a long way from infallible, as I grieve to know.

But, however it may have been with regard to Bash-Bish, Miss Sedgwick is certainly good authority for the assertion that the Swiss colony gave the name of Mount Rhighi to the locality where they settled, in honor of the famous mountain they had left behind. She was a descendant of the most prominent of the early settlers of southern Berkshire, and was likely to be well informed in regard to its history.

One more preliminary. The brown hematites, which abound in Berkshire, from Mount Washington to Lanesboro' and Cheshire — as well as here at Copake, and in the neighboring Connecticut town of Salisbury — are among the most precious of iron ores. They are among the most beautiful, also, when, as they often do, they assume the stalactical form. The black and glossy bubbling shape of many specimens gives the impression that they were made by heat; but the real agency was water. The hematite beds were certainly deposited from the decomposition of primitive, or magnetic, ores which once lay at points higher than they. Break one of those glossy pieces, and you shall see the stalactical crystalization in exquisitely delicate and symmetrical radiation. It is worth one's while, even in the region of rarest landscape, to stop curiously by the side of a rusty ore-heap. There is nothing more admirable in the painting of the loveliest flower, nothing more wonderful in the upheaval of the mightiest hills, than you may find in the formation of those myriad crystals, about to be cast by rude hands into the seven-fold heated furnace.

When the fields were first cleared these ores, scattered in boulders over the surface, or not deeply buried, were easily accessible, and iron works sprang up everywhere: not the costly and massive structures you now see, but forges, scarcely more in appearance than expanded blacksmith shops; although they made iron that was iron. It was this slightness of structure and consequent change of location as often as convenience required, that renders it impossible for me to tell you precisely where the forge and iron-master's dwelling of my story stood: but you will observe that it could not have been far from the Bash-Bish gorge; perhaps — who knows? — on the very site of the present Copake furnace.

Doubtless you think this a queer, matter-of-fact introduction to a love-story. But this will not be much of a story, after all. You must recollect that it might have been a field-meeting report. And, moreover, the love-stories in this volume are, none of them, mere things of fancy; but the genuine growth of this Berkshire soil — or, at the least, fixtures attached to the reality.

And there is poetry in the iron-master's trade. Listen to but one verse of a spirited song put into his mouth by J. E. Dow:

"I delve in the mountain's dark recess,
    And build my fires in the wilderness;
    The red rock crumbles beneath my blast,
    While the tall trees tremble and stand aghast.
    At midnight's hour my furnace glows,
    And the liquid ore in red streams flows,
    Till the mountain's heart is melted down,
    And seared by fire is its sylvan crown."

Yes, the monotony of woodland excursions by day is grandly relieved by a visit to an iron furnace by night. And the ladies should know that the light from the glowing metal is a great intensifier of some kinds of beauty.

And now to my story.

It must be more than a hundred years since there lived near the base of the Bernese Jura, two men quite opposite in character, and — as one of them, at least, conceived — of somewhat different ranks in life. Peter Goubermann earned a moderate livelihood in a narrow recess of the mountain, which, besides the necessary room for his forge and dwelling, had barely space for a modest garden, and pasturage for a single cow. It was a laborious and humble life he led; but he had little ambition to exchange it for one of more wealth and ease; and none at all to rise in the social scale above the station which his fathers had occupied before him for he knew not how many generations. Content that he was secure in the reasonable comforts of his home, and that it was safe from the terrors of the avalanche — whose crash sometimes roused him from his peaceful slumbers to utter a thankful prayer and fall quietly asleep again — almost his sole pride was in his forge, whose iron was unrivalled in the Berne market, and his garden which, for its rods, had not an equal in the canton.

But, if he exulted in these, his chief pride was his pretty daughter, Annette; not his pride alone, but the pride of the whole neighborhood; its pride and flower, by the consenting voice of all, except an envious few. And the envy must have been base indeed, which could sour those whom it possessed against one so unspoiled by flattery as Annette Goubermann — the gentlest, kindliest and most unassuming, as well as the most beautiful, of Bernese maidens: as all accounts agree.

The moral antipodes of that Swiss Valley-Forge was only a mile and a half distant from it, where the possessions of Anton Von Stachel, the great landed proprietor of that region began. The rich man had commenced life with Peter Goubermann; and as plain Anton Stachel, the poorer of the two. But he was of that class against whom the prophet Isaiah pronounced the curse:

"Woe unto them that join house to house,
That lay field to field, till there be no place,
That they may be placed alone in the earth."

And he succeeded so well that it seemed as though he would finally leave no place in his mountain microcosm for any neighbor. The superstitious people said he had discovered the philosopher's stone, or possessed some talisman of that sort: and so he had; but it was only his own stony heart, that grew harder and harder every prosperous year. There are many people who prosper under the same potential charm; but wise old Isaiah knew what he was prophecying: it is but a bitter woe to them all at last.

As the rich man grew in wealth, he increased also in vanity, and either discovered, or pretended to discover, some far-away connection with a gentle German family; whereupon, assuming gentility to himself, he jerked an aristocratic syllable into his plebeian name, and became Anton _Von_ Stachel. That is, he so called himself; and all the neighbors, who held him in awe, so addressed him, although the high and mighty council of the canton contemptuously persisted in enrolling him simply as "Stachel, yeoman." And he almost bit his tongue through with vexation when he was compelled to answer to the .humble patronymic of which his honest father had been proud.

In republican Switzerland, the legitimate distinctions of social rank are not very marked; but, as in republican America, the craving for them, such as they are, often half crazes the unfortunates upon whose vanity it takes hold; and poor, rich, Stachel — now with, and now without, the " Von " — was a very sad case of this mental malady. His social ambition possessed his soul almost equally with his avidity to add field to field in what he called his "domain." Indeed the two seemed only different developments of the same consuming passion.

The gossips said, in whispers among themselves —

that he had worried his poor wife to death by his attempts to make her conform to his notions of gentility, assume superiority over the friends of her youth, and even half disown her own family relations. It is certain that, what with his vanity, his tyranny and his absurdity, he led her a most unhappy life, in a vain attempt to conquer her aversion to falsehood and pretence, and check her generous charities. It is certain moreover that, with all due submission in things reasonable, she made a brave, honest, and womanly resistance to wrong and folly, while she could. And then she died.

Whether the gossips were right as to the cause of her death, I shall not at this distance of time pretend to say; but in their mysterious female Vehme-Gericht — that shadowy tribunal which prevails in all lands, and holding its secret sessions undetected in the midst of crowds, deals doom to high and low, as insidiously and irresistibly as the viewless angel of the plague — in this grewsome conclave, the gossips continued to mutter judgments. And none among them was more positive than this; that Madame Stachel had left a son who had a deal of the mother in him — or, as the more emphatic put it, "was all mother" — and that he would one day worry the life out of the old man, unless he forestalled him in that pleasing process.

As the boy, Hermann, grew up to be a fine, bold, generous-hearted young man, it began to look as though the doom pronounced by the feminine

Vehme-Gericht against the house of Stachel, would
befall it. The whole neighborhood rang with stories
of the wrangles between the father and the son; although even the old man's most cringing adherents
were compelled to admit, when pressed to the wall,
that Hermann was disobedient only to his most
odious commands.

Of course in due time, the young man lost his
heart to the Pride of the Valley. There was nothing
strange in that; all the youth of the canton suffered
in the same way. The peculiarity of this case was
that the honest Annette, rather than Hermann should
be robbed, gave her own in exchange.

There was a little halcyon period of courtship;
but when the betrothal was fully determined upon,
neither Father Goubermann nor the young people,
were of the mind to make a clandestine affair of it.
That was not in their truthful natures. Perhaps,
too, they did not anticipate the stubborn and violent
opposition with which the elder Stachel received the
announcement of his son's intentions. To be sure,
the iron-master was not rich, and not even the prefix
of, " Von," could make the name of Goubermann
sound otherwise than peasant-like; but then he could
afford his daughter a decent dower; and, as for his
name, there was not one in all Switzerland which
stood higher for the integrity and sterling worth of
its owner. And, then, everybody knew that Annette might have gone to the best mansion, or one
of the best, in the city of Berne, as the bride of the
wealthiest young burgher there; and what was more,

a right worthy fellow.   But the Valley-Forge match
would have thwarted one of the fondest schemes of
Stachel's ambition, and he set his face against it as
flintily as though it had been his heart.

I need not tell in detail the story of the long
months of waiting and hoping, loving and hating,
threatenings and defiances.   Suffice it, that Father
Goubermann would not hear of any marriage without the consent of Father Stachel, at least until
further effort was made to obtain it; nor would he
listen to Hermann's plan of learning the iron-maker's
art, in order that he might make himself inde-
pendent.

Six or eight months had passed in this manner
when, in an interval of comparative peace — doubtless cunningly prepared — his father commissioned
Hermann to attend to some affair in connection with
his mother's family in a remote section of the con-
federacy; and, after a tender parting with his be-
trothed, he set out on his errand without suspicion
of treachery.   But he had scarcely crossed the borders
of the canton when the storm which had long
been brewing burst upon the household he loved so
well.

In his life-long course of evil-dealing, Stachel had
necessarily secured legal tools, as reckless of right
and mercy as himself; and now, having determined
to break off his son's marriage at any cost, he put
the business into the hands of one Beza, a weasel-
faced lawyer of Berne.   Even the ferret-eyes of the
attorney, squinny them as he would, could discover

nothing in the conduct of Annette upon which the most harpy-like slander could fasten; and that resort was speedily given over. Nothing remained but, by some device, to bring the iron master into the power of the oppressor; and the unimpeachable integrity of the man forbade all hope of effecting this by criminal accusation, or by enticement into any rash act. Thus far, the righteousness of the threatened household was a wall of defence round about them.

But, almost mad with the ill success of his wicked schemes — which did not even come to the knowledge of those against whom they were plotted — Stachel spurred on his agent with new promise of reward: and not in vain. Beza discovered, or forged, some flaw in the Goubermann title to the iron-works and the land attached to them; and his employer hastened to purchase the rights of the person in whom the property would vest, if the flaw should prove fatal: and no efforts were spared to make it so. Before Hermann departed on his journey, the new claim had become so well fortified, although no hint of it had spread beyond the circle of the conspirators, that it seemed impregnable; and, as soon as the young man was well out of the way, the masked battery was uncovered.

The revelation came upon Father Goubermann like a thunder-bolt from a clear sky. That he rightfully and legally owned the property of which he had so long held undisputed possession, he had no more doubt than he had of his own existence: and that any man should attempt to deprive him of it, seemed

to his simple and honest nature, too monstrous **for**
belief.　But there lay, staring him in the face, **a**
formal — a very legally formal — demand that **he**
should, not only surrender it, but also account **for**
long arrears of rents — making an astounding sum
total.　And the claimant was Anton Von Stachel, who,
more than once, had found means to wring from **an**
unwilling tribunal, a decision which, though legally
correct, the judges knew to be essentially unjust: **a**
man of many well concocted appliances in resisting
the right, was Von Stachel.

That night, it needed no thunder of the avalanche
to rouse Goubermann from his slumbers: it found him,
for the first time, restless on his bed at midnight.
No sleep came to him; and, with the earliest dawn, he
started for the city, to consult an honest lawyer — his
long-time friend.　He found small consolation there.
Herr Zwingli had no doubt that Stachel's claim was
fabricated and fraudulent; but to resist it would involve a ruinous and doubtful law-suit.　Nevertheless,
he advised resistance, as affording some small hope,
and at any rate postponing for awhile the ejectment
of the Goubermann family from their home.　The ruin
of resistance could be no more complete than the
ruin of submission.

Stachel, who had anticipated this legal consultation and its results, met his victim as he was returning home, laden with this woeful counsel.　He had
waited for this before seeking an interview; and now,
conscious that the hypocrisy of any attempt to give
his purpose a friendly coloring would be instantly

detected, he came bluntly to his proposition, which was substantially this : that the Goubermann family should leave Switzerland at once, to remain for a given number of years; that they should leave no trace of their course, nor ever in any manner, communicate, so that it could reach Switzerland, the place of their retreat. On these conditions, Stachel offered to pay the iron master such a sum as would enable him, in England or elsewhere, to establish himself in a better position than he left, and consenting, moreover, that he might take with him such personal property as would not betray his course.

Goubermann listened to these cruel terms silently, and as if in a dream; but they were stamped upon his memory as if branded with a hot iron; and, no less, the savage warning, uttered by his enemy as they parted, of the probable consequences to his invalid wife of a rejection of this his offer.

There was another sleepless night at Valley-Forge — a night of agony and prayer, in which the daughter shared, but not the mother, who slept unconscious of the impending evil. In bitterness of soul the father wrestled with his own spirit, and sought counsel of his God. What thoughts possessed the young girl, conscious that her innocent but unhappy love had brought about all this misery, I leave you to imagine; what rebellious thoughts to be crushed back, what youthful longings to be repressed, what pitying compassion for her lost lover; before the victory was won. I do not say that Annette's dream of happiness and Hermann was altogether dissipated by her silent vow; but she said quietly to herself, "If it pleases the good God, it will all come to pass yet; as for me I will perform this present duty which He imposes upon me, without murmuring." And then with a saintly smile, she said:

"Father, we will go."

The father half smiled, half sighed, his blessing and his assent.

When Hermann returned from his journey, he could learn little more from the sorrowing people of the neighborhood than the deserted cottage had already told him. The Goubermann family had been missed from their home, one morning, a week previous. They had departed without farewell or explanation; which was strange in such honest and kindly folk, and only to be accounted for as the result of something connected with Stachel's claim upon their property, which Lawyer Zwingli made public with a free expression of his opinions as to its rascality. It needed but an incautious word, dropped by his father in the heat of passion, to enable Hermann to divine all the rest.

In looking for the success of his plot the father had counted too little upon the depth and constancy of his son's affection for the noble peasant girl, and altogether failed to comprehend the strength and faithfulness of his whole nature, as well as his quickness of perception. His own experience in hearts led him to believe confidently that, the object of Hermann's youthful fancy, once sent away, would soon be forgotten, and the young man ready to receive the impression of new charms. It was not the only mistake he made. In sending Hermann on that trumped-up errand, he was the unwitting means of his obtaining a considerable sum of money in hand, and a large bequest afterwards, from a maternal uncle who regarded him with affection for both his moral and personal likeness to his mother. Hermann now found this gift much to his purpose: and thus a good Providence justified the faith of the pious and submissive maiden, and made the device of the wicked help to the very end it was intended to prevent.

It was but a day after his return before Hermann disappeared as secretly as the iron-master and his family had departed. But the smiling and smirking gossips made no ado in guessing upon what mission he had gone. Nobody feared that he had plunged rashly into the lake, or laid himself down in the path of a glacier — as unhappy people, now-a-days, do before a rail-road train.

Probably Stachel had counted as much upon his son's inability to follow the exiles, as upon his measures to conceal their route and hiding-place; but the uncle's gift — which the young man did not deem it needful to boast of — was an obstacle to that element in the plot.

In the region of passports and police with which Switzerland is surrounded, there is no great difficulty for one disposed to use money with moderate — not to say lover-like — liberality, in tracing any body

whom the government is not disposed to hide. Still
it took the inexperienced youth some little time to
ascertain that the objects of his pursuit had passed
through France on their way to Great Britain. A
wearisome and heart-sickening search there ended,
by mere chance, in the discovery that — Father
Goubermann not taking kindly to the ways of his
rude English fellow-craftsmen — the family had
sailed for America. No one could tell him for what
port they embarked; but, by good luck, the first ship
up was bound for New York; and, impatient of
delay, he took passage.

At New York, he was bewildered by the report
that little iron-works, like those I have described, and
similar to the well remembered forge in the Jura —
were springing up everywhere in the wild woods of
Pennsylvania, New York, New Jersey, Massachusetts and other provinces. It was a discouraging
out-look; and, with a heavy though determined
heart, he resumed his loving pilgrimage, resolved
that it should end only with success or death.

But now, fortune — which, in storm and sunshine,
with his consciousness, or without it, had still been
urging him towards the haven where he would be —
again came visibly to his aid. As the sloop in which
he had taken passage lay becalmed on the Hudson,
a barge, heavily laden with iron from above, dropped
alongside; and the skipper, questioned as to the
source of his cargo, shouted: " From Mount Rhighi !"

Hermann was startled almost into crying out: but
the barge floated out of hailing distance, and he was

only able to gather from the sloop's people that she was from Kinderhook, and that Mount Rhighi must be somewhere in the same vicinity.

Had he known the remarkable way New York people had of appropriating foreign names, he would have understood that the clew was of the faintest! but, for once, ignorance helped him to a correct conclusion. The idea that this Swiss name would lead him to a colony of his countrymen, and finally to those he sought, seized upon him so forcibly that he sprang on shore at Kinderhook with a lighter step and heart than he had known for months.

The village was not large, and he easily found Peter Van Schaack, the merchant who had shipped the iron; a warm-hearted gentleman who listened with sympathy to the broken English of the young Switzer's story, and overwhelmed him with joy by expressing his belief that a certain foreign family who had, a few months before, passed through town to Mount Rhighi, were none other than his friends. Mr. Van Schaack pressed him to accept his hospitality for a day or two, until he could have conveyance to the iron-works; but he would not have been the true lover he was, had he not set out at once, and — since that was necessary — on foot, to make his way through the wilderness.

On the second afternoon after this interview, Annette Goubermann was standing thoughtfully upon the brow of Sunset Cliff in the Bash-Bish gorge. Whether she had come down the mountain to enjoy the sunny outlook, or had gone up the glen to revive

her Alpine memories, will be determined when some
field-meeting or other shall fix upon the locality of
the Goubermann forge. But, there, on Sunset
Cliff, she certainly stood, looking dreamily towards
the Catskills, and doubtless meditating such things
as befit such a maiden at such an hour and on such
a spot; when she suddenly uttered a piercing cry,
and fell, senseless, to the ground.

In an instant her lover was by her side, and, by
the aid of the appliances immemorial in such cases,
she was soon restored to consciousness; although it
was a long while before Hermann was sufficiently
sure of her full recovery to suspend the use of his
restoratives; and, even after that, imminent danger
of a relapse seemed frequently to recur. I count it
selfish on their part — unless Annette's health positively compelled it ; which, Hermann admitted,
her complexion did not indicate — for the pair to
keep Father Goubermann and his good wife so long
from sharing their felicity; but the evening shades
had sent him in search of his daughter before they
thought of leaving their meeting place. The rock
which was their seat that evening, and many a
happy hour thereafter, is still there on Sunset Cliff.
The antiquarian may still detect it by the fact that
it is just long enough for two, and, unless time has
effaced it, by the inscription, HERMANN STEIN. If
it has become obscure with age, some " Old Mortality " should restore it.

I need not paint for you the joyous meeting with
the father and mother, nor the mutual explanations

which preceded the speedy nuptials of Hermann and Annette. But I trust you will be glad to learn that the whole family lived with delightful harmony in their new home, that Hermann became a very skillful and renowned iron-master; but took with him father and mother, as well as his beautiful wife and children, when he was called back to Berne, to enjoy the property which became his by the death of his father; including the old forge whose fires were now relighted, not from necessity, but out of love for the noble art.

Stachel fully intended to bequeath his whole estate to some hospital or other public institution; but, like all prosperous and self-important men, he conceived that life would be long with him, and delayed his preparation for death until it came upon him fearfully and suddenly: for he never recovered from an apoplexy with which he was struck upon learning that the supreme court of the canton had adjudged a poor wretch, whom he thought in his clutches beyond rescue, not bound to Anton Stachel yeoman, by an obligation given to " Anton Von Stachel, gentleman." Rank and name had real meaning in those days. Lawyer Zwingli, who made the point, had come so utterly to hate the old usurer that he smiled, with grim satisfaction, when he heard the fatal result of its success; but the gentle Annette wept that her enemy was cut off in the midst of his sins.

Such is one story of the Swiss occupation of

Mount Washington and the Alpine gorge of Bash-Bish.

The Dome of the Taghconics.

While we are in this romantic mountain corner it would be the most unpardonable lese-majesty, not to pay our homage to the kingly Dome of the Tagh-conics.   And yet — I confess it with shame — never having been presented at that court myself, I am disqualified for introducing you, and must request Mr. Headley to act as usher, with that golden rod, his eloquent pen:

"Two or three miles from Bash-Bish, is the Dome of the Taghconics, a lofty mountain rising, precisely like a dome, from the ridge of which it forms a part. It is in our estimation, far superior to the Catskill, for you have from a single spot, a perfect panorama below you : you have only to turn on your heel, and east and west, north and south, an almost endless prospect spreads away on the vision. You are the center of a circle at least three hundred and fifty miles in circumference ; and such a circle ! The mountains that stretch along the horizon between the Connecticut and the Hoosac river on the north-east, fade away as the northern Taghconics, the Berlin and the Canaan Mountains greet you in the north-west ; and these in turn are forgotten as your eye falls on the dark mass of the Catskill showing its huge proportions against the weste n horizon.

" And then, between is such a wealth of scenery. The valley of the Housatonic, for miles and miles, spreads all its loveli-ness before you. There, too, are the two settlements of Canaan, and, further up — a mere spot on the landscape — Sheffield ; and, still farther up, Great Barrington, hardly visible amid its forest of old elms, while the white cliffs of Monument Moun-

tain shut out old Stockbridge from view, and the distant spire
of Lenox church closes the long train of villages.

"Old Saddle-Back of Williamstown (the Greylock Range
in Adams, North Adams and Williamstown) stands up to its
full height against the misty mountains that repose further
off in the horizon — a peculiar feature of the landscape. Egremont stands alone in the valley of the Green River, but its
sloping land and swelling hills present a still lovelier variety.
A low line of mist is dimly seen stretching along the black
base of the Catskills, so indistinct that you would scarcely
observe it; and yet that is the lordly Hudson, heaving its
mighty tide seaward, laden with the commerce of a nation.
A mere pencil mark in the landscape, here, it gives no token
of the haste and busy life on its surface. Close under the
foot of the mountain on the south, sleep the sweet lakes of
Salisbury, while other lakes dot the horizon in every direction.

"But I cannot tell you of the prodigality of beauty which
meets the eye at every turn. You seem to look on the outer
wall of creation, and this old dome seems to be the spot on
which nature set her great compasses when she drew the
circle of the heavens. A more beautiful horizon, I have never
seen than sweeps around you from this spot. The charm of
the view is perfect on every side — a panorama, which becomes
a moving one, if you will but take the trouble to turn round."

21

XVIII.

GREYLOCK.

Greylock, cloud-girdled, from his mountain throne,
  A voice of welcome sends;
And, from green summer fields, a warbling tone,
  The Housatonic blends.— *Frances Ann Kemble.*

Spirit of Beauty! Let thy graces blend
With loveliest nature all that art can lend.

  *   *   *   *   *   *   *   *   *

Come from the steeps where look majestic forth
From their twin thrones, the giants of the north
On the huge shapes that, crouching at their knees,
Stretch their broad shoulders, rough with shaggy trees.
Through the wide waste of ether, not in vain,
Their softened gaze shall reach our distant plain;
There, while the mourner turns his aching eyes
On the blue mounds that print the bluer skies,
Nature shall whisper that the fading view
Of mightiest grief may wear a heavenly hue.— *O. W. Holmes.*

Greylock is the figure-head of the county of Berkshire. I might say that it is the figure-head of the Commonwealth of Massachusetts, if some Boston critic would not cry out that the hill-folk are trying to run the ship of state stern foremost. But the figure-head of the county, it plainly is; and a noble one. What a grand terminal it affords for the mountain bulwarks that so grandly sweep up, to it on either side the symmetrical valley. How proudly it lifts itself against the northern sky; the crested front of the mighty landscape !

We see it from a myriad points of view, varying its aspect with the different stand-points of the spectator, and with the perpetual changes of the atmosphere; although the general directness of the perspective from the south renders the apparent alterations in its contour, from change in the line of vision, to be much less frequent than with most of our mountain shapes.

The isolated mountain range between the Hoosacs and the Taconics, now generally known as the Greylock Range, is not so much a chain as an intertwisted cluster of mountains in the towns of Adams, North Adams and Williamstown; from which a spur strikes southward through New Ashford, Cheshire and Lanesboro', to Pittsfield. The main cluster has a length, from east to west, of about six miles, and an average altitude of perhaps twenty-four hundred feet above the surrounding valley. It consists of six or seven distinct peaks and ridges rising above a common base. The highest peak — the Greylock, from which the cluster takes its name — is upon the east, and has an elevation of thirty-five hundred feet above the sea level, or twenty-six hundred above the valley of the Hoosac, at its base on the north and east.

The twin peak on the west, less in height than Greylock by three or four hundred feet, commands no view, being covered by woods and having its nearer outlook cut off by surrounding summits. Nor has it any generally recognized name. But it is more conspicuous from the south than its taller brother, and, being of a graceful contour, will make a capital monument, if nothing else; and, for one, I heartily approve the proposition to christen it "Sy-MOND'S PEAK" in honor of the grand old Williams-town Colonel who led the "embattled farmers" of Berkshire in their glorious fight at Bennington.

The combination of these peaks in the view from the south, bears a rude, but rather striking, resem-blance to a saddle, which suggested to the early settlers the name of Saddle-back Mountain by which the cluster was long called; but the comparison was prosaic; and, besides, a similar likeness had caused the same name to be given to mountain ridges in more than one locality. A finer imagination early seized upon the likeness to the grey locks of an old man, which the top of the highest peak presents when whitened by the snows or frosts of the late fall or early spring, while the body of the hill is clothed in dark forests; and that summit became Greylock: one of the most poetic names which ever added grace to the loveliness of nature.

The rudeness and lack of distinctive meaning of the name "Saddle-back," as applied to the cluster, have caused it to be gradually disused, and the pret-tier designation has been extended to the whole group, with the addition of "group," "range or "mountain;" so that the name "Saddle-back" is rarely heard.

except from lips which say "his'n" and "hern" for "his" and "hers." But you will observe that there is a difference between "Greylock" and "Greylock Mountain" or "The Greylock Group."

You recollect Grace — the wild and witty Berkshire girl, we met one day down by the borders of Pontoosuc Lake. Well, a while ago, a geologist deeply enamored of her and Berkshire rocks, after showing her a wonderful piece of contorted strata by the road-side near the lake, was explaining that it was really the most marvellous specimen he had ever met: when the saucy thing threw him completely off his balance by exclaiming, with eyes distended in mock astonishment: "What a twistification! Isn't it nice, though? It looks just like half-worked molasses candy. Did you ever help pull candy, professor? Its awful jolly!"

"Awful" and "jolly," I ought to explain, are words which Grace reserves for the sole purpose of extinguishing over-exquisite admirers; but I have no doubt that, if I were to set her to explaining the queer interlacings of the Greylock ridges, she would dash me with something like this: "What a twistification! Its just like one of cook's dough-nuts Arn't there some in the lunch basket? Let's have them out!" And I feel very much inclined to dispose of the matter in the same way. In quiet earnest, the peaks and ridges, the ravines and cascades, the rugged notches and picturesque nooks of this, as yet only half-studied, mountain group, are food for a season, rather than a tit-bit for a hasty excursion.

They seem moreover to belong to the peculiar domain of the Williams College people, and the summer denizens of Greylock Hall; to whom I commend them, although it sounds very like a stranger commending to a man, the charms of his own wife. Such counsel is not always superfluous.

The rest of you, nevertheless, must come with me through the more noted and striking scenes whose beauty boldly challenges us on the peaks, or lies hid in the recesses, of this loftiest and most picturesque mountain of Massachusetts.

One who has not climbed to the top of Greylock has taken no very high degree as a Berkshire excursionist; and, to be initiated into the highest, he must pass a night there. If you are an invalid, or have any other very valid reason for it, I will, however, help you to take your degrees by proxy: although, for the more convenient connection with what is to follow, I must give the story of my two ascents of the great mountain in reversed order.

Night and Morning on Greylock.

It was a laughing, sparkling, companionable, well-assorted party that, passably well supplied with brains, and thoroughly well versed in the matter-in-hand, met one evening in the most deliciously comfortable of parlors, to organize — as the summons of our queenly chief put it — for a new crowning of Old King Greylock. There is much good in these preparatory meetings. In the first place a successful excursion must be organized by somebody. However you may tumble into it at hap-hazard, somebody has planned and prepared for it. The victories which nobody organizes are no more to be counted upon, in any undertaking, than the fortunes that fall to lucky people from forgotten Californian uncles. And, least of all, can you trust to chance for the successful issue of a day and night mountain excursion, where a single fault in the commisariat or the quarter-master's department may cause infinite disaster. To be sure, some considerate or generous persons generally provide all things necessary; but it is every way better to do it in merry committee of the whole.

If there were no other reward for this equitable course, it is enough that it doubles your pleasure; which you take in two installments; the first being in hand, and sure: to whatever fate, foul weather or other misfortune may bring the second. And, by and bye, when both come to be alike far-off memories, you may doubt which was the richer, and more real. And then, again, in this cosy and informal preliminary gathering, you assimilate your party; which — particularly if there happen to be new elements in it — is very desirable. It saves much delay and awkwardness on the morrow. Nobody is distrait, as strangers are apt to be, when you meet for the start; and sometimes very pleasant unexpected pairing results — permanent or otherwise.

Our council in preparation for Greylock had no perplexing subject of debate. A railway ride to Adams, where carriages to the mountain-top had

been engaged, disposed of the matter of transportation. Apparatus for open-air cooking, we always
had ready; and supplies of cold meats, boiled eggs,
sandwiches, fruits and all manner of pic-nic fare
were reported in quantities that only mountainous
appetites could expect to do away with. It only
remained to provide for protection against the night
dews, and the mists of the mountain top; and that
was soon carefully arranged. In view of the pro-
spective fatigues of the morrow, only a very small
allowance of dancing was allowed; and then, to
help our anticipations and dreams, Henry Thoreau's
graphic account of his night and morning on Greylock was read. It is an episode in his charming
"Week on the Concord and Merrimac," from which
I shall presently quote a paragraph; but you should
read the story in full, with the characteristic moral
and philosophical observations of the great Secular
Solitary.

His conveyance and commissariat were even simpler
than ours, and much more self-reliant. "I had
come over the hills on foot," he writes, "on foot
and alone in serene summer days, plucking the rasp-
berries by the wayside, and occasionally buying a
loaf of bread at a farmer's house; with a knapsack
on my back which held a few traveller's books and
a change of clothing, and a staff in my hand. * * *
Reaching the mountain top, I had one fair view of
·the country before the sun went down; but I was
too thirsty to waste any light in viewing the prospect,
and set out directly to find water. First, going

down a well-beaten path through a scrubby wood, I came to where the water stood in the tracks of the horses which had carried travellers up. I lay down flat and drank these dry, one after another — a pure, cold, spring-like water; but yet I could not fill my dipper, although I contrived little syphons of grass-stems, and ingenious aqueducts on a small scale; it was too slow a process. Then, remembering that I had passed a moist spot near the top, I returned to find it again; and here, with sharp stones and my hands, in the twilight, I made a well about two feet deep, which soon filled with pure water; and the birds, too, came and drank at it. So I filled my dipper, and making my way back to the observatory, collected some dry sticks, and made a fire on some flat stones which had been placed on the floor for that purpose; and so I soon cooked my supper of the rice I had bought at North Adams, having already whittled a wooden spoon to eat it with." With Mr. Thoreau's resources one could afford an extended tour.

Mr. Thoreau ascended the mountain, from North Adams through "The Notch," a savage cleft between Greylock peak and a lower hill upon the east. Through this rugged pass, dashes a crystal brook, which supplies to the village waterworks, an abundance of pure water; and also, with its foaming cascade and other brookly beauties, affords an attractive as well as accessible resort for citizens and strangers. At its southern end, where the narrowing notch " slopes up to the skies," it is called "The

Bellows-pipe." In our wild northern storms, the fierce winds bellow through it in thousand-fold concentrated fury.

Our ascent, from Adams, was much more prosaic. We sacrificed a little romance, for the sake of a good deal of ease: still we we were often tempted from our comfortable conveyances into groves, glades and recesses among the rocks by the road-side. There was no need of haste. Even after a socially prolonged dinner, enjoyed in full view of a magnificent, but comparatively narrow, landscape, we had ample time to ascend the observatory and enjoy the stupendous scenery which presented itself in every direction.

We were in rare good fortune. The atmosphere was exceptionally pure, rendering the view as clear and distinct as one of such vast proportions ever can be. Approximately to measure that vastness in your mind, consider that the diameter — not the circumference — of the horizon revealed to you, is some three hundred miles. Away in eastern Worcester, you see Mount Wachusett; the Grand Monadnock in south-western New Hampshire; the lofty peaks of the northernmost Taconics in Vermont; the Adirondacs of New York in the north-west, and the Catskills in south-west. In the south, the far-away hills of Connecticut melt dimly into the Soundward slope. From Mount Tekoa, Mount Tom, and Mount Holyoke in the Connecticut valley, successive ridges rise continually, to the Columbian Mountains of New York; pile after pile in most admired disorder, for a breadth of more than sixty miles: longitudinally, some seventy miles southward; and northerly as far as the eye can reach.

Mr. Gladden, quotes President Hitchoock as saying: " I know of no place where the mind is so forcibly impressed by the idea of vastness, or even of immensity, as where the eye ranges abroad from this eminence: " and it is not for us, in the immediate presence of this majestic over-view, to look for a rival to it in Alps or Sierra.

The nearer and gentler, but still bold and commanding, view is close upon the south, where the great Berkshire valley lies spread out before us: in its centre the streets and spires of Pittsfield, with their fair cordon of glassy lakes glittering around them, and, on every side, half-hidden villages and village churches gleaming white upon the verdant back-ground of woods and fields; conspicuous among them the fine old meeting-houses of Lenox and Dalton — while, most distinct of all, almost under our feet, and so close to the mountain's base as to seem a very part of it, lies the thriving, busy and handsome town of Adams. A scene, take it all in all, to be tenderly yearned over by the children of that glorious valley, and to be lovingly admired by the merest chance-comer to the hill-top.

While we lingered dreamily over it, the sun went down, leaving on that transparent sky, no such cloud-shapes of fantastic gorgeousness as often veil his parting; but, along the whole western horizon, one, broad, uniform band of glowing light — softening,

from richest orange through all golden tints, until it
melted from liquid amber into crystal chrysoprase,
and then was lost in the prevailing azure.

The gold paled from the western heavens: and
then the grey was absorbed in the blue. The evening
shades filled the valley; crept up the mountain side;
enveloped grove and tower, and the little group who
silently awaited their coming.

"Darkness upon the mountain and the vale ;
The woods, the lakes, the fields are buried deep
In that still, solemn, star-watched sleep :
No sound, no motion, and o'er hill and dale,
A calm and lovely death seems to embrace
Earth's fairest realms and heaven's unfathomed space.

The forest slumbers; leaf and branch and bough,
High feathery crest, and lowliest grassy blade.
All restless, wandering wings are folded now,
That swept the sky, and in the sunshine played.
The lake's wild waves sleep in their rocky bowl :
Unbroken stillness streams from nature's soul,
And night's great star-sown wings stretch o'er the whole!"

Mrs. Kemble.

As was fitting, even in the merriest party, we
yielded for awhile to the solemn promptings of the
hour; but it is not fitting, even were it possible, that
they should long curb the glee of a mountain excursion. The voice of our chief reminded us that we
had promised our friends at home to signal our
presence on Greylock by a blaze which they could
see. The appointed hour had come, and the beacon
was lighted. Our friends were kind enough to believe they saw it beaming like a star, or a light in a

distant window. Perhaps they did. It certainly
cast a strange, wild, red glare upon the old tower and
the overhanging foliage; and invested the ladies, who
gathered around it, with a weird, gypsy beauty that
was very enchanting.

The little grotto of light, we had wrought out in
the great darkness, had hardly disappeared, when
the white moon rose up the eastern sky, revealing
new realms of splendor. Little by little, the hills and
valleys emerged from the shadow ; reposing in the
pallor, or gleaming in the silver sheen, of the white
radiance. There was no longer any color in the
picture. It was drawn in crayon — all light and
shade. Nor was there day-light's sharpness of outline: the landscape lay in broad surfaces and heavy
masses, except in the close foreground. There is
something altogether delusive in the brilliance of
moonlight. It dazzles, but cannot illuminate. It
will light you gaily to your serenade; but you cannot read a sentence by it, at its brightest, as you
can by a very dim twilight. You need the yellow
rays of the spectrum for that; as you will discover
by attempting to read in a church whose "dim religious light" streams through stained windows, and
then in one where the garish light of day is rendered still more garish, by being strained through
ground glass, which eliminates most of the yellow
from it. You will observe the same difference,
although in a less degree, between the yellow flame
of a kerosene lamp, and the white blaze of a gas-jet ;

22

the eye tiring much the quicker under the latter. But it was not dread of spoiling our eye-sight which led our prudent chief to order us to our couches. Indeed the glamour of that illusive splendor seemed magically projected on the scene for our immediate enchantment and witchery. But the white mists which first traced, in delicate lines upon the dark surface, the curves of the river and the lurking places of the lakes, had filled the lower valley, until as we looked down upon it, it lay outspread like a great snow-shrouded plain. And now tall, ghostly, phantom-like shapes upreared themselves on the mountain side. We knew that their embrace was uncanny, if not deadly, and we fled before the advancing specters, screaming — with laughter.

The floors of the two stories of the tower had already been spread with elastic boughs, of balsamy odor, from the near woods; shaggy bear and buffalo robes, army blankets and rubber coverings were now liberally distributed. Generous draughts of hot coffee were dealt out. Prayers were read. Then stillness was enjoined upon the wakeful, and soon those not too much excited by the novelty of the scene slumbered peacefully. Before morning all enjoyed a healthful sleep, undisturbed except, once or twice, by a fitful cloud-rack which drifted through the open windows — just to remind us how near we were to heaven.

Before I tell you of our awakening, I will read you what Mr. Thoreau says of his:

"I was up early and perched upon the top of the tower to see the day break; for some time reading the names that had been engraved there before I could distinguish more distant objects. An 'untameable fly' buzzed at my elbow with the same nonchalance as on a molasses hogshead at the end of Long Wharf. Even here I must attend to his stale humdrum. As the light increased, I discovered around me an ocean of mist which reached up by chance exactly to the base of the tower, and shut out every vestige of the earth; while I was left floating on this fragment of the wreck of a world, on my carved plank in cloudland: a situation which it required no aid from the imagination to render impressive. As the light in the east steadily increased, it revealed to me more clearly the new world into which I had risen in the night: the new *terra firma* perhaps of my future life. There was not a crevice left through which the trivial places we name Massachusetts, Vermont and New York could be seen; while I still inhaled the clear atmosphere of a July morning — if it were July there. All around me was spread for a hundred miles on every side, as far as the eye could reach, an undulating country of clouds, answering in the varied swell of its surface to the terrestrial world it veiled. It was such a country as we might see in dreams, with all the delights of Paradise. There were immense snowy pastures apparently smooth-shaven and firm, and shady vales between the vaporous mountains; and, far in the horizon, I could see where some luxurious misty timber jutted into the prairie, and trace the windings of a water course, some unimagined Amazon or Orinoko, by the misty trees on its brink.

As there was wanting the symbol, so there was not the substance, of impurity: no spot nor stain. It was a favor for which to be forever silent to be shown this vision. The earth below had become such a flitting thing of lights and shadows as the clouds had been before. It was not merely veiled to me; it had passed away like the phantom of a shadow, σκιᾶς ὄναϱ, and this new platform was gained, As I had climbed above storm and cloud, so by successive day's journeys I might reach the region of eternal day ; aye,

> ' Heaven itself shall slide,
> And roll away like melting stars that glide
> Along their oily thread.'

But when its own sun began to rise on this pure world, I found myself a dweller in the dazzling halls of Aurora — into which poets have had but a partial glance over the eastern hills — drifting among the saffron-colored clouds, and playing with the rosy fingers of the Dawn, in the very path of the Sun's chariot, and sprinkled with its dewy dust, enjoying the benignant smile, and near at hand the far-darting glances, of the god.   The inhabitants of earth behold commonly but the dark and shadowy under-side of heaven's pavement ; it is only when at a favorable angle of the horizon, morning and evening, that some faint streaks of the rich lining of the clouds are revealed.   But my muse would fail to convey an impression of the gorgeous tapestry by which I was surrounded ; such as men see faintly reflected afar off in the chambers of the east.   Here, as on earth, I saw the gracious god

> ' Flatter the mountain tops with sovereign eye, * * *
> Gilding pale streams with heavenly alchemy.'

Never here did ' Heaven's Sun ' stain himself.   But, alas, owing as I think to some unworthiness in myself, my private sun did stain himself, and

> Anon permit the basest clonds to ride
> With ugly wrack on his celestial face ;

for before the god had reached his zenith, the heavenly pavement rose and embraced my wavering virtue, or rather I sank down again into that ' forlorn world ' from which the celestial sun had hid his visage."

Mr. Thoreau, descending the mountain, soon found himself in the region of clouds and drizzling rain; and the inhabitants affirmed that it had been a rainy and drizzling day wholly.

Our party had a somewhat different experience, yet with a general likeness. A bugle, surreptitiously carried to the mountain top, roused us with pleasant surprise by a wild reveille as soon as light began to kindle beyond the Hoosacs. The surface of the mist-sea which filled the valley, lay calm and level some two hundred feet below the summit on which we stood; everywhere dazzling-white, except upon its extreme eastern verge which flushed with rose-red — changing soon to gold, and then to golden blaze. The sun came up and added new splendor to the glowing scene before the morning breeze began to disturb its serenity.

'From the first, three or four distant peaks were seen, like far-off islands in a foaming ocean. Now the mist began to lift itself with the breeze, and roll away into the blue sky; while new islands, promontories, capes, began to appear, until the green earth lay again beneath us, revealed in all its summer beauty. So, to some angel, worshipping in awe and wonder, the broad scene of creation may have been revealed when God said, "Let the waters that are under the heavens be gathered into one place, and let the dry land appear : and it was so."

I made an excursion to Greylock prior to the one I have just attempted to describe; and I recall it now for two specific purposes. After the visit to the natural bridge at North Adams, of which I gave an account some while ago, my companion and myself walked to Williamstown, where we passed the night. In the morning we walked to South Williamstown, where, being told that the "Hopper" would be intolerable on a day so intensely hot, we abandoned our intention of exploring that torrid gulf, and went up the mountain. We had no guide, nor any but very obscure directions as to the path we were to pursue; and, making our way pretty much at random, we found ourselves first upon Symond's Peak. Rectifying our mistake, we reached the tower on Greylock, at about one o'clock: not at all fatigued by our tramp. Nor were we unpleasantly wearied when we reached the hotel at New Ashford in the evening, or after our walk to Pittsfield the next day. I make this point to correct the impression that the ascent to Greylock is either difficult or unduly fatiguing to persons of ordinary health and powers of endurance.

I have also taken you to the top of Greylock again, to tell you of our descent from it on that first trip, and how it brought us into

The Heart of Greylock.

It was not until the middle of the afternoon that we yielded to the stern fact that lack of supplies and camp equipage would repress our noble rage to pass the night upon the mountain top; and we shaped our course homeward, taking our bearings solely with reference to directness.

> " Straight is the line of duty,
> Curved is the line of beauty;
> Follow the first and thou shalt see
> The other ever follow thee."

And that, we found true. Our straight course brought us to the verge of a precipitous descent of something more than a thousand feet, but with sufficient inclination to give root-hold to a moderately thick growth of trees.

Down this sharp descent, we dropped rapidly, clinging for support to the branches and undergrowth, and deliciously refreshed by frequent draughts of the cold and limpid water which gushed from a thousand springs, and sometimes dripped its coolness luxuriously upon our heated, upturned faces.

At the foot of the precipice, a brook brawled its way between banks which afforded a narrow grassy glade in the midst of the dark woods. As we stood in this sunny opening, we gazed above and around us in utter amazement and delight. The chasm into which we had been chance-led, was, in shape, an inverted cone, truncated at its reversed apex by the little plain intersected by the brook. The walls, at least a thousand feet in height, and all over enamelled with the richest forest green, appeared to us as perfectly circular and their tops presented a line as level against the sky, as though we had looked up from within some unroofed round tower or castle — of the Titans, for instance. Lost in astonishment at the strange beauty of the spot, and, still more, that whisper of it had never reached us, we pursued our way down the stream, to be still more amazed when the people who lived near, told us that, so far as they knew, it had neither name nor renown.

Finding afterwards, however, that the persons of

whom we sought information were not very intelligent new-comers, I resumed my pursuit of knowledge, and finally learned from a good old family of the neighborhood — besides some pleasant legends which I have carefully stored away — that the names we sought were "Money Hole" and "Money Brook," which were given in respect of a tradition that, in Revolutionary times, a gang of counterfeiters used to haunt their obscure recesses. I do not know how well founded the tradition is; but it is strongly fortified by the fact that, half a century ago, the little stream gained the soubriquet of "The Specter Brook," because the ghosts of the departed rogues were often seen keeping watch and ward at the entrance of the glen, while mysterious noises were heard within. I can well believe the phantom part of the story; for, to this day, the banks of all our mountain streams are all alive, if that is not a bull, with sheeted ghosts,

> In the moonlit mist restoring
> Vanished forms of long ago.

The roguish name assigned to what it seemed should be rather a classic than a criminal haunt, did not altogether please me, and I was glad to discover, a year or two later, that Professor Albert Hopkins — that gentle, but enthusiastic, spirit to whose fine influence Williamstown and Williams College owe so much of their esthetic interest — had christened it "The Heart of Greylock."

I was told, too, at the same time, that, had we, on

our chance visit, followed the brook up, instead of down, its course, we should have soon come to the Erēmite or Hermit Cascade — a waterfall at the least as picturesque and wild as Bash-Bish, and which I have since heard praised by other admirers in similar exalted terms. As I have not yet seen it, my memories of Mount Washington are not disturbed; but, what with a Specter Brook and a Hermit Cascade, the Heart of Greylock certainly offers a fine field for an old-fashioned imagination.

If you are now ready to climb the mountain again, I will take you to the summit whose shaven head gives it the name of

BALD MOUNTAIN,

and also enables it to afford a finer view of the Williamstown valley than can be obtained from the higher peaks. Seven or eight years ago a party composed chiefly, it seems, of college professors, clergymen and other gravely-gay characters — such as much affect Williamstown for a summer resort — with a feminine element of the same caste, dwelt for a while in leafy tabernacles in a sheltered nook of this summit, and one of the party sent a spirited account of their joys to the New York Observer, of all papers in the world: dating from "Camp Dew-Dew" as if the reverend writer were wholly oblivious of Don Juan and correct orthography. However, his spectacles were good, and we will take a look through them from the mountain top.

"Our camp lies in this sheltered spot upon Bald Mountain,

so near the summit of Greylock that sunset and sunrise
parties go out daily, and our artists and botanists climb its
sides in search of views and botanical treasures * * * Select
what point you choose of these commanding hills, and below
you lies the wide valley, the faint blue line of the river winding past Williamstown, Blackington, and Adams — the whole
framed by the encircling sweep of the blue mountains; while
far away is the white shaft of the observatory on Mount
Anthony, and farther in the distance still, overtopping all
nearer summits, loom up the dark hills of Vermont. And this
landscape is never twice the same: always bold and varied."

These views are not all to be witnessed from Bald
Mountain, which is over-topped on the north and
east by Prospect Mountain and Greylock. I did
not bring you here, however, for the sake of the
views; but that you might look down from its
northern edge into

The Abyss,

upon which the name of "*The Hopper*" was early
inflicted by that unimaginative imagination whose
horrid mission seems to have been from the first to
curse this picturesque mountain group with the most
common-place nomenclature. I grant that, as you
look down into the abyss, it has a striking likeness
in form to the hopper of a grist mill; and that this
comparison is the readiest mode of conveying to the
mind of a stranger some idea of its shape; but mere
form is not the most essential element in the description of any natural object; else were the old
likeness of the moon to a green-cheese felicitous and
poetic. It seems to me that the one idea which that

likeness of the abyss to a hopper ought to have suggested was to cast headlong into it, the wretch who first conceived the thought of making use of it in naming this grand work of nature, and let him take his chances of being well ground up on the rough mill-stones at the bottom.

You will start back in affright lest some such fate may befall yourself, if you approach unwarned the brink of the chasm on the edge of Bald Mountain. Unless nature has favored you with firmer nerves than she grants to most men, or you have plied some such dreadful trade as the samphire gatherer's, it will cost you some effort; with much probability of failure, to prepare yourself to observe the abyss from above with any calmness, or without absolute danger of fatal dizziness. It is thus, however, that you best comprehend the terrific grandeur of the scene.

Having obtained this apprehension, it will be as well if you pursue your study of the place from below. To do this, you will enter it from the Williamstown road, passing through a narrow valley and ravine, penetrated by a rocky brook, which, now I think of it, used to furnish capital trouting. Reaching the floor of the chasm, you will discover that it does not come to a point, as distance deceived you into thinking when you looked from above, but affords a level, though rock-cumbered, surface. Here you will find yourselves surrounded by four precipitous mountain walls over a thousand feet in height, or more than twice as high as the crags of Monument Mountain, although not, like them, abso-

lutely perpendicular and bare. On these rough and
shaggy sides you will see here huge and bare cliffs,
there ragged trees clinging to steep ascents and
scanty soil, and there patches of richer wood, but
still of precarious foothold; here the broad path of
the land-slide, and there, piled and scattered below,
its mighty ruins. Vastness and desolation will be
every where about you; and, if you can rid yourself
of that disennobling association with a mill-hopper,
I think you will feel that this great abyss in Greylock is both terrific and sublime.

KING GREYLOCK'S MOUNTAIN HEIGHT.

With jollity, jollity, ho, to-night,
To scale King Greylock's mountain height!
While many a wild recess profound
Sends, rattling back, the echoing sound,
As we startle the sleepy forest glades
With the joyous rout of our madcap maids:
For never a merrier band than they
E'er climbed at eve this mountain way!

Chor.—Then, ho, on our rude, steep path, away!
With the morrow's light on the topmost height,
We must hail the coming pomp of day!

Oh, whether the height in sunshine lie,
Or glamour moonlight cheat the eye,
'Tis a laughing light on the mountain side,
That owl-eyed care can never abide;
And his worldly weight, that worldlings bear,
Is loosed at the magical touch of our air;
Earth's spell is broke — and the heart is free,
As childhood's in its frolic glee!

Chor.— Then, ho, on our rude, steep path, away !
   With the morrow's light on the topmost **height,**
   We must hail the coming pomp of day !

  Our beacon fire this night shall glow,
  A gem on the monarch mountain's **brow,**
  Or far to our dear home valley gleam —
  A new found love-star's gentle beam.
  Then sweeter couch ne'er wooed to rest,
  Than the springy boughs of the green hill's **crest,**
  Whose leaves our fragrant bed shall be,
  With the starry night for canopy !

Chor.— Then, ho, on our rude, steep path, away !
   With the morrow's light on the topmost **height,**
   We must hail the coming pomp of day !

23

XIX.

WAHCONAH FALLS AND A TRADITION ABOUT THEM.

How throbbed my fluttering pulse with hopes and fears,
To know the color of my future years.— *Rogers.*

A little way off the main road in Windsor, a pleasant farming town on the highlands, some ten miles from us, are Wahconah Falls. I had heard their praises spoken by one who had an affinity with beauty which sought out its kindred in all hidden nooks; and on a bracing Autumn day I sat out to seek them.

There are few drives through a more agreeable region. The villages of Dalton, through which you pass, form a handsome town with a fine old meeting-house on its ample, lawn-like green. You are enticed to linger as well by the dark rushing river, where you see the groaning locomotive toiling up the steep ascent above you. And there, too, the quaint-looking paper-mills by the river side, go far to make up a pretty and novel scene. It is said, that as bright glances are sometimes thrown from the windows of these oddly shapen manufactories as from any balcony, lattice or verandah whatever

The paper manufacture, a great leading interest of

Berkshire, was here introduced into the county in 1799, by Zenas Crane, whose sons and grandsons still carry it on, making among other styles the paper upon which the bonds and bank bills of the United States government are printed. One of them, Hon. Zenas M. Crane, is the proprietor of Wahconah Falls, of whose romantic beauty he is one of the most enthusiastic admirers. Leaving behind us the pretty villages of Dalton, and its prettier belles — a production for which it was famed long before it gained renown for paper-making — we soon come to The Falls, a romantic miniature cataract, just far enough from the highway to be sheltered from the too careless eye.

Wahconah Brook, one of the larger of the numerous eastern branches of the Housatonic, here pours through perpendicular cliffs of dark grey rock, a considerable volume of water, which, in two or three leaps, makes a descent of seventy or eighty feet. The dark, precipitous cliffs form a striking and sombre vista, and the black and glossy surface of the water affords a fine contrast with the silvery white of the foam into which it breaks. But the peculiar charm which wins the place so many and so constant admirers is indefinable.

One may be sure of passing a pleasant hour at such a spot. The swift, smooth gliding of water always brings a pleasurable sensation, and there is rare music in the dash of a waterfall free from the discordant clatter of machinery. Alas, too rare in manufacturing Massachusetts! I confess to a malicious

joy in looking upon the blackened ruins of an old
mill which used to stand here, but perished long
ago in some fierce conflict with the insulted elements.
Heaven send thee no successor, thou grim and grin-
ning skeleton !

It is in such places as this, that sensible people
cut up all manner of boyish antics. Never be over
nice about dignity when in near pursuit of the
better thing, woodland or rural enjoyment; leave
gravity and etiquette at home, in your wardrobe,
with all other starched and flimsy articles of ap-
parel, and all the flummery of life. Get astride an
island rock, that midway divides the stream; where
the torrent shall throw its spray over you, and the
current dash by on either side your slippery foothold. Shout ! Rival the noisy, angry stream at its
own game. Observe now how superior is organic
sound to any mere inarticulate noise: your voice
lost in the thunder of the cataract, so that you cannot hear your own words, comes out clear and distinct, to your friends upon the shore. So the voice
of true and prophetic genius, lost now in the mad
roar of the multitude, shall ring its message clearly
in the ear of the listening future.

This cascade makes good its claim to be called
beautiful by gaining constantly upon your affections. You come again and again to sit by its ebon
pools, and let your eye glide with the fall of its
glossy sheet, and sparkle with the glittering fragments into which it breaks among the rocks. I like
these minor cataracts, which do not oppress you

with their sublimity, where your soul is not absorbed by any awful grandeur. They are like those plesant books where something is left for the imagination of the reader. There is room for the delights of an " if: " if it had been hung in air like the white ribbon of a bridal bonnet; if it had been swollen to mighty bulk, and curved like a horse shoe: if it had fallen from so far that it had lost its way to earth, and so flown back on iridescent wings to heaven. Why, one has a whole cabinet of possible picturesques in that little germ.

There is a tradition about these falls which I heard, long years ago, from a young Indian of the civilized Stockbridge tribe, who had come back from the western exile of his people to be educated at an eastern college. I hope it will please you.

WAHCONAH.

At the close of the great Pequot war in 1637, you will recollect that the remnant of that gallant but unhappy nation were driven from Connecticut, and scattered abroad, as they plaintively said, " like the autumn leaves which return not, though the tree grow green again." In this sad exodus, a majority of the fugitives went to swell the Onuhgungo and other fierce tribes of Canada which afterwards took such dreadful vengeance upon the western border settlements of New England. But some bands chose to pause by the way in the valleys of the Housatonic and the Hoosac, where the brotherly kindness of the Mohegans and the Mohawks granted them homes in which game was plenty and hunters were few.

One of these small parties, under the lead of a young brave, called Miahcomo, built their frail village in that part of the valley now called Dalton. Here, for forty years, they lived in peace, and, begetting sons and daughters, increased in numbers far beyond the red man's wont. The hill-side, where they buried their dead; the glen, whose thick woods reflected the red glare of their council fire, became dear to them as home; but above all, the inaccessible mountains were prized, as the hunted man only can prize the strength of the hills.

Almost forty years had passed since the little tribe fled from the flames of Fort Mystic, when the great sachem of the Wampanoags came to them. With strong logic, and glowing eloquence, he painted the rapid encroachments of the white man, and passionately besought them to join in that league which, in the following year, well nigh swept the English colonists from the soil of New England.

The young braves grasped their tomahawks as they listened, and the sympathetic eye of woman kindled with almost martial fire. But the rulers in savage, as in civilized life, can sometimes be prudent men. The chiefs crushed with cold words of sympathy the hopes which had quickened in the smiles of the people. Miahcomo — the same who had led the tribe from the pursuit of the English — still ruled them; and the young warriors muttered that the horrors of the last night of Fort Mystic, had turned his blood to water at the thought of the Long Knives — although bold as an eagle towards aught else. In more cautious tones they whispered, that if ever a spark of the old fire rekindled in Miahcomo's breast, the wily and cowardly priest Tashmu was always at hand to quench it. Thus the mission of Philip failed, and the tribe continued in peace.

In the early summer, nearly two years after the visit of Philip, Miahcomo and his warriors were summoned to meet the Mohawks — to whom they had become feudatories — beyond the Taghconics. Trusting to the quiet of the valley, the village was left in charge of the women, and a few decrepit old men. Among the former was Wahconah, the old chief's favorite daughter, a young lady of singular personal attractions, and skilled in all the fine arts in vogue among her countrywomen — especially in that of angling.

What with all these accomplishments, and the high rank of her father, it is little wonder that Wahconah was the idol of all the young men of the village, and, although yet almost a child in years, had — so the rumor ran — received offers matrimonial from a certain mysterious Mohawk dignitary. This latter worthy, the wigwam gossips unanimously agreed, would carry off the prize, whenever he came in person to claim it — for it was a thing unheard of in Indian wooing, that a brave of fifty scalps should sue in vain.

The young gallants of the Housatonic did not, for all this, remit one whit of their attentions, so that, while they were over the border with her

father, the hours hung heavily on the hands of
Wahconah. It was, perhaps, to while away the
tediousness; perhaps to get a nice dish for her
lodge, that the maiden, one sunny afternoon in
June, took her fishing lines and wandered up the
river to our cascade. Before the sun went down,
her success had been abundant, and she only waited
for one more last prize — a habit which I notice is
still invariable with successful people, be they
anglers, speculators, or what not.

But Wahconah did not, after all, seem to have
fully set her heart upon this final prize. On the
contrary, she lay luxuriously back upon the soft
greensward, playfully twining a few scarlet columbines in her dark hair, and smoothing softly down
the gay feathers of the oriole and blue bird that
decorated the edges of her white deer-skin robe —
a garment which, it must be confessed, was rather
excessive in its Bloomerism, considering the primitive nature of the wearer's pettiloons; but that
was the fashion of the day, and no fault of Wahconah's.

The child-like maiden revelled in the very fullness
of delightful revery. With a gentle, undisturbing
thrill, she felt the richly colored clouds fill her with
their delicious warmth; she dipped her little foot
in the stream and laughed aloud to feel the soft
caresses of the current; she mocked the black-bird
that sung upon the oak, and the squirrel that chirped
upon the hickory; she threw flowers and leaves upon
the wave, and smiled maidenly when two chanced

to meet and float together down the stream — for that was a love omen. That must have been a pleasant sight in the summer twilight, almost two hundred years ago.

Pity if it had been lost ! — as it was not; for all the while a young warrior had been looking on, from the shelter of a wood on the other side of the stream. It was certainly indelicate in him to play so long the spy upon a maiden's reveries, but one cannot find it in his heart to blame too severely, when he considers the temptation; and, besides, that the offender was but a mere savage, who never had the advantage of the counsels of Chesterfield, Abbott, or any "Young Man's Friend" whatever. The promptings of nature, however, did at last suggest to him the impropriety of his course; or perhaps he grew impatient. At all events, he hailed Wahconah, in the flowery language of Indian gallantry, "Qua Alangua !" that is to say, "Hail ! Bright Star ! "

Wahconah, startled at the sudden appearance of a strange warrior, in the absence of her tribesmen, sprang to her feet; but preserving the calmness befitting Miahcomo's daughter, replied "Qua Sesah ! " that is "Hail ! Brother ! " "Nessacus," continued the stranger, introducing himself, "Nessacus is weary with flying before the Long Knives, and his people faint by the way. Will the Bright Star's people shut their lodges against their brethren ? "

Miahcomo has gone toward the setting sun," replied the maiden — who by this time had pro-

bably come to the conclusion that Nessacus was
a very handsome young man, and well behaved —
"but his lodges are always open.' Let my brother's
people follow, and be welcome."

A signal from the young chief brought a weary,
travel-worn band to his side, and Wahconah led the
way to the village, while Nessacus related to her the
sad story of Philip's defeat and death. "They waste
us," he said, "as the pestilence which forerun them
wasted our fathers."

"The Manitou is angry with his red children,"
said Wahconah; "He makes the white man mighty,
by the strength of the long knife and the fire bird."

"It is not that," responded her companion bitterly,
"but the traitor's tongue at our council fires, and the
traitor's arrow upon our war-path."

Wahconah remembered what the people whispered
concerning Tashmu, and was silent.

Thus they came to the village; but I must let pass
the welcome, and the housekeeping as well, until
Miahcomo's return. Suffice it that in those pleasant
days in that moon of flowers, the young people did
precisely what you and I would have been likely to
do: fell violently in love; and, what was more, in
utter disregard of Indian notions of propriety, confessed it to each other — a breach of aboriginal
etiquette, you will the more readily pardon, if you
know experimentally, as I have no doubt you do,
how dementing is the glance of a bright eye and the
bloom of a damask cheek in the soft light of a June

evening, when your heart is as full of love as the air
is of fragrance.

Four suns had ripened the passion of our new
lovers, and a fifth was shining genially upon it, when
a messenger came in, announcing the near approach
of Miahcomo; and, as the custom was, all the people
went out to meet him. What visions of happiness,
our dreamers had built up in their barbarous way, I
cannot tell: nor do I know whether, as a rule, Indian
sires have such a fatal way of laying siege to air-
castles, as more civilized fathers use: so you can
guess as well as I, whether any tremblings troubled
the hearts of our young friends, akin to what young
Squire Mansfield and old Banker Barker's daughter
might experience in corresponding circumstances.
But, remember, one love is much like another.

Wahconah and the chief of her guests stood together on a shaded knoll as, just up the valley, the
returning warriors came in sight. Their leader is
described as a fine old hero as one should desire to
see. His tall sinewy frame was scarcely bent by the
snows of seventy years; every wrinkle in his face
was firm as if it were a new sinew of added strength;
his eye, keen and piercing as that of his youngest
archer.

By the chief's side, walked a different figure;
meek even to cringing, with an uncertain step, and
weak, restless, unquiet eye. It was the priest, Tashmu — one of that strange caste, often hated, sometimes despised, but always feared by the aborigines.
This Tashmu was a constant attendant upon Miah-

como, and, it was said had acquired a mysterious and powerful influence over the sachem's mind.

Wahconah shrank from the presence of the wizard as the summer flower shrinks from the north wind; but his, was, for once, not the most unwelcome figure which met her eye. With her father and his spiritual adviser, came a burly warrior, not positively old, nor absolutely ugly — only a little smoke-dried or so, and marked by transverse and obverse scars, which, although doubtless honorable, might have been dispensed with as matters of mere beauty. Grace would have likened his face to a smoked ham ornamentally slashed. He was evidently conscious of his renown, and wore the scalps which hung dangling in profusion about him, as proudly as ever civilized hero his jewelled star or blushing ribbon. Wahconah guessed but too shrewdly, that this was her Mohawk suitor — although he was far too dignified a character to conduct his wooing in the unceremonious manner which suited his young rival. Perhaps it had been awkward work had he tried.

When the parties met, a few words explained to the chief, the character of the strangers, and why they were his guests; which ensured a hearty confirmation of the welcome extended them by his daughter. Whatever may have been his meditations upon learning the new disasters of his race, and however bitter were the memories they recalled, they did not hinder his holding high revel that night upon the banks of the brook; where feasts were celebrated and athletic games held in honor at once of all his guests. Such was the courteous custom of the woods. I leave you to guess whose eyes brightened as Nessacus carried off all the prizes for daring feats, and skillful; and whose darkened as the brawny arms and square frame of the Mohawk,' Yonnongah, excelled all in their marvellous strength. There was yet another eye stealthily and intently watching every glance and motion, and divining the thoughts of careless hearts. For Tashmu was already, by his evil instinct, the enemy of the young exile.

Nessacus was no laggard in love nor in business. Early on the morning after the feast, he repaired to the lodge of Miahcomo, and the two remained long in conference. The visit was again and again repeated, but still the nature of their consultations did not transpire: only the name of Wahconah was mixed in the gossip concerning them; and it was surmised that the courtship of Yonnongah was perhaps getting in a bad way. The young chief was certainly gaining the favor of the old, and, as the people hoped, undermining the influence of the dread-inspiring Tashmu: love was casting out fear. But the Mohawk was powerful and the priest crafty; and both were busy and dangerous enemies. For the present it was the part of the latter to discover the desires and plans of Nessacus, and bring them into the open day, where his ally could attack them with his might.

There was no great difficulty in effecting the revelation; for there was no longer any purpose or possibility of concealment. And two propositions soon came to be national affairs, for discussion at the tribe's council fires: the first was for the marriage of Nessacus and Wahconah; the second for the migration of the tribe to the west, beyond the reach of the white man's encroachments.

To the first, Miahcomo gave his support; but he clung to the spot where he had ruled so long and so happily.

On the other hand, Yonnongah demanded the maiden for his fourth wife, on the strength of some ancient promise of her father ; and denounced the far-reaching vengeance of his nation, if their tributaries should attempt to migrate beyond their jurisdiction. The amorous old warrior seemed immovably bent upon securing Wahconah for his lodge; alternately employing threats and those sweet promises, of which even an Indian lover can be so profuse — especially in the ripe experience of his fourth courtship. This was no matter of jest with the sorely perplexed father and sachem; for Yonnongah was a man of might in his nation, and would have scant scruples of delicacy in carrying out his threats. All which, Tashmu lost no opportunity for urging upon his dismayed chief, to the great detriment of our hero's suit.

Nessacus soon saw how matters were tending, and took a bold, impetuous man's short way out of the difficulty, by challenging his rival to decide the issue by arms. Yonnongah, who, to do him justice, was as fearless as Nessacus himself, closed at once with the proposal; but the priest was not thus to be balked of his chance for villainy. Signs and potents multiplied marvellously: not a bird could fly, or a fish swim, or a cloud float, but each and all were pregnant with divine prohibition of the proposed duel. The powers above and below combined to forbid it. The thunder muttered the supernal veto; the winds breàthed it; the stars winked it. If one could put perfect faith in Tashmu, never was such a commotion in heaven and "elsewhere," as the coming combat had created. The ordeal of arms was abandoned.

It was only fair, since the gods had issued their fiat against one method of solving the tribe's perplexity, that they should provide another. So thought Tashmu, and exclaimed in the council, " Let the Great Spirit speak ! "

" Let the Great Spirit speak, and we will obey," repeated Miahcomo reverently.

And Yonnongah said: " It is well ! "

It was then proclaimed that Tashmu would, by divination, enquire that night, in the Wizard's Glen, how the will of the Manitou should be ascertained; and a " bad spell " was denounced against all who should disturb his incantations, by going beyond the precincts of the village.

Many predicted ill to Nessacus from this committal of his fate to the hands of a well-known enemy; but none ventured to remonstrate against a decree recognized by law as heaven-inspired: and still more venturesome would it have been to rebel against the edict, if it emanated, as some believed, from authority the reverse of heavenly.

A few rods below the cataract of Wahconah Falls is, or was, a sharp rock which midway divides the stream. At the date of our tradition, the current flowed smoothly and evenly on the two sides of it, and it had often been used, like the flight of birds, the aspect of clouds and other simple objects in nature, to ascertain the will of heaven. Upon the night of Tashmu's supposed divination in the "Wizard's Glen," that respectable minister of religion might, instead, have been seen here, assisted by the stronger arms of his Mohawk friend, tugging away at certain great rocks which lay near the shore, and which they finally contrived to place in the water, so as to impede the current upon one side.

At this same spot, by the river side, a day or two afterwards, the tribe were assembled, and it was announced to them that Manitou had delegated the spirit of the stream to settle their difficulties. In other words — a small canoe, curiously carved with mysterious hieroglyphics, was to be launched midway in the river and, as the current chanced to carry it on one side or the other of the dividing rock, the questions in dispute were to be decided. This was a mode of solving knotty points by no means uncommon, and which, therefore, excited no surprise, except that the priest's chances for trickery seemed to be lessened. Simple souls ! who knew not that what appears the fairest field often affords the best harvest to accomplished knaves !

An "era of good feeling" seemed now to dawn. All parties hastened to adopt this as a "finality." Tashmu, in oily words, wished well to his brother Nessacus; and Nessacus resigned himself unreservedly, to the care of his brother Tashmu. The priest was as much puzzled as pleased at this sudden access of confidence; but it, at least, made his part easy to play.

A solemn feast was now held; and the magical bark, freighted with so many hopes, was then poised in the middle of the stream. Miahcomo was placed in savage state, at a conspicuous point, while Yonnongah and his rival were assigned separate sides of the river.

"Let Manitou speak!" exclaimed the priest; and the sacred canoe, released from its moorings, floated steadily down the stream — inclining now to the right hand, now to the left. All eyes intently followed its course, hardly doubting that, by some charm or other, Tashmu would at last cause it to pass near Yonnongah. You will guess that none counted more confidently on such a result than that worthy himself. Still the bark floated regardlessly on, until it touched the magic rock — hung poised there for a moment, then seemed to incline toward the Mohawk; but, the inconstant current striking it obliquely, it swung slowly round, as upon a pivot, and passed down the stream, by the feet of Nessacus.

" Wagh! the Great Spirit hath spoken, and it is good?" exclaimed Miahcomo; and the people whose

hearts the young chief had somehow gained, shouted
"Ho ! It is good ! "

The priest and his accomplice gazed at each other
in silent astonishment, that Heaven could possibly
decide against arguments of such weight as they had
used. The former, for a moment, began to suspect
that a great God might possibly, in reality, rule in
the affairs of men — making him to bless whom he
would have cursed. But the idea was too mighty
for him, and he recurred, naturally, to a suspicion of
treachery. I need not say, however, that he had his
own reasons for not pressing an immediate investigation. I do not know that it ever occurred to him
that Nessacus might have been a witness to his pious
midnight labors, and improving upon the hint, rendered them abortive.

The assent of all parties was accordingly given to
the proposed marriage; and the time which inter-
vened between the trial and a " lucky day," was to be
filled up with feasting and revelry. The disappear-
ance of Tashmu from the scene added to the hilarity
of the occasion, and all was wild merriment.

But alarming intelligence interrupted their festi-
vities. The terrible Major Talcott, with his soldiers,
had pursued the brave sachem of Quaboag across
the mountains, and slain him with more than two
score of his best warriors, at Mahaiwe, on the banks
of the Housatonic, not thirty miles from the settlement of Miahcomo. Even their temporary security was gone; the mountain barrier was already
passed.

The fugitives from the battle at Mahaiwe came thronging in, but at last brought intelligence that the invaders had returned. A party of them brought, also, the missing Tashmu, whom they accused of having offered to lead the enemy to the refuge of Nessacus. The evidence of his guilt was complete, and the fate of the criminal was not delayed by any unnecessary judicial forms.

Only a want of provisions had prevented Major Tallcott from accepting the wizard's kind offer, and he might now return, at any moment, to profit by it. The best haste was accordingly made in their migration, and before the November winds blew, Nessacus had led them to a home in the west, where they became a great tribe, and flourished for many generations, before they again heard the white man's rifle.

As for Wahconah, the story of her happiness comes down to us, through Indian traditions, faint and far, but sweet as the perfume which a western gale might bring from a far-off prairie.

XX.

MAPLEWOOD AND BERKSHIRE'S BEAUTY.

Strowed with pleasaunce, whose fayre grassy grownd,
Mantled with greene and goodly beautified
With all the ornaments of Flora's pride.— *Fairie Queene.*

It is like a picture in an old story book about France *la belle*, with arching trees in front, a temple and château in the back-ground, and maidens and peasant-girls in all — is the scene at our Young Ladies' Institute, of a pleasant summer twilight. All its light hearted inmates are out in full glee, with circling games and ringing laughter—the truest children of health, content, and innocence.

But all are not in the giddy group: some have separated from it, and, in couples, with arms affectionately inter-twined, are slowly walking down the long paths, pouring into each other's ears the precious secrets of maiden confidence — all the hopes, the dreams, the fears which can find a lodging place in pure hearts. Very precious are those hopes and fears; although neither may ever be realized, yet shall they be a part of life and a part of the woman in all her future. In this life of ours, we pile dream upon dream, effort upon disappointed effort, until the apparent fruitlessness attains to some sort of fruition and reality. There are few things in poetry more beautifully and truthfully said, than these lines of Henry Taylor:

> "The tree
> Sucks kindlier nurture from a soil enriched
> By its own fallen leaves; and man is made
> In heart and spirit from deciduous hopes,
> And things which seem to perish."

Under the vine shaded bowers, or by the sparkling fountain, sits here and there a solitary maiden, with thoughts, perhaps, far away in a happy home; striving to bring to her fancy the family group as it is in the old homestead at the pleasant close of day. She may well be pardoned if, even in this pleasant home of learning, she steals a little while from young companionship, to let the warm but not bitter tears run freely down her cheeks. She will soon rejoin the merry circle, not the least merry there.

I used constantly to attend the examinations, exhibitions and concerts in the pretty chapel. I don't go so often now. The fact is the girls get my poor mind into a fearful muddle with their sines, cosines, sonatas, arias, ballads, tangents, French nasals, subjectives, German gutturals, objectives, and all the rest; till I go home and dream that "Ah, non giunge," is Greek for the segment of a circle, and that some delicious voice is trilling out in notes that reach E alt., $a + b - c = x$! How it did wring my heart one anniversary day — that is the feminine of "commencement"—to see a venerable Doctor in Divinity utterly non-plussed by a saucy Miss whom he had under cross-examination as to her theology. "You did not learn that here!" he exclaimed in astonishment at some startling heterodoxy." "Oh dear, no sir!" was the pert response, "I knew it a long while before I came here!" The good man laughed a polite little laugh; but he looked much less the great divine he certainly was, than his conqueror did the little divinity she very possibly was not.

It was not so in the good old times; but now we are required to believe that beauty and brains are as natural concomitants as strawberries and cream. "Well," as I once heard two astute politicians of opposing schools, agree as they went out from one of Wendell Phillip's lectures on Female Suffrage, "Well, I suppose we must submit to the inevitable." But they did not vote for it, nevertheless.

The grounds of Maplewood are very beautiful. Nothing in our village is more fascinating to the stranger's eye than its lawns, groves and winding avenues, with their rich ornamentation of bowers, fountains, vases, and flowers; and, grouped in the center of all, the classic chapel, the balconied dormitories and the elephantine gymnasium. The latter, by the by, was the grand old church in which Thomas Allen, the Bennington battle-parson, President Allen of Bowdoin College, President Humphrey of Amherst, Rev. Dr. John Todd and other noted divines once preached as pastors, and in which Dr.

Holmes first read his " Ploughboy." Maplewood is also historical in another point; occupying the grounds which in the war of 1812 belonged to the cantonment where thousands of national troops gathered for the campaigns on the northern border; and in which the prisoners of war, taken in those campaigns, were confined: fruitful subjects for the young ladies' themes, as it seems to me. After the war, Professor Chester Dewey, the eminent naturalist, established here a boy's school of high reputation; and, in 1841, Rev. Wellington H. Tyler founded the present institute, and soon gained for it a grand reputation.

The world has found out the picturesque charms, and not unpicturesque comforts, of Maplewood; and now, from June to October it is permitted to invade the sacred precincts with its fashions and pleasures. Even the dance — tabooed in term-time, or masked as "steps and figures" — treads gently the tempting floor between the Corinthian columns of Gymnasium Hall; and serenades sweetly thrill the balconies sacred from such follies for the rest of the year. Maplewood Institute becomes Maplewood Hall: just as you may have read in weird story of enchanted persons who passed their lives alternating between two widely different shapes.

It is all very odd, and it's all very charming; but I did not bring you here on that account. You asked me, sometime ago — yes: I am sure you did — " What is it, after all, that makes this Berkshire so very beautiful ! Now come to the tower of this

gymnasium, which stands practically in the center
of our glorious amphitheatre of hills, and I will
show you.

Yes, the views certainly are comprehensive and
superb: we will attend to them in a moment. But
first listen to Mr. Ruskin, whom I suppose you will
recognize as a competent interpreter of the laws of
beauty.

"That country is always the most beautiful which is made
up of the most curves."

That is the great teacher's absolute dictum directly applicable here : and listen to another, applicable by indirection but clearly pertinent.

"In all beautiful designs of exterior descent, a certain regularity is necessary ; the lines should be graceful, but they
must also balance each other, slope answering to slope, and
statue to statue."

And now observe what may be considered Mr.
Ruskin's application of the first-quoted law. It
forms part of his ideal description or characteriza-
tion of " the picturesque blue country " of England;
that is, a country having a blue distance of mountains:

"Its first and most distinctive peculiarity is its grace ; it is
all undulation and variety of line, one curve passing into
another with the most exquisite softness, rolling away into
faint and far outlines of various depths and decision, yet none
hard or harsh ; and, in all probability, rounded off in the
near ground into massy forms of partially wooded hill,
shaded downward into winding dingles or cliffy ravines, each
form melting imperceptibly into the next, without an edge or
angle. * * * * * * * *

"Every line is voluptuous, floating and wavy in its form; deep, rich and exquisitely soft in its color; drowsy in its effect, like slow, wild music; letting the eye repose upon it, as on a wreath or cloud, without one feature of harshness to hurt, or of contrast to awaken."

I cannot quote the whole description; but you will find it in the Essay upon the Poetry of Architecture; and grand reading the whole book will be for Berkshire summer days.

But look around you now. Mr. Ruskin might have written the quoted passages sitting here upon this tower; and been guilty of nothing worse than almost Pre-Raphaelite precision. The landscape is literally all curves: there is not a straight or ungraceful line in it, except it be of man's making. In what graceful sweeps those mountain walls were thrown up. Into what an endless and infinitely varied succession of interlacing loops and curves, the old glaciers scalloped their crests and indented their ravines. The meanderings of the countless brooks, the serpentine windings of the Housatonic, the wavy and sinuous contours of the lakes, soothe the eye by the multitude of their luxurious curves. The bare morains, the wooded knolls, the mossy maple-groves and clumpy stretches of willow, are all soft and rounded. The shadows which lie under the solitary trees on the hill side, have no harsher shape than that which the fleecy passing cloud casts near them. Nay, Nature, compelling man to her own sweet mood, forces him to bend his railroads and highways gently around the circled bases of her mountains. Even when he makes his

25

ways straight, "Nature soon touches in her picturesque graces," and covers his streets and his habitations with her swelling drapery. Berkshire, as you see it here, surely answers well to Mr. Ruskin's definition of "the most beautiful country."

And as to the demands of the second passage which I have quoted, and to the general requisitions of his essay; I repeat what I have said elsewhere:

" A lovelier landscape one might not desire to see; and when satiated with long luxurious gazing, the spectator seeks to analyze the sources of his delight, all the elements of beauty justify his praise. To the eye the valley here presents the proportions which architects love to give their favorite structures. The symmetry, too, with which point answers to opposing point, exceeds the attainment of art.

" Variety, the most marvellous, but without confusion, forbids the sense to tire. Colors, the richest, softest and most delicate charm the eye, and vary with the ever-changing conditions of the atmosphere. Fertile farms and frequent villages imbue the scene with the warmth of generous life; while, over all, hangs the subdued grandeur which may well have pervaded the souls of the great and good men who have made Berkshire their home from the days of Jonathan Edwards down."

And now, in order that we may get back to the Institute, and, as I am in moderately good humor to-night — and moreover as it seems half-way pertinent to the subject — I will give the young ladies a little sermon, upon a German text, or variation upon a German theme — as they may elect to call it — which I made a long while ago — in fact, before any of them were born. It had a little adventure once, which may improve its flavor. After it had duly gone the rounds of the newspapers, and been consigned, as I supposed, to its long home—the limbo of fugitive verse — it suddenly reappeared; being communicated to a " spiritual " journal by some great departed, through a female medium of Chelsea. It was tricked out in grave clothes of very flowery prose, but I recognized the familiar thing in a moment, and have restored it to its original versiform dress. Still I beg that you will treat it with the regard due to one who has come back from the tomb for your instruction.

SCATTER THE GERMS OF THE BEAUTIFUL.

" Streut eifrig in empfängliche Gemüther,
  Des Guten und des Schönen Samenkörner,
  Sie keimen und erblühen dort zu Baümen,
  Die goldne Paradiesesfrüchte tragen."

———

Scatter the germs of the beautiful;
  By the wayside let them fall,
That the rose may spring by the cottage side,
  And the vine on the garden wall.
Cover the rough and the rude of earth
  With a veil of leaves and flowers,
And strew with the opening bud and cup
  The path of the summer hours.

Scatter the germs of the beautiful
  In the holy shrine of home;
Let the pure and the fair and the graceful there
  In their loveliest luster come:
Leave not a trace of deformity
  In the temple of the heart,
But gather about its hearth, the gems
  Of nature and of art.

Scatter the germs of the beautiful
　In the temples of our God;
The God who starred the uplifted **sky**
　And flowered the trampled sod.
When he built a temple for himself,
　And a home for his priestly race
He reared each arch in symmetry,
　And curved each line in grace.

Scatter the germs of the beautiful
　In the depths of the human soul;
They shall blossom there and bear **thee fruit,**
　While the endless ages roll.
Plant with the pure and beautiful
　This pathway to the tomb,
And the pure and fair about **thy path**
　In Paradise shall **bloom**

XXI.

QUAINT OLD STOCKBRIDGE.

Of silence is the thunder born.— *Gerald Massey*.

So much has been written about the fair old
town of Stockbridge that the tourist finds almost
every rood of its soil already storied ground. Sel-
dom does genius owe so much to its dwelling place,
and still more rarely is the debt so richly paid.
The scenes which have received their fame at the
hand of Bryant or Miss Sedgwick need no new celebration here; nor does the town which has been the
theater of so much curious history, and the home or
birth-place of so many men of intellectual power.
Yet the interest which already attaches to such
places communicates somewhat of its own zest to
whatever may be newly written concerning them.
The world has a singular craving to know more of
that of which it already knows much, rather than
to follow the traveller in "fresh fields and pastures
new." You may have noted that the gaping crowd
always have the readiest and loudest laugh for
their orator's stalest jokes. They are prepared for

the point the moment it comes, while the brightest of them will not seize the gist of the most sparkling original witticism until the opportunity to laugh at it is long past. So, always, the world feels a comfortable security in enjoying that which has before pleased and interested it: that is the advantage that one has in following the path which has already been broken out by genius. And in some such fashion we will explore old Stockbridge.

There are many objects and localities here, the mere mention of which suggests to you a story or a picture, although the story may never have been written, and the picture may never have been born of pencil or camera. "Old Stockbridge on the Plain" is full of these thought-compelling objects. Cradled between hills, enriched by frequent costly villas, picturesque cottages and handsome ornamental grounds, the world-renowned model village of New England lies stretched for a mile along a level surface formed in great part by a singular embankment of the Housatonic, which, although doubtless the work of nature, half deceives you by its regularity into the belief that it is artificial. The river here moves in its most exquisite curves, and is bordered by its richest meadows. Bryant in his Reminiscences of Miss Sedgwick — published in her "Life and Letters" edited by Miss Dewey — thus describes the scene as it first met his eye in the October of 1816, on his first visit to southern Berkshire.

"The woods were in all the glory of autumn, and I well remember, as I passed through Stockbridge, how much I was struck by the beauty of the smooth, green meadows, on the banks of that lovely river which winds near the Sedgwick family mansion: the Housatonic whose gently flowing water seemed tinged with the gold and crimson of the trees that overhung them. I admired no less the contrast between this soft scene, and the steep craggy hills that overlooked it, clothed with their many colored forests."

Wealth and time have, since Mr. Bryant's picture was drawn, done something to adorn the original; nothing to mar its wild beauties or its soft luxuriance. It is still sought by the beauty-seeking artist. Before artist or poet, when the pine and the oak outnumbered the elms, the Mohegan also loved it well.

Through this superb cradle of the hills, extends, on the north side of the river, the noble avenue which, with a few fine subsidiary streets, forms the old village of story. This avenue is nearly, or quite, straight: but the variation in the spacious court yards, with their rich shrubbery, and in the planting of the great trees, wards off any impression of stiffness. The elms, in particular, many of them of more than a century's growth, are among the most magnificent in New England. Miss Sedgwick, in one of her letters, gives the following characteristic instance of her remembrance of them on the other side of the Atlantic:

"One of the cultivated women of England said to me, in a soothing tone, on my expressing admiration of English trees, 'Oh, you will have such in time, when your forests are cut down, and they have room for their limbs to spread.' I smiled and was silent; but, if I saw in vision our graceful, drooping elms, embowering roods of ground, and, as I looked at the stiff, upright English elm, had something of the

Pharisaic 'holier than thou' flit over my mind, I may be forgiven."

Stockbridge Street — I believe that is the recognized name for this grand avenue — is sprinkled all along with spots of historic or romantic interest. At its western extremity is the old burial ground of the Mission Indians; the scene of Bryant's poem, "An Indian at the Burial Place of His Fathers."

> "It is the spot I came to seek —
> My father's ancient burial place
> Ere from these vales, ashamed and **weak,**
> Withdrew our wasted race.
> It is the spot — I know it well —
> Of which our old traditions tell.
>
> For here the upland bank sends out
> A ridge towards the river side ;
> I know the shaggy hills about,
> The meadows smooth and wide —
> The plains that, toward the southern **sky,**
> Fenced east and west by mountains, lie.
>
> A white man, gazing on the scene,
> Would say a lovely spot was here,
> And praise the lawns, so fresh and **green,**
> Between the hills so sheer.
> I like it not — I would the plain
> Lay in its tall old woods again."

This ancient burial-ground has long been sacred from the plow, and now has its proper enclosure and monument. A few rods east of it, on the broad church green, is the monument erected to Jonathan Edwards, who was pastor of the Mission church here, from 1751 to 1757: the period in which he wrote his most celebrated works.

The story of this Indian mission — the most successful in New England — is entirely fascinating, and is worthy of a volume. Indeed Miss Electa F. Jones has compiled an interesting book from its records. But I must pass the story with the briefest allusion. It was established in 1734 at Great Barrington, but was removed in 1735 to Stockbridge where the Indians were collected: the whole township being granted by the General Court for that purpose.

A very few carefully selected white families were admitted to aid in.the civilization and christianizing of the neophytes; which the wise managers conceived could be most readily accomplished by initiating them into the art of agriculture. The Devil — or whatever may be his other and true name — well understands the godly influence of a farmer's life; and why should not they also whose mission and endeavor are to thwart him in his wiles. I hope you recollect how, a great way back in the history of our family, Satan, in the likeness of a serpent, set about the seduction of grand-father Adam by disgusting him with his excellent situation as a gardener, and putting it into his silly head that he could shine in one of the learned professions, or perhaps all: and again, how the same cunning tempter, under the name and style of Mephistophiles, played the deuce with poor, vain Faust's virtue by persuading him that a farmer's life would be degrading to a man of his spirit and genius. The founders of the Stockbridge mission showed that they had the scriptural com-

bination of the serpent's wisdom and the dove's innocence when they employed the plow, as one of the
weapons of their warfare against Hobomoko; whom
I take to be the same old Diabolus under an aboriginal alias. The white families who were sent out
on picket in this semi-spiritual warfare did their
duty faithfully, and the mixed red and white church
which resulted was harmonious and healthful, besides being strikingly picturesque. But the exceptional success of the Stockbridge mission was without
dispute, due to its first pastor, the Rev. John Sergeant, who evinced as wonderful capacity for that
work as his successor did for metaphysics. The
mixed church flourished until 1785, when the Indians
accepted a new home among the Oneidas of New
York: the separation seeming best for both colors.
We will not pry too curiously into the ultimate
cause of that voluntary exile; but the tribe has twice
since migrated from state to state — flying from the
vices or driven by the cupidity of the race which
gave them their religion — and are now in Minnesota,
a moral and intelligent community, but mysteriously
unworthy of American citizenship.

To return to their metaphysical pastor, Rev. Jonathan Edwards: who was installed August 9, 1751;
got cleverly at work just one year later on his long
contemplated "Treatise on the Freedom of the
Will;" in nine months nearly finished the rough
draught of what he originally intended; completed
the work before April, 1753, and published it in
1754. From July, 1754, to January, 1755, he was

incapacited by the chills and fever incident to all new lands, but long since banished from Berkshire. Between the spring of 1755 and the fall of 1757, besides smaller works, he finished his two essays upon "God's end in Creation" and "the Nature of Virtue." The biographers say that he gave to these labors, the leisure left him by his pastoral duties: one would rather infer from the amount of his literary work, that he gave to those duties the leisure left him by his pen; and the steady declension of the mission would tend to the same conclusion. But his correspondence shows that he was "in labors abundant" for the good of his flock; and the decline of religion among them must be traced to other causes than absolute neglect, although the great author could hardly have been so absorbed in the interests of the mission as the simple pastor had been.

People often talk also of the profound quiet and seclusion in the midst of which President Edwards was able to compose his subtile and recondite works. They must have conceived that notion, some dreamy summer afternoon, to the lulling music of rippling fountains and rustling foliage, and after listening perhaps to a less rugged sermon than the mighty Calvinist was wont to preach: there was no room for it in the Stockbridge of 1753–7. The year 1752, following the deceitful peace of Aix-la-Chapelle, was indeed a season of some quiet on the border, and the new pastor seems to have used it to get settled to his work. After that, came troublous times. From Stockbridge northward to the haunts of the fierce and hostile savages of Canada, the forest was broken only by Fort Massachusetts and the soon-interrupted settlements of Lancsboro' and Pittsfield. The Mission Indians were restless, and in the spring of 1753, the homicide of one Wampaumcorse by white men, whom they thought insufficiently punished, roused to fury the still savage passions of the young sannaps. The emissaries of the French and the Canadian Indians took advantage of the ferment. Plots and suspicions of plots, for the destruction of the town, followed. Horrible orgies, stimulated by large supplies of rum from Kinderhook, were kept up for days in the woods west of the village, for the purpose of further inflaming the rage of the young red-men. The pastor, together with the magistrates, was constantly busy, enquiring into the nature and reality of these affairs, and, when they were found genuine, in ascertaining who and how many, of the native Indians were engaged in them; and what real or supposed grievances had disaffected them: striving in every way to sooth the passions and allay the storm which had been raised with sédulous cunning. At the same time Mr. Edwards, by letter after letter, piteously implored the Provincial government to come to the relief of the frontier by a commission of such imposing character that it would salve the wounded pride of the Indians, and also with money, after the aboriginal custom, to wash out the stain of blood.

He succeeded at last. But quiet had hardly descended once more upon the troubled valley when, one August evening in 1754, two Mohegans who had been out on a hunting excursion came flying home with the startling report of burning and massacre they had seen at Dutch Hoosac which had been utterly destroyed by five hundred Canadian Indians, who were doubtless bent southward on the same bloody errand. All was consternation; messengers were sent northward to call in the exposed settlers at Pittsfield and Lanesboro'—southward and eastward, to summon aid: everywhere to alarm the country. This was on Thursday, the 29th of August, and by Saturday night the town was full of armed men. Still, on Sunday afternoon, the fugitives who came in from Pittsfield, on horses sent from Connecticut to bring them off, reported that the woods were full of the enemy, who repeatedly fired upon them, killing one man while the woman on the pillion behind him barely escaped by the aid of the only settler in Lenox. What was worse, they had picked up on the hill above Stockbridge village a fatally wounded child, and on investigation had discovered that, while the people of the town were mostly at church, two Indians had entered the house of one Chamberlain, killed a hired man named Owen, who stoutly resisted them, dashed out the brains of one child, and left another with its head cleft by a tomahawk, near the roadside, where it was picked up.

The terror which ensued all along the border was pitiable beyond description, and it was months before it was allayed. The veteran Colonel, Israel

Williams, declared he had never known its equal.
The large body of the enemy which destroyed
Hoosac proceeded no further south; which raised
the grave suspicion that the murders in Berkshire
were the work of resident Indians. The report that
they were the guilty parties spread all over the
Province, and in New York, till it became the duty of
their mission-pastor to sift the evidence and learn
the truth. He did so, and satisfied of their innocence
manfully become their warm defender; which —
in the excited state of popular prejudice outside
of Berkshire, and among the soldiers sent thither —
was no easy or brief task. But he gave himself
to it, and was also the helpful assistant of the civil
and military authorities as long as he remained in
Stockbridge; for during all that time it was on a
more or less threatened frontier of a province which
was constantly sending through it troops for the
war in New York and Canada.

Such was the secluded leisure and the peaceful
quiet which favored the composition of the Treatise
on the Will, and other great works of Jonathan
Edwards. I think that, if ·we look the grand cata-
logue carefully over, we shall find a considerable
number of illustrious books which were written
without much aid from ease, leisure, quiet seclusion,
intellectual appliances or literary companionship.

The missionary, Sergeant, first lived in a house
which still stands upon " The Hill;" but, before his
death, he built another in the village, which was
purchased by his successor, and is one of the mem-

orable points upon Stockbridge street, through which we are making such slow progress. It is now the property of a classical and philosophical German gentleman, whose dreams are probably not badly disturbed by belief in the calvinistic dogmas of its original owner. Still the house is scrupulously preserved in its pristine condition, and you can still, if you are not very portly, sit in the little closet, about six feet square, which President Edwards called his "study," and in which he did such gigantic intellectual work. It would be scarcely ample for the easy chair and commodious desk which modern students require; and the walls would only hold the scantiest of libraries — so far as number of volumes go.

You may even perhaps sleep in the chamber, where, in the wakeful midnight hours which must often have been his, the most severe, as well as the most subtile, of metaphysicians must have shuddered under the contemplation of his own terrible reasoning, with its awful logical results. For my own part, his doctrines gave me too many cruel hours in my boyhood, for me to desire ever again to come under their dreadful shadow, even in dreams; but, if you like, and have strong nerves, you may sleep comfortably in the mighty reasoner's bedroom: for his home is now but a summer hotel.

On the pleasant church green, between the Indian burial place and the Edwards Homestead, is the site where stood the plain meeting house in which the missionary, Sergeant, first preached the gospel to his parti-colored flock. A handsome tower, surmounted by a chime of fine bells — given to the town by Hon. David Dudley Field in 1878—marks the site. And, as their silvery music rings out daily among the echoing hills, it marks also time's changes since the huge East Indian conch-shell, the gift of the pious people of Boston to the mission, and blown by stout David Nau-nau-nee-ka-nuk in tones which "resounded from center to circumference of the town," summoned the white man and the red, to worship their common Creator in one rude but sufficient temple.

Passing, without comment, some interesting historic localities, and also the handsome marble library building among whose treasures some rich relics of the old times are preserved, we come to bold, beautiful, half rock, half grass-clad, oak-crowned, laurel-wreathed Laurel Hill; upon whose southern verge we shall find the "Sacrifice Rock." Miss Sedgwick thus described both hill and rock in "Hope Leslie," where she first introduced them to fame.

"They [the chief Mononotto, his prisoner, daughter, and warriors] had entered the expanded vale by following the windings of the Housatonic around a hill, conical and easy of ascent, except on the side which overlooked the river, where half way from the base to the summit, it rose, a perpendicular rock, bearing on its beetling front the age of centuries. On every side the hill was garlanded with laurels, now in full and profuse bloom, here and there surmounted by an intervening pine, spruce or hemlock, whose seared winter foliage was fringed with the bright, tender sprouts of spring."

For the story which attaches to the spot, you must look in Miss Sedgwick's enchanting novel. The hill, on which the oak is now, if not the most abounding, the most conspicuous, tree, was given by the Sedgwick family, many years ago, to the Laurel Hill Association, to be forever preserved as a public resort. This famous institution — which holds a place among village improvement societies like that which the Berkshire Agricultural does in in its own class of organizations — owes its existence to this gift, and it has not only managed the donation with rare good taste; but has been a chief instrument in making the village of Stockbridge the perfect thing it is.

Every year the Association here celebrates its anniversary, with many true, pleasant, and often brilliant, words, both of eloquence and poetry. But it seems to me that the grandest gathering the old hill ever saw, was when, after the laying of the first Atlantic cable, the people of Berkshire assembled by thousands to welcome Cyrus W. Field back in triumph to his native town, and the home of his leisure. That looked to me like a triumph worth having; and I still seem to hear the massive sentences — amid whose rugged strength, poetic beauty bloomed like Alpine roses — with which the venerable President Hopkins, Mr. Field's fellow-townsman by birth, congratulated him upon an achievement which he classed, in character and magnitude, with that of "the world seeking Genoese."

The stranger who comes to Stockbridge to dream away some slumberous summer hours, and finds it excellently well adapted to that purpose, may fancy that he has come into that land

> " In which it seemed always afternoon,
>   Around whose coast the languid air did swoon."

But the insight of a little familiarity with the place will teach him better than that. The repose of Stockbridge is the repose of caste, not of lymphatic vulgarity. Its luxurious leisure, so indolently but refreshingly enjoyed, is for the most part either a lasting peace conquered in the hottest life-battle, or the interval of needful rest between two periods of hard work — and probably of hard knocks as well. Frequently it is more even than that; it is a season of quiet preparation: the pause of the lion before the leap; nay, it is the silence before the thunder-peal — they have been forging thunder-bolts here, from the troubled era when Jonathan Edwards hurled his lurid theology upon the world, down to this present peaceful summer of — whom and what, you will learn if you read carefully the New York dailies of next winter.

They have a " Laura's Rest," here in Stockbridge: it is far up a mountain steep. Had it been in Italy, now, they would have placed it in some fountain-lulled, luxurious vale, into which the languid maiden could have lounged listlessly to her siesta. But Stockbridge Lauras must climb before they rest. Is not that the moral of it?

The repose of Stockbridge is the repose of caste.

The same air of quiet, well-bred, refined enjoyment, and of modest, well-bred pride, invests both the place and its people. Of the class of cottages in which it becomes cultivated people of moderate tastes to dwell, Mr. Ruskin says, that in them " we naturally look for an elevation of character, a richness of design and form, which, while the building is kept a cottage, may yet give it an air of cottage aristocracy." We might paraphrase this instruction for application to the class of villages to which Stockbridge belongs. They must be kept villages: to make anything else of them would be to take away their charms. But they must retain also their air of village aristocracy: a widely different thing — be it noted — from the aristocracy of a village. This quiet dignity has been well maintained in the building up of old Stockbridge, both on the plain and on the hills.

The influence which gives tone to society here is that of the old South-Berkshire Federal gentry, which has come down in much perfection of spirit in spite of the constant influx of city folk. I do not say that there have not been vast changes in manners and in personnel, as well as in habits of thought, since gentlemen went staidly about Stockbridge street in cocked hats, knee-breeches and silk stockings; and ladies, who called their hoop-skirts farthingales, played "Washington's March" upon London-made Clementi pianos, that sounded like a modern music-box. But the spirit of the old social life and the old breeding — together with very much

of the old blood — still survives. Whatever modi-
fication it has received has come to it, not from any
absolutely extraneous source, but from those circles
of New York society which originally were chiefly
made up of, or took their color from, men and women,
who went to them from Stockbridge, Great Barrington, Sheffield and Lenox: the Sedgwicks, the
Dwights, the Fields, the Bryants, the Deweys and
others of like character. Stockbridge society, as it
now is, may have been passed, for its refinement,
through a metropolitan crucible; but, if so, it was at
least one of its own making, and its own firing.
Undoubtedly both Stockbridge and Lenox have attractions peculiar to themselves, in their locations
and scenery: but quite as certainly the great mass
of the hundreds who resort to them every summer
are governed in their preference by social considerations. In the case of Stockbridge, there is super-
added in many instances the love and pride of successful descendants of the old village families, who
return to the home of their fathers, to enjoy and
adorn it; while acquaintanceship, and kindred tastes,
draw after them many to whom life here may prove
as familiar as the landscape is strange.

And this brings me back to another historic spot
on historic old Stockbridge street: the mansion in
which was born, and where lived and wrote, one
whose pen has done more to render Berkshire soil
storied and classic ground than even Bryant's; and
the charm of whose presence has drawn here more
men and women of rare mind and character than

have come under any other personal influence: Catherine Maria Sedgwick.

Miss Sedgwick was born here in 1786. Her father, Theodore Sedgwick, served with credit in the Revolutionary war, and won the warm friendship of Gen. Schuyler with whom he had many points in common. He was the leader of the Federal party in Western Massachusetts, which made him the first representative in Congress from Berkshire, the first United States Senator from Western Massachusetts, and a Judge of the Supreme Court of the Commonwealth, in which office he died while attending court at Boston in 1813. He was a man of much self-assertion; and in that queer piece of portraiture, "The Mirror of the Berkshire Bar in 1799," is dashed off as "Duke Ego the Bully." In the "Shays Rebellion" he was a leader against the insurgents who handled him roughly and pillaged his house. He had an intense dread of popular rule, and held that a Jeffersonian Democrat was of necessity an enemy of the country. He conceived that there was a great gulf between him and the people; yet, in such personal relations as he had with them, he was benignant and kind. His family affections were of the warmest and most tender conceivable: a peculiarity which was inherited by all his children, and especially by Catherine. All his sons nevertheless became Democrats, although of the anti-slavery type. His abilities as a statesman, although the admiration of his household and his party, do not appear to have been more than re spectable, and were exceeded by those of at least one of his sons — the second Theodore — who, if he did not, as is probable, first conceive the idea of a railroad across the forbidding hills of Berkshire, was at least its ablest early advocate.

Miss Sedgwick's mother was a daughter of Brigadier General Joseph Dwight, who won distinction as commander of the artillery at the siege of Louisburg, and afterwards settled at Stockbridge, as the trustee of the Mission School. When the county of Berkshire was established in 1761, he became its first chief justice of the Common Pleas, and was thus the head of the provincial magistracy as well as the military officer of the highest rank in Western Massachusetts; so that, when his daughter married young Esquire Sedgwick, she was her husband's superior in social rank, as well by these considerations as perhaps by family connection otherwise; just as Miss Abigail Smith as bride outranked the young lawyer, John Adams, as bridegroom. Lawyers did not stand very high *per se* in the social scale of Provincial times. It required office to lift them.

The Sedgwick family was harmonious and united, and the strong ties of affection and esteem between its members were among the chief influences in forming Catherine's character, and shaping her life. Many of her intense likings and antipathies — not to say loves and hatreds — were based upon the relations of men and things to her brothers or sisters: although it is true that her fine capacity for righteous indignation, and a happy faculty for appreciating

the noble in character and intellect, and the right in
morals, generally prevailed in matters of high consideration.   And if she exceeded measure in her
praises of what she admired, or in her denunciations
of that which she condemned, that is not without
precedent or apology. Miss Sedgwick was a liberal
of the liberals; and I think you will remark, if
you observe closely, that, so far as words go, there
is no intolerance so unsparing as that of liberalism,
in whatever department of life or morals it may
profess itself.

I do not, however, purpose to discuss Miss Sedgwick's life or character at large. All this is merely
passim : being suggested by hearing, the other day,
that "they are getting tired of Sedgwick-worship at
Stockbridge"— which I apprehend can be true only
as to a limited circle: and as to that, I trust, only
refers to disgust with over-weaning and exclusive
consideration, and not to the withholding of high,
grateful and perpetual regard from one to whom it
is grandly due from all Berkshire: one to whom, at
the great Berkshire Jubilee, there was aptly applied
the scriptural commendation: "Many daughters
have done virtuously; but thou excellest them all ! "

Catherine Sedgwick was a thoroughly Berkshire
woman. Her many virtues, her few foibles, were
all of an intensely Berkshire type; although their
manifestation was sometimes in novel directions; as
when she revolted against Calvinism with the same
boldness and vigor which her Calvinistic ancestry
exhibited in their revolt against popery. She loved

the mountain county with all her heart—loved its soil, its scenery, its people; and sought its welfare untiringly. What she has done for its fame, all the world knows; but what she did to make it better worthy of fame is not so often told. Yet the good she effected in mollifying the harsher characteristics of its people, in softening the asperities of their lives and opinions, in doing away uncouthness of manner, in implanting or extending esthetic tastes, and in similar gentle missions, is beyond estimate.

She resented bitterly the coarse exaggerations of Mrs. Trollope, and the impertinent criticisms of Basil Hall regarding Berkshire and American life; but she knew precisely to what extent they were founded in fact, and she did what her pen could to remove that foundation. And her success was great: one instance may illustrate it. Mrs. Trollope declared that all the bigotry in America was concentrated upon the Berkshire Hills. There can be no doubt that she found a great deal of it here. But there is as little doubt that it was reasonably mitigated when Dr. Channing, the great apostle of Unitarianism in America, was able in 1842 to deliver his last public discourse in the Othodox Congregational church at Lenox, and when an eloquent eulogium upon his life and character, written by Miss Sedgwick, was received with profound feeling and universal approval by the great throng of Berkshire people at the Jubilee of 1844. Another incident of the same occasion shows how the clouds of bigotry were at that very time lifting from these hills.

Macready, the tragedian, recited, at the table, Leigh Hunt's well known poem, "Abou Ben Adhem," to express his reciprocity of the feeling which invited him, an Englishman, to participation in this peculiarly local festival. And the committee, of which orthodox Dr. Todd of Pittsfield was chairman, did not hesitate to insert it in the printed record of the occasion, in spite of numerous protests against so doing on the ground that the poem placed love of man before love of God. A good illustration, that, both of what had been, and what was passing away. And in causing it to pass away, Miss Sedgwick's writings had a large share.

So, in other directions, was her influence greatly felt in making the life of Berkshire more genial, as well as in developing the spirit of its natural beauties. The local popularity of her writings inspired a more general taste for elegant literature, and associated it with what every day met the eye and the ear. At a later period came her more direct teachings of the good and beautiful in what are termed the practical virtues. But in the interval she cultivated, for her people, by precept, by illustration, by conspicuous example — by indirect as well as by direct induction — a love for all that is graceful in life.

The home of such a woman is, a spot to attract the feet of all who love what she loved and taught so well. It stands — a plain, square, brown, old fashioned mansion — "somewhat back from the village street," in the center of broad, level, elm-shaded grounds. An old green-house — the first, I believe, in Berkshire — is seen in the court yard; and reminds us that, among Miss Sedgwick's manifold services to this region, was the introduction of new varieties of flowering plants and stimulating the taste for floriculture in many ways. Some of the flowers and shrubs planted by the hand which wrote Hope Leslie were growing rank, and seemingly wild, in the old garden in the rear of the homestead, when I, with a field-meeting party, last visited it.

Behind the mansion, with a broad strip of rich meadow between, winds the blue Housatonic — at this point some six rods wide. If you cast your eye westward, up the river, as you pass it on the Housatonic railroad, you will get a full view of the old place, and, if it be in summer, in one of its pleasantest aspects.

Here Miss Sedgwick passed her youth and the summers of her early womanhood; and under that roof were written Hope Leslie and her other tales of peculiarly local interest. By and bye we will follow her to Lenox. But first we will visit two or three of the spots to which she gave name and fame.

With the exception of Monument Mountain there is no locality in the vicinity of Stockbridge so widely known as

Icy Glen.

I had long impatiently anticipated a visit to this celebrated ravine, before I was able to gratify my longing: and now that I have repeated my exploration more than once, I almost as impatiently wait for the next. It is a deep, narrow gorge cleft in what is known as Little Mountain, a considerable hill a little south of the river, whose meadow-banks here intervene between it and Laurel Hill. The roughly-wooded sides of the glen descend abruptly to the base of the mountain, which it completely penetrates from south to north. The bottom — an eighth of a mile long — is everywhere thickly cumbered by enormous boulders and the great trunks of fallen trees; all mossy and slippery, all piled in huge and wild confusion, so as to leave great cavernous recesses, and an often impeded passage for a brawling brook.

The air is dank, the shade gloomy and the clambering arduous; so that, while attractive to the point of fascination for an occasional visit, the gorge is not a place to invite loitering. But when — after tumbling and stumbling, climbing and sliding, over and under, and among, these devil's playthings of rocks, for a mortal hour — one emerges, just at sunset, upon the mellow rural scene without, he is prepared to welcome ecstatically the smiling landscape.

The glen sometimes presents a scene of grotesquely picturesque delight; when some hundreds of people with flaming torches and pealing music — and many of them in fantastic costumes — traverse the ravine at night in such broken procession as, over that crazy pathway, they can. In that chasm of impervious shade, it matters little what the moon and

stars may be doing on their far away rounds: the
red glare of the torches flashes from the rugged
surface of the rocks to the fair faces of the ladies —
never so fair as in such fitful radiance — and if, in
the uncertain light, some light foot shall slip, the
little shriek which announces the disaster, has an
invariable echo of silvery laughter. I remember
well, one night, when our sole music was merry shouts
and ringing laughter, how the mad glen re-echoed
with a thousand Babelish discordances, until our
senses were almost dazed when we came out into
the moonlight that rested upon the dewy meadow
and mist-wreathed river.

It was a queer looking crowd we were: the gilt
paper rent from the cambric-clad cavaliers and their
glittering tin spear-heads bent with frequent service
as climbing staffs; the spangled fairies in still more
dismal plight; the phantoms with their ghastly
robes in tatters; and all sorts of all possible and impossible characters in sore disorder.

> Yet each and all could soothly swear,
> No merrier troop ere rambled there.

There are four lakes in the township of Stockbridge, but at some little distance from the village:
Mahkeenac, Averic, Mohawk and Agawam. All are
very lovely; but we will, for the present, confine
ourselves to that which they now call Mahkeenac,
on the authority of an old Indian who came back
from the west some years ago to insist that this was
its Mohegan name: meaning The Great Water. But

as Mahkeenac won't work into poetry, nor very well into prose, and as our Indian friend did not seem to be perfect in the grammar of his own language, I prefer the designation given by Miss Sedgwick:

THE STOCKBRIDGE BOWL.

This lake, which lies on the road between Lenox and Stockbridge, one of the most charming in the whole county—is a mile and a half long, and by many is thought to be the most beautiful sheet of water in Massachusetts. I have intimated a moderate dissent from that opinion; but however it may be as to that, there can be no doubt that it is the most famous. Celebrated by the loving pens of Miss Sedgwick and Mrs. Sigourney, it has long had associations which our northern lakes lack.

And, later, another and higher honor, has fallen to it: in that on its northern shore, Nathaniel Hawthorne lived, while he wrote the "House of the Seven Gables," and the "Blithedale Romance." His home was a little red, scantily furnished cottage, loaned him by an admirer. Notwithstanding the success of the Scarlet Letter, his pecuniary means were still slender; but I suspect that the years passed here were among the happiest of his life. I am told that he honored the mountain and the lake with far more of his attention than he bestowed upon his other neighbors. Herman Melville, at Pittsfield, Mr. W. A. Tappan at Lenox, and J. P. R. James, the English novelist, who then resided at Stockbridge, were among his friends; but, for the most part, he lived in great seclusion. One is not much surprised to learn that the creator of Hester Prynne, and Little Pearl, Zenobia and the Pynchons, did not find his highest pleasure in the chit-chat of fashionable circles, or even in literary coteries. Nor need it surprise us that a touch of melancholy, or even at times seeming moroseness, tinged his manner. The knowledge of the soul's anatomist is that which "by suffering entereth in."

But that Mr. Hawthorne's heart was warm and tender, I am well assured by more than one circumstance, which I do not know that I am at liberty to recall here. But there can be no wrong in mentioning the origin, as I have heard it, of the brotherly friendship which existed between him and Herman Melville. As the story was told to me, Mr. Hawthorne was aware that Melville was the author of a very appreciative review of the Scarlet Letter, which appeared in the Literary World, edited by their common friends, the Duyckincks; but this very knowledge, perhaps, kept two very sensitive men shy of each other, although thrown into company. But one day it chanced that when they were out on a pic-nic excursion, the two were compelled by a thunder-shower to take shelter in a narrow recess of the rocks of Monument Mountain. Two hours of this enforced intercourse settled the matter. They learned so much of each other's character, and found that they held so much of thought, feeling and opinion in common, that the most intimate friendship for the future was inevitable.

I have heard of another odd interview with Hawthorne. A lady from a distant state had expressed an intense desire to meet the great author, and it was arranged that her wish should be gratified at a Pittsfield dinner table; she not at all anticipating that he would know her feeling. But it seems that some friend, with a turn for teasing, apprised him of it; and as they were sitting down at the board opposite to each other, an expressive glance from the tell-tale made known to the lady that her secret had been exposed. The result was that two pairs of remarkably fine eyes were very unquiet and that two uneasy people had their dinners spoiled. But I dare say that the appearance of the wine restored ease.

They are beginning to appreciate the honor conferred upon the county by Mr. Hawthorne's residence in it; and now have treasured up in the historical museum of the Athenæum at Pittsfield, the desk upon which he wrote the House of the Seven Gables, The Blithedale Romance, and probably other works. It is a plain, solid, handsome piece of mahagony furniture, with an abundance of drawers, and seems exceedingly well adapted to novelist's work. It has a host of visitors.

But we have been drawn far away from Stockbridge and its lakes. Let us return, and sing in the praise of Mahkeenac, if you still insist upon calling it by the name which appears upon the map, the verses composed in its honor by Mrs. Lydia H Sigourney, and read at the Berkshire Jubilee:

The Stockbridge Bowl.

The Stockbridge Bowl !   Hast ever seen
   How sweetly pure and bright,
Its foot of stone and rim of green
   Attract the traveller's sight ?
High set among the breezy hills
   Where spotless marble glows,
It takes the tribute of the rills
   Distilled from mountain snows.

You've seen, perchance, the classic vase
   At Adrian's villa found,
The grape-vines that its handles chase
   And twine its rim around.
But thousands such as that which boasts
   The Roman's name to keep,
Might in this Stockbridge bowl be lost
   Like pebbles in the deep.

It yields no sparkling draughts of fire
   To mock the madden'd brain,
As that which warmed Anacreon's lyre
   Amid the Teian plain —
But freely, with a right good will
   Imparts its fountain store,
Whose heaven replenished crystal still
   Can wearied toil restore.

The Indian hunter knew its power,
   And oft its praises spoke,
Long ere the white man's stranger plow
   These western vall ys broke.
The panting deer that, wild with pain,
   From his pursuers stole,
Inhaled new life to every vein
   From this same Stockbridge bowl.

And many a son of Berkshire skies,
　　Those men of noble birth,
Though now perchance their roof may rise
　　In far or foreign earth,
Shall on this well-remembered vase
　　With thrilling bosom gaze,
And o'er its mirrored surface trace
　　The joys of earlier days.

But one that with a spirit glance
　　That moved her country's heart,
And ba le from dim oblivious trance
　　Poor Magawaska start,
Hath won a fame whose blossoms rare
　　Shall fear no blighting sky,
Whose lustrous leaf be fresh and fair
　　When Stockbridge Bowl is dry.

XXII.

MAHAIWE.

"Here I have scaped the city's stifling heat,
  Its horrid sounds and its polluted air;
And, where the season's milder fervors beat,
  And gales, that sweep the forest-borders, bear
The song of bird and sound of running stream,
  Am come awhile to wander and to dream,

Ay, flame thy fiercest, sun! thou canst not wake,
  In this pure air, the plague that walks unseen.
The maize-leaf and the maple bough but take,
  From thy strong heats, a deeper, glossier green.
The mountain wind, that faints not in thy ray,
  Sweeps the blue steams of pestilence away."—

Bryant.

I think I will escort you, this brilliant morning, to a region worthy of the goldenest sunlight that ever came from Heaven's alchemy — down that Washington Street of railroads, the tortuous Housatonic, to Great Barrington, the greatly beautiful early home and foster-mother of Bryant's genius.

Henry Ward Beecher extols without measure the scenery which borders the Housatonic railroad, particularly between Bridgeport and Lenox — being careful to exclude from his commendation the little

four miles above what was his home. And it is worthy of ecstatic admiration. Still I think it clearly surpassed by that through which the Boston and Albany road passes between the Connecticut and Hudson rivers; especially in the magnificent gorges between Chester and Washington. I know of no route, rail or highway, which excels this; except possibly the famous old Stage road over the Hoosac Mountain between Deerfield and North Adams; the same which filled Henry Clay with such amazed delight, when he passed over it fifty years ago on his visit to Berkshire and his friend Henry Shaw.

Between Pittsfield and Westfield, the Boston and Albany Railroad follows substantially the old Indian trail — Unkamet's Path. Early surveyors and government messengers made great use of it; and tradition asserts that one or two adventurous and spirited women traversed it. The faithful old guide, from whom it took its name, lived near the railroad crossing of the east branch of the Housatonic river in Pittsfield, and has left it also attached to a brook and a meadow in that vicinity, where a street has also received the same designation.

But the Boston and Albany railroad will never take us to Great Barrington. We might, however, drive thither — twenty-one miles — through Lenox and Stockbridge. If we did so we should find scenery rivalling that on either of the routes which I have mentioned, here or elsewhere. It is certainly richer in the tokens of wealth, as well as in historical and personal associations. A host of notable

critics firmly hold that it is easily first of all in
Berkshire. But, that we may sooner reach Great
Barrington, where we shall find natural beauty to
satiety, we will adhere to our purpose of going by
the Housatonic railroad, which, for its many ex-
cellencies, is a sort of pet, here.

We might, however, pause a long while, on our
way, at the fine town of Lee, the widely famed seat
of the paper manufacture, and also of the great
quarries of white marble from which the grand extension of the Capitol at Washington was built, as
well as many other noted structures. The marble
of Berkshire extends through the whole length of
the county, and some of it, particularly that of Lee,
Sheffield, North Adams, and West Stockbridge, is in
the highest repute as building-stone. The remarkable dark blue compact limestone of Great Barrington,
of which the uniquely beautiful Athenæum at
Pittsfield is built, is not properly a marble. You
may see it in place at Mount Petra, whose picturesque
little rocky knoll, near the main street of Great
Barrington, Dr. Clarkson T. Collins has set apart
for the pleasure of the public. And a nice place it
is from which to obtain a view of the grand old
street and other pleasant prospects. But we are not
yet at Great Barrington.

The marble quarries of Lee, interesting to every
intelligent visitor, afford a most inviting field to the
mineralogist, although, I believe, the old deposit of
the much sought bladed tremolite is exhausted.

Fern Cliff, which holds the place in Lee which

Laurel Hill does in Stockbridge, is a handsome eminence near the village. I passed a pleasant May morning there once, and gathered a fine collection of large and rare mosses. But the pride of Lee's romantic scenery is Laurel Lake, a much prized sheet of water, nearly a mile long, which lies on the border of Lenox, a mile and a half from Lee Park, and at the head of a precipitous mountain-stream thickly studded with busy paper-mills. It is proof of the profusion of splendid scenery in Berkshire that it is only through a recent introduction by the late Rev. Dr. Gale, that the merits of this fine lake with its pleasant surroundings have obtained general recognition. It seems not likely now to fall into neglect again.

A great deal of the romance of reality might be wrought out, not only from the secluded haunts of Lee, but from its peculiar material resources and industries; and that without any exhaustive brainwork. But it occurs to me at this moment that we are bound for Great Barrington, where we shall find romance ready made, to our hands: and so much of it that we must confine ourselves chiefly to that which arises from the life and work there of Berkshire's great poet. Berkshire's poet: for if Mr. Bryant's birthplace was not in the county of Berkshire, it was on the Berkshire Hills — a region whose bounds were fixed by a wiser and mightier power than that which defines county lines. It was in a Berkshire college that he was educated, so far as such minds receive their education from colleges; and it was in one of the loveliest of Berkshire towns that he passed his choicest years — those in which some of his best work was done, and during which his fame became national, or more: the culminating years of "a youth sublime."

I have already quoted from his own account of his introduction in 1816 — when he removed to Great Barrington — to that fair region with which his name was forever to be inseparably connected, and over which he has thrown an imperishable charm.

It cannot be said that the scenery of Southern Berkshire inspired Mr. Bryant with that intense love of nature which informs the best of his poems. *That* had already been awakened by the scenes among which his boyhood was passed, and strengthened by the majestic hills and romantic valleys by which Williams College is surrounded. *These* had been the nurses of his infant thought, and the tutors of his youthful imagination: they, with Shakespeare, Spenser and Milton for text-books — nay, with Homer and Virgil also.

But Southern Berkshire furnished the already ripened poet of nature with fitting themes in abundance, and fitting accessories of tradition for his faithful portraiture of landscape: the Mohegan at the burial place of his father; the maiden of Monument Mountain; the murdered traveller of the lonely glen between old and West Stockbridge.

It may be pleasant, as well, for youthful lovers who wander under the noble elms which give so fine a charm to Great Barrington streets, or on the

willow-shaded brink of the Housatonic, the Green
river or other of the frequent streams, to remember
that here was the scene of the poet's wooing; that,
perhaps under the very branches which over-hang
them, or on the same verdant bank where they sit
by the brook-side, William Cullen Bryant first read
from the manuscript, to her who was afterwards his
bride, some of those pleasant poems they now delight
to read together there. Does it not, my young
friends, add to your own joy in so reading Mr.
Bryant's verses, to think that he may have thus
read them on this very spot more than fifty years
ago ?

During Mr. Bryant's residence in Great Barrington — from 1816 to 1825 — only a small portion of
his time, comparatively, was given to letters. He
took a creditable part in the affairs of the town, of
which he was clerk from 1820 to 1825. In 1818 he
delivered the address at the first anniversary of the
town Bible Society. He was an ardent politician
of the Federal school, and in the old files of the
county newspapers, we often find his name as secre-
tary or committeeman of party meetings. He was
an active, learned and rather fiery young lawyer,
with more practice than usually fell to the lot of
men of his age at that period. He might have become distinguished, could he have overcome his
disgust with a profession in which — in his day
much more than at present — law was not synony-
mous with justice. Finally he struck upon an experience which, if the well supported tradition of

the Berkshire bar can be trusted, was so intolerable
that he relinquished practice altogether. The case —
"Grotius Bloss *vs.* Augustus Tobey of Alford" is
recorded in the 2d volume of "Pickering's Reports."
Mr. Bryant lost his case through a mere technical
omission in his declaration which did not in the
slightest obscure its meaning. That his client's
cause was just, the court admitted practically; Chief
Justice Parsons prefacing the adverse decision by
remarking: "It is with great regret, and not without much labor and research to avoid this result,
that we are obliged to arrest judgment."

Mr. Bryant's just indignation against an adminis-
tration of the law which compelled its servants to
do acknowledged wrong to those who sought justice
in its highest state tribunal made him ready to
seek a more congenial pursuit at the first opportunity.

The famous first cattle-show of the Berkshire
Agricultural Society at Pittsfield occurred during
his junior year in Williams College, and strongly
impressed his susceptible youth. He continued the
warm friend of the institution, and wrote two odes
for its anniversaries. One, which was sung in 1820,
is included in his published poems, and commences
with the lines,

> " Far back in the ages
> The plough with wreaths was crowned."

The second, sung in 1823, seems equally worthy
of preservation, and is as follows:

> Since last our vales these rites admir'd,
> Another year has come and flown,

But where her rosy steps retir'd,
   Has left her gifts profusely strown.

No killing frost on germ or flower,
   To blast the hopes of spring, was nigh;
No wrath condens'd the ceaseless shower,
   Or seal'd the fountains of the sky.

But kindly suns and gentle rains,
   And liberal dews and airs of health,
Rear'd the large harvests of the plains,
   And nursed the meadow's fragrant wealth.

As if the indulgent power who laid,
   On man the great command to toil,
Well-pleased to see that law obeyed,
   Had touched, in love, the teeming soil.

And here, while autumn wanders pale
   Beneath the fading forest shade,
Gather'd from many a height and vale,
   The bounties of the year are laid,

Here toil, whom oft the setting sun
   Has seen at his protracted task,
Demands the palm his patience won,
   And art has come his wreath to ask.

Well may the hymn of victory flow,
   And mingle with the voice of mirth,
While here are spread the spoils that show
   Our triumphs o'er reluctant earth.

Of the spots in Berkshire to which Bryant's pen
has given fame, the most noted is Monument Mountain, which rises near the highway between Great
Barrington and Stockbridge; being within the former town, but considerably nearer to the village in

the latter. No description of it could be more precise than that given in Bryant's poem :

     " There is a precipice
That seems a fragment of some mighty wall,
Built by the hand that fashioned the old world
To separate its nations, and thrown down
When the flood drowned them. To the north, a path
Conducts you up the narrow battlement.
Steep is the western side, shaggy and wild
With mossy trees, and pinnacles of flint,
And many a hanging crag. But, to the east,
Sheer to the vale, go down the bare old cliffs.—
Huge pillars that in middle heaven upbear
Their weather-beaten capitals, here dark
With the thick moss of centuries, and there
Of chalky whiteness where the thunderbolt hath splintered
  them."

The mountain has an elevation of five hundred feet above Stockbridge Plain, or twelve hundred and sixty above the sea level. The cliffs rise perhaps four hundred and fifty feet, perpendicularly or a little beetling at the top. Their face is slightly curved inward and their height gradually decreases to the south. At their foot immense piles of angular flinty fragments, which have fallen in the course of ages, are heaped up in confusion; and a detached pinnacle, known as the Pulpit Rock, together with a few other grotesquely shaped crags, relieve the uniformity of the grey old wall. The pulpit is after the tall old fashioned type which made the attentive congregation look like a crowd at a balloon ascension. Cliff and fragment, and isolated crag are all formed of compact granular quartz — technically " quartzite "—the same mineral which, further north when disintegrated by some process known only to nature, becomes the silicious sand of commerce. Rumor of this fact had reached the glass-makers, and I was sent to see what could be made of it: so that my first visit to this old poetic mountain was not for the most poetic of purposes. No matter: it is quite easy to weave a little sentiment into any excursion to a place like this.

The precipice extends northward to about the middle of the mountain, where it disappears, although the hillside continues very abrupt. The geological character of the rock also changes, if my slight observations were correct, to mica-schist. At the junction rises the path mentioned in the poem, and by which I reached the summit. In its track, I found some pretty crystals of black tourmaline. Climbing this ascent, which is quite difficult enough to give a zest to it, I bent my head dizzily over the abyss.

> " It *is* a fearful thing
> To stand upon the beetling verge, and see
> Where storm and lightning, from that huge gray wall,
> Have tumbled down vast blocks, and at the base
> Dashed them in fragments ; and to lay thine ear
> Over the dizzy depth, and hear the sound
> Of winds, that struggle with the woods below,
> Come up like ocean murmurs."

The summit commands a noble prospect :

> " The scene
> Is lovely round ; a beautiful river there
> Wanders amid the fresh and fertile meads,

> Tho paradise he mado unto himself,
> Mining the soil for ages.   On each side
> The fields swell upward to the hills ; beyond,
> Above the hills, in tho blue distance, rise
> The mighty columns with which earth props heaven."

The scene is fair to look upon, but I confess, that, after the mountain and its immediate surroundings, I was most interested in peering down to its base at a black speck, which my guide assured me was G. P. R. James, the novelist, who then thought of building a residence there, and was at that moment engaged in investigations as to the probabilities of clarifying a muddy pond.   When I used, in school-time, to steal the moments due to drier studies to peruse, in the old "National Reader," the poem of Monument Mountain, with

> "Its sad tradition of unhappy love,
>   And sorrows borne and ended long ago,"

I little dreamed that I should ever stand at its base in the glorious light of a Berkshire morning to compute the marketable value of its "bare old cliffs;" and quite as little that I should look down from its summit upon the wizard — a wizard still, though years brought disenchantment to me — whose creations seemed to my boyhood, quite as marvelous as those of Walter Scott.   Ah, happy period of childhood's indiscriminating enjoyment: what an appetite I must have had !

The pile of loose stones which led to Bryant's poem, and gave name to the mountain, was destroyed in wantonness or idle curiosity many years ago.   I

have been told that the pious contributions of visitors — who adopt the Indian custom of casting a
stone upon it as they pass — have restored it. I did
not see it; for my guide, a very literal person, insisted that there was no monument, nor ever had
been. In fact the hard-headed Yankee had very
little respect for the romancings of Kate Sedgwick
and Cullen Bryant, as he somewhat familiarly de-
signated two distinguished personages.

Green River, which Mr. Bryant seems to have
taken to his heart with the fullness of poetic affection, has its fountain among the rocky hills of Aus-
terlitz, New York; passes through the fine pastoral
country of Alford and Egremont, and across the richer
agricultural section of Great Barrington, until it
joins the Housatonie near the Sheffield border. It
was a favorite stream with the Mohegans. The
green tint from which it takes its name is communicated by a peculiar clay of which some portion of
its banks is composed. Mr. Bryant intimates that
it was the favorite haunt of his leisure:

> " When breezes are soft and skies are fair,
>   I steal an hour from study and care,
>   And hie me away to the woodland scene,
>   Where wanders the stream with waters of **green,**
>   As if the bright fringe of herbs on its brink
>   Had given their stain to the wave they drink ;
>   And they whose meadows it murmurs through
>   Have named the stream from its own fair hue."
>
> ' Yet pure its waters — its shallows are bright
>   With colored pebbles and sparkles of light,
>   And clear the depths where its eddies play,

And dimples deepen and whirl away,
And the plane-tree's speckled arms o'er-shoot
The swifter current that mines its root,
Through whose shifting leaves, as you walk the hill,
The quivering glimmer of sun and rill
With a sudden flash on the eye is thrown,
Like the ray that streams from the diamond **stone.**
Oh, loveliest there the spring days come,
With blossoms, and birds, and wild-bee's **hum ;**
The flowers of summer are fairest there,
And freshest the breath of the summer air ;
And sweetest the golden autumn day
In silence and sunshine glides away."

" Yet, fair as thou art, thou shunnest to **glide,**
Beautiful stream ! by the village side ;
But windest away from haunts of men,
To quiet valley and shaded glen ;
And forest, and meadow, and slope of hill,
Around thee, are lonely, and lovely, and **still.**
Lonely — save when, by thy rippling tides,
From thicket to thicket the angler glides ;
Or the simpler comes, with basket and **book,**
For herbs of power on thy banks to look ;
Or, haply, some idle dreamer, like me,
To wander and muse, and gaze on thee.
Still — save the chirp of birds that **feed**
On the river-cherry, and seedy reed,
And thy own wild music gushing out
With mellow murmur and fairy shout,
From dawn to the blush of another day,
Like traveller singing along its way."

There ! I positively will not disturb that **exquisite**
picture.

You will find much of Mr. Bryant's poetry — not
only of his earlier but of his later years, colored by

the scenes among which he lived while a lawyer at Great Barrington; and one finds it an interesting and agreeable study to wander through those scenes, with his volume in hand, and compare the one with the other. I am sure you cannot but enjoy taking with him " A Walk at Sunset; " deciphering by the aid of book or memory, the Inscription at the Entrance of a Wood; tracing " The Rivulet; " gathering " The Yellow Violet " and the Fringed Gentian, and joining in all his rural pleasures.

In dwelling thus upon the scenes in Great Barrington which have been illustrated by the genius of Bryant, I do not mean to intimate that there are none of merit which he left unsung. The village, which since his day has grown to a large and handsome town, has characteristic charms beside those of its noted elms, in the graceful irregularity of its streets, in some fine and tasteful buildings, and a general mingling of the pleasant features of town and country. There are other gentle streams to wander by, besides Green River, and majestic hills besides Monument Mountain.

. Great Barrington is also an old historic town. It was the north parish of Sheffield, the first settled town in the county, and when incorporated it was the first shire town of Berkshire. The Indian mission was first established here. Here, first in Massachusetts, the King's Courts were over-thrown by the people in May 1774, with such results of kindling feeling that General Gage wrote home to his government, " A flame has sprung up at the extremity of the Province "— "The popular rage is very high in Berkshire, and makes its way rapidly to the rest." Here also the greatly erring but also greatly wronged Shays rebels obstructed the Courts of Commonwealth; and on the borders of the town they met their final defeat.

XXIII.

TOWN, COLLEGE AND SPA.

Ages and climes remote to thee impart
What charms in genius and refines in art;
Thee in whose hands the keys of science **dwell,**
The pensive portress of her holy cell;
Whose constant vigils chase the chilling **damp**
Oblivion steals upon her vestal lamp.
* * * * * * * * * * * * * *
They in their glorious course, the guides of **youth,**
Whose language breathed the eloquence of **truth;**
Whose life, beyond preceptive wisdom, taught
The great in conduct and the pure in thought. —

Pleasures of Memory.

My first visit to Williamstown was made in the
company of Samuel Bowles. It was in the days
when Mr. Bowles did some of the best reporting for
his own journal personally; and he was on his way
to the commencement at Williams College, an institution to which he gave love and honor such as
he did not scatter wastefully, and whose faculty
well appreciated his friendship. I was bound upon
a similar errand, and intended to go by railroad and
stage through North Adams, but Mr. Bowles would
not hear of that route; and insisted upon a drive up
the valleys of Lanesboro' and Williamstown, and

29

over the ridge of hills at New Ashford, which he
pronounced the most enjoyable ride possible. I
was glad enough to accede to the proposal, and we
started at the early dawn of the most delicious of
summer mornings.

The drive was all that had been promised of it.
My companion, relieved for a time from his exhaustive journalistic work, was in the height of
life and spirits, and descanted upon the scenes
through which we passed with all that enthusiasm
and those quick perceptive powers which, in after
days, rendered his stories of travel across the continent so wonderfully attractive: and perhaps with
even more *abandon*, and freshness of feeling. He
seemed all alive with the spirit of the morning.
Nothing escaped his glance, from the mist-wreaths
on the surface of Pontoosuc lake and the butterflies that fluttered about our path, to the contours
of the Greylock group which seemed to change inces-
santly as we approached and rode along its base.
After these many years, I recall perfectly the kindling
of his fine eye, and the rich tone of his voice, as he
pointed out one striking picture after another. He
fairly joyed in the morning glories of the lake; but
reserved his most ecstatic praises for the lovely
valley in which lies the village of South Williamstown.

By the road-side in the north part of Lanesboro' is
a little grove, long familiar to myself and other lovers
of pic-nic. The river murmurs gently through a
green and level space; there are grey old rocks and

mossy trees; and, when we passed it, a broken table, a dismantled bower, and other relics of recent revelry, elicited from Mr. Bowles quaint and genial comment that showed his hearty sympathy in the simple pleasures they gave token of. Again, he drew rein long, to admire the nice grouping of bosky woods and single trees on a sunny hill-side. But to tell of half the pleasant things of that July morning ride would tire you in the reading, fleetly as they passed in the riding.

Mr. Bowles's fondness for this region was further exemplified the next morning when, in full view of the laborious day before us, he was up at day-break for a two mile walk to the Sand-Springs — the present site of Greylock Hall. I have a theory that, to fully enjoy sunrise views, they should not be taken in too quick succession, and I kept to my theory and my bed. But the vigorous early-riser came back at breakfast-time all aglow with such descriptive eloquence that to this day I have not for-given myself that ill-timed indolence.

In some of his despondent moments of discourage-ment or disgust with political affairs in those years, Mr. Bowles often spoke of relinquishing his interest in a daily newspaper, and retiring to the charge of a weekly journal in Berkshire. Whether he ever seriously contemplated so great a change, or it was a mere passing fancy, I do not know; but I hear that he gave much of his most arduous and most loving work to the weekly edition of his own paper: and he certainly had a warm

liking for Berkshire. Angels perhaps, better than
men, may judge whether it would have been well
for him to yield to that mood of longing for a quiet
life, rather than, by the tremendous intellectual
pressure which he finally chose, to condense the
alloted three-score-years-and-ten of man's growth
and effort into little more than fifty of measured
time. For him, however, it may be that no other
result was possible than that which came: no other
choice than that he made.

The impression of Williamstown gained under
the pleasant circumstances which attended my first
visit, was of an old-fashioned, quiet, uniquely beautiful village. It had at that time little to boast in the
way of architecture; but, I do not know how it is,
it seems to me that, make your college edifices as
ugly as you can — and the old architects had immense capacities in that direction — still, if you
plant them, with reasonable surroundings of fine
trees in a pretty New England town, they soon
acquire a classic and tranquil air which goes far to
mollify the exasperating effect of brick-red and
right-angles upon sensitive nerves. I remember
that the tumble-down, cheap, old wooden chapel of a
certain salt-water down-east college had an awe-
inspiring aspect in my boyish eyes, which I fail to
find intensified by the granite and gothic piles which
have supplanted it: and I have a similar experience
with Williamstown in its new architectural estate.

Nevertheless the improvements both in town and
college, have been made with such unexceptionable

good taste that the result has been a genuine growth in beauty, until Williamstown has come to rival Stockbridge as the model village of New England. Its appearance from within is peculiar — unique so far as I have knowledge — which comes chiefly from a singular and very artistic unity of arrangement. It is in effect a broad park, of perhaps a mile in length, subdivided into shapely plots and wide un-fenced court-yards of verdant turf, with shaded avenues between: and all compassed within a rim of college edifices, churches, hotels, private dwellings and business structures; while, on the moderate elevations to which the ground rises towards the western extremity, a church, two or three college buildings, and a soldier's monument surmounted by a statue, stand out in bold relief. There are some pieces of exceedingly creditable and pleasing — even of striking — architecture. The scrupulous care with which the village society, modelled on the Laurel Hill Association, keeps every thing in exact order, as well as the perfection of grass, flower and foliage everywhere maintained, increase the attractiveness of the scene. But the characterizing element is the unity and harmony of plan which seems to embrace at once town and college, and to have its counterpart in the life of those who dwell in that charmed circle.

Outside of itself, Williamstown has another peculiarity of landscape, as a college town, in the near neighborhood of Greylock and other mighty hills. Our down-east friends will have their badinage at

"Fresh-water colleges." But what to the student is the ocean, whose ordinary acquaintance he makes through the fragrant medium of the Back-Bay — his more familiar intercourse being confined to sea sickness on brief holiday excursions — what, for a neighbor to the languid student, is this moody old sea, oftenest making his august presence known by the heralding of east winds and slimy odors, compared with the mighty mountain shapes, which greet his eye with every rising sun, and send him health and vigor in every breeze.

Thoreau recognized the strength of the hills; writing, thus, from the top of the tower which once capped Greylock, but was accidentally burned:

"This observatory is a building of considerable size, erected by the students of Williams College, whose buildings may be seen by day-light, gleaming far down the valley. It would really be no small advantage, if every college were thus located at the base of a mountain; as good at least as one well-endowed professorship. It were as well to be educated in the shadow of a mountain as in more classic shades. Some will remember no doubt, not only that they went to the college, but that they went to the mountain. Every visit to its summit would, as it were, generalize the particular information gained below, and subject it to more catholic tests."

In the Hoosac Valley — of which the Williamstown is an expansion — the mountains assume a very different expression from that which they wear in the central portions of the great Berkshire basin: they make one feel that they *are* mountains, and not — as at Pittsfield, for instance — mere graceful lines in the landscape. Everywhere in this region one gets an inadequate idea of the magnitude of its mountainous character, failing to realize that in Lanesboro' and Pittsfield, he stands upon the summit of a solid mass eleven hundred feet high, whose base extends from the sound to the St. Lawrence, and from the Connecticut to the Hudson: so that nearly one-half the real altitude is lost before the base of the mountains as here visible is reached. The apparent height of the mountains, as seen from Central Berkshire, is further diminished by another circumstance. The ranges upon the east and west are continuous ridges, cleft here and there into domes and peaks, with indentations between, comparatively so slight as to leave the crest not serrated, but in wavy or scalloped relief against the sky.

The valleys which separate the different hills are for the most part, properly, only what are known in English and Scotch landscape, as "Hopes:" that is valleys open only at one end. They give the hills grace rather than grandeur. If the Hoosac and Taconic ranges were sharply divided to their bases by distinct transverse valleys, they would convey an impression of vastly greater magnitude than they now do, although in reality it would be less.

These weakening influences do not exist to the same extent in the more northern valley. There the mountains press closer upon the villages; the surface of the great swell of land which underlies them is four hundred feet lower than its maximum; and the contours of the mountains are more sharp and distinct. The result is a great gain in grandeur, whatever may be lost in other regards. ' The landscape is more imposing; you feel the might of Greylock, and the magnitude of the neighboring summits, here at Williamstown, at Adams and North Adams, as you do not feel them in the more open valley at the south.

Notwithstanding the distance which separates them, Williamstown seems specially affiliated with Stockbridge, of the towns in the county, by social influences which date very far back. Colonel Ephraim Williams, the founder of the college, was the son of Col. Ephraim Williams, one of the four farmers sent to Stockbridge to aid in civilizing the Indians; and was himself for a time a resident there. Some of the most distinguished early trustees lived in the same town. The long-time President — the massive minded Mark Hopkins — was born in Stockbridge; and so was his gentle brother, Professor Albert Hopkins — a gentle spirit his, however obscured to any by severity of aspect and manner — to whose fine tastes and elegant scholarship the college owes as much in one direction as it does to the sterner qualities of the great President in another. Nathan Jackson, John Z. Goodrich, David Dudley and Cyrus W. Field, and other of the late liberal benefactors and zealous friends of the college were Stockbridge men, although Mr. Jackson was a native of Tyringham, and Mr. Goodrich of Richmond. '

Through these and other causes, the influence of the older, upon the younger town — perhaps I should

say their reciprocal influence — has been powerful.
Indeed I am not sure but that, if the spirits of
Parsons West and Field should come back to Berkshire for a summer visit they would find themselves
quite as much at home in Williamstown as on Stockbridge street. At all events the sort of people most
attracted to the college town for rest and recreation,
are grand and reverend seigniors of the old Stockbridge gentry-class, who can make merry on mountain excursions with college professors, or lend their
aid, if need be, in the village Sunday school and
weekly conference meetings. There are among
them, I doubt not, gentlemen who find a real luxury
in being wakened by the college bell to the con-
ciousness that they are no longer subject to its
brazen summons; some of them having the added
delight that their sons are still *bond-knechts* of
learning: which does not mean, young gentlemen,
that there is anything as yet especially knightly
about you — although there may be — but that, for
four years, you are the bound servants of a noble
mistress, of whom you may, when freed by your
baccalaureate, become, if you will, gallant and devoted followers — and who, whether you will it or
not, will not wholly forsake you to your life's end,
nor, as I reverently believe, even then.

The grave and reverend seigniors, permanently
or transiently resident here, give tone to Williamstown life the year round. To be sure, their sons
and daughters are not, as a rule, so grave and reverend: but if you meet Ralph Royster Doister and

Miss Flora McFlimsey sauntering up the street—
she dangling her parasol and giving back the saucy
sun, glances as good as he sends; he twirling his
tortoise shell cane and sheltering the delicate blossoms of his complexion with a blue veil — you may
set these interesting young persons down in your
note book as, for certain, erratics from some other
summer social sphere.

Thus much, of the old college town. The scene
changes two miles to the north; where a fashionable
watering place has within a few years started up
around some mineral springs which have long had
local repute. The analysis of the waters gives a
result similar to that of Lebanon Springs; but some
old farmers of the neighborhood, who were kind
enough to be my guides, on a visit "out of season,"
told wonderful stories of old-time cures of rheuma-
tism and cutaneous disorders; which would indicate
a resemblance to the Missisquoi Springs on the
shore of Lake Champlain. To be candid, however,
whatever may be the virtues of the waters, the
people who come here do not look as if they had
anything to be cured which would not be speedily
remedied by mountain air and free exercise in the
old balsamy woods; and I apprehend that health-
seeking is a thin excuse for enjoying a few weeks in
a delightful and picturesque spot, and with pleasant
associates: an apology for that which needs none.

Greylock Hall, the hostelry of this novel watering
place, stands on an elevation well up to the base of
the Vermont border-mountains, whose forest-covered

sides furnish a strong back-ground for the large, showy building, while a soft foreground is supplied by the groves, gardens, bowers and fountains of the Hall; a roomy park, carved, as it were, out of the forest primeval, and converted to culture by some eccentric magician. The world of fashion, delighting in sensational contrasts, has here retreated towards the rudest recesses of the mountains, as far as it well could without absolutely making its abode in them. Greylock Hall is a slice of metropolitan life and luxury taken up — students of the "Arabian Nights" know how — and dropped right down in the wilderness.

Behind, stretch wild and scraggy mountains with a highly inviting look of native savagery, not a little suggestive of bears and catamounts, although I believe the sportsman must be content finally with much less exciting game; and, before the Hall, lies a rural country with few farm houses. But, only two miles away, one gets a picturesque glimpse of Williamstown spires, and he knows that, six or seven miles down yonder rich and busy valley, lies the great town of North Adams. At his elbow he hears the click of the telegraph and close at hand, the jar of the locomotive with its train. Ah, that is the charm of it! The world of fashion, hide itself in what nook or wilderness it may, does not willingly loose its grasp of the telegraph and the railroad, and wants its daily metropolitan journal as regularly at Greylock Hall as at the Buckingham or the Clarendon. And with all this mixture of life and loneliness, civilization and savagery, lore and luxury, freedom and comfort, social pleasures with a rural zest and woodland sports with a citizen's relish for them; with all these, I conceive that the liking that the world's people — to use a Shakerism — manifest for Greylock Hall, is abundantly accounted for.

XXIV.

LENOX — THE ONLY ONE.

The wales through which my weary steps I **guide**
In this delightful land of Faëry,
Are so exceeding spacious and wyde,
And sprinkled with such sweet variety
Of all that pleasant is to ear and eye,
That I, nigh ravisht with rare thoughts delight,
My tedious travell do forget thereby ;
And when I gin to feele decay of might,
It strength to me supplies, and chears my dulled spright.
Faerie Queene.

And now, what of Lenox? Of Lenox, whose name has so long been associated with so much of the grandest and most beautiful in Berkshire scenery, the noblest, purest and most graceful in Berkshire life, the most admired and most loved in Berkshire genius: which, not many years ago, absorbed almost entirely whatever attention an influential portion of the outer world had to bestow upon the great highland county of Massachusetts — Stockbridge alone closely rivalling it in the eye of these fashion-setting folk.

Lenox is a puzzle; and the mystery with which it challenges us, is the hidden spell that, irresistibly as

it seems, yearly compels hither an ever-increasing
number of men and women of a superior intellectual—not necessarily literary—caste, and of exceptionally pure and natural tastes: an annual
assemblage whose social life is governed by idiosyn-
crasies—perhaps indefinable—that distinguish it
from every other summer-social circle. It is natural
enough, and for the better enjoyment of all, that
every section of society, should gather itself together, each after its own kind, and in its own place;
but it is not often that the result is so homogeneous
as that which is, every summer, reproduced at
Lenox. The characteristics of life there are con-
sequently more individualized and pronounced than
in looser and more temporary social organizations:
some of them indeed amounting to polished eccen-
tricity.

I wish it to be understood that my opportunities
of observing this peculiar phase of society have
been, for the most part—in recent years altogether—
from without; and I am aware that the aspect of
social formations, like the apparent contours of our
mountains, vary strangely with the varying point
of view. Whether my own stand-point in this case,
being a distant one, has enabled me to borrow any
enchantment for my picture, I am not able to say.
It was once my privilege, for a single season at a
certain theatre, to go nightly behind the scenes—
where I learned a great deal, to be sure: but it hardly
fitted me to prepare a more appreciative morning
critique upon the presentation of the play.

I do not however purpose the absurdity of attempting, with my plentiful lack of data, an analysis of life at Lenox; but simply, in incidental connections, to hint at possible sources of its more patent peculiarities, and some of the elements in that mysterious spell which the spot casts upon its habitues. But I may speak from more thorough information of that remarkable natural scenery which steadily holds the first place in the love and esteem of so many constant beholders, whose tastes have been moulded or corrected by extended travel at home and abroad: scenery whose charms seem to me to consist more in an unusual combination of satisfactory qualities, and freedom from blemish, than in any specific splendor of landscape — however striking instances of the latter may here and there present themselves.

I think that, to obtain a better first effect, we will approach this scenery by a circuitous route. Immediately south of Pittsfield, there rises a short, but — as seen from that town — a conspicuous, and exceedingly picturesque, chain of mountains. The hastiest glance will show the traveller who mounts to the foot-bridge at the Union Depot, how much the landscape owes to the fine shaping of its three great hills. In this regard the Greylock group is not more worth. These hills, of which there are four visible from Pittsfield, are a part of the Lenox range, which, as I told you sometime ago, is a spur thrown off by the Taconics at Egremont. It terminates with Melville Hill, which lies in Pittsfield, between the new and old roads to Lenox, its eastern slope being the farm formerly owned by Hermann Melville. At its foot, upon the north, is the fine old mansion — now almost in its hundredth year — whose hospitable roof, under the successive mastership of Henry Van Schaack, Elkanah Watson, Major Thomas Melville, and J. R. Morewood, has welcomed a long and rare array of guests, from Alexander Hamilton and Philip Schuyler to Nathaniel Hawthorne and Hermann Melville. The grounds of this mansion enclose Melville Lake — the prettiest little lakelet possible, with its crystal-clear wave and rim of green woods. One for whom Berkshire skies should weep, used to call it "A Tear of Heaven;" they who love best the pure white flowers on its placid breast, speak of it as "The Lilly Bowl." There is, upon its eastern shore, a cool and mossy path completely overarched by spreading, thick-leaved boughs:

> "No more sky, for overbranching
> At your head than at your feet."

Rarely, through that leafy screen, the green and golden light streams down with transmuted gorgeousness. There is an exquisite wealth of color in some of those woodland tints. I can never forget the rich purple hue which a few struggling rays of summer sunshine imparted to a little spot of black earth as I walked once in this cool retreat, while it was fierce noon-tide without. The very figures painted on the mould, in that royal coloring, are vividly present to me now, while so much that pro-

mised to endure has faded from existence, and is
fading from memory.

The first conspicuous eminence in the Lenox
Range is South Mountain: a mile from Pittsfield
Park, and deservedly the favorite of such towns-
people as enjoy a moderate walk, through pleasant
avenues, to an alluring goal. No other spot within
easy distance presents so many enticements to the
devotee of the romantic in natural scenery. From
several points upon it, you will get the best views
of the town of Pittsfield to be had: except, perhaps,
one from Day Mountain in Dalton. The rocky
natural terraces on its north-eastern side afford
strolls of novel beauty, and rich in wild-flowers:

> "Flowers, purple, blue and white,
>
> Like sapphire, pearl and rich embroidery."

Mount Osceola, next in the range, is a large and
shapely mountain, playing an important part in the
landscape, and interesting, although not especially
so, to the excursionist.

Beyond Osceola, and an intervening valley, the
Lenox range rises to its greatest altitude, one thousand and sixty-five feet above the track of the railroad at the Richmond Depot, or twenty-one hundred
and fifteen, above the sea level. Rising sharply from
the Richmond valley, its contour is more clearly defined than that of any other mountain — Greylock
always excepted — which is visible from Pittsfield.
In this view it assumes a distinctly pyramidal form,
which gives it great prominence; but the summit is
not often visited by pleasure-seekers, as thick woods·

obscure the prospects which would otherwise be among the most magnificent in Berkshire. A spectator perched among the boughs of some tall and favorably located tree, looks directly down in different directions, upon the Lenox and Stockbridge, the Pittsfield, Lanesboro' and Dalton, and the Richmond and West Stockbridge valleys, as well as away to the Catskill and other distant summits. But such an observatory defies the daring of the most adventurous young woman in the maddest of our Alpine clubs — not to impugn the aspiring courage of the masculine mountain-climbers — and it behooves the tasteful people of Lenox or of Pittsfield, to erect here, in some suitable clearing, a stone tower of liberal dimensions. Visible from every train of the Boston and Albany railroad, it would soon become as famous as the Wadsworth tower near Hartford, and render the peak the favorite mountain resort of central Berkshire.

I once passed a delicious summer-day here with a party of rare climbers, who believed that we were upon Perry's Peak. We were sorely disappointed in not finding the superb views we had been promised: and the disappointment was aggravated by the tantalizing glimpses, some of us succeeded in getting after much effort. Nevertheless we had a day of memorable enjoyment by the aid of some freely-voiced music, and readings from the poets by one who had a rare gift that way:

When we came to learn that we had not been upon Perry's Peak at all, but only upon the nameless "highest point of the Lenox Range," we felt that so grand a feature of the landscape deserved a less awkward designation: and we agreed upon one. It was a noble and fitting name: but I shall not tell it to you; for it is best to avoid confusion in such matters — and be-thinking ourselves that, as the peak is in the bailiwick of Lenox, its christening by us might be resented as discourteous intrusion, we did not proceed with it.

Afterwards, however, I mentioned the incident to a brilliant Lenox woman — a Lenox woman by virtue of a residence of several summers, and, I believe, winters also — who spoke of a name which is certainly not alien to this region:

YOCUN'S SEAT.

Yocun was a noted Indian chief of the vicinage, who, with his fellow-chieftain, Ephraim, sold to the grantees from the Province, the rights of their people in the township now divided into Lenox and Richmond; but which as plantations were known as Yocuntown and Mount Ephraim. When Richmond was incorporated as a town in 1765; and Lenox in 1767, the sachems were, in very unceremonious fashion, deprived of their honors, in order that they might be bestowed upon Charles Lenox, Duke of Richmond: the friend of Horace Walpole, and the early defender, in the House of Lords, of American colonial rights.

This seemed to Mrs. X. and the lively circle about her, a very sad case of robbing Peter to pay Paul;

and she proposed to rectify the ancient wrong in part, by giving the old Lenox sachem's name to the highest point of Lenox Mountain.   And she was the more satisfied of the rightfulness of this tardy and partial restitution of stolen honors, when she unearthed — for aught I know, from the rich stores of her friend, Miss Sedgwick — a tradition that Chief Yocun, in his later years, was wont often to seek this commanding summit, and, seated there in kingly sorrow, to gaze long and sadly over the fair realms which, partly by his own act, had passed from the sway of the red man.

If you think with this justice-loving woman, Yocun's Seat, let it be.

But, by the by, and before I forget His Grace of Richmond entirely, it may relieve the minds of some hypercritical people, of whom I often hear, to tell them that, although there is a Scottish region known as "The Lennox," the charter of the Berkshire town follows correctly the spelling of the ducal family name in using only a single "n.'

The pyramidal appearance of Yocun's Seat, as seen from Pittsfield, is deceptive; it being only the terminal presentation of a ridge which descends very gradually for some miles to the south-west. The chain is continued by connected elevations through Alford to the main range of the Taconics in Egremont, although the elevation at the last becomes so slight as hardly to be recognized; giving the spur the appearance of an isolated chain of hills. These mountains — many of which command superb views — are generally known by the names of the towns in which they lie; but, upon the border between Alford and West Stockbridge, Tom Ball rises abruptly, and proclaims itself one of the most notable of the great mountains of Berkshire. President Hitchcock speaks of the Lenox spur of the Taconics as here attaining its highest elevation, but he does not state the height of Tom Ball, nor whether he refers to its elevation above the sea, or above the bottom of the neighboring valley. I think that the latter is intended, and that Yocun's Seat, which rises from a valley level two hundred feet higher than the more southern mountain has, is, in regard to the sea level, the higher altitude; although the difference can hardly be more than one hundred feet.

But we have now to do only with the northern portion of the Lenox spur, which, bending around the Lenox and Stockbridge valley, separates it from those of Pittsfield, Richmond and West Stockbridge. By the Lenox and Stockbridge valley, I do not mean the Housatonic valley in which the villages of Lenox Furnace, Lee and Stockbridge on the Plain are built. Lenox has, besides its farming districts, two thriving villages. Lenox Furnace, the seat of the glass and iron works, lies directly upon the Housatonic river and railroad. Westward from this the ground rises rapidly, four hundred and fifty feet, in two and a half miles; at the end of which commences a shelf of rolling upland, extending into the elbow formed by the Lenox range of mountains on the north and west; southward, this upland de-

clines a mile and a half to the Stockbridge Bowl,
and, past that noble sheet of water on the right,
and Mount Deokook on the left, to the brow of the
hill which descends abruptly to Stockbridge Plain.
And this, from the northern mountain wall to
Stockbridge on the Hill, is the far famed Lenox and
Stockbridge valley.

Upon the upland shelf and its slope to the lake —
which you may call Mahkeenac if you are bent upon
it — are built the village, and most of the villas, of
Lenox-on-the-Heights; the favorite haunt of that
summer-life of which I have spoken.

And, now, let us approach Lenox, from Pittsfield,
by the circuitous route of which I told you so long
ago. Following the pleasant road which skirts the
northern bases of the Lenox range, we shall come, ·
after a drive of a half dozen miles, to the highway
from Lebanon Springs, through Richmond to Lenox,
which here crosses the southern slope of Yocun's
Seat. The same route was followed very long ago
by some very distinguished tourists to whom I introduced you in the story of Perry's Peak.

Descending the ridge upon the east, you will
obtain the best view of Lenox; a white village, half
hidden by embowering trees and seated upon a
gently sloping and richly cultivated swell of land.
In various directions you will see picturesque villas
and cottages in park-like grounds, although the most
costly are not in this view. On an eminence at the
farther end of the village, rises the fine old-fashioned
New England meeting-house in which **William**

Ellery Channing delivered his last discourse, and which bears on its front the clock presented by Frances Anne Kemble. On your left you will look down the luxurious Lenox and Stockbridge valley. It was the view from this point which compelled from a band of Hungarian exiles the shout, "Beauty! Beauty!" Their English could go no farther than that; nor was more needed.

I shall not attempt to describe for you the nice points of Lenox scenery: there are too many of them. Lenox summer-folk — the most energetic of pleasure seekers — are always trooping to some of them: hill-top, cliff, lake-side or glen — "And small blame to them!" said an Irish friend of mine who had in his student-life been familiar with all that is best in Italian and German landscape — "and small blame to them; for this Lenox beats the world for grand going-places." "Going-places" was a new phrase to me; but I do not think that it needs interpretation. Of these Lenox going-places, one of the most admired is so central as the village church yard. Indeed you can hardly walk a dozen rods without coming upon a new phase of loveliness which in regions where beauty is not so freely lavished would be deemed wonderful. The favorite points are those which, like Church Hill, The Ledge, and Bald Head, look down the rich vista of the Stockbridge Valley, with the blue Dome of the Taghconics rising in the distance. But the spot which glows most vividly in my remembrance is "The Old Judge Walker Hill." I passed a glad summer afternoon there, years ago, and made a deliberate effort to fix the landscape in my memory. I do not know how much has, nevertheless, faded; but I still seem to see a rolling country, of mingled wood, field and meadow, intersected with shaded avenues; with Stockbridge Bowl and Laurel Lake gleaming in blue and silver amid the broad verdure; a pretty glimpse of Lee village in the middle distance; and, still beyond, great mountains, whose personality I did not recognize. It was a bewildering excess of beauty.

But grand and lovely as are the natural attractions of Lenox, they are not so pre-eminent as to account for the place which it holds in the esteem of those who give tone to the world's opinions. That has been gained by social influences of exceptional power: which it may not be profane to consider briefly. And among those influences we must concede that a large share were derived primarily from the Sedgwick family: not, however, to the extent of admitting that, in 1821, they went to the shire town of Berkshire, missionaries of culture among a rude people.

In 1821, Mr. Charles Sedgwick was compelled by his duties as clerk of the County Courts, to remove to Lenox.

Mr. Sedgwick was the youngest and favorite brother of the authoress, between whom and his wife there was also a very tender friendship. For the two years succeeding his marriage,. they had lived as one household in the old Stockbridge homestead, and the change, in 1821, was very distasteful to Miss Catherine, whose judgment of her brother's new place of residence was characteristically warped by its connection with the disruption of the pleasant family circle, over which she moaned disconsolately in her correspondence. Her biographer — doubtless receiving her impressions from the writings or conversations of Miss Sedgwick — describes the Lenox of 1821, as "a bare and ugly little village, perched upon a desolate hill at the end of six miles of rough and steep driving;" and, while admitting, to the full, the native beauties of Lenox scenery, she thinks that to a "native and lover of the rich valley of Stockbridge, with its soft and graceful variations of meadow and wood, its gentle river and sheltering mountains, and the appearance of refinement even then given to its dwellings, Lenox must have seemed dismally bleak and uncouth."

There was certainly some foundation for these strong expressions, but they, as certainly, owe their extreme bitterness to the great liability of Miss Sedgwick's judgment to be disturbed by the relations of men and things to the House of Sedgwick. Lenox-on-the-Heights stands three hundred and fifty feet higher than Stockbridge-on-the-Plain: full one-quarter of the rise being within a mile of the Sedgwick homestead on Stockbridge street. The height of Lenox above Pittsfield Park is one hundred and forty-three feet. The present denizens of the place decidedly pique themselves upon its altitude. Tradition tells dismal stories of the Berkshire roads a half century ago, and the soil of Lenox is not favorable for road building. The drive from Stockbridge, now so wonderfully delicious, was beyond question very different at certain seasons of the year 1821.

President Dwight, who visited the village in 1798, thus describes it:

"Lenox, the shire town of the county, is principally built upon a single street, on a ridge, declining rather pleasantly to the east and west, but disagreeably interrupted by several deep valleys crossing it at right angles. The soil and the buildings are good, and the town exhibits many marks of prosperity. The public buildings consist of a church (the same which now crowns the hill), a court-house, a school-house and jail."

Not a glowing description, nor yet, on the other hand, repulsive. And the place must have improved in the twenty-three years between 1798 and 1821. Still it cannot be denied that the Lenox, even of the latter year, bore but a sorry comparison with either the present urbanized Lenox or the Stockbridge of sixty years ago. In 1821 the commonwealth had few villages of which the same cannot be said, with at least equal force.

In regard to social life, the superiority of Stockbridge was less marked; amounting, to put it at its strongest, to no more than was to be expected in the older, richer, and more populous town. Lenox had even then a social circle of culture, exceptional even among larger towns.

As early as the beginning of the present century,

as we may fairly infer from the correspondence of
so competent a critic as Henry Van Schaack, men of
much more than ordinary refinement, information
and breadth of thought were accustomed to meet
around the hospitable board of Major Eggleston.
In 1821, Lenox had been for thirty-four years the
county seat of Berkshire; and it was then the custom for the judges — more numerous than now —
and, at least the leading members of the bar, to remain in town through the long sessions of the
courts: a fact which must have greatly benefited local
society. And it is no unmeaning jest to add, that
some of the most cultured citizens of other sections
of the county were often compelled, as prisoners for
debt, to pass long periods in Lenox, in its legal
capacity as " jail limits." The Lenox Academy, one
of the most successful high schools in the state, had
flourished since 1803, and in 1821 was under the
charge of scholarly Levi Glezen: and it, too, must
have had its mollifying effect upon men and manners.

Among the permanent citizens were the elder and
the younger Judge Walker, County Treasurer Joseph
Tucker, Rev. Dr. Shepard, Doctors Worthington and
Collins, and James W. Robbins who, with others of
like merit, betoken a very respectable elevation of
village society.

I think, therefore, that the picture which appalled
Miss Sedgwick's imagination when she first learned
the necessity for her brother's removal to the seat of
the county business may be sufficiently softened to

leave us a prosperous, and rather pleasant, county-town, with a population of some refinement, very considerable liberal culture, and much intellectual power: comparing quite favoraby with most of the New England county-seats of that era. The six miles exile of the county-clerk and his family fell far short of Siberian severity: as his sister found, when, some ten years later, she consented to share it.

It was about the year 1831, that Lenox became the chief summer residence of Miss Sedgwick, who in winter made her home with either of two brothers resident in New York, as she might elect. In the interval between 1821 and 1831, Lenox village had improved in appearance, and its society had received some valuable accessions; particularly in the family of Henry W.—afterwards Judge—Bishop, Mr. Sedgwick's life-long friend. A coterie composed largely of gentlemen holding county-offices, and their families, had grown, or was growing, into a remarkable social body, distinguished for intellectual graces, and the marvel of .all observers for its fraternal friendship and close alliance. In this circle, the love-compelling qualities of Charles Sedgwick and the queenly powers of his accomplished wife made them conspicuous.

But, as yet, Lenox had only provincial distinction. The great world took little note of the superb scenery, still less of the life, of the little mountain town. The residence of Miss Sedgwick soon began to change all this. Her literary fame, the social distinction of her family in the metropolis, and more than all, her sympathies with humanity — which were as world-wide as her local affections were intense — soon began to attract to her country home, men and women of the more intellectual class every where; and especially those most deeply engaged in efforts to speed the world towards its better future. Not only the champions of freedom and humanity in the great centers of American effort, but the higher order of republican exiles from Italy and Hungary, made pilgrimages to the home of a family whose sympathy with embattled right was not limited by nationality. The keen and friendly interest of the whole Sedgwick family of that generation in the struggles of European republicanism was, by the bye, in violent contrast with the sentiments of their father.

The singular merit of the family school for young ladies which, begun by Mrs. Charles Sedgwick in 1828, grew to great fame, also largely influenced the gathering and moulding of the summer society peculiar to Lenox; and not less did the accession of Mrs. Kemble, who became, first a frequent visitor of the Sedgwicks, and afterwards a permanent resident, zealously active in promoting the good of the town.

In a letter, of November 1842, Miss Sedgwick hints the characteristics of the social life which grew up under these and similar influences and became so wonderfully attractive.

"You have heard of Channing's death, and perhaps that he passed the summer at Lenox, and in a free and happy condition of mind and body, such as he often said he did not remember to have enjoyed since childhood, and such as his friends had never before observed. He seemed to have thrown off every shackle, to be rid of his precision ; and he was so affectionate and playful with the young people that those who did not before know him wondered why any one should fear Dr. Channing. He liked our anti-conventionalism; our free ways of going on — our individual independence of thought and action ; he enjoyed, as if he had come to his father's house, the forever-changing beauty of our hills and valleys, and he went away with more than half a promise to return to us next summer."

I find this letter, which is addressed to Rev. Dr. Orville Dewey, in Miss Sedgwick's "Life and Letters." In the recently published correspondence of Charles Sumner, there are two or three letters which illustrate the unconventionalism of Lenox life from another point of view. In the latter summer of 1844, Mr. Sumner visited Hon. Nathan Appleton in his country-seat at Pittsfield, reinvigorating his impaired health, and "enjoying much the meadows, green fields, rich country and beautiful scenery," in rides upon a horse loaned him by his host's neighbor, Hon. E. A. Newton. He gave his impressions freely in letters to George S. Hillard and Dr. S. G. Howe, who had been his companions during part of his visit. Under date of September 10th, 1844, he writes thus to Mr. Hillard concerning two rides to Lenox:

"He [Mr. Samuel G. Ward] jolted us in his wagon to view the farms, one of which he coveted. Afterwards, we looked on while, in a field not far off, the girls and others engaged in the sport of archery. Mrs. Butler (Fanny Kemble) hit the

target in the golden middle. The next day was Sunday, and
I was perplexed whether to use Mr. Newton's horse, as I presume the master never used him on Sunday. But my scruples
gave way before my longings for the best of exercises. I left
Pittsfield as the first bell was tolling and arrived at Lenox
some time before the second bell. I sat in Miss Sedgwick's
room ; time passed on. Mrs. Butler joined us and again time
passed on. Mrs. Butler proposed to accompany me to Pittsfield on horse-back. I stayed to the cold dinner, making it a
lunch. Time again passed on from the delay in saddling the
horses. We rode the longest way, and I enjoyed my companion very much."

Again on the 12th Mr. Sumner writes to Mr.
Hillard from Pittsfield:

" I wish you were still here. Your presence would help me
bear the weight of Fanny Kemble's conversation. I confess
to a certain awe, and a sense of her superiority, which makes
me at times anxious to subside into my inferiority, and leave
the conversation to be sustained by others."

The glimpses into the Lenox life of a generation
ago, afforded by these extracts, convey a better idea
of its peculiar charms than I could give you in any
other way. The passing away of that generation of
the Sedgwick family, and of most of their associates,
together with the removal of others, consequent upon
the change in the county seat, has taken away, for
the most part, the local frame work, upon which the
summer society of Lenox first formed itself. But
it had already outgrown that frame-work. The
flood of life which poured towards these romantic
heights as they became more and more known, was
perplexing in its variety. Millionaires, artists, poets,
politicians, scholars and statesmen came in yearly

succeeding waves. Some found themselves in harmony with the genius of the place and affiliated themselves with it: others, after a more or less brief trial, sought a more congenial resort elsewhere. In the meanwhile, villas and cottages have sprung up on all manner of beautiful sites; and such luxurious appointments as metropolitan tastes demanded have in some measure been supplied. Society has of course much modified its usages to accommodate itself to these changes. What the exact result has been, as I warned you at the first, I shall not attempt to tell, or even myself to understand, but it is at least something unlike any other social life; and I believe it to have so far retained the old spirit, that Lenox-on-the-Heights — in spite of stately mansions, showy equipages and fashionable clubs — still remains the Paradise of unconventional good-breeding.

L'ENVOI.

To thee, perchance, this rambling strain
Recalls our summer walks again;
When doing naught — and to speak true,
Not caring to find ought to do —
The wild unbounded hills, we ranged,
While oft our talk its topic changed,
And, desultory as our way,
Ranged unconfined from grave to gay:
Even when it flagged, as oft would chance,
No effort made to break the trance,
We could right pleasantly pursue
Our sports in social silence, too.— *Walter Scott.*

We must finish here our rambles upon the summer-enchanted hills of Berkshire, which we have ranged, as I hope, not altogether without pleasure, or profit. But I feel that my neighbors will complain, with reason, if I forget the multitude of our own enticing " going-places," which, are, at least, not exceeded in number or loveliness even by those of Lenox. To some of them, I have already conducted you; but there are others quite as choice, which it would be unpardonable in one who owes to them so many days of exquisite pleasure, to neglect, for wanderings to the end of the county. And even if I cannot now go with you to them, you too, would have cause for complaint, if I left you totally uninformed of their existence.

If, coming to us for a single day, you should ask, what ride, of all others to select, the answer would almost certainly be: "To Potter's Mountain!" This bare and lofty Taghconic summit lies some six miles north-west of us. When it was very difficult of access it was a frequent and favorite resort of Herman Melville and his companions in picnic. A new highway to Hancock, now renders the ride to its mossy top, perfectly easy, and the whole town seems to have gone mad over its fine and comprehensive views of mountains, valleys, lakes, streams, villages and groves.

A most alluring "going-place" for young people, in pairs and parties, is Lulu Cascade, in a lonely nook between two Taghconic hills, some two miles north-west of Lake Onota. It is almost the exact counterpart of the little water-fall of which I told you in the story of Undine's Glen, which was ruined years ago by the wood-choppers. A silver-white column of water falls fifteen feet over dark rocks, into a broad black pool, overhung by a huge grey boulder. Below is a ravine, shaded half with rocks and half with trees, and a rippling brook. The merriest of all parties linger to lunch upon its banks.

A cool and pretty wood-road leads up the southern bank of the brook, and if, after pursuing it for perhaps half a mile, you climb a moderate hill upon your left, you will find upon its top a basin in which lies Berry Pond: the gem of mountain lakelets. Its shore is a favorite camping ground for those who seek a brief interval of woodland life. Berry Pond and Lulu Cascade are not to be omitted in any programme of Berkshire summer excursions.

And yet the ride upon which I should best love to take many of you is different from either of those which I have described. What is known as the old, or east, road to Lanesboro'; and is now little used, runs for a great part of its length along the crest of an upland ridge, noted for its fertility. The drive along this road is exceedingly pleasant, with its border of rich farms, over which we look on every side to noble mountain landscapes. After a five-mile drive along this ridge and in a picturesque valley, we rise to the summit of the road on the southern slope of Prospect Hill in Lanesboro', with the village below us and a magnificent over-view stretching to the Lenox Hills. We may now descend to the village and pursue our way home, past Pontoosuc Lake. But it would be better to turn down the eastern descent to Berkshire village, the seat of the Crystal Glass Manufacture, where, at the foot of Crystal Mountain, we should find, great heaps of white silicious sand, which if it were winter, you could not distinguish from snow-drifts. Then we would enter the works where this beautiful material is transmuted into glass, clear as crystal, or of any, or all, the colors of a summer rainbow. I think some of you would enjoy that excursion.

I should be glad to show you these and a host of

other beautiful and interesting spots which lie
close about us. But for the present at least, our
rambles are ended.

I cannot, however, part with you, without re-
moving some false impressions, which a reading of
the printed pages leads me to fear that I may have
given you. I had no wish in telling the story of
John Chandler Williams, to rob Dr. Benjamin
Franklin of the glory of securing the Hutchinson
correspondence in England. The letters obtained
by the young student-hero must have been supple-
mentary to the Franklin acquisition. You will find
the authority for my story in the Journals of the
Provincial Congress, and in the History of The
Williams Family, where it is given in the words of
Hon. Edward A. Newton, Mr. Williams's son-in-law.

In the account of the Dedication of the Pittsfield
Soldiers' Monument, the prominence given to Gen.
Bartlett by the circumstances of his subsequent early
death, led me to the use of language which may be
construed as meaning that his brief, but noble, address
was the chief feature of the ceremony; whereas in
fact the grand address was one of that series of ora-
tions by George William Curtis, which, if collected
would form at once the most glowing eulogium and
the most philosophical commentary upon the War
for the Union.

In another place, I see that, quoting very carelessly from memory, I have put the warning, "Let
him who hath a dead hand take heed how he strikes,"
into the mouth of Lord Chief Justice Selden. My

cooler recollection is that it came from the lips of quaint old Fuller.

I make these corrections after the wisdom of Sir Richard Moniplies of Castle Collop, whose rule was to speak all the ill he knew of his family: being quite sure that if he did not some ill-natured person would be sure to detect and publish it.

And, now having confessed and asked absolution for these and all other sins of omission and commission, I beg your kindly reciprocal

Farewell.

32

INDEX.

TALES.

MAPLEWOOD INSTITUTE.

One of the most widely and longest known features of Pittsfield, physically and socially, has been and is, its school for young ladies. Founded in 1841, it soon reached a national patronage and fame.

Here first, liberal provision was made for the healthful exercise of young lady pupils, a gymnasium ninety feet by fifty-five being established in the spring of '51. Dio Lewis, visiting it about a dozen years ago, declared with great emphasis that not a school on the continent was doing as much for the physical development of its pupils.

The grounds about the buildings, always of rare attractiveness, are now more beautiful than ever, magnificent elms and maples of fifty years' growth, and fountains, flowers and shrubbery adding every year to its beauty.

As regards intellectual training, Maplewood well maintains its position. With its regular collegiate course, of four years it has of late also a special classical and mathematical course for those desiring to be fitted to enter Smith College, or any similar institutions and also a music course with diploma. It also gives more prominence than formerly to drawing, sketching from nature, and studies designed to fit pupils for the practical duties of life.

Its aim is to make a thoroughly home-like place for a limited number of students, in marked contrast with those institutions which receive and educate several hundred, all mature enough to be fully able to take care of themselves. The principals with their families and most of the instructors reside within the institution.

THE BERKSHIRE ATHENÆUM.

The trustees of the Berkshire Athenæum were incorporated in 1871 for the promotion of education, culture and refinement by means of libraries, reading-rooms, cabinets, lectures, etc. Previously established libraries and cabinets were combined in their hands. A costly and capacious building has been erected on Park Square. The library now numbers about eleven thousand valuable books; and there are an historical museum and a mineralogical cabinet; each with a large number of rare and interesting specimens. Reading rooms for reviews, magazines and newspapers have been opened.

All departments of the Athenæum are open daily, and the library and reading rooms every evening; and the use of all is entirely free to the public, under such rules only as are needful for the protection of the books and other property.

The trustees solicit donations of contributions to the library and cabinets; especially of books, manuscripts and other articles illustrative of the civil, military, or natural history of the county.

The edition of the report of the proceedings at the dedication of the Pittsfield Soldiers' Monument, including the oration of Hon. George William Curtis, has been presented to the Athenæum, and copies will be sent post-paid, to any address on the receipt of the retail price, 25cts. The report is a very handsome octavo pamphlet of 72 pages, with a photographic view of the monument.

THE BERKSHIRE LIFE INSURANCE COMPANY,

Incorporated in 1851 — is one of Berkshire county's solid institutions. Its directors are prominent men, in the county, of various callings. It does not emulate the large city companies in the extent of its business, but it is none the less sound on that account, as the personal supervision of its officers can be, and is, given to all its business operations. Ex-Governor George N. Briggs was the first president and was succeeded by Thomas F. Plunkett, who had a wide reputation for sound and practical business sagacity, and the conservative principles impressed by these men on the company have been followed to the present time.

The institution is one that should find especial favor with New England men everywhere ; and command the confidence of Berkshire's sons.

It has agents in most northern states ; but application can be made to the company direct, at its home office in Pittsfield, Mass.

It aims to give to each policy holder a fair contract and to honestly perform its part of it. It has maintained through a commercial depression, unexamped in the history of this country, a surplus of cash assets for the benefit of its policy holders, and the published statements of the company honestly and fairly represent its financial condition. It has never undertaken expensive methods for obtaining new business to the detriment of present members.

THE HISTORY OF PITTSFIELD,

From 1734 to 1876, by J. E. A. Smith, was prepared and published at the expense of the town, whose property it still is. It consists of two handsomely printed volumes with an aggregate of 1,243 octavo pages, illustrated by a map, 35 wood cuts and sixteen finely executed steel portraits. The work met with extraordinary favor from the press, from whose opinions we make a few extracts.

From the Boston Congregationalist.

It is seven years since the first volume of this work, bringing the history of the town to the beginning of the present century, was issued. We then expressed our sense of its great excellence and interest, as we are now glad to do of its continuation, to the present time. These two volumes furnish a memorial, for which any town might be grateful, and of whose so successful preparation any author might be proud. * * * We do not know where any man could go for so accurate and graphic a minute picture of the best New England life at the beginning of the present century as in the first fifty pages of the second volume.

From Harpers Monthly.

The admirable history of Pittsfield, Massachusetts, by Mr. J. E. A. Smith, one of the most elaborate, thorough and accurate of local histories.

From the Springfield Republican.

The Benedict Arnold episodes in this volume (the first) are among the best parts of it, and contain much that will be new to the reader. The whole book when completed will be the pride of the town, and of great service to all students of American history.

The work can be had of the subscriber, agent for the town at the following prices: First volume, 518 pages, in cloth, $2.40, in half morocco, $2.80; or it will be sent by mail in cloth at $2.60, in half morocco, $3.00; Second volume, 725 pages, in cloth, $2.80, in half morocco, $3.20; or it will be sent by mail in cloth for $3.10, in half morocco for $3.50: The set complete in cloth, $4.00; in half morocco, $4.80, by mail cloth, $4.50; half morocco, $5.30.

S. E. NICHOLS, *Bookseller, Pittsfield.*